# Twisted

A HARP SECURITY NOVEL

*Laura K. Curtis*

## BY LAURA K. CURTIS

THE HARP SECURITY SERIES
*Twisted*
*Lost*
*Echoes*
*Mind Games*

THE GOODY'S GOODIES SERIES
*Toying with His Affections*
*Gaming the System*

For Mike, who was patient, and for Lydia, who was not.

# CHAPTER ONE

When Momma died, Timmy and I ran. The way I saw it, any man who'd stab a woman five times, then slit her throat and leave her lying on the floor, blood soaking into the worn carpet and running in rivulets down the ancient grout between the kitchen tiles, wouldn't hesitate to get rid of any other little inconveniences in his life.

FROM *A BAD DAY TO DIE*
BY LUCY SADLER CALDWELL [DRAFT]

EVERY BATTLE CALLED for a specific weapon, and over the years Lucy had become accustomed to carrying at least one at all times. Now, without the weight of a pistol at her hip or back, the reassuring bite of a sheath at her ankle, or even the knowledge of a can of Mace in her purse, she felt supremely vulnerable. But she could hardly walk into a police station armed to the teeth, no matter how much she might prefer to.

So instead of checking the bullets in a magazine, she patted the tight bun restraining her wavy hair, spritzed her neck with a touch of eau de toilette, and gave her appearance one last once-over in the rearview mirror. Good to go.

Sliding out of the Range Rover in a pencil skirt and high heels wasn't easy, but when she turned to walk up the steps to the station house and caught a man on the sidewalk doing a double take, satisfaction swirled through her. The costume had been worth the effort. As she swung open the heavy iron-and-glass door, she nodded at the man, who narrowed his eyes and frowned. The disapproval radiating from him almost made her laugh, and she entered the building on a wave of renewed confidence.

Her first challenge sat behind a long counter directly ahead of her and just inside the door, ostensibly guarding against unauthorized personnel. In reality, the barrier—and guardian—were flimsy.

Lucy could have vaulted the counter and knocked Marge Bollingham flat on her butt in less than a second. Marge looked up from the crossword puzzle in front of her, and Lucy saw recognition darken her eyes and pale her skin.

"May I help you?" Marge asked, her voice stiff and decidedly unhelpful.

"I'm here to speak to Chief Donovan." Lucy kept her own tone as friendly as possible.

"He's busy."

Indeed, behind the counter, beyond the six desks that comprised the bullpen of the small department, Lucy could see what had to be the chief's office. The door was open, and a dark-haired man sat behind a desk talking to a uniformed officer.

"I'll wait," she said.

Marge's lips flattened. "I'll buzz him," she said at last. And then, as if it had only just occurred to her, "Who shall I tell him is waiting?"

Games. Why did everyone have to play games? But if Marge wanted to waste time, Lucy would oblige. "Lucy Sadler Caldwell," she said. Then she glanced ostentatiously down at the nameplate on the counter between them. "Marge."

The woman stiffened, but didn't reply. She pushed some buttons on the phone in front of her and Lucy saw the man in the office pick up his phone.

"Someone's here to speak with you, Chief," said Marge. "Her name's Lucy Sadler."

At the name, the cop who'd been talking to the chief whipped around. Lucy was too far from them to make out anything distinctive, but she was surprised to see feminine features beneath the short blonde hair.

Donovan must have asked her to come back, because without further word Marge hung up and pushed a button beneath the counter and a section swung inward to let Lucy pass. Lucy carefully closed the barrier behind her and gave Marge a smile before walking back toward the office. The uniformed cop had disappeared, and Donovan was standing when she arrived. Christ, the man was tall. Even in three-inch heels, she had to look up to him, a fact she vaguely resented. Black hair fell in a shock over the front of his forehead and grazed the neck of his khaki uniform shirt, and for a split second furious heat blazed in his green eyes. But it was gone so fast, she might have imagined it.

He held out a hand. "Ms. . . .Sadler, is it? I'm Ethan Donovan, Dobbs Hollow's chief of police."

"Actually, it's Lucy Caldwell. Lucy Sadler died a long time ago." She took the hand, willing her own to stay cool and steady as Donovan's gaze sparked with interest at her statement.

The phone buzzed, and Lucy turned to look out at Marge. But Donovan hadn't released her yet, and he had to have felt the involuntary clench of her muscles when she saw the man standing in the bullpen as if he owned it.

Donovan let go of her hand, his calloused palm sliding against her own where every nerve in her body had suddenly focused. "Excuse me just a minute," he said, stepping out from behind the desk and leaning out the office door.

"I'm busy at the moment, Mayor Dobbs," he said, his body blocking the doorway. "Can I get back to you in an hour or two?"

Lucy couldn't hear the mayor's response, but it went on for quite some time. Eventually, Donovan nodded. "That'll be just fine." A moment later, still blocking her view, he asked Lucy whether she minded if someone else sat in on their meeting. "A precaution, you understand," he said with a disarming smile that slashed deep grooves in his cheeks. "I'd like to close the door against interruptions, but nowadays that's not such a smart move, even in small-town departments."

Laughter bubbled up in Lucy's throat. Was he worried about being accused of sexually harassing her? *Her?* In *this* town? Far more likely, *she'd* be accused of seducing *him.* But he'd find that out soon enough without her enlightening him.

"Not a problem," she replied. "I completely understand."

"Excellent." He waved to someone in the bullpen, and a minute later the same blonde cop who'd been in his office came to the door. It took Lucy a full second to recognize her.

"Tara Jean!" She leapt from her seat, practically tripping over the blasted high heels in her shock. "Look at you!"

Tara Jean grinned back at her. "Look at *you*," she retorted. "The famous author returns."

"Hardly. You don't get famous writing true crime." And then the words sank in. "How did you know?"

"Why don't we all sit?" Donovan suggested, drawing her attention back to him.

For a moment, she'd forgotten he was even there, forgotten the whole point of her visit to the police station. "Of course." She took her seat, and TJ settled in the chair next to hers while Donovan went back around the desk.

"Shall we start again?" he asked.

"Sure." She swallowed. "Would you like me to go first?"

"That might be best."

"You asked my name. When Tara knew me, it was Lucy Sadler. Now, it's Lucy Caldwell. I had no idea anyone knew Lucy Sadler of Dobbs Hollow and Lucy Caldwell, true-crime chronicler, were the same person."

"I recognized you from the author picture in your third book. In fact" — she broke off and looked at Donovan, who nodded — "I was talking to Ethan about you when you came in."

"You were?" Lucy recalled the way Ethan had reacted to

Marge's message, cutting short his meeting and double-checking her last name when he introduced himself.

"Ellen Wilson recognized you this morning driving through town. She called me to see if I knew why you had come home. I wanted to explain who you were, since Ethan's only been here a few months."

*And he'd be getting complaints the minute word got out she'd returned.*

"How far did you get?"

"Not far. She only called a minute or two before you arrived." Tara Jean reached over and laid a hand over hers. "I hadn't gotten past the fact that you used to live here, and now you're a famous

writer."

"I can't believe you actually read my books."

"Of course I did. They're incredible. I bet even Ethan's read them."

Lucy glanced across the desk, and Donovan's lips twisted into a wry smile. "'Fraid not. I surely will, though. But name and occupation aside, was there a reason you came to see me today? Something you wanted to talk about?"

"Yes." Lucy pulled a sheaf of papers from the black tote bag she'd laid next to her chair and pushed them across the desk at him. "I wanted to give you these: copies of my permits, the concealed-carry license, and the registration numbers."

Donovan didn't look down. Instead, he held her gaze with his own. In the deep, forest green of his eyes, she saw that same spark of interest he'd shown when she declared Lucy Sadler dead burn even brighter.

She dropped her eyes, squelching the urge to fidget by spreading the papers across the desk with a fingertip. "The rest are from departments I've worked with over the past few years. The names and numbers are for people there who can attest to the quality and legitimacy of my work."

She leaned down and reached into her bag once more, pulled out four books, and laid them in front of him, covers up.

"If you skim them, you'll get an idea of what I'll be doing while I'm here."

"I'll read them." Still, he never even glanced at the books, never took his eyes off her. "But how 'bout you give me a little preview."

Lifting her chin, she met his gaze solidly with her own.

"I'll be investigating my mother's murder."

# CHAPTER TWO

No one was surprised at Momma's murder. Lots of folks figured she had it coming. She was, after all, a woman of few scruples and fewer morals. She drank and slept around and had two kids with no fathers. But she was my mother. Mine and Timmy's. And we loved her.

FROM *A BAD DAY TO DIE*
BY LUCY SADLER CALDWELL [DRAFT]

"TELL ME." ONCE Lucy had dropped her bombshell and taken off, Ethan had sent TJ's partner out on patrol alone. An itch at the base of his neck he'd learned at no small cost to trust warned him his days chasing addicts, drunks, and teenagers had come to an end.

"Lucy's mother was . . .well, as they used to say back then, at least in our hearing, 'no better than she had to be.' When they thought we weren't listening, the words they used were less generous. I don't think either Lucy or Timmy knew their fathers, and Cecile had no visible means of income."

"And she was murdered."

"You should have asked her about this." TJ shifted, clearly conflicted about revealing her friend's history.

"You know better than that. Once I have a grip on what we're looking at, I'll get details from her. But I don't want her interpretation as my introduction to the case."

"Yeah, I know." Still, she took a minute before she continued. "Cecile was stabbed to death seventeen years ago. When Lucy was fifteen and Tim was around three. We never saw Lucy or her brother again. Sheriff Pike's daddy was chief then, and he didn't give a tinker's damn about who'd murdered the town whore, so eventually the talk died down and the whole 'unpleasant incident' was forgotten."

"Doesn't seem like Marge has forgotten. Or Ellen Wilson." He touched the papers on the desk. "And given the amount of firepower your old friend brought with her, it doesn't seem as if she expects other people to have forgotten, either."

TJ took a deep breath and let it out slowly. "Small towns are all about family and family names." She chewed a thumbnail as she spoke. "Mine's good, so it can take a beating. People even forgave me for taking a real job when I should have been home baking cookies and making babies. But the Sadlers couldn't do anything right. More than that, no matter what they did, they couldn't escape their name.

"Marge's niece, Ginny, got pregnant when she was sixteen. We're talking" — she stared off, lips moving slightly, silently, as she counted back in time — "eighteen years ago. Ginny told her mother she'd been forced to sleep with her boyfriend, because if she didn't, he'd . . ." Her mouth twisted.

"He'd find someone else."

"One of the Sadlers. The threat was pretty common back then, and Lucy and Cecile were interchangeable."

"Jesus, TJ! You were what, ten? And Lucy was fourteen?"

"I was twelve. Two years behind her."

"How did you even hear about a thing like that?"

"Middle school and high school shared a building here up until seven years ago. Anything that went on in the high school, the younger ones found out. Plus, I heard Drew pull that same shit on his girlfriend once.

"But that's neither here nor there. Marge, and everyone in Marge's family, blamed Lucy for Ginny's 'disgrace.' It was easier than shunning Ginny, who was super popular and whose family owned the only bookstore in town. A lot of other women Ginny's age did things in those days they'd rather not take responsibility for. Since Lucy wasn't here to defend herself, she became the scapegoat for all of it."

Ethan tapped his fingers against the desk. "Huh. And now?"

"I wish I could say for sure. Some people are likely happy to have the sacrificial lamb back in

town, while others probably don't care for the reminder of what they did years ago. What happened back then . . . parts of it aren't mine to tell. But the day—the week, really—of Cecile's death was one of those times you never forget. For me, it was like realizing I'd been living in Stepford all my life, that people I'd thought were mildly annoying were actually evil and the others went along because it benefited them in some way. The Pikes, my own family, the whole damned town. I was happy Lucy had escaped."

"Whatever it is you're not saying, Lucy doesn't seem to have held it against you, though she certainly doesn't care for your father. You should have seen her face when he walked in demanding an audience. What does she think of your brother, Drew?"

TJ laughed, her troubled blue eyes suddenly cold and flat. "If he had a heart, she'd probably put a stake through it. But if he turns up dead, I'll swear on my mother's grave I never said that."

Ethan's curiosity clamored, but long-unused instinct warned him he couldn't press without TJ shutting down entirely, so he changed the subject. He touched the books on his desk.

"You knew she'd written these, even though she didn't use the name Sadler."

"Strictly coincidence. I picked up *Seven, Eight* because it was recommended reading in my criminal justice class. I didn't realize till I saw her picture inside the cover that Lucy Caldwell and Lucy Sadler were the same person. There was no missing it, though. Her father must have had weak genes, 'cause Lucy could be Cecile's clone. Once I discovered she'd started writing true crime, I knew sooner or later she'd try to find out what happened to her mother."

"I'll have to take a look at the file. Cecile Sadler?"

"Aside from a couple of photos and the autopsy report, the file's only two pages long. There's some physical evidence—bits of blood and hair—but they never came up with a suspect to match it to. Like I said, her murder wasn't high priority. Most common belief was that a stranger did it, some man she'd picked up in a bar. But I never believed that. I always thought Lucy took off out of fear the guy would do the same to her and Timmy as he had to Cecile, then changed her name to stay out of sight."

"And you just happen to know the report is two pages long?" Just how deep did TJ's relationship with the enigmatic Lucy Sadler Caldwell go? And despite Lucy's anger and determination, would her arrival actually change anything? Seventeen years was a long time for a case to be cold. Not that even older cases hadn't been closed. Perhaps her killer had been caught for some other crime in the meantime, his DNA logged into the system. If there was anything left to test from Cecile's case, he could check.

"You remember how when I came on board six months ago I went through the files to . . . uh . . . familiarize myself with how everything in the department worked?"

"Yep."

"Well, I familiarized myself with Lucy's case, too."

"You went back a ways to do that. I checked the last ten years myself when I was hired. In all that time, we have five unsolveds. You know what they are?"

"One homicide, when the Gas 'n' Go clerk got shot; one missing person; an arson; and two armed robberies. If you'd gone a little further than that, you'd have found another arson—though Al Pike insisted it was an accident, cause unknown—Cecile's murder, another missing person, and two rapes. I went back twenty years."

"Good job. I knew you were thorough when I hired you, but that's above and beyond."

TJ blushed a little at the compliment. "Of course, unless Lucy finds a way to connect them to her mother's murder, none of the other unsolveds are apt to matter, so there's no reason to review them. But when Miz Wilson called, I knew it was all about to start again. And, to be blunt, it scares the hell out of me. If Cecile's killer *is* still in town, I could lose a friend all over again. This time for good."

It scared him, too, Ethan reflected as he shut the door behind TJ. It also explained the quality and quantity of firepower Lucy Sadler Caldwell owned. He picked up the earliest of the books she'd left him, *Finding Sarah*, and the list of precincts she'd given as references. Matching one to the case described in the book, he dialed the number. Rather than asking for any of the men she'd named specifically, however, he explained that Lucy was in town doing an investigation, and asked to speak to whoever could give him the best background on her. As he'd suspected, the man he was transferred to was not on Lucy's list.

"I don't suppose Lucy gave you my name, Donovan, so I've got to ask myself how you come to have it."

Ethan heard tapping in the background. Artie Buck was checking on him. No surprise; he'd do the same in Buck's shoes.

"The Sarah Lowell murder case was the subject of Lucy's first book. To get what she did from your department, someone had to have vouched for her, which meant she had a personal connection. No one talks that openly to a writer with no previous credits unless someone's gone to bat for her."

Buck was silent so long that if it hadn't been for the steady sound of keys tapping in the background, Ethan might have thought he'd hung up.

"You'll do," he said finally, with a bark of harsh, smoker's laughter. "What can I tell you?"

"I'll take whatever you'll give me."

"You read her books?"

"Not yet."

"Tell you what. You read one. Not the first, though. It's good, but it won't give you what you need. Pick one of the others, then call me back." He gave Ethan his cell phone number. "Don't worry about the time. I'll be up."

HER BROTHER WAS mowing the lawn in front of the house when Lucy pulled up and, as always, her heart twisted at the sight. Tim hated her fear of his disease, hated how tight, how close she held him, but she couldn't help herself. He frequently reminded her that, at twenty-one, he no longer needed a mother, and he was probably right. But she needed him. He was the only family she had left, the only person she trusted right to the bone.

A genetic mutation, the doctors had explained three years before, when the symptoms had begun to appear. Spinal muscular atrophy occurred approximately one time in ten thousand, usually the result of having two parents with the recessive gene for it. Since Tim hadn't noticed the persistent weakness in his shoulders and thighs until he was eighteen, they'd classed his case as adult-onset, the form with the best possible prognosis. In fact, he might live an almost normal life. Then again, he might not.

He cut the motor when she climbed from the car.

"I hope you're planning to help rake all this stuff up," he groused. "I told you no one would have done a lick around here in ages."

"Yeah, yeah. You were right to insist on bringing the mower. I admit it."

"Hah!" He did a crazy little victory dance that made her giggle as she watched from under half-closed lids. She'd learned the art of evaluating his health without appearing to. He hadn't pushed too hard; he just wanted her to get her hands dirty, too. "Okay. Let me get changed, and I'll give you a hand."

In the house, Lucy pulled off her suit and let her hair down from its punishing knot. She'd been determined not to let Dobbs Hollow's self-righteous citizens see her sweat, and not to let them believe—even for a moment—she'd take the kind of abuse they'd given her mother. Lucy Caldwell might look like Cecile Sadler, but there was a world of difference between them. For a moment, she flashed back to Ethan Donovan and the way he'd held her hand when she'd introduced herself.

She wished she knew what she'd revealed to that fathomless, assessing stare. She hadn't missed the first flare of heat in his moss-green eyes, but he'd banked it, flattened his gaze almost immediately. And it didn't have to mean anything. Some men reacted that way to all women. Perhaps that was Donovan's weakness, the flaw that had left a man so apparently strong and smart vulnerable to a shark like Mayor Andrew Dobbs.

The house had only two bedrooms, so Lucy had taken Cecile's old room and given Tim the one they'd shared as children. Her sleeping bag lay on the floor where a bed would rest soon enough, and two suitcases lay open next to it. She selected a pair of shorts and a tee and ducked into the bathroom to change. Nothing in life had ever felt as good as peeling off the horrible, hot nylons and shaking her hair loose.

She splashed cold water on her face and tied her hair back into a loose ponytail. The light in the bathroom sputtered and went out. She hadn't thought to bring bulbs, so focused had she been on bringing only the essentials. Well, she could go shopping later.

She pulled on the work clothes in the darkened room and went back downstairs. Even now, after living with it for a day, she had a hard time reconciling the living room with the picture she held in her memories. Someone had replaced the olive-green shag with a tan-and-chocolate cut-and-loop that wouldn't show dirt, and had painted the walls a pale cream.

In most cases she'd written about, she had extensive crime-scene photos to work from. She doubted she'd be offered that kind of courtesy from the Dobbs Hollow Police Department, and she refused to get Tara in trouble by asking her to go behind her boss's back. The lack wasn't particularly important. She'd found her mother's body; the image wasn't likely to fade.

The emotions were another matter entirely. She'd stuffed those down so deep she wasn't certain she could access them again even if she wanted to. And she did want to. To write a good book, she needed to.

She shook off the troubling thoughts and stopped in the kitchen for two glasses of the iced tea she'd made that morning, then went out to join her brother. Tim had separated trash from the leaves, and was stuffing junk into a contractor's garbage bag when she joined him.

"Some kids around here are gonna be upset we've moved in," he said, holding up a bong he'd found loosely hidden in a pile of leaves. "This seems to have been the local party spot."

"They'll find another. They always do."

"What was it when we lived here?"

"Like I would have been invited to the party spot?" She laughed, punched him lightly in the shoulder, and turned to work, avoiding the question. Tim didn't need to hear about his sister's teen angst, her imaginary friends. Parts of the past she'd have to admit to him before she finished the manuscript, but not all. Never all.

They were sitting on the front porch, sweating, laughing, and drinking tea while looking with satisfaction at the seventeen leaf bags they'd filled with grass, leaves, and twigs when a dusty, blue, crew cab pickup pulled into the driveway. They were unable to see who was driving, and Lucy sent Tim inside to get the shotgun. Not that she expected trouble. Not so soon. But it didn't hurt to let people know she wouldn't take any flack. If Ellen Wilson and Marge Bollingham knew she had come home, so did the whole town of Dobbs Hollow.

Tim stepped back outside just as Ethan Donovan unfolded himself from the vehicle, and Lucy motioned to her brother to set the gun aside. She didn't know what to make of Donovan—she wouldn't until she could press a few friends for details, and find out who he was and why Andrew Dobbs had hired him—but she didn't figure he posed an immediate threat. The cable company was due that afternoon, and she'd check him out on the Internet once they'd installed everything.

He nodded to Lucy, then held out a hand to her brother. "Ethan Donovan. You must be Tim. TJ told me Lucy had a brother."

They shook hands, two wary male animals assessing each other. "Who's TJ?"

"Tim doesn't remember the people from around here. He was too young when we left." She put her arm protectively around her brother's waist, but he shrugged her off.

"Well, then. TJ—or Tara Jean, as your sister calls her—is a cop. And, if Lucy didn't explain, I'm Dobbs Hollow's chief of police." Ethan spoke easily, casually, as if he greeted every new member of the Hollow personally. Lucy estimated he had an inch or so on her brother's six feet, putting him almost a foot over her own five three. His clean, pressed, tan shirt stretched only slightly to cover his wide shoulders. She'd noticed that at the police station, but she'd missed the fact that his jeans, while neat and clean, were old enough to have molded to a very nice pair of thighs.

All in all, he presented an intimidating front, especially with the duty belt circling his waist, badge, gun, radio, and cuffs all in place. Could be he donned it any time he was farther than a block or two from the station, or could be he was trying to make a point about the official nature of his visit.

Either way, Police Chief Donovan she could handle; it wasn't until he glanced her way and Ethan the man peered out through the cop's eyes that she found herself backing up a step. It was there again, the slicing heat that suddenly made her conscious of how little she was wearing. She straightened her back. This was her home. She'd dress how she liked. She was not her mother, and no one, *no one* would ever make her feel cheap.

He took a long stride forward, narrowing the space between them, and for a moment she had the completely irrational urge to flee, along with the equally ridiculous idea that he could see exactly what she felt. He held out a manila envelope.

"A copy of the file on your mother's death," he said. "I'm afraid there's not much there. We have some physical evidence. I'll get it pulled and sent to the county lab."

For a moment, simple shock robbed her of words. He'd brought her the file? Without her even asking? Beneath the gratitude, suspicion nagged. What did he want? And physical evidence . . . that was more than she could have hoped for. But it couldn't stay in the county.

"Thank you," she said at last. She carefully avoided touching his hand as she accepted the envelope, remembering the calloused heat of it from their first meeting. "And you have no need to apologize. I'm glad to have whatever I can get." And she was, regardless of his motive. After all, Billy Pike wouldn't have given her the time of day, let alone the report on her mother's murder. But if Ethan thought such a simple action could win her over, he had another think coming.

"As long as you're being so cooperative, though, is there one more favor I could ask?"

"I guess that depends on what it is."

"Would you mind sending the DNA tests to the state lab rather than the county one?"

He tilted his head to the side and surveyed her in silence for a full minute. "You want to tell me why?"

Lucy swallowed. "Not so much. Like I said, it's a favor."

After another long examination, he nodded. "State it is. I hope you'll trust me enough one of these days to tell me why. They'll take longer, though. They always do."

"That's okay. I've waited seventeen years."

His lips curved into a crooked half smile. "I guess you have, at that."

The glass of the windows caught the afternoon sun and Ethan nodded to the plywood leaning up against the side of the house. "You're not staying out here, are you? This place has been abandoned for years."

"It wasn't exactly abandoned." Lucy bristled. "We just couldn't get here before."

 

ETHAN CURSED HIMSELF for a fool. *Caldwell.* He'd spoken to the man himself after the third time kids had broken into the place. The man had apologized, and a week later a crew from out of town had rolled in and repainted the place, cleaned it up, nailed fresh plywood boards over the windows, and installed new deadbolts and padlocks on all the doors. He flicked a glance at Lucy's left hand, but she had jammed it into the pocket of her jeans. Could Caldwell be her husband? She hadn't been wearing a ring that morning. He would have noticed. He'd sure as hell noticed everything else about her from the wisps of blonde hair escaping an almost painfully tight bun to the pointed heels he was pretty sure weren't her usual footwear.

But maybe she'd left the ring behind for some reason. Perhaps she'd split from her husband even while keeping his name for professional reasons. Even so, how could a man who'd ever cared about her let her come out here with only her brother for protection? A brother who, unless his instincts had atrophied completely, wasn't quite what he should be.

"So the two of you are going to live here?"

"That's the plan."

"I suppose there's no point in trying to talk you out of it?"

Tim snorted. "Good luck, pal. I've been working on that for months."

Lucy frowned at her brother, and Ethan restrained a smile. She wouldn't thank him for it, but he appreciated Tim's point of view.

"Ah, well. No point in arguing a lost cause, so I'll be on my way. I wouldn't stay outside too much after dusk if I were you. With the woods right across the street and the lake less than half a mile from here, the mosquitoes are killer this time of year. Don't hesitate to call if you need anything." He nodded to both of them as he climbed into the truck.

Time for him to get home. He had reading to do.

ERIC ALLENBY WAITED, slowly becoming one with the stillness of the woods. He lived in a small house on two acres of land, worked late as a security guard in an empty factory, and yet he never felt as alone, or as right, as he did surrounded by the scrub cedar and tall, straight oaks. His heart beat with the night, and he took a deep breath, inhaling the very forest into his body.

Eric heard the rumble of Jed Martin's SUV as it pulled up. Normally, supplying the prey for their hunts was Eric's job. He knew how to take them at places and times they wouldn't be missed. But that required planning, and Jed had wanted to hunt tonight. He'd found the perfect prey, he claimed. Eric hoped he hadn't done anything stupid.

But surely he wouldn't have brought Lucy Sadler out.

Not yet. He wanted to, that much Eric understood, which was why he'd scheduled tonight's hunt so precipitously. Jed needed to reassert his power. That was the essential difference between the two men: Eric hunted for the joy of outsmarting the prey, for the thrill of the chase. Jed was in it for the kill. Night-vision goggles, waiting for moonless nights, duct-taping the prey's hands behind its back, all were fair in Jed's book. Eric preferred a more equal fight. But it wasn't worth ending their partnership over, especially since, beneath his genial good-old-boy persona, Jed Martin was violent as hell. Eric never let himself forget that.

Jed pulled up next to him and opened the back of the SUV. "Give me a hand with this."

The back of the SUV held a large black trunk with chrome latches. Eric held a gun pointed at the trunk while Jed popped the locks. The woman inside remained utterly still.

"Get up, you stupid cow," said Jed. "You're not fooling anyone with the unconscious act."

Slowly, the woman raised her head. Big, brown, pleading eyes stared out at them. Doe eyes. Eric hoped she proved more of a challenge than the average deer, or the hunt would be completely unsatisfying. Duct tape had been wrapped around her mouth, preventing her from calling out for help.

Putting a knee up on the bed of the SUV, Jed dropped a cloth bag over her head. She began to struggle then, but he managed to keep her down and tie the drawstring around her neck. When she could no longer see, Eric tucked his gun back into the holster at his side and helped Jed drag her from the trunk. They couldn't begin the hunt so close to the road. Even at one in the morning, she might find her way to civilization before they could trap her.

They half dragged, half carried her deep into the forest. Then they pulled the hood up and off.

"You get a full minute head start. After that, we're coming after you." Eric repeated the words in Spanish. When she just stood there, Jed pulled a knife, and she finally got the idea. With a single, desperate, backward look, she took off into the forest.

"She's quick," Jed observed.

"Yeah, but she's headed in toward the lake. No way she survives more than a half hour, max."

"Yeah." Jed pulled the night-vision goggles over his face. "Well, time to play."

They surged off into the darkness, splitting up after a few steps. Eric was an excellent tracker, and the woman was terrified, making no effort to hide her trail. But he preferred to give her a bigger head start, to give himself more of a challenge. He wasn't likely to lose her, not with all the noise she made. Clearly, she'd been a city dweller once, wherever Jed had found her. He yawned and stretched. Over to his left, Jed was making almost as much noise as the prey.

Suddenly, everything quieted. Interesting. What could the woman have done? What could she be planning? He began following her trail. Carefully, slowly. They always let the prey keep their clothes. Eric knew determined prey could make weapons out of shirts, shoes, even socks. He never underestimated them.

He got about a half mile into the woods, and the trail ended. Just ended. Her shoes were there, next to the end of the trail, a pair of cheap, worn-out running shoes. Why would she have discarded them? He tied the laces through his belt so the sneakers hung down at his side. Children and adults walked these woods by day; nothing could be left for them to find.

The woods were too silent, with the notable exception of Jed's heavy boots off to Eric's right. Eric sniffed the air, thick with humidity and heavy with the scent of decay. A storm was coming. As long as it didn't descend tonight and ruin the hunt, Eric didn't care. But the heavy air made scenting her difficult.

He squinted and turned in a slow circle. There. To the

right. A tree limb bent awkwardly forward. She'd been through here. Or had she laid a false trail? No, she was too urban and too scared. She'd run; she'd just decided to be quieter about it. He slipped after her, following the bent and broken branches and crushed leaves on the ground.

Now he was closer. He could hear her breathing, harsh in the night. But he could hear Jed, too, moving in from the side. He'd obviously spotted her with his thermal imaging goggles.

She'd changed direction and was headed for the road; in another few minutes, she might have reached it. Not that anyone traveled the byways of Adams County in the middle of the night, but anything was possible.

No need to concern themselves with that now, though. Eric circled around to cut off her escape and, they converged on her mere yards from the blacktop. In daylight, she might even have been able to make out the end of the forest. But tonight she saw only Eric as he stepped out in front of her, blocking her path. She jerked to a stop, freezing like the deer he'd first thought her, and let out a little yelp. She'd removed the duct tape somewhere. He'd have to go back along the trail and find it—Jed would have left fingerprints when putting it on her.

He grinned, and she spun on her toes, only to run smack into Jed, who'd come up behind her. She screamed in earnest then, and Jed clocked her. The woods went silent once more.

# CHAPTER THREE

It has been twenty-four years since Janie Talbot's murder, twenty-two since her father was convicted of raping her and strangling her with her own jump rope, eight since he was stabbed to death in prison, and four since he was exonerated. Tilly Watkins, Janie Talbot's best friend, has three girls of her own. They are the only children in their neighborhood who don't skip rope.

FROM *SEVEN, EIGHT, SHUT THE GATE: THE JANIE TALBOT STORY* BY LUCY CALDWELL

LUCY ROLLED OVER, watching the lights pass her bedroom window once again. Every time she managed to doze off, a noise or a light would startle her awake. Was someone out there, watching? Or was she just so unused to the country that its once-familiar rhythms now set her on edge? The stress of the day had taken its toll. She was exhausted, but sleep eluded her.

Giving up, she hauled her body out of bed and slipped downstairs. A light still shone under Tim's door, and the clatter of keys gave away his occupation. Video games, online chatting sites, and instant messages opened a world to him that remained opaque to her. He had a Facebook page, but when she'd asked whether she could be his friend, his horrified look had said it all. And his studies . . .he'd gone to college to get, of all things, a business degree. Nothing could be more foreign to Lucy.

So she slipped past his door, leaving him to his late-night journeys, and tiptoed down the creaky stairs to study her mother's case file.

She still couldn't get over the ease of its acquisition. She'd been prepared to fight to get her hands on the information, not to have it handed over. Had it been sanitized? Was that why Donovan had turned it over so lightly? If so, it had likely happened long before his arrival. But no, chances were better that the investigation had simply been shoddy from the beginning. Al Pike never worked harder than absolutely necessary, and a prostitute's death wouldn't have merited missing his golf game.

She flipped on a lamp and opened the folder. The pictures were on top, curiously flat against the vibrancy of her own memories and dreams. She would study them by day, though, since the living room lights didn't provide a great deal of illumination.

Next up, the autopsy report. She tried, really tried to see her mother as just another victim. But the clinical words defeated her. Cecile had suffered defensive wounds on her arms and hands and four shallow stab wounds on her back before the final coup de grâce. Bruising on her face indicated she'd been beaten. The medical examiner hadn't bothered with a sexual-assault exam. Lucy didn't recognize the man's name, but she wrote it down. Maybe she could dig him up and talk to him about the exam, see if there was anything he hadn't put in his notes because he hadn't believed it to be relevant.

As she scribbled questions she wanted to ask, she realized her eyes had filled with tears. She rubbed them away. She couldn't afford side trips into sentimentality. If she wanted to find her mother's killer, she had to stay calm, professional, and alert. She'd no sooner reminded herself to stay cool than a car passed by, the moron behind the wheel leaning on the horn and practically scaring her out of her skin.

Fury shut off the tears. Two in the morning, there was nothing for the guy to honk at. Probably no real reason for him to be on the road. Just some idiot with an axe to grind.

Still, he'd gotten her adrenaline flowing, and now it was even less likely she'd manage any sleep. She turned the page and began to examine the names of the men Al Pike had interviewed in her mother's case.

ETHAN RUBBED HIS eyes and winced as the grit beneath his lids scratched against his corneas. Two thirty in the morning. Not the time to call his sister and force her to be certain his nieces — Allison, age eight, and Emily, age five — were safe in their beds, no matter how much he might want to. Artie Buck, however, was fair game.

"Been waiting," he said when Ethan identified himself. "Which one did you choose?"

"I read the Talbot book. Skimmed the others."

"You like them?"

"Not particularly, no. Why would anyone spend her life immersing herself in other people's pain and misery?"

"You do. I do."

"We're cops. We have to."

"She's a victim. Maybe she has to, too. And she's good. If something happened to me, I'd want her to tell my story."

"I'll give you that." Ethan rubbed his hands over his arms where goose bumps had risen. "Those books were creepy as hell. So what can you tell me about her?"

"Not much, given how long I've known her. She was just a kid first time I saw her. Scrawny, but scrappy. My partner, Todd Caldwell, he caught Lucy stealing stuff for her little brother. More than fifteen years ago now. Todd and Karen, they couldn't have children, so just like that he took those two home and made them his own. Probably wasn't legal, but who was gonna complain with the system overloaded as it is? Karen got sick. Died a couple years later. Tim was still a kid, and Todd wouldn't leave him with anyone, so he pretty much grew up in the house."

"She watches him too carefully. There's something off there. At his age, he should be spending the summer with his buddies, not his sister."

A scratchy sound, then a long inhalation told Ethan that Buck had lit a cigarette.

"Observant bastard, aren't you? I'd heard that, but it's good to have it confirmed.

"It's not my business to say what's between Lucy and Tim. I doubt he's happy she's hunting a murderer, since he's lost three parents already. Probably went along because he figured he could protect her. Hell, he might be right. Fact is, Lucy worries more about him than she needs to. He couldn't pass the academy physical, but he's not going to drop dead any minute, either."

*Some people have bad luck and others have no luck at all.* Lucy fell into the latter category.

"And your partner? You said three parents."

"Punk stabbed him in the kidney one night a couple months back when he was buying cat food. Dumb fuck shoulda gone to the grocery store, not the damned gas station."

"I'm sorry."

"Me, too." Silence fell between them. On the job or off, cops' lives always seemed to end badly.

"When we caught the three-time loser who killed Todd, we told Lucy. Wanted her to know we were bringing him in. It was courtesy, you understand?" He did. "She walked right up to him in booking—no one thought twice about her being there—and told him he had two choices: he could make a deal with the DA to plead guilty if they took the death penalty off the table, and he'd have a chance at getting out before he hit fifty, or she'd save the state the cost of a trial and kill him before he saw twenty-five."

"Surely he complained?"

"Not a peep. He believed every word she said. I did, too. She doesn't much care what happens to herself, which makes her a damned effective investigator but gives me heartburn." And more, Ethan guessed. Artie Buck might sound casually disinterested about Lucy and Tim, but they were his partner's kids, which made them his.

"She got the estate settled—Todd had a solid life insurance policy, so they should be doing okay in that respect anyway—and then took off. Didn't tell me where she was headed. She decided it was time to go home, huh?"

"Seems like."

"You gonna watch out for her?"

"With all due respect, sir, the woman travels with an arsenal. She can watch out for herself." But it couldn't hurt to be sure.

⤳

ETHAN'S PHONE RANG at seven, a scant four hours after he'd crawled into bed, and he debated the wisdom of answering it. Keith Arlen had the morning shift, so Ethan didn't have to be at the station until one, but in Dobbs Hollow "working hours" didn't seem to apply to the chief of police. If folks couldn't find him at the station, they just called him at home.

A glance at the caller ID, though, showed TJ's cell.

"Hey, boss," she said when he picked up. "I'm parked outside the Sadler place. I stopped by to bring them muffins this morning. Thing is, someone beat me here."

Ethan paused, unable to speak as he pulled his T-shirt over his head. "What happened?"

"A couple hours ago, someone tossed a couple bricks through the front window, wrapped in paper with explicit instructions to get out of town."

"They okay?"

"Yeah. Pissed off, but not hurt. According to Lucy, she swept up the glass, reboarded the window and went back to bed."

"Why the hell didn't they call it in?"

TJ's silence answered for her, and he blew out a deep breath to ease his frustration. Okay, so Lucy's distrust of the Dobbs Hollow residents included him. He'd led plenty of investigations where suspects, witnesses and even victims didn't trust him. "Fine. I'll be there in a couple minutes."

Ethan elected to forgo the lights and siren, not wanting to draw attention, but he drove as if using them, ignoring most of the stop signs, as he was alone on the road. When he skidded to a stop, he saw Lucy—standing on the porch with TJ, surveying the damage—jump. TJ put her arm over her friend's shoulders, and Lucy relaxed a bit.

Ethan, on the other hand, found every muscle in his body frozen into place. He'd seen Lucy in a business suit and he'd seen her in shorts, but this morning she appeared to be wearing nothing but an oversized Cowboys football jersey. Her hair fell about her shoulders in a golden tangle, shimmering in the morning sun. Christ on a crutch. How was he supposed to concentrate on a crime scene with her looking like she'd just crawled out of bed? Which, come to think of it, she probably had. He hadn't had such an immediate physical reaction to the sight of a woman since . . . well . . . since Betty Ramsey had invited him into her room while her parents were away when they were in high school.

Just then, Lucy noticed his gaze. She glanced down, and a hot blush swept up from her ankles all the way up to her face. In a flash, she disappeared inside the house, freeing Ethan to climb from his car.

The front window, from which Lucy and Tim had removed the plywood only the day before, was once again boarded up. In addition, two red paint bombs had been tossed at the house, exploding against the wall and dripping down the white siding like blood. Lucy couldn't have missed the similarity. Ethan walked over to check out the source of the paint, expecting paintball shells or balloons. Instead, two broken condoms rested below the red streaks. Lucy couldn't have missed that, either.

"I'm sure it was just kids," she said, coming back out to the porch. She'd donned jeans along with a T-shirt, and pulled her thick, honey-colored hair up into a high ponytail. Her feet were still bare, however, her toenails polished a pale pink.

Ethan dragged his gaze from the fascinating glimpse of feminine softness provided by those touches of pink back up to her face. "No, ma'am, I don't think so. Kids, they might TP your house, or spray random slogans, or even go for the shock value of an inverted pentagram or two, but the kids around here don't know you. They've got no reason to bust out your windows and send notes telling you to go home."

Lucy's eyes closed for a minute, and she took a deep breath and blew it out slowly. "My mother wasn't liked in this town. I don't aim to be liked, either. You don't need to come out here every time some fool gets it into his head to try to aggravate me into leaving, or you won't have time to help anyone else."

He shrugged. "Not much crime around here, anyway. So go on and call when things like this happen. I get too busy to pay attention, you'll be the first to know." He could see her getting ready to argue, so he turned away and spoke to TJ.

"Drive over to Redmond's and see if anyone's been buying red paint the last couple days. Check Dumpsters, too, in case any of the dimmer bulbs threw away empty cans with prints on 'em. Anyone still owe on com serve hours?"

TJ thought for a minute, then smiled. "Yeah. Tommy Jenkins and Roy Lighter still owe ten hours apiece for destruction of school property." She turned to Lucy. "They made good on generations' of kids promises to burn the Dobbs Hollow Dragon costume."

Lucy laughed, and Ethan felt as if someone had thrown one of the window bricks at him, knocking all the air from his lungs.

"I'd think that would be considered a good deed, not a crime."

"Yeah, well, Coach Barnes and the school board didn't see it that way." TJ switched her attention to Ethan, who'd lost track of the conversation. Damn, Lucy Caldwell was a dangerous woman. "You want me to get Tommy and Roy over here?"

"Yeah." He practically shook himself back on track. "Have them scrub this garbage off the wall before the mayor has himself a heart attack about the town's lack of decorum."

TJ grinned, but Lucy stiffened again at the mention of Dobbs' name and protested. "I can handle this myself."

"You want to involve your brother in cleaning up this mess, right after he helped you get the whole yard done yesterday? Because you know he won't let you do it on your own."

A muscle flexed in her jaw.

"I didn't think so." If he'd ever seen two people so determined to protect each other, Ethan couldn't remember it. But he could, without any guilt whatsoever, use that protective impulse.

"Why don't you take him over Maxie's Diner for breakfast. I'll have this fixed before you get home."

"You don't have to do that."

"Well, now, I figure I know that. Being a detective and all."

"Give it up, Luce. You're not going to win. The chief does what he *wants* to do, not what he's *supposed* to do."

Lucy didn't look convinced, so Ethan asked her whether she or her brother could handle a screwdriver. The seeming non sequitur stopped her argument and wrinkled her brow.

"Sure. Why?"

"'Cause I have a trade in mind. The kids will deal with your house. You tell Maxie I said to let you and Tim replace the hinges on her door. She has the tools and hardware, but her husband's a dead loss when it comes to even the simplest home repairs. It'll keep your brother out of the way for the morning and get Maxie off my back at the same time."

*Proud*, he thought as she nodded slowly. She wouldn't take charity, but she'd make a deal. He wondered whether she'd even have been willing to go that far if he hadn't brought up Tim's name.

⌒

HALF AN HOUR later, Lucy found herself seated in the back booth of Maxie's Diner with Tim opposite her and Maxine Allen next to her. When Ethan had told her to speak to the diner's owner, Lucy's imagination had produced a frumpy woman with overly dyed hair, crepe-soled shoes, and more than a few extra pounds. Maxie, however, appeared to be in her late forties, and she dressed to match her diner's fifties-chic decor. The cinch-waisted dress she wore suited her height and her narrow, elegant figure, as did her low-heeled pumps.

"I can't believe Ethan put y'all to work on your first day here! Or, technically, I guess it's your second." Maxie laughed, a throaty, sexy sound Lucy bet brought men from miles around to eat in the restaurant.

"Oh, it's not a problem. He's helping out with some stuff over at our house, and Tim's very handy."

"Which is great," Maxie said with a wink, "because Buddy certainly isn't."

"This place . . . I don't remember it."

"No, you probably wouldn't. I only opened it a few years before your mother died. Y'all didn't spend much time in town." Now there was an understatement. Cecile didn't encourage her children to stray far from the house, and the other kids didn't welcome them in their hangouts.

"Have you always lived here?" Lucy asked, trying to keep to her usual, calm pace of questioning instead of rushing ahead. Cecile's ghost seemed to inhabit the booth with them, begging her daughter to hurry, hurry, hurry.

"Oh, heavens, yes," Maxie said. "Grew up just down the street at the corner of Willis and Oak. Not that you care about my history. Word is, you've come to find out about your momma. So you probably want to talk about her, not me."

"Oh no. Well, I mean, yes, of course. But I want to hear about you, too. I love to talk to people about their histories. If I didn't write true crime, I'd probably be a biographer."

"Well, I don't believe in talking on an empty stomach. So let me get Buddy working on breakfast. We don't do fancy here. For that, you gotta go up to Barney's. He's got a brunch on Sundays so good I close the diner so I can eat it myself."

Lucy laughed. "Tim usually does all the cooking. I bet he's just glad to have a breakfast he didn't have to make himself for once."

"You like to cook?" An avaricious gleam entered the older woman's eyes.

"If it weren't for me, we'd both starve," Tim confirmed with a smirk.

"Well, then you should come on into to the kitchen with me and meet my husband. Buddy makes a mean cheesy egg casserole. If you don't mind leaving the two of us to our girl talk, that is."

"Not at all." Tim had never acquired a taste for Lucy's research.

Maxie returned a couple of minutes later with two cups of coffee, taking Tim's seat so she could

look at Lucy while they spoke.

"He really enjoys cooking?" Lucy nodded. "Then, if he needs a job, he can work here. Like I said,

the food's plain, but we could use a hand, and if he wants to try out a few more complicated recipes, well, I'm open to that, too. The Hollow's coming up in the world, and people here have more sophisticated tastes these days."

"I bet he'd love that. But I have to warn you: not everyone's overjoyed to have us back. Someone already threw a pair of bricks through our window, and I wouldn't want you to have trouble because Tim worked here."

Maxie laughed again. "Honey, having that boy here will make me a rich woman. Everyone in town's heard y'all have moved back, and they're going to want to keep their eyes on the both of you at all times. The ones who actually know you 'round here these days are a minority. A very vocal minority, I'll give you that, but still. The rest will want to come in to find out what all the fuss is about. I foresee a huge increase in business."

"In that case, I'll certainly talk to him."

"Good. But I'm guessing right now you want to ask me about your momma."

Lucy sucked in a deep breath, let it out slowly. "Did you know her?"

"Sure. Not too well, though, since she was a couple years younger than me. I'm fifty-one. Near as I recall, she'd be forty-nine."

"That's right." Lucy had to force herself to ask the next question calmly, not to jump all over Maxie in delight at having found someone willing to speak to her. "Did you grow up together?"

Maxie looked at her oddly. "She didn't grow up here at all. Didn't you know that?"

"No. It never even occurred to me. . . ." Lucy's excitement evaporated, and she wanted to slam her head into the table. How could she not have researched such a basic thing? She'd planned to get her mother's birth certificate eventually—it was precisely the kind of thing that made for interesting photographs in a book—but she'd been so focused on the end of Cecile's life, she hadn't spent time yet on the beginning.

"I'm sorry."

"No, it's fine. That's exactly the kind of thing I came to find out. When did she move here?"

"Well, you were just a little thing. Three or four, I think. And she was twenty-one. I remember because Buddy and I had just gotten married. He was home on leave, and he left again not a week after she got here. She took an apartment in town at first, and got a job over to the drugstore. Doc White, he was the pharmacist, he let her bring you to work with her."

Lucy forced her mind back, but couldn't remember being a child in an apartment, or playing in a drugstore, let alone a life before those things. "How long did that last?"

"Not too long, actually. Not even a year. She said she'd inherited a little money, then bought the house way out on the post road. It was considered unsociable, when there were houses for sale much closer to town. When you went into first grade, she quit her job at the drugstore."

"Inherited? So we had other family?" Everything Lucy thought she knew was crumbling. They had family? Maybe cousins? Someone she and Tim could have gone to who would have taken them in? Was it even possible? Why would her mother have kept such important information away from her?

"I never heard any details. Just she inherited money. That was when the talk began. Here was this woman with a child who had no father anyone knew of, which was pretty bad in those days, and then she up and quit her job. The gossips began wondering just how much money she had and how she might be making more."

"Especially since she drank an awful lot of it away."

"Yes." Maxie's gray eyes carefully hid any sign of pity, for which Lucy was grateful. "And when your brother came along, it just confirmed the rumors. A couple divorces got blamed on her when she started showing, including Andrew Dobbs."

"Mayor Dobbs got divorced because of my mother?" Her

research had turned up an obituary for Marianne Dobbs, but nothing about a divorce.

"If you want my opinion, Marianne Dobbs just used Cecile as an excuse to kick that no-account bastard out of the house. If there'd been more to it than that, she could have insisted on a paternity test once the kid was born, and she didn't. In fact, they never even finalized the proceedings, so I figure Marianne didn't really think her husband was Tim's daddy, she just wanted leverage if she did have to go through with the divorce. After all, the man ran around on her all the time, but he was too concerned with his public image to let on he'd had to pay for sex." She winced. "Sorry, sugar."

Lucy shrugged. "She was what she was." But maybe that was why Andrew Dobbs *Junior* had hated Lucy so much. Not an excuse for what he'd done to her in high school, but maybe an explanation.

And the paternity test . . . if Marianne Dobbs had kicked Dobbs Senior out over Cecile's pregnancy, why hadn't the mayor—or the state senator, as he'd been at the time— insisted on one to prove his innocence? Possibly, he'd hoped the whole scandal would just die faster if he didn't provide any more grist for the gossip mill, but, still, it was a thread Lucy would have to find the time to tug.

Tim came out of the kitchen carrying a tray of food, effectively putting an end to the conversation. But Maxie had given Lucy a great deal to think about, and the facts gnawed at her as she picked at her food, and continued to do so while she and Tim fixed the diner's door.

Once they were through, Lucy took Tim home and checked to be sure there had been no uninvited visitors during their absence. The boys Ethan had sent over to scrub the walls had almost finished, and she told Tim to invite them in for iced tea and ice cream when they were done. She still resented Donovan's interference in her life, but she had to admit the house did look better, and it was a distinct relief not to have to concern herself with Tim's well-being in the brutal Texas summer heat.

Leaving the house and boys in Tim's hands, Lucy drove herself to the library. While in Dallas, she'd gathered any information as she could on the Hollow, but although the town had its own website, the local paper did not. Back issues of the *Dobbs Digest* would have to be accessed on paper or maybe on microfiche. Luckily, she wasn't trying to hide her research; she could walk up to the information desk and ask for copies.

Of course, nothing could be so simple.

# CHAPTER FOUR



I remember, in grade school, examining all the childless men in the neighborhood, wondering which one was my daddy. It didn't occur to me until after Timmy was born that our daddies might have other children, other families. I asked momma once whether she'd divorced our daddies and that's why they weren't around. She just laughed and said she'd never had that kind of luck.

FROM *A BAD DAY TO DIE*
BY LUCY SADLER CALDWELL [DRAFT]

ETHAN HAD EXPECTED a pile of memos on his desk. He hadn't expected to find Sheriff Billy Pike in his office. The man sat in Ethan's chair, resting crossed ankles on Ethan's desk and sorting through files from Ethan's inbox. When Ethan had been hired, Pike had let him know in no uncertain terms that the sheriff in Adams County outranked the Dobbs Hollow chief of police in every way.

If Ethan hadn't needed a job so badly, he'd have gone back to Houston on the spot. It had taken a while, but eventually he and Pike had come to an uneasy détente. Now, it looked as if that was over. Ethan leaned against the doorjamb, refusing to show his irritation.

"Good morning, Sheriff. What can I do for you this fine morning?"

"Mayor Dobbs tells me there's a new resident in town." Cold hazel eyes assessed Ethan, and he found himself shifting his weight from leg to leg. He forced himself to remain still and kept his voice casual.

"Several, since the last time I've seen you. The apartments over on Archer are almost full." What was it with these people and Lucy Sadler? Sure, it wouldn't be comfortable having the old murder raked up, especially since Al Pike hadn't done a damned thing to determine the culprit, but was a little embarrassment worth trying to run her out of town? And if what TJ had said was true, Billy Pike had more than likely benefited from Lucy's poor reputation when they were younger—if Drew Dobbs had held Lucy over his girlfriends' heads, no doubt Pike had done the same.

"Don't be a fool. I'm trying to give you advice here. You never met the girl or her mother, don't know darling little Lucy like the rest of us do. Liars, she and her mother both. Say anything and screw anyone to get what they want."

For the first time, Ethan realized TJ hadn't explicitly denied the rumors about Lucy's promiscuity. He felt vaguely ill. He had a hard time picturing a fifteen-year-old girl as a seductress. Especially a fifteen-year-old girl who'd grown into a woman determined to solve her mother's murder as well as care for her sick brother. And who painted her toenails baby-girl pink. He shook off the thought and focused on Pike.

"Exactly what is it she wants she'd have to lie to get? I've already given her a copy of the case file on her mother's murder."

If the statement startled Pike, he gave no sign. "If that's all she was after, she could have called and asked for it. Maybe the visit's a PR stunt. Maybe her books aren't selling all that well and she needs a boost. I have no idea, but you mark my words, that woman is trouble."

Trouble for who? Ethan examined Pike with critical eyes. The man appeared relaxed, but he'd had years of practice as an actor, any career cop had. No way was he merely here to do Ethan a favor, though. Something else was at stake. Probably whatever had made Lucy insist Ethan send any evidence in her mother's case to the state, rather than the county.

"Okay, fine," Ethan said easily, watching for any reaction. "But even if Miz Sadler isn't the town's most upstanding citizen, she's hardly county business."

Pike smiled, a tight, transparently thin grimace, not intended to signify humor in any way.

"Now, see, that's just plain shortsighted. As I recall, you have about three months left on your contract. If things don't work out here and you, say, find another position more appealing, it'll be up to me to watch out for the town until we find your replacement. So, naturally, I'm keeping an eye on the situation. In case it isn't resolved satisfactorily before then."

A threat? But Dobbs Hollow's chief of police was hired—and fired—by the mayor, with the approval of the town council. Which meant that both Pike *and* Dobbs had pawns in play. The itch at the base of Ethan's neck sharpened into pain, and he straightened from his casual slouch in the doorway. "You trying to tell me something, Sheriff? 'Cause if you are, you're going to have to be a little clearer. I'm a simple guy, so spell it out for me."

Pike rose, tossing the files he'd been perusing onto Ethan's desk, scattering papers everywhere. "Just passing along some advice," he said. "Y'all have a good day, now."

When Pike left, Ethan set about sorting through the scattered sheets and trying to process the conversation. What on earth were Dobbs and Pike hiding that they were afraid Lucy's investigation would expose? Not murder. That much he was fairly sure of. A murderer would merely have killed Lucy, disposed of her the same way he'd disposed of Cecile, and he'd have done so before anyone connected them.

⌒

"Come on, Eulie," Lucy said, forcing a strained smile at the woman behind the library's circulation counter. They'd been arguing for almost half an hour. "What am I likely to do to the microfiche machine? I promise, I have plenty of experience using them."

"Rules are rules," the woman replied with a sniff. "Once the *Dobbs Digest* goes to film, we have no other copies. We have to protect it."

"I'm a writer, for goodness sake. I treasure words. I'm the last person who would destroy them. Besides, you'll be able to keep an eye on me the whole time." Lucy gestured to the glassed-in enclosure at the rear of the library. It contained a computer, a printer, a copier, and the microfiche reader.

Not that she actually believed Eulie was worried about the films. This argument, like many others she expected to have in Dobbs Hollow, sprang from her mother's lifestyle. "I'm not saying you can't look at the microfiche, just that you need a library card like everyone else. I understand you're used to preferential treatment, but around here you're no one special."

If only that were true, but Lucy could hardly accuse Eulie of treating her badly if she wanted the woman's cooperation. And she did. Not that Eulie was likely to talk about the fact that her high school sweetheart had cheated on her, or the fact that both she and Jed had been interviewed after Cecile's murder, but Lucy wouldn't shut down a potential source.

She counted to ten, then did it a second time. "So you need what, exactly, before you'll give me a library card?"

"Proof you're a Hollow resident. Bills in your name at a local address, property tax receipts, that sort of thing. It's really not that complicated."

And if she went home to get the installation paperwork from the cable company, would the issues of the *Digest* she'd requested still be available when she returned? Or would they mysteriously have disappeared or been damaged? Perhaps she could have Tim bring her the bill, though he'd have to call a cab to do so.

She was about to pull out her cell phone when a deep voice sounded behind her, sending an unwelcome thrill up her spine.

"Now, Eulie, I'm sure you can come up with a way around this. You've too fine a mind to be flummoxed by a tangle of bureaucratic red tape."

"Chief Donovan, I never thought I'd hear you advocating breaking the rules." She sniffed again, and Lucy gave silent thanks for having left town when she did. Dobbs Hollow had apparently turned Eulie into an old woman before her fortieth birthday.

"Well, not so much breaking them as bending them. I can vouch for Miz Sadler, here. Surely you wouldn't want to deprive her and her brother of the joys of reading?"

Eulie frowned and glanced down at her hands but finally gave in with a huff, taking Lucy's twenty-five dollars and issuing her a card. Lucy restrained both a smirk at her success and a laugh at the library card, which was little more than a business card with her name and address on it. Her phone number was her library identification number—luckily, she'd written it down when the telephone company had assigned it, since the equipment itself was not yet in place—and Eulie's signature completed the ID. Glaring, Eulie passed the card through a laminating machine and handed it over.

"I'll get started, then," Lucy said, but even that couldn't go smoothly.

"It's five minutes to twelve. The library closes between twelve and one. I have to have my lunch."

Lucy ground her teeth together to keep from threatening Eulie with strangulation. The scathing remark on the tip of her tongue died, however, when Ethan Donovan laid a large, heavy hand on her shoulder.

"Course you do, Eulie. I'll bet Miz Sadler, here, needs to get some food in her, too. How 'bout it, ma'am? Care to join me for a bite? There's a burger spot about five miles down the road. Wouldn't have been around when you lived here, and Josh Edgar makes a mean cheeseburger."

The outraged expression on Eulie's face gave Lucy her

answer. Summoning her best smile and batting her lashes just a tiny bit, she hooked an arm through Ethan's and rested her fingers against his biceps. If claiming the man made his life a bit difficult, she couldn't afford to care. After all, she imagined the burger wouldn't be the only thing grilled at the restaurant.

"Why, Chief Donovan, what a lovely invitation. Of course I'll have lunch with you." Her slight stammer, she told herself, had nothing whatsoever to do with the disconcerting strength and heat of the muscles flexing beneath her fingertips.

⌣

WHAT IN HELL *had he been thinking?* Bad enough he'd played simpleton to the sheriff's good-old-boy routine, which was pretty much guaranteed to come back and bite him in the ass, but he'd just insured the biggest gossip in town would spread the word he'd taken Lucy Sadler Caldwell's side in a battle he didn't even understand.

As they left the library, she dropped her hand from his arm. Her fingernails were painted the same color as her toes. Did the polish or the attitude represent the real Lucy? The way she'd pressed her small breast against him when she slid her hand around his arm argued for the attitude—and for Sheriff Pike being right about her man-eating ways. But the deep breath she took at the bottom of the four steps down from the library's door, and the way she stretched her fingers as if her hands had been curled in tension, argued for the fingernails.

Once upon a time, he'd been a pretty good judge of character. Of course, that was Before. But he wouldn't—couldn't—let himself believe anything had changed. So he'd take this disconcerting woman to lunch and practice his rusty skills on her.

"Thank you." He stared down into those expressive blue

eyes and realized she meant for more than simply opening the door to the cruiser for her. But she'd never say it. Like her agreement to take Tim to breakfast while he arranged for her siding to be scrubbed, the thanks were offered grudgingly.

Edgar's Bar and Burger Joint wasn't crowded, but the few patrons at the scarred picnic tables salvaged from a long-deserted roadside park eyed him and Lucy avidly. He wondered whether Eulie had called ahead. He wouldn't put it past her. When Mayor Dobbs and his secretary—whom not even the most charitable believed had been hired for her typing skills—coincidentally wandered in for lunch, his suspicions were confirmed.

"I'm sorry," he said.

Her smile was half-mocking, half-bitter. "Then we're even. I'm sorry you're caught up in this. It's not your fight."

"Why don't you explain it to me. Let me decide whether I want to take it on." He didn't. He was no knight in shining armor. He'd moved to a small town to be chief of police to get away from the troubles and battles of the city. Why should he involve himself in a fight neither side seemed to want his help with? And yet, the same sensation he'd experienced in the diner, the call of anticipation and adrenaline, still coursed through him. And now it was laced with a protectiveness he didn't much like but couldn't deny. The cold case intrigued him, but even more than that, Lucy needed him. In a town where most of the crimes involved addicts and dealers, he'd forgotten how good that could feel.

Josh Edgar himself came over to take their order before Lucy so much as opened her mouth to reply. It wasn't an interruption; she hadn't spoken for the full two minutes between Ethan's request and Josh's arrival.

Josh's arms were covered with prison tats. When Ethan introduced them, she held the big black man's hand in her own as she traced the inked spider web between his thumb and forefinger with one delicate, pink nail. Transfixed by the sight, Ethan took three quick sips of water to ease the sudden dusty dryness of his throat.

"What happened?"

Josh raised one eyebrow so high it would have disappeared under his hair had he not shaved his head perfectly smooth on a regular basis.

"Now, usually, pretty ladies like yourself don't ask me that."

"Oh, I bet ladies ask you all kinds of questions, Mr. Edgar." Lucy flashed him a coy smile from under thick, sooty lashes, and Ethan took another swallow from his glass. Who could have guessed the woman could flirt? He couldn't decide whether to be offended or relieved that she chose not to practice her wiles on him. Josh laughed, the rolling boom drawing both attention and censure. One more strike against Lucy: she'd chosen to befriend the only recognizable convict in town.

"No bets, ma'am. None at all. And you can call me Josh."

Once Josh left, Ethan set his elbow on the table, propped his chin on his hand, and, without taking his eyes off Lucy, began to hum. He'd have preferred to whistle, but the picnic benches had no backs to them, and whistling while sitting straight up didn't feel right.

Lucy stared at him as if he were crazy for about two bars, then she burst into laughter. He hadn't been certain she'd recognize "A Policeman's Lot Is not a Happy One" from *The Pirates of Penzance*, but the sparkle in her eyes, and the all-out laugh that heated his blood and made the muscles in his stomach clench, were worth the chance of being thought insane. When she quit grinning, however, the sparkle died, and her whole expression went still and watchful.

"What are you doing here, Chief Donovan?"

"Ethan. And I'm taking a pretty lady to lunch."

"I didn't mean here at the restaurant; we can get to that in a minute. I meant here in the Hollow. You and your show tunes and your willingness to sit down with the likes of me and Josh Edgar don't belong."

"How 'bout we make a deal. I'll tell you how I got here if you tell me why no one wants you to stay."

She cocked her head and studied him far less kindly than she had Josh's tattoo.

"Artie called while Tim and I were rehanging the diner door this morning." She looked as if she expected an answer, but Ethan remained silent. "Between what he told you and what I said about my reasons for coming back, you should be able to figure out why at least one person, or one group of people, doesn't want me around. As for the rest . . ." She shrugged. "I suppose I remind them life isn't all sunshine and roses. My mother's very existence posed a threat to the clean, conservative image Hollow residents held of themselves and their town. Just by living in a nice house and feeding and clothing two kids, she reminded them that people have secrets, that spouses stray, and that attending church of a Sunday, which we always did, was no guarantee of righteousness."

"The sins of the mother are visited on the daughter?" Not according to TJ, but she'd also warned him Lucy might not be aware of what had been said about her. But then, why the vague and evasive answers? He couldn't push, not yet. But there was more to the story than she was telling, and he'd find it out sooner or later.

"Possibly." But her eyes shifted from his face. "So, Ch—Ethan, what brought you to lovely little Dobbs Hollow?"

"A bullet." He could do half truths as well as anyone. "I took disability retirement from the Houston police three years back after knee-replacement surgery left me incapable of working on the street."

"And then you just happened to look in the help wanted section of the *Dobbs Digest?*"

"According to Artie Buck, you'd know that's not how it works. Mayor Dobbs put out the word when his last chief retired, and someone gave him my name."

"Not to be crass, but why would he give the job to a man with a handicap?"

"Sweetheart, you figure that out, you let me know." She'd probably think he was handing her a line, but he'd never been more serious. Half the town mistrusted him because he'd been recruited from Houston when they thought the job should have gone to Ellen Wilson's nephew, Johnny, who was Sheriff Pike's chief deputy.

Josh brought their burgers, and Ethan bit into his, the rhapsody of hot meat and cold ketchup bursting on his tongue, a reminder that he'd skipped breakfast. If it had been polite, he would have groaned with joy.

"What does Dobbs have on you?" Lucy asked.

He swallowed wrong and choked. Struggling to draw breath, he wondered whether Lucy would perform the Heimlich maneuver or let him suffocate. When he regained control, he gestured to Josh to bring him an iced tea and glowered at Lucy until it arrived. After a long draught, he spoke.

"What the fuck are you accusing me of?"

"Not a damned thing." She matched him glare for glare, a fact he had to respect. She took a deep breath, then laid out her opinion in a clinical, detached tone. "But I know Andrew Dobbs, and he would never hire a man he couldn't control absolutely. So he bought your gambling debts, has pictures of you with an underage girl or a prostitute, knows about your drug habit. You don't want to tell me, that's fine."

"For crying out loud—"

She held up a hand. "But let me get this over with: you're trying to help me now. I get that. I really do. But sooner or later, it may very well come down to the Madges, the Dobbses, and the Pikes of this town versus me, and when it does, the mayor will turn whatever screws he has. It's only fair you understand up front that whatever he can do to you is nothing compared to how far I am willing to go to find out who killed my mother."

The words were emotionless, cold, but over the red rage that filled him, Ethan noticed the rise and fall of Lucy's chest, how her breath came faster and her chin rose even as she half flinched, expecting the violence in him to take physical form. Why would she deliberately provoke such a reaction? Did she even believe what she was saying? He already knew she didn't trust him, so perhaps this was nothing more than another test.

Artie had been right. Lucy's single-mindedness would get her into trouble in an inhospitable town with secrets to hide. She might not want a protector, but she was going to need one. Why Ethan felt drawn to the duty himself, well, that was still up for debate. He gritted his teeth and forced the anger down.

"For the record, if Dobbs has blackmail material on me, he hasn't seen fit to share it." But she'd put an end to his curiosity; Ethan now understood exactly why Dobbs had hired him. What he would do about it was another matter.

He nodded to the corner where Dobbs and his companion sat. "Maybe I should ask him."

OH, LUCY WAS so tempted to call his bluff. Nothing in Ethan's direct gaze indicated he was being less than perfectly truthful, but Lucy had spent half her life around cops and recognized their masks. The flat eyes, the complete lack of emotion told her he was lying, either in fact or by omission.

He hadn't reacted to her accusations, which only meant she probably hadn't hit on the right one. *Who are you, Ethan Donovan?* She should have looked into his background before she left Dallas, but involving the police in a sinkhole of corruption like Dobbs Hollow had never crossed her mind. When she got home from the library, she would go online and dig into Police Chief Donovan's background.

Then she would decide how far to trust him. Usually, she wouldn't second-guess her own judgment; she'd honed her evaluative skills to scalpel sharpness over the years and rarely mistook foe for friend. Those instincts told her that, despite his caginess, Ethan was more ally than enemy. But Dobbs Hollow had a way of clouding her mind, and she didn't dare rely on Ethan until she knew for sure where his loyalties lay. Not when he worked for Andrew Dobbs and couldn't be completely honest about his past.

So she ate silently, watching him over the enormous cheeseburger Josh had brought her.

After lunch, Ethan dropped her back at the library. Eulie's attitude had not improved, but there was nothing she could do to prevent Lucy from viewing older issues of the *Dobbs Digest*. Originally, Lucy had planned to begin with the murder and work her way backward a few years, looking for items mentioning Cecile or anyone involved with her. As her mother had always met her "dates" out of the house, Lucy had no idea who the men were. She'd been hoping the gossipy nature of the *Digest* would reveal a few clues.

Maxie's revelation about Cecile's origins, however, had altered Lucy's strategy. Now she wanted to know exactly when her mother had arrived in Dobbs Hollow, where she'd come from, and how she'd chosen this particular spot to settle. So she began the year before Maxie estimated Cecile to have arrived. If a specific event had drawn her, Lucy hoped she'd recognize its importance.

Like many small-town papers, the *Digest*'s staple fare consisted of births, deaths, weddings, and school-sports scores. It also featured a page of gossip, one of local politics, and a "crime beat" column. Cecile's arrival had made the gossip section. The writer of the day, one Marcia Stillman, inserted the information as an "item of interest to young local men."

Lucy stayed longer than she expected in the library, but that often happened when she was researching her books. Only when Eulie flicked the lights and announced the library's imminent closing did she look up from the screen. Stuffing a huge pile of printed sheets into a file folder—another habitual problem, as she never knew at the beginning of her research what might turn out to be pertinent—she grabbed the three books she'd found before lunch and approached the desk. Naturally, Eulie objected to her checking out the Hollow history books.

"Those are irreplaceable. They don't leave the building."

"Then why do they have checkout cards in the back?"

"That's library policy. All books need inventory numbers. Even those not to be removed from the premises."

Lucy sighed. "You know, if you won't let me take these home, I'll have to spend a lot more time in your personal little demesne here." Apparently, the pleasure of hamstringing Lucy's investigation surmounted the pain of having her so close, however, because Eulie remained firm.

"Well, then," Lucy said with determined cheer, "I guess I'll see you tomorrow." She even managed a little wave as, slinging the bag full of papers over her shoulder, she left.

Lucy had parked a mere hundred feet from the library, but as she approached her car, the distinct lean told her the precaution hadn't been enough: both the driver's side tires were flat. Part of her wanted to scream. Part of her wanted to cry. All of her was hot and tired and severely tempted to call a cab and come back and deal with the car in the morning. But leaving the Rover on the street overnight would only invite further vandalism.

She looked up and down the street, but no obvious culprits lurked in the vicinity. Should she call the police? No, TJ had been at her house far too early that morning. She'd surely be off duty by now, and Lucy didn't trust anyone else on the force. Besides, if she called in a complaint over such a trivial event, everyone might consider her helpless.

The library was only a few miles from her house. She

could walk it with no problem, and the exercise would be good for her after having been so long cooped up in the microfiche lab. Once there, she could look up a tow company to come and deal with the car. She called Tim and explained the problem, then set out along the road.

She'd been walking only twenty minutes when she heard a car slowing behind her. She stepped off the asphalt and reached into her satchel for her pepper spray. No sense making herself an easy target for a hit-and-run, though the game was still in its early stages, so she didn't expect violence. Her grip tightened on the spray.

"Which is it," an amused voice asked as the car pulled even with her, the window rolling down with a hiss, "the Glock or the S and W?"

"Just pepper spray." Unreasonably relieved, she halted and faced the cruiser.

The creases beside Ethan's eyes smoothed out as the smile slid from his lips. "I'm glad you have that. Word's out you're a bit of a sharpshooter. I've gotten half a dozen calls from businesses asking whether it's a violation of state law to post 'firearms prohibited' signs."

"Including the library?"

"Including the library. I went by there to tell you, but Eulie'd closed up early."

"She what?"

"It's Saturday. The library's usually open an extra half hour. Common practice, you understand, nothing mandatory, so the kids have extra time to get their books. But I was there at ten after six, and the place was locked up. I saw your car and called your house. I also called Brad and had him order you new tires; the old ones are slashed, so they can't be repaired. He'll tow the car and change them out tomorrow morning. I told him you'd stop by the Gas 'n' Go tomorrow to pick it up."

Lucy wasn't sure how she felt about him taking charge

of the car repair, but decided to focus on the more pertinent question. "You called my house?"

He winked. "Got the number when you gave it to Eulie for your library card. Your brother said you'd be home in about an hour, so I figured you'd be walking. Hop in, I'll give you a lift."

Lucy closed her eyes and sighed as she sank into the air-conditioned interior of the cruiser. If she'd known she would be walking home, she would have worn shorts rather than jeans.

"I'm going to have to remind Tim not to give out information like that when I'm working. My research tends to irritate people."

"Could be he's decided I'm trustworthy." One beat. Two. "There's nothing wrong with the kid's judgment."

The slight emphasis on the last word told her Artie had explained Tim's condition. The betrayal stung, especially after a day under the weight of Eulie's bitter scrutiny, followed by the vandalism of the Rover and Tim's disregard for her privacy. Was there no one left she could trust?

"Dammit. He had no right." She reached for anger to combat the tightness in her throat, the burn at the back of her eyes, but she couldn't summon it.

"He cares about you. Both of you. That gives him the right."

Kindness could be her undoing. She pushed it away. "No—"

"Yes. Wouldn't you reveal Tim's secret yourself if that's what it took to protect him?"

She had no answer and wouldn't meet his eyes.

"If it helps, he didn't give me any details, and he checked me out first. I've gotten calls from three guys I worked with at HPD. Your friend was very thorough."

"But not thorough enough to uncover whatever you're hiding."

Ethan debated just telling her and getting the whole mess over with. But if he did, he'd lose any ground he might be gaining. Hell, he barely trusted himself, how could he expect anyone else to rely on him once they knew the truth? Especially Lucy, who already considered him a candidate for the mayor's blackmail. No, better she suspect him of holding back than she know the details.

"We all have secrets. I promise, mine won't hurt you." He hoped.

Lucy stared straight ahead, as if riveted by the view of the flat, Texas landscape. She didn't speak, and as they pulled up in front of her house, he saw her lower lip tremble slightly. Unable to stop himself, he reached over, grasped her chin between his thumb and forefinger, and turned her to face him.

"Maybe your brother and Artie are smarter than I am. Maybe they knew before I did I'd end up on your side in this war you've got going."

She swallowed hard, blinked rapidly, and he hoped with an emotion akin to desperation she wouldn't cry. He'd never been able to handle women's tears. One drop and he'd probably do something colossally stupid, like pulling her close and making promises he didn't have a prayer of keeping. But she took a deep breath and, letting it out slowly, stiffened her spine.

"You don't understand the stakes."

"Because you won't explain them. But that's okay. I can figure them out on my own. Besides, I have an edge: I know things you don't."

"What do you mean?"

"You're too hung up on your mother to see what's right in front of you."

"That's what you call taking my side? My mother was *murdered*." Her eyes flashed blue fury, and he relaxed. Anger, he could handle.

"Yup. Maybe even by someone in Dobbs Hollow, though

you haven't let on what makes you so sure of that. But what-ever she may have been, or may have done, it doesn't explain the level of animosity directed your way almost twenty years later. Face it, however important Cecile Sadler was to her kids, she didn't have enough of an impact on anyone else to turn this whole place against you.

"So, maybe I'm keeping secrets, sweetheart, but I'm not the only one. And mine aren't the kind that get people killed." Maybe if he said it often enough, he might begin to believe it.

# CHAPTER FIVE

Two days a week that year, Timmy had preschool in
the morning. The other three, he went to a sitter and
I picked him up when I was through with my classes.
I couldn't carry him on my shoulders that afternoon,
could barely manage the walk myself. So by the time
we got home, Timmy was crying and I was furious with
both him and Momma. What little of my childhood
she hadn't destroyed, he'd stolen with his neediness.

FROM *A BAD DAY TO DIE*

BY LUCY SADLER CALDWELL [DRAFT]

*YOU'RE TOO HUNG up on your mother to see what's right in
front of you.* Ethan's words pricked at Lucy all night. Again,
she couldn't sleep. Again, a car had passed by, its lights gliding
across the room, pausing for a moment each time. The first
time, Lucy's muscles tensed. The second, realization struck:
Ethan had set the night shift to keep an eye on her. Because
he worried, or because he didn't trust her?

She tossed and turned all night, finally dozing lightly, only
to awaken as dawn spread its first fingers over the sky. Coffee.
Today called for lots and lots of coffee. As the machine hissed
and dripped, she picked up the card Ethan had given her
when he dropped her off and flipped it over and over between
her fingers. Could he be right? Could she be too wrapped up
in the past to consider the present? Why *did* people want her
to leave? Didn't she have more reason to hold a grudge against
them than the reverse?

She settled herself in front of the computer and put
Ethan's name into a search engine. The first link was to an
article in the *Houston Chronicle*: Hero Cops Gunned Down
in Street. And Ethan was a hero. He was also a survivor.

Unconsciously, Lucy brought her knees up beneath her chin and wrapped her arms around them as she read.

Three years earlier, Ethan and his partner had been arresting a killer when the man's girlfriend arrived. She'd shot both detectives before the uniformed backup officers had even managed to draw their weapons. Ethan's knee had been shattered. His partner had been killed. The half-hand-cuffed murderer had managed to grab a gun, and the patrol cops had been occupied trying to bring him down, so Ethan had been forced to fire on the girlfriend. She'd died on the way to the hospital.

Had killing the woman bothered him? Was that why he'd decided to move to a small town? Did he think he'd have less crime in Dobbs Hollow than in Houston? And if so, did he resent her for bringing death back into his life?

She turned back to her research. Nothing in the *Chronicle* or anywhere else suggested any dirty laundry in Ethan's past. He had degrees in both criminal justice and psychology. A true do-gooder, he'd even served a stint as an EMT between college and the police academy.

He'd been thirty-three at the time of the shooting, divorced—to be expected, as law enforcement personnel had a much higher divorce rate than the general population—with an outstanding service record. The knee had been his second injury in as many years; many men would have quit after the extensive shoulder surgery he'd endured the year before when a knife had sliced through one of his tendons.

She rubbed her breast where a scar marked her own knife wound. It had hurt like hell. From the article's description, Ethan's had been devastating. How did a person go back to work knowing such a thing could happen again at any time?

The photograph of Detective Ethan Donovan in the *Chronicle* article, clearly taken long before the shooting, showed a man whose features were softer, less worn than the man she'd met, but no less attractive. The poor quality and color of the old photo did nothing to diminish his sex appeal. She remembered his loose-limbed stride, only slightly uneven, his long fingers and rough, heavy hands, and shivered. Sex hadn't ever been a priority for her, but neither of the men she'd chosen to sleep with had affected her the way Ethan Donovan did.

Which brought her right back to the present and the puzzle of a man who seemed too good to be true. The only ripple on the otherwise perfect surface was the lack of information about him after the shooting. She'd learned from the Hollow's website that he'd been hired in October, which left two years unaccounted for, two years in which to get into whatever trouble had left him vulnerable to Andrew Dobbs's blackmail.

Still, she wanted to trust him. He'd given her Cecile's file, and he had even pulled her from the past and forced her to reevaluate the Hollow residents' present reactions to her.

The rumble of truck wheels drew her to the window; the movers had arrived right on schedule. Lucy had arranged for them to bring only the most basic items, leaving the remainder in Dallas, where three of Tim's college buddies were staying at the house for the summer.

By one o'clock, the movers were gone. Lucy and Tim had finished unpacking and were sitting at the kitchen table working out a shopping list when the doorbell rang. She handed Tim the Glock 19—on which she'd had a custom three-and-a-half pound trigger pull installed, making it easy for him to handle even on bad days—and waited for him to give her a ready nod before putting her eye to the peephole. It was a routine they'd practiced many times while living with Todd.

As she peered through the fisheye, fire ran along Lucy's nerves. Alert to her moods, Tim shifted into a firing stance as she unbolted the door.

"Well, well," she said, opening the door wide and stepping aside to give Tim a clear view of—and shot at—their visitor, "if it isn't little Andy Dobbs. What brings you out this way?"

"It's Drew these days, Lucy."

"Drew? Drew Dobbs?" She tried a laugh. "Do you mind if I call you DiDi?"

He sighed, the long inhalation accentuating his broad shoulders. If Lucy hadn't had firsthand experience with the fetid ooze beneath his fashionable exterior, she might have found him attractive. Khaki pants showed off long legs and short sleeves revealed muscular forearms, while tousled, sandy hair added an air of boyish innocence and hid the water moccasin slithering silently behind his pale blue eyes. He'd succeeded so far in politics, where style trumped integrity. Lucy wondered whether there was any way to stop his ascent.

His eyes shifted over her shoulder to take in Tim's pose.

"That's hardly necessary. I didn't come here to cause a problem."

"Of course not." But she nodded at Tim, who lowered the pistol, slipping his finger out of the trigger guard to automatically reactivate its safeties. Todd had recommended the Glock for exactly that reason: unlike most semiautomatics, its hammerless construction was quick to use and easy to de-cock.

"So," she leaned an elbow against the doorjamb, blocking the door. This man would never enter her house. "Why *are* you here?"

"Actually, I wanted to apologize." He flashed a politician's smile, teeth professionally straightened and bleached. Too bad he hadn't spent as much time working on his inside as he had on his outside. "I know we were . . .awful to you in school."

*Brass balls. The man had brass bloody balls coming to her house and making a statement like that.* Lucy straightened from her casual pose as her muscles tensed, and she struggled to cap her anger. She didn't dare respond.

"I can only speak for myself when I say how sorry I am for my behavior in those days." And yet there was no humility in his stance, no apology in his tone.

She found her voice. "Get. Off. My. Property." Eyes never

leaving his face, she reached behind the door for the shotgun. "Now."

"Jesus! You fucking crazy bitch!" Drew backed away, and Lucy would have relished the sight of his blanched face if she'd been capable of seeing it beyond the black rage and sick fear clouding her vision. She slammed the door and slid down it. Tim settled beside her.

"That went well," he teased.

"Hell. I'm not sure I can do this, Timmy."

"Then don't. Let me call the movers and have them come back." For the first time since Todd's death, she debated backing down, putting an end to the crusade. But the reasons for which she'd set out to uncover her mother's killer were too important. Justice—and, if she were honest, vengeance—took precedence. And if she could topple a few upstanding figures like Drew Dobbs at the same time, so much the better. Too bad he hadn't been the one to murder Cecile; she'd have loved to watch him fry. Preferably right alongside his best buddy, Billy.

"I'll be all right. Just give me a minute. It's been a long couple of days."

"Sure. You stay here and I'll get us some tea." He loped to the kitchen. Over the swish of the refrigerator opening and the clink of ice in glasses, Lucy heard his voice.

"What did you say? I can't hear you!"

"Nothing," he called. "Be there in a second." And he was. He laid the iced tea on the coffee table and gave her a hand up. "Now, let's get back to the important work. We need to make a shopping list."

The doorbell rang again while they were debating Heinz versus Hunt's.

"Cripes, Luce, I doubt a murderer would ring the doorbell," Tim grumbled when she gestured for him to once again take the Glock.

"It's about appearances. Remember what Todd said: if

word gets out you're prepared for *everything*, no one will try *anything.*"

"Fine. Then you get the shotgun. I'll get the door." Instead, Lucy reached for the pistol he'd returned to the kitchen counter.

With a cursory glance through the peephole, Tim flipped the deadbolt, then flung the door open wide.

"HELL OF A welcome mat you've got there," Ethan said, nodding to the weapon pointed at his head. "Glad you don't have an itchy trigger finger."

Lucy relaxed her stance. "What are you doing here?"

"Didn't you know? I'm a celebrity stalker. I heard our esteemed state senator was here, and I wanted to get a picture." He grinned. The expression had often been called disarming, at least Before, but it had no appreciable effect on the woman in front of him. Maybe he was out of practice.

Lucy rounded on her brother. "Kitchen. Now." Ethan noted that, even in anger, she handled the Glock with respect, laying it softly on a table in the far corner of the room that seemed to function as a desk.

She wasn't so gentle with him. "Sit," she commanded, pointing to the couch.

"Yes, ma'am. I should probably stay, right? How about lie down? Fetch? Play dead?" Her shoulders lowered infinitesimally as she rolled her eyes at him. Better. Tim had been right; Drew's visit had unnerved her. Ethan's desire to make him pay for doing so surprised him. Lucy was a mess, and he'd given up on messes when he left Houston. These days, he liked things simple. And going after State Senator Dobbs would be anything but simple.

He could hear her and Tim in the next room, her tone

agitated, his reasonable. The conversation was apt to take a while. Absently humming "Sit Down, You're Rocking the Boat" from *Guys and Dolls*, Ethan wandered over to the desk to have a look at the pages on top of which the Glock lay, a lethal paperweight.

He flipped through the papers, hoping to find personal data on Cecile Sadler. There'd been nothing in the case file to suggest she was anything more than an anonymous victim, no indication she'd been an active member of the community. Although, come to think of it, maybe she hadn't been a member of the community. Certainly, no one had welcomed her daughter home with open arms.

"What the hell do you think you're doing?"

*Damn.* "Looking into a cold case." He went for a friendly smile. "There's been renewed interest in a seventeen-year-old murder."

Before she could respond, Tim swung out of the kitchen. "I called a cab. I'll have them drop me at the car, then I'll drive it to the store. Be back in couple hours." He turned to Ethan. "Hey, come for dinner. I'm going to buy a grill today and throw on a couple steaks. I'll get extra."

Lucy's eyes narrowed and fired poison-tipped arrows at her brother. Ethan bit the inside of his lip to suppress a laugh. Was the kid just making sure his sister had a bodyguard, or was he playing matchmaker? On the phone, Tim had seemed really shaken up by whatever had happened with Drew Dobbs. Whatever history Lucy and Drew shared, Tim didn't know about it, and he'd never seen his sister so close to meltdown. Ethan had no idea how he'd earned the right to get the call, but he but he had questions of his own, and he'd take Tim's help getting answers.

"Can't turn down an offer like that. Name the time."

"Eight." Tim escaped through the front door before Lucy could prevent him.

Glaring at the door, Lucy ran her fingers through her hair.

Ethan imagined his own hands doing the job and gritted his teeth against a surge of frustrated desire. Lucy stalked toward him, eyeing the stack of papers he'd been examining.

"You can go. I have no idea why Tim called you." She'd come so near he could taste her scent. Something light and citrusy, cool on the hot, close air.

"Really? He was pretty straightforward with me about his reasons. You get too caught up with your work and wouldn't hear an army in full battle mode approaching, let alone one individual bent on doing you harm." *And Drew Dobbs scared you.* But she wouldn't appreciate being forced to admit that.

"I'm careful!"

"I'm sure you are. But what could an extra pair of eyes hurt? If you're serious about solving your mother's murder, you should be glad of the help."

"I suppose." He'd hoped for a more enthusiastic response, but he'd take what he could get. His rusted instincts were slowly creaking to life, and they told him TJ hadn't exaggerated the problems Lucy Sadler would bring home. He'd enjoyed nine months of relative calm as chief of police; he was ready for some action. And the duty wouldn't be a hardship. Despite her wariness, or perhaps because of it,

Lucy Sadler Caldwell tugged at him.

"Another thing your brother told me?" She arched a brow. "When you're working, you forget to eat."

"I do not!"

"No?" He stepped closer, waiting for her to back away. When she didn't, he let his eyes wander over her body. Some men might find her too thin, but he'd lay odds if he could get her out of those ratty jeans and loose T-shirt, he'd find solid muscle. His blood heated and his whole body tightened at the image. Damn. The woman had done nothing, *nothing* to encourage him. She'd probably be thrilled never to see him again. Besides, he reminded himself, he'd sworn off complications.

He was having a purely hormonal reaction. Had to be. After the shooting, he hadn't wanted company. Then he'd been off his game for a couple of years. So, yeah, it had been a while.

"You look a little on the skinny side to me." The flash of hurt in her expression surprised him. Didn't she recognize teasing when she heard it? Who'd have thought a woman who answered the door holding a 9mm would be so sensitive? He gentled his tone. "I apologize. I get cranky when I'm hungry. So even if *you* don't want to eat much, why not let me take you to lunch? We can go over your research together."

"Why would you care what I find out? Planning to tell Mayor Dobbs?" Her chin had popped up again. Always ready for a fight, this one.

"Nope. I care because I spent six years as a detective before moving here, and cold cases fascinate me. Your mother's death didn't get the attention it deserved the first time around."

Her jaw set. "She was a prostitute. The crime was NHI."

*No humans involved.* "You don't believe that and neither do I. Let me prove it."

She studied him a long time before nodding. "All right, then. Take me somewhere my mother would have gone."

"I didn't know her. And I didn't live here in those days."

Lucy walked over to the table and pulled out the file he'd brought over the first day. She sorted through the papers inside, and shoved one of them at him.

"The list of men Al Pike interviewed about Cecile's murder. I want to talk to them, or at least meet them. Where can I do that while you eat?"

"This list is meaningless, Lucy, you know that. Anyone whose name came up for any reason is on it. Hell, even Buddy's here."

"What?"

"Robert Barnwell. That's Buddy's real name."

A muscle spasmed in Lucy's jaw, and Ethan wondered

what she was thinking. She'd hit it off with Maxie right away. The fact that Maxie hadn't mentioned Buddy being questioned, well, he didn't figure that would do much to improve Lucy's ability to trust.

"Look, you know how it works. Anyone they talk to has to go in the file, no matter what. It's just procedure. Chances are, Chief Pike didn't have a good reason to suspect any of these men. Their names came up for one reason or another, and he had to clear them. He didn't arrest them, didn't even make extensive notes on any one over the others."

"I'm not wasting my time; either we go somewhere useful, or we stay here. Or, actually, I stay here and you leave."

He should leave, he told himself. Get away from everything about Lucy Sadler Caldwell and go back to a life uncomplicated by visits from the mayor and the sheriff. "Rosalita's," he heard himself say against his better judgment.

"Good thought. I'd planned a visit there anyway. It was the only real bar in town when we lived here, so I know my mother spent time there."

"And the owner, Ron Hess, is on the list. More than likely, Al Pike only interviewed him because Cecile hung out at the bar, but it's a place to start. Plus, they do fairly decent chicken wings there."

"Fine." Lucy gathered the papers from the desk and stuffed them into her black satchel.

⌒

ROSALITA'S SAT ON the very edge of Dobbs Hollow proper, and as they drove up Lucy examined the giant shed that housed her mother's home away from home. What had drawn her to the place? Was it just the booze? Or had there been a particular patron, or employee, she'd followed there? Perhaps it was simply a place where she could be one person among many who were all there for the same purpose, rather than a marked pariah.

Inside, the cool, dark room had been divided into sections. In the back, Lucy saw pool tables and a small area for darts. In the front, the scarred and stained bar ran along the right, tables filled the center, and booths lined the left wall. The yeasty smell of beer hung in the air along with the faint odor of cigarettes, probably soaked into the wood from all the years before Texas had banned smoking in public places.

A couple sat in one of the booths, eating food from red plastic baskets. A single man with gray, frizzy hair sat at the far end of the bar staring down into his glass as if it were a crystal ball. A woman stood behind the bar polishing glasses, smacking chewing gum in the way of one who'd far rather be smoking. She looked to be in her early fifties, and Lucy immediately began formulating questions about whether she'd known Cecile. Ethan put a hand on her shoulder, however, and held her back.

"Hey, Charlene," he said easily.

"Ethan! What brings you out this way?" Her eyes shifted to Lucy and her smile disappeared. "And what are you doing with her?"

"Charlene Davies, this is Lucy Sadler. Lucy, Charlene." He walked steadily toward the bar as he made the introductions, his fingers digging into Lucy's shoulder so she would keep pace and keep quiet. "I'm sure by now you've heard that Lucy is here trying to find out about her mom."

"That's nothing to do with me."

They'd reached the bar, but Ethan didn't allow Lucy to sit.

"Come on, Charlene," Ethan coaxed. "You had to have known Cecile."

"Oh, I knew her." The woman turned pale green eyes on Lucy. "She looked just like you. And she figured that was all she needed. Wave her little ass around, get whatever she wanted. She was a first-class bitch."

Lucy recoiled from the venom in the woman's words. "I'm terribly sorry if she hurt you," Lucy offered. "I'm under no illusions about her. She was an alcoholic, and alcoholics don't make great friends."

The woman leaned over the bar. "Maybe you're not understanding me. She wasn't my friend. She didn't have the power to hurt me."

But she had; Lucy was certain of it. So she switched gears. "Have you worked at Rosalita's for long?"

"Damn near thirty years," Charlene answered.

"Has it changed much? Or has it stayed pretty much the same? Pool tables, darts, same kind of look and feel?"

Charlene laughed. "The day this place changes is the day they start serving iced tea in hell."

"And back then, Cecile was a regular?" Charlene nodded grudgingly. "Did she have a regular spot?"

Charlene gave her an incredulous glare. "That's what you want to ask? Where she fucking *sat*?"

"For starters. I'd like to see the place through her eyes, you know? Try to understand what she felt. Besides, I thought it might be the only question you were willing to answer."

Lucy waited while the other woman mulled over the question. Eventually, she nodded.

"She sat in the back corner booth. Don't know why. Not as easy to pick up men there as it would have been here at the bar. Guess she liked her privacy." Lucy waited, hoping for more. It came. "Of course, men found her anyway. Woman looks like her . . .like you . . .men always do." This came with a glance at Ethan that inexplicably made Lucy's face heat. She forced herself to ignore the innuendo. "Any particular men that you remember?"

"A few. But you want to know what I really remember? I remember she didn't care who they might have belonged to."

"I'm sorry," Lucy said.

Charlene continued to glare for a minute, then glanced

down. "Shit." She shrugged. "I don't guess it's your fault. Not like I coulda kept him for long, anyway."

"Kept who?"

Charlene's eyes slid away. "Chief Pike."

Lucy felt her legs weaken and practically give way. Al Pike. Al fucking Pike? How was it even possible? Her stomach revolted, and the room spun slowly as black spots began to impede her vision.

"Lucy?" Ethan pushed her onto a barstool. "Hey, Lucy! Pour her a soda, will you, Charlene? I think that came as a bit of a shock."

A minute later, a cold drink was placed in front of her, and Lucy sipped at it. The sugar fizzed through her bloodstream. She steadied her breathing, and her stomach settled.

"Wow. Color me officially surprised," she said, trying for a light tone. "Al Pike and my mother were involved?"

"His wife died when Billy was still little. He tried a lot of women on for size after that, but he always came back to me. I really thought he might marry me one day, even if it was only to take care of his kid. Until he started seeing Cecile."

"People knew? They knew he was . . .and they let him investigate her murder?"

"Oh, it was over between them long before that."

Al Pike. Lucy couldn't get her head around it. It was like she had taken a step back in time, with the Pike family and the Dobbs family haunting her every footstep.

"Look," Charlene suggested, obviously uncomfortable with the subject, "why don't y'all go sit in the booth and get a sense of what she saw, like you said."

"Yeah, okay." Lucy still felt dazed and a bit sick.

"Is Ron around?" Ethan asked.

"He's in the back. But he sure as hell isn't going to want to talk about Cecile."

"Why not?"

This time, it was Charlene who flushed. "Ron's wife took

off when she caught him in the back room with Cecile. That whole 'takes two to tango' thing didn't seem to occur to Ron, and he tossed Cecile out and told her never to come back. That was about six months before the murder, so Chief Pike dragged him over the coals pretty good."

But Ron hadn't been charged. Because he was innocent? Despite Charlene's assertion that he'd been extensively questioned, the notes on his interview said only "alibied."

"Could you ask him to come out and talk to us anyway?"

"Your funeral. Go on and sit in the booth. I'll get him."

"Can you bring two orders of wings and a black coffee, too?"

"Sure thing."

"Thanks." Ethan winked at Charlene and led Lucy back to the corner booth.

The couple in the other booth watched them with unconcealed curiosity. Lucy recognized neither of them.

While they waited for either Ron or the food to show up, Lucy pulled the files from her bag and began to make notes on what she'd learned. A few minutes later, the front door to the bar opened, and Lucy leaned around the corner of the booth to see the dark silhouette of a man in the entryway.

He paused there for a few seconds before heading straight for their table. A few steps away, Lucy recognized Billy Pike, and her stomach went back into freefall. She bit down on her tongue until the coppery taste of blood filled her mouth. Swallowing, she picked up her soda and gazed down into it as if she had no idea of the coming confrontation.

"Afternoon, Sheriff," Ethan said as the man reached the table.

"Donovan. Miz Sadler."

"Billy."

Pike seemed to take her greeting as an invitation. He pushed his way into the booth beside her and picked up a piece of paper from the table—the very one on which she'd written his father's name. He tapped it against his chin several times before speaking.

"I understand you're looking for your mother's killer."

"That's right." Lucy stiffened her spine, waiting for his reaction. But he remained surprisingly polite.

"You don't think my father did enough?"

"I don't think he did a damned thing. And since he wasn't overburdened by an abundance of other criminal activity, I'd love to know why."

From the corner of her eye, she saw Ethan's attention shift from her to Pike. He'd read the file. He had to be curious about the shoddy work, too.

Pike's eyes narrowed. "You were just a kid, and you didn't stick around long enough to watch the investigation. There was nothing to go on. Not then, certainly not now. You should have come to see me." He jerked his head in Ethan's direction. "He wasn't even in town back then. He can't tell you anything."

She looked away from Pike, directly at Ethan, whose eyes met hers calmly, steadily. Deep curiosity lurked there, but he was letting her control the conversation.

"I don't consider a person's usefulness before spending time with them."

Ethan's gaze grounded her. Why, after all these years, did Billy Pike and Drew Dobbs still make her skin cold and her stomach queasy? She wasn't a kid any longer; she could— and would—destroy either of them should they lay a hand on her. But she couldn't control her instinctive, shrinking reaction.

Pike rose. "I have to get going. You won't believe me, but I'd like to see Cecile's murder solved, too. If the department can be of any help, you give us a call." He nodded abruptly and left, pausing to joke with Charlene on the way out. Lucy wished she could tell the woman the truth, that she hadn't missed out on a thing not being Billy Pike's stepmother. Of course, if Charlene had gotten her wish, maybe Billy would have turned out better.

The minute Pike was out the door, Charlene came by and dropped off the wings and the coffee.

"Guess Ron asked the sheriff to do his talking for him," she said. "I hate to say I told you so, but . . ."

"Yeah, you did."

When Charlene left, Ethan finally loosed his curiosity. "So, you want to tell me what that was really about?"

Amazingly, she did. But she wouldn't.

"It's old business. Maybe some other time." She stuffed a chicken wing in her mouth to keep from having to say anything more.

For a hungry man, Ethan ate slowly. He kept slanting long looks up at her until she could bear the silence no longer.

"What?" she burst out. "Do I have hot sauce on my cheek or something?"

Ethan grinned, the expression turning her insides liquid and warm, but the grin gradually faded as his eyes fixed on her mouth. "Or something," he said, the words deep and husky. Then he shook his head and smiled. "So you won't talk about Billy. Tell me about your foster father."

"Todd?"

"Sure. His partner said he adopted the two of you off the books."

"At first. After a few months, we had to make it official so I could go to school and we could get on his insurance."

"Must have been tough to do."

"Not so much." She shifted in her seat, unused to having to discuss her past. "Todd's position helped. He knew a lot of people in social services and in the court system. I'd given him a fake last name—Simmons—when we first met him, so we stuck with that story."

"But there had to be things like social security numbers, birth records . . ."

Lucy shrugged off his comment, though the old pain of denying her whole life ate away at her. "We lied a lot. I told them I didn't know where I'd been born, didn't know my social. I was only fifteen, so I didn't have a driver's license or anything. All the lies, the denials, being put back a grade so I could pretend I'd never been to a proper school—it was all worth it to see Karen with Timmy. She loved him. He was finally safe."

"And you?" The intensity of the velvet darkness of his voice caught her attention, pulled her from her memories.

"What about me?"

"Tim was a kid. He didn't understand the cost. He got a safe, comfortable home with people who loved and cared for him. What did you get?"

"The same."

"You got that for him. What about for yourself?" When she didn't answer, he changed tacks. "They were good to you, Todd and Karen?"

"They were the best. When Karen died, I thought . . . Karen had been the driving force behind the adoption. She'd wanted a baby so badly, and Timmy clung to her right away."

"You thought once she died, Todd would kick you out?"

"No!" But she had. She went hot with shame, cold with fear all over again.

"Okay." He quirked a gentle smile at her. "It would have been natural if you had, you know."

"I've had plenty of therapy. I know it was natural." She shrugged. "So, yeah. I did worry that we would be out on the streets. But I was old enough to support us. Twenty. I told Todd he didn't need to take care of us, that I would quit college and get a job."

"He had other plans."

"Oh, yeah." She remembered how offended Todd had been. "He said we were his kids, and a man didn't abandon his kids."

"He was right." Ethan pushed away his empty basket of chicken wings and rose. "I'm going to wash up before we look through the information you have. Don't want to get hot sauce all over your research."

As he walked away, Lucy guzzled her soda and tried not to stare. Ethan Donovan looked as good going as he did coming, and he had a smile that could make a woman forget her entire purpose. He also had a way of getting her to talk about things she shouldn't, of tugging on her emotions. And she couldn't afford that. Not now. She wiped her hands with the little towelette that had come with the wings and began once again to make notes.

ETHAN STARED AT his reflection in the cracked and spotted bathroom mirror. He needed to get hold of himself. He didn't understand his reaction to Lucy. He'd met her only two days before, and in that time he'd taken her to lunch twice, and he planned to be at her house for dinner that evening. Of course, she hadn't invited him, her brother had, but still. He couldn't remember sitting down to so many meals with a woman since his marriage.

On the other hand, watching her eat those chicken wings accounted for a lot. The way her delicate fingers had pulled the meat from the bones, then slid each morsel between plump lips, had made him uncomfortable in more ways than one. And the sight of those lips sucking the last bits from both bones and fingers . . .

Christ. This wasn't a date. Something was coming—his every instinct screamed it—and she was at the heart. If nothing else, her reaction to the sheriff convinced him of that.

She'd turned pale, and her features had gone slack, as if the essence of woman had simply faded out from inside her skin. She'd recovered nicely, but whatever lay between her and Pike had deep and disturbing roots, and it looked like it was still growing, sending out poisonous tendrils. Still, Pike had been a kid when Lucy's mother had been murdered, so perhaps he should ignore the antagonism between them and assume it was irrelevant to her investigation and his own.

After splashing water on his face to clear his head, Ethan returned to the table. Charlene had removed the baskets, and Lucy's papers were spread over the surface in small piles. He picked up one pile, leaned back in the booth, and began to read. Within minutes, he found the first clue.

"Check it out. Under the PTA news." He passed the page over the table. A small blurb mentioned that the grade school would be instituting a children's fingerprinting program on the suggestion of new PTA member Cecile Sadler, whose daughter had just entered the first grade. Ms. Sadler had gotten the idea from the schools in her hometown of Palo Pinto.

"Do you know where that is?" Lucy's eyes were shining, and her whole body vibrated with excitement.

"Nope. But let me pay for lunch and we can go find out." He winked. "Want to stop by the library and ask Eulie for a Texas map?"

"Not hardly." Lucy flashed him a conspiratorial smile, and he drank the last of his coffee to quench a sudden thirst. He'd just laid cash on the table when his cell rang. He ignored it.

"Shouldn't you answer that?"

"It can wait. I'm off duty." But no sooner had the call gone to voice mail than the phone began to ring again. The display showed the station's number. "Dammit."

"Go ahead. You forget, I've lived law enforcement almost twenty years. If you have to go, Tim can pick me up."

"Thanks." He didn't like leaving her at Rosalita's, especially after the incident with the sheriff, but the phone buzzed insistently, reminding him of his duty. He touched the back of Lucy's hand lightly before he stood and walked outside to take the call.

"Thank God I found you," Marge said when he answered. "TJ and Keith are out at Miller's Lake. A couple of kids were out grubbing around, and they found a body."

"A what?"

"You heard me. A body. Keith says she was murdered. And not long ago. Maybe yesterday."

"Fuck. Okay. Tell Keith I want a twenty-foot perimeter, unless he thinks it needs to be even bigger. Outside that, they can start looking for evidence once the kids are gone, but inside nothing gets touched. And I mean *touched*, Marge. Call Scott and have him pick up the kids and bring them to the station. I don't want them scared more than necessary, but I want them separated. Call the parents and get them over to the station, too. Keith's already called Bobby O?" Bob O'Reilly served as medical examiner for all of Adams County. The hospital—and the morgue—were in the county seat at Prattville, thirty-five miles away, but O'Reilly himself could be anywhere.

"It's his day off. He was fishing over to Bardwell Lake, but I got hold of him because I didn't think you'd want an assistant on this one. He'll be a while, but he's on the way."

"You're a gem, Marge. Tell Keith and TJ I'm in route."

"Can I help?" The soft voice and the tentative hand on his shoulder startled him, yanked his mind from the gruesome duties ahead.

"No. I have to go. I'm sorry. I should drop you at home, but . . ."

"But it's not on your way and you need to go. It's okay, Ethan. Really." The acceptance in her eyes proved an unexpected relief. "I'll tell Tim to count you out for dinner."

"Don't do that. It's only three, and I don't have any idea

what I'm walking into. If it looks like I won't be able to make it, I'll call you."

"You sure?"

"Positive." He couldn't afford to take the time to figure out why.

ONLY A QUARTER of the property at the edge of Miller's Lake belonged to Dobbs Hollow proper; the rest was Adams County jurisdiction. Ethan had hiked the whole perimeter, some eighteen miles, when he'd first been hired. His bad knee had been crippled for two days thereafter, barely able to make it up the stairs to his second-floor apartment, but he considered the experience worth the pain. He'd learned as a beat cop that there was no better way to know your territory than to walk it.

A thick stand of oaks on the Hollow side of the lake provided shade, enticing swimmers and fishermen alike. Although the murky water hid an uneven bottom and the occasional poisonous snake, every sunny day found children of all ages diving from the taller rocks at the lake's edge or splashing in its shallows. Today, however, no laughter or high-pitched voices drifted toward him as he maneuvered his truck down the narrow path to the shore. Only hushed adult conversation broke the silence.

The woman lay atop an outcropping of limestone like a sacrifice posed on an altar. Her blonde hair flowed down the rock, the tips drifting over the water, the constant sway almost mesmerizing. For a time, Ethan stared at those strands of gold, glinting in the dappling sun. It was hard, so hard, to follow them back to their source when he knew what he would see.

Her throat had been slashed, but the blood had slid down

the side of her neck rather than spraying her face and body. Her heart had stopped pumping before the knife had severed her trachea. She was naked. Flies congregated around her head, a mobile black mask, and across her belly where the killer had scrawled WHORES DIE in what Ethan assumed to be her own blood.

Both Keith and TJ were pale but composed. Ethan send up a brief thanks to whatever powers had ensured they had been the ones to find the body. Any of the others on the force would have panicked. And would have, more than likely, thrown up, further contaminating the crime scene. In a bigger department, the two wouldn't have been out together at all, given that, Ethan aside, Keith was Dobbs Hollow's only detective.

"I know we have to wait for Bobby to confirm," Keith said as Ethan circled the body, "but look close at her neck. I think she was strangled before she was cut."

Ethan squatted, waving his hand slowly to dispel the swarm of flies without disturbing the body itself, and peered at the abrasions.

"Either of you recognize her?"

Neither did.

"We picked up a load of trash." TJ indicated the cruiser sitting off to the side, its open trunk filled with evidence bags. "But you know how this place is. Since school let out, it's been packed every day. And if you check out the general area, it's been fairly well trampled. It's possible he chased her out here. Keith stayed with the body and I followed a couple of trails where it looked as if someone had come through. About a half a mile down one of them I found this." TJ held up a plastic evidence bag with a wet sheet of paper inside. At the top it read *Martin and Sons Autoplex*, and appeared to be a checklist of cleaning chores.

"You think she worked there?"

"Could be. That's Jed Martin's place. You know him?"

"Heard of him. Know his ex," Ethan replied, remembering Eulie's adamant rejection of Lucy. "Does that count?"

"Hell no," Keith replied. "Everyone knows Eulie."

"No kidding." Ethan rubbed a hand across his face. "Okay, so we have a piece of paper from Jed Martin's business. He's what, forty-five minutes or so from here?"

"'Bout that."

"So it's a bit odd that we'd find this here, but not unheard of. Our victim might have dropped it. Our killer might have dropped it. Or it might be unrelated to our case. No point in jumping to conclusions."

"So let's think this out. If you were going to kill someone, why would you leave the body where it would be found so quickly?"

"And by kids." TJ's expression held both disgust and sorrow. "They'll be traumatized for ages."

"Shock value," Keith suggested. "The whole town will be up in arms."

Ethan considered the golden drape of the woman's hair, so like Lucy's. Something inside him popped with a snap like the sudden tear of a ligament shattered by a shard of bone, and the tingle at the top of his spine increased. He cracked his neck, but found no relief.

"A lot of unusual things happening around here these days." He kept his tone carefully neutral. He could be imagining the similarity.

"Shit," said TJ. "She looks like Lucy."

Nope. Not imagining. "The thought had occurred to me."

"The Sadler woman? How does she fit in?"

"Possibly she doesn't. Just like the paper. But I can't say, as I like the fact that we get our first murder since Cecile Sadler's only days after her daughter arrives. And that the victim happens to have her build and hair color."

"And Cecile's throat was cut," TJ reminded him. "You don't think Lucy's in danger, do you?"

"Too soon to say. Nothing's going to happen here till Bobby's done with the body. Why don't you pack up the evidence you guys collected and have Marge ship it out to the state labs. Then take a run out to the Sadler place and have a chat with Lucy and Tim. Print out a picture of the victim and take it with you. We'll send whatever we get off the body separately."

"County lab's pretty good," Keith objected. "Why involve the state?"

"When it comes to murder, 'pretty good' doesn't cut it." And if the killing turned out to be connected to Lucy, Ethan didn't want Sheriff Pike within a mile of the evidence. He couldn't say he trusted Lucy completely, but nothing about her set off the alarms the scene with Pike in his office had. "Once Bobby and his boys get here, I'll call for someone else to take over and come down to the station to talk to the kids. Give them food, whatever they want before then, but they don't get to talk to each other and they don't get to go home. Okay?"

"Yes, sir." Gratitude shone in TJ's eyes. Ethan refused to let recognition of it show, refused to admit even to himself that he wouldn't be able to concentrate on the murder unless he knew Lucy was safe.

LUCY WAS RESEARCHING her mother's hometown when the doorbell rang. Tim poked his head out of the kitchen, but she glanced at the security monitor he'd installed and waved him off. Tara Jean stood on the doorstep, shifting from foot to foot. Lucy shut off the computer and ran over to open the door.

"Tara Jean! What are you doing here? I'd think Ethan would have you running all over town, dealing with whatever emergency called him away." Her heart dropped suddenly. "He's okay, isn't he? Nothing's happened to him?"

"No, no. Ethan's fine. Actually, I'm here on official business. Sort of. The boss sent me to check on you. Plus, he wanted me to ask you a couple questions. Can I come in?"

"Oh God, of course. Where are my manners?" She ushered TJ into the house, and Tim popped out of the kitchen. "You remember Tim?"

"Wow. Not this Tim. Sheesh, last time I saw you, you were a toddler!"

Tim sighed dramatically. "And my sister still thinks I am." He punched Lucy lightly in the shoulder. "Do me a favor and remind her frequently of the fact that you can see the difference, 'kay? Can I get you a drink? Tea? Water? Soda?"

"Water would be great."

Tim disappeared into the kitchen, and Lucy and Tara Jean settled onto the couch.

"So what happened?"

"We found a young woman murdered in the woods."

"Oh no! Oh, Tara Jean, that's terrible. Did you know her?" Lucy reached over and touched Tara's hand.

"No, no. She's not from town."

"Well, that makes it a little easier, I guess. What do I have to do with this murder?"

"As the chief said, probably nothing at all. But we haven't had a real murder since your mother was killed. A couple domestic disputes turned deadly, a convenience-store shooting, and a few drunk-driving fatalities, but not premeditated murder. From what we can tell so far, the woman died late last night or early this morning, so she'd have been killed less than two days after you came back to Dobbs Hollow."

"He doesn't think *I* killed her, does he? For God's sake, he had a patrol car coming by on a regular basis last night, so he knows I didn't leave."

TJ blanched, and Lucy felt her own blood freeze. She

knew what her friend was about to say. "Luce, Cal Wilkes and Aaron Barrett were on last night, and I saw their report this morning. They spent most of their shift chasing down a Peeping Tom at the Archer apartment complex on the other side of town. They weren't anywhere near here. I'm calling Ethan." TJ pulled her cell phone from its belt clip.

"No." Lucy laid a hand over TJ's, struggling to keep her composure. "He's got a murder to contend with. Whoever drove by here didn't hurt us. He was probably just looking for another window to break."

"He'll want to know." Tara's chin set, and Lucy knew she would tell Ethan anyway.

"Please, Tara Jean, leave it lie."

"And would you stop calling me that? How am I supposed to present myself as a tough, no-nonsense cop with a name like Tara?"

"Hey," said Tim, handing her a bottle of Ozarka. "I think Tara's a pretty name."

"You keep out of this, toddler boy. 'Pretty' doesn't exactly scream 'competent police officer.'"

Lucy laughed. "Yes, ma'am, Officer Dobbs."

"Better. But TJ will do fine."

"I guess I can get used to that. So what did Ethan want you to ask me?"

"Hang on a sec." TJ leaned over to open the bag at her feet. From its depths, she removed a file containing the four photographs she'd printed at the station. Without speaking, she laid them on the coffee table in front of Lucy.

"Oh." Lucy picked up the headshot and ran the tips of her fingers over the woman's face. "You poor, poor thing."

"You don't know her? Either of you?"

Tim examined the photograph over Lucy's shoulder, and both brother and sister shook their heads.

"Do you have a close-up of her throat?"

"Let it be!" Tim's voice was filled with a sharp warning, but the girl in the photo had already captured Lucy's mind and heart. "She's not one of yours."

"She could be."

"Jesus, Luce, do you think for once you could choose to live with the living rather than with the dead?" With a curt nod at TJ, he swung out the front door, slamming it behind him. Lucy stared at the spot for a long moment, loss flooding through her. He was growing further from her every day. Closing the pain away with the ease of long practice, she returned her attention to TJ.

"Do you? Have a close-up?"

"Not with me. Why?"

"I wanted to see the abrasions around her neck. She was strangled?"

TJ nodded. "We think so."

"He crushed her windpipe." Lucy ran her forefinger back and forth across the photo. "And then he took a knife to her throat. The strangulation, that could be rage, if he'd used his hands. But the marks here don't look right for manual strangulation."

"You can tell that from a printout? The quality's crap."

"Which is why I want a closer look. Here's the thing: hands leave bruises, not scrapes. So I'd guess rope. Probably hemp or the like, to cause abrasions like these. Definitely not nylon. But to cut her when he'd already taken her life.... What was he trying to say?"

"Maybe he wasn't saying anything. Maybe he's just nuts."

"The two aren't mutually exclusive. I interviewed a pathological liar for *Finding Sarah*. You couldn't trust a word out of his mouth. Still, he passed three lie-detector tests, fooled numerous experienced police officers and a couple of psychiatrists, because he believed his own lies. You probably would have called him nuts—in fact, he ended up in a psychiatric hospital—but there was a certain logic to his fabrications. In the end, that logic was what trapped him."

"I remember."

"Ah, right." Lucy forced a grin. "My biggest fan. Your guy here considered slitting his victim's throat once she was dead rational. As was stripping her, writing on her, and leaving her in a public place." She ran her fingers over the picture once more. "She's a billboard."

"A billboard? Cripes, Lucy."

"To him, that's her purpose. An advertisement. A medium for getting his message across."

"Did you miss the fact that she looks like you?"

"Does she?" Lucy flipped the pages to examine the head-shot. "I can't see it."

"Well, I can. And so can Ethan. He's worried about you."

Lucy blinked. Focused. "He shouldn't be. I can take care of myself. He needs to concentrate on *her*. If he can't determine what her killer meant, the guy may feel the need to make a . . . more pointed statement."

"You think he's a serial, like Amicone or Paxton?" The subjects of Lucy's last two books, Craig Paxton and Nico Amicone, had each taken more than eight lives before being captured.

"I don't like the term 'serial killer.' Most of these guys don't see themselves that way, and dehumanizing them through labels is a surefire way to miss out on understanding who they are as people."

"But you rarely go into depth on their humanity. You concentrate more on the victims."

"I have to." Lucy scrubbed a hand over her face. "If you read Paxton's story, you'll remember Jacob Nolan."

"Of course."

"He lived in Paxton's head, and it destroyed him. Two weeks after the trial ended, he dropped off the grid. He hasn't worked since. That kind of burnout isn't uncommon, and it's why I focus on victims. Or, as Tim so eloquently put it, I live with the dead. I'm not strong enough to drink with the devil.

"But that's not what you asked. You wanted to know whether I thought the man who strangled this woman, sliced open her throat, and used her body as a banner would do the same again."

TJ nodded.

"Then, yes. In my opinion, if no one can interpret the message he's left, he'll leave another."

"What do *you* think he's saying?"

"I have no idea. I'm not a detective. I come in at the end. Or, if I'm lucky, I document the investigation as it progresses, the way I did with the Paxton case. People like you, like Ethan, like Jake Nolan, you do the interpreting."

# CHAPTER SIX

The average human body holds only about a gallon and a half of blood. It doesn't sound like much until you see it spread in prints and smears and pools on the floor you play jacks on every day after school.



"It's ten o'clock," the radio announcer informed him. "Do you know where your children are?" Ethan swore. He'd forgotten to call and tell Lucy he wouldn't be able to make dinner. As soon as O'Reilly had arrived to take charge of the body, Ethan had returned to the station to question the twelve-year-old boys who'd found her. They could tell him nothing, and had seemed more interested in her nudity than the fact that she was dead.

Then Ethan and Keith had driven out to Palestine with a couple of pictures of the dead woman's face, along with a copy of the cleaning checklist found in the woods. No one at Jed Martin's dealership recognized the woman, so Ethan hadn't expected much of a reaction when he showed Martin the chore list.

But Martin's eyes widened at the sight of the list in a way they hadn't when he was shown the picture. He placed the photocopy of the list back on his desk as if it might bite him, then kicked back in his chair, elaborately calm.

"I have no idea where that came from," he said with a dismissive shrug. "We have an outside service that comes in once a month—Carmine's Commercial Cleaning—but other than that we handle everything ourselves, and we don't use a checklist. Maybe they do."

"Are these the things they're responsible for?"

"Well, some of them, yes. They scrub the bathrooms, of course, and they disinfect all the surfaces and mop the floors, but they also shampoo the carpet on the showroom floor and clean the windows, and those aren't on here."

"You only clean your bathrooms once a month?"

"No, no, of course not." His genial smile set Ethan's teeth on edge. Of course, the guy was a car salesman, so he probably didn't know how to smile naturally. Still, his movements were too jerky, too abrupt for Ethan's comfort. "But we only have Carmine's do it once a month. We handle it ourselves the rest of the time. When the economy was better, we used to have Carmine's crew come in every week, but we don't get enough traffic these days to warrant it. Frankly, I'd let them go entirely if I could, but inevitably people want to car shop when it's raining and muddy, so the carpets get bad. Plus, my employees aren't janitors. By the time the month is over, the place needs a professional cleaning.

"Maybe if you told me where the paper came from, I could come up with a reason?"

"It was in the woods, not too far from this woman's body." Ethan tapped the picture of the blonde girl's face. They had no name yet, but Scott Allenby and Cal Wilkes were working on an ID back at the station.

"From the body?" Jed's hands shifted on his desk—he was clearly unwilling to touch either the girl's picture or the list—and finally grasped a letter opener. He turned it over and over, running his finger along the edge. Ethan would bet that sweat had begun to bead beneath his carefully styled hair.

"I have to ask you, Mr. Martin. Where were you last night?"

And just like that, as if a puppeteer had put down his crossbar, Jed Martin leaned back into his chair and relaxed. "Saturday night we're open until nine, so I was here. After that, I went to play poker with Eric Allenby, Chuck Hemming, and Bob Redmond. We played until maybe one in the morning. Then I went home."

"Don't suppose anyone can verify what time you got home?"

"I don't know. I have an alarm system. If the company keeps track of what time things are activated and deactivated, that would show it, but otherwise, no. I live alone."

O'Reilly had estimated the time of death between one and three in the morning. He'd have a more precise estimate after the autopsy. Martin could have done it. Ethan made a note to check into the alarm situation, but he doubted they'd have adequate records to conclusively prove or disprove the man's guilt.

"So, what do you think?" He asked Keith when they'd finished at the dealership and were headed back to Dobbs Hollow.

"He's hiding something, but I can't say I peg him as the killer. He honestly didn't seem to recognize the woman, but he'd seen the list of chores before."

Unfortunately, Ethan agreed. He'd have loved to solve his first murder in Dobbs Hollow in mere hours. Then he might feel as if he'd earned the citizens' trust. He hadn't had a clue what he was signing on for when he took the job, but it turned out that being Dobbs Hollow's chief mainly meant breaking up meth deals, quelling meth-or-alcohol-fueled domestic disputes, or investigating the occasional burglary. Usually, that turned out to be meth-related, too.

Murder, however, was a different situation entirely. And as much as he was glad to be sharpening long-unused skills, he was sorry for the situation that brought them to the fore.

Scott Allenby called when they were on their way back from Jed Martin's with an ID on the dead girl.

"Her roommate called her in as missing," he explained. "Her name's Renee Josephs. Twenty-one. From Corsicana."

"Damn." Ethan thought for a moment. "They're what, half an hour from here? Forty minutes? You know anyone in the department there we can liaise with?"

"Yeah," said Scott. "Royce Beaton and I went through the academy together. I'll give him a call."

"Do that. I'll drop Cal at the station and head down there so we can break it to the parents."

Which was why, instead of having dinner with Lucy and Tim, at eight o'clock Ethan found himself in Corsicana, giving Mr. and Mrs. Josephs the news that their daughter wouldn't be coming home.

"It's not possible," Mrs. Josephs kept saying, though Ethan had shown her a carefully edited photograph that only revealed the girl's face. "It can't be." She shook her head and refused to meet his gaze, as if seeing the truth there would destroy any protection she could pull around her. Her husband wrapped an arm around her, but they both swayed, and it wasn't entirely clear to Ethan who was supporting whom.

"I'm very sorry, ma'am." Denial was natural, but he had to get beyond it in case the woman had useful information.

"Why don't we go in the kitchen and get you some water?" Detective Beaton asked.

Mrs. Josephs looked up at him, her head still shaking slightly, as if she would say no, then she finally acquiesced. He led her away, leaving Ethan alone with Renee's father.

"She'll never get over this," the man said. He'd aged twenty years in the few minutes since inviting Ethan in. "Renee's our only child."

"I'm terribly sorry. But I need to ask you a few questions. Just a few."

"Of course." Mr. Josephs sat heavily in a slightly ragged easy chair and gestured for Ethan to take a seat on the couch. Leaning forward, resting his elbows on his knees, Ethan asked the first in the endless series of questions.

"Did your daughter have any enemies?"

"No. She was popular. People liked her." Mr. Josephs wouldn't look at him, either, but Ethan didn't figure the man was hiding anything beyond a broken heart. God, he hated notifications.

"Maybe an ex-boyfriend?"

"No. She didn't date."

"Are you sure? She was a very pretty girl."

"I'm as sure as a father can be. She always had a lot of friends who were boys, but she never talked about one more than another. We were glad. Maybe we shouldn't have been. Maybe if she'd had a boyfriend, he would have been looking after her. . . ."

"Mr. Josephs, you can't think that way. Seriously. What happened, well, it happened. It wasn't your fault or Renee's fault, or anyone's except the man who took her. You and your wife need to remember that."

"We did our best." But the unsaid portion echoed silently through the living room — *it wasn't good enough.*

"You did. And her roommate says she loved you and knew you loved her." Adele, the roommate, had said no such thing, but Ethan figured she would have, and it would give the Josephs a little peace to hear it.

"She also told us Renee was a waitress at Wally's Tavern."

"Yes. She'd just started, but she liked it. She said the people were friendly and they tipped well. I was worried because she got off so late, but she told me the bartender always walked the girls to their cars."

"Did she drink?"

"A bit. Like any college kid. But we taught her never to drink and drive. We told her she could always call and we'd pick her up, no matter what." The tears that had filled the man's eyes finally escaped and began to track long trails down his cheeks. He didn't seem to notice.

And the question Ethan hated to ask. "What about drugs?"

For three full breaths, Josephs didn't answer. "She didn't do drugs. I know you have to ask these things, but no. She wasn't that kind of girl."

"Okay." He'd ask around a bit more, but the girl hadn't looked like an addict or a drunk. She'd been beautiful. He thought about the word scrawled in blood on her abdomen. Had she been a flirt who'd angered the wrong man?

"She never mentioned anyone giving her a hard time, did she? Like maybe someone who was jealous of her popularity?"

Josephs wrinkled his brow. "She never said anything to me or to her mother. But you should ask Adele."

"We'll do that."

Ethan rose as Detective Beaton came out with Mrs. Josephs, who was still shaky. She held a glass of water in her hand. Ethan helped her to sit in his place. A quick glance at Detective Beaton let Ethan know he'd gotten everything he thought he could from the woman.

"Let me give you my card," Ethan said. "Anytime you want to call, you do it. If you remember something, or have a question, or even just feel the need to know what's going on."

"I'll give you mine, too," said Beaton. "I'm right here in town, and I can come over any time."

"You won't . . .forget about her, will you?" asked Mrs. Josephs in a small voice.

"No, ma'am," Ethan promised. "We won't."

$\backsim$

ON HIS WAY back to Dobbs Hollow, Ethan stopped into Wally's Tavern, where Renee had been working. No one had anything negative to say about her, though most admitted they didn't know her well. She'd started less than two weeks before and had kept to herself. Men came on to her, as they did to all the waitresses—the women wore short shorts and midriff-baring tops—but Renee had been good at blowing them off without hurting anyone's feelings. She hadn't talked about having a boyfriend, and they hadn't seen her with anyone while she'd been working. As Mr. Josephs had said, the bartender, a bruiser named Orel, walked the waitresses out to their cars every night.

Dead ends. Everywhere. And every one sent the tension in his body higher. He pulled the cruiser to a stop in front of Lucy's house. Okay, so he could have called in his apology. But TJ had discussed Lucy's night visitor with him, and the drive-by pulled the knot in his gut too tight to be ignored.

She answered the door in the jersey he'd seen her in the previous morning, this time paired with black leggings, and the knot in his stomach became hotter and more urgent. Her hair was up in one of those things that always reminded him of bat wings with teeth. He remembered his ex-wife calling them hair claws. Lucy's pink-nailed toes were bare, and for once her hands were empty.

He exploded. "It's ten-thirty at night, a girl's been murdered, and you answer the door without any kind of protection? What the hell are you thinking?"

"Relax. Tim picked up a wireless camera when he was out. It's set behind the motion-sensor security light. We have monitors in the kitchen, the living room, and at the top of the stairs. I knew who you were before you rang the doorbell, and told Tim he could keep on instant messaging with his friends."

He closed his eyes, scrubbed his face with one hand, and let out a long breath. "I shouldn't have yelled at you. It's been a bitch of a night. I really only stopped by to say I'm sorry for missing dinner."

"Did you eat anything?"

He had to think about it. "Not unless you count a PowerBar on the way out to Corsicana."

"Then come in. One of our dinner guests didn't show up, so I just so happen to have a leftover steak in the fridge. I'll fix you a sandwich."

"You don't have to do that."

"I know." She reached for his hand, tugged gently. The feel

of her soft skin against his, the honeysuckle clean scent of her after the grimness of the day—they entranced him. He almost missed her words. "Come on into the kitchen. You can tell me about Corsicana while I throw the sandwich together. That's where she was from?"

Ethan had learned during his brief marriage to keep the details of his work to himself, so he was surprised to find himself going over everything—not merely the facts, but the feelings and hunches as well—while he ate.

"There's so much we don't know. She drove to work every night, but her car isn't in the lot and it's not at her apartment. So, where the hell is it?"

"You're thinking wheel-poppers? Like the South Dakota guy?" Robert Leroy Anderson had attempted to use the devices to flatten his victims' tires to make them vulnerable. Once it had worked. Twice it had not. "He moved the car so no one would know where he abducted her from?"

"Maybe. Or maybe someone came along, realized the car had been abandoned, and stole it. Either way, it's gone. Until it's found, we won't know if there's anything in it or on it to point to the killer."

"I take it there aren't any like crimes showing up in ViCAP?"

"No, although . . ."

"Although?"

"This isn't exactly dinner-table conversation."

"Then it's a good thing we're not exactly having dinner."

He took a bite of his sandwich, getting his thoughts in order as he chewed and swallowed. "As you guessed, I had Keith put in a ViCAP request. Three, actually, with different levels of specificity. What I got back . . . I can't explain it. Things fall through the cracks. God knows, that's the point of ViCAP. And the first search, the one where I input all the parameters—the posing, the strangulation, and knife work— it didn't return anything.

"But the fact is, this part of the state presents a couple

of statistical anomalies. First, we have too many missing females. Couple of teenagers, but the rest are grown women. They could have left their families, walked away on their own, but none of them have turned up, and a couple of them left kids behind. One, Beverly Jackson, lived right here in Dobbs Hollow and has been gone long enough to be declared legally dead. Her husband remarried last year.

"And then, there is a rape pattern that appears in several cases from Adams and surrounding counties. But the women who were sexually assaulted weren't killed." He pushed the remains of his sandwich away, appetite gone.

"It's possible, of course, that those two sets of statistics have nothing to do with each other. Women disappear. Women get assaulted. The two don't have to be related."

"Or the missing women might have been killed by the same guy who raped the others."

"The same guy or guys. I haven't seen the reports themselves yet, just the numbers. Only a few of them made ViCAP as being pattern."

"What were the elements that made the pattern?"

"First, abduction from a public place by a man or men. In three of the seven cases, the victims claim there might have been more than one man, and in all those instances the women were penetrated anally as well.

"Second, the victims were blindfolded. Duct tape was used to keep the blindfold on for the whole time they were held. That amounted to several hours at the minimum, more than a day at the max. Between the rapes, the women were dosed with a drug that left their systems fast and left them extremely confused. Most of them don't remember the abduction itself at all. The one who did said a smelly rag had been put over her mouth. Probably chloroform.

"In each case, the man or men also beat the woman, and muttered the whole time, accusing her of being a whore.

"Finally, all the pattern rapes took place outside, and the

women were left bound, gagged and naked by the side of a highway."

Lucy nodded slowly, and Ethan examined her face, trying to get a handle on her thoughts. But it was oddly blank. "And how long has this been going on?"

"The earliest one of the ViCAP cases was eight years ago. It's been one a year ever since. Not on a regular enough basis to consider it predictable—not full moons, or the second weekend of September or anything—but pretty much one a year."

"And the others?"

"We have ten years of data on hand without resorting to paper files. The numbers of missing women didn't go up until more recently. Three years back." He watched her closely, waiting for her to shrug off the crimes as unconnected to her mother's case, but she did not. Instead, her face still inscrutable, she finally met his eyes. Something dark and haunted lurked behind her carefully composed features, but he didn't dare question her about it. Not yet.

"The ViCAP victims . . . did they look like Renee Josephs?" She rubbed absently at a spot below her left shoulder and his eyes followed the motion, noticing against his better intentions the way the cloth of her shirt shifted over her breast.

He swallowed. "All different. Two blondes, three brunettes, a redhead, and a Hispanic woman. He might not have known she was Hispanic, though. She had very light skin. Which would mean he had at least a single racial/ethnic profile, even if the women had different hair color. All of them were slim, though, and pretty. The missing women, too, for what it's worth. He has good taste." Lucy frowned, her eyebrows drawing together. Had he gone too far?

"I'm sorry. I—"

But she surprised him. "Renee wasn't bruised."

"Not much. She had one large perimortem bruise on the side of her head, probably from being knocked unconscious."

"But he didn't beat her."

"You have a very analytical mind. No, he didn't."

"So chances are, it's not the same guy, though it's hard to tell, given that he crosses ethnic boundaries, which is highly unusual. Even so, the precedents are pretty clear: the change of MO is too radical for Renee to be the victim of the rapist or rapists. Assuming the missing women were abducted, and not by the rapist, why would Renee have been left to be found instead of being hidden like the other women? It seems more likely that her case is unrelated to the others." She yawned.

"I think you're right." He stood, and she followed suit. "I also think I've kept you up too late."

"You've probably had less sleep than I have. Are you okay to drive home? I don't even know where you live. Maybe I should make you a cup of coffee?"

"I'm fine." And then, because she didn't seem any more anxious for him to leave than he was to go, and because he'd been thinking about it since the moment they'd met, he reached out and cupped her cheek in his right hand, running his thumb across her full lower lip.

Lucy's eyes widened, pupils dilating as her gaze met his. Her entire body vibrated.

Shock? Arousal? Fear? Ethan was lousy at interpreting women's body language, and Lucy, recklessly bold in some areas, desperately shy in others, was more difficult to read than most. So he moved slowly, cautiously, allowing her plenty of time to pull away as he slid his hand to the back of her head and urged her closer.

He'd intended the kiss to be slow, too, but when her lips parted beneath his own, his restraint shattered. His left arm locked around her waist, pulling her tight against him. He devoured her, sucking her lower lip between his teeth in a nip that caused her to whimper and writhe against him. All he could think about was getting her naked and listening to those little cries as he licked and sucked and nibbled his way down her body. God, they were going to be good together. Better than good.

He palmed her breast through the jersey and she froze, a reaction even he could interpret. Lost in his own fantasies, he'd pushed her too hard, too fast. He loosened his grip, easing back slightly. She tried to wriggle completely free, but he kept her near. If he allowed her to step away, it would create a rift he'd never bridge.

Besides, he wasn't ready to let go. He wasn't at all sure hanging on to her wasn't the only thing keeping him standing.

"I'm sorry." It was barely a whisper. She kept her head bowed, forehead resting against his chest. "I'm not very good at this. I didn't mean to be a tease."

He slid a knuckle beneath her chin and forced her head up.

"Sweetheart, that was not a tease." And if he ever found out who'd told her it was, the guy was in for a serious hurt. But he supposed growing up with an alcoholic prostitute for a mother gave a girl strange ideas. And if her foster father had been like most cops, he would have had a rather jaundiced view of human relationships.

"No?" Lucy's blue eyes finally met his.

"No. That was the highlight of my day. Hell, of my year." Of more than three years, but he had no intention of saying so.

"You really don't mind?"

"I'm not going to lie to you." At least not about this. "Do I want more? Hell, yes. But it's your hand, Lucy. You play it however you want." He took a deep breath, let it out slowly. He was going to need one long, cold shower when he got home. He wasn't looking forward to it.

"Now, I do believe we were discussing the lateness of the hour. So walk me out and lock up behind me." At the door, he pressed a quick, hard kiss on her lips. No point in pretending he wasn't coming back for more later, because he for damned sure was. "I'll call you tomorrow, and we can talk about your mother's case, since we didn't get to it tonight. And Lucy?"

She looked up at him.

"Don't think you're not on the hook for not calling me about the drive-bys. I told you, I want to know when things happen. Especially to you."

⁓

LUCY HAD TO force herself out of bed the next morning. Ethan's hands, and his mouth, had haunted her dreams, and she had woken twice, her breathing ragged, her body aching for fulfillment. The man turned her inside out, and part of her relished the new, super-feminine sensation. But she still didn't trust him.

Why had he kissed her? A man who looked like Ethan Donovan, especially one whose position of authority announced his acceptance by the Hollow's elite, could have his pick of women. Of course, lunching with convicts and outcasts probably knocked him out of the running for a few ladies in town, but it only served to further arouse Lucy's interest.

What if Ethan's friendship with Josh was merely a way of keeping track of a potential troublemaker? And what if his kisses were designed for the same purpose? Or, more disturbing still, what if he simply believed she'd fall into bed with him based on Cecile's reputation? Still, he'd been more than gentlemanly when she'd pushed him away.

She was sipping coffee and trying to banish the memory of Ethan's kiss by MapQuesting directions from Dobbs Hollow to Palo Pinto when Tim came downstairs. He blinked the sleep out of his eyes and peered over her shoulder.

"You're going to check out where Cecile grew up?" For Tim, Karen would always be "Mom," Cecile a faint and distant shadow. Even as a baby, he'd been closer to Lucy than to their mother, and he'd been Karen's "precious baby boy" for almost three years before her death.

"Tomorrow. Today, I'm going back to the library to pull anything I can find on the town and see whether anything strikes me as a reason for her to leave. I'd love to get hold of the papers from Palo Pinto itself, but I'll probably have to settle for references to Palo Pinto, town or county, in the larger press. Still, you never know unless you try."

"Uh-huh. So what did the chief want last night?"

Heat crawled up Lucy's body and she raised her mug as a shield against her brother's speculative expression. She took her time blowing on the hot liquid before taking a swallow.

"He wanted to apologize for missing dinner without calling. And TJ, damn her eyes, told him about the car that kept passing by here the other night."

"Ah. So he didn't stick around, then?"

"We discussed the murder a bit. He'd been to see the victim's parents. That's why he couldn't make dinner."

"He seems like a good guy." Tim's tone held both speculation and approval.

"It's not like that."

"No? Maybe it should be. After that bastard Sean and that wuss David, you could do with a good, solid guy in your life."

"What was it TJ called you? Toddler boy? Stay out of my love life."

"Jeez, Luce, I wasn't talking about your love life. I was talking about your sex life."

Lucy choked, sputtered. "Tim! You're my little brother, for God's sake! You're not supposed to be thinking about sex at all, let alone as it relates to me."

"Uh, Luce? I'm twenty-one. Everybody knows guys my age think about sex nonstop. And since I'm here with you, rather than in Dallas with my girlfriend, I can't spend much time worrying about my own sex life or I'll get really depressed."

"Wait. Back up. You have a girlfriend? What's her name? Why haven't I met her?"

"Who do you think I spend all night with online? Her

name is Amy. But quit trying to change the subject. We're talking about you. You need to get your head out of the past and take a look at the present before it passes you right by."

No wonder her brother approved of Ethan. They thought alike.

"I am not having this conversation with you. I'm going to the library." She printed out the directions and stuffed them into the folder with the rest of the papers she'd accumulated. "Actually, get your shoes on. Since I don't feel like replacing the tires again so soon, you can drop me off in town. I'll walk home."

"With everything that's been going on, is that a good idea?"

"Hmmm. If you don't think so, I guess you'll have to pick me up."

"You witch! You never had any intention of walking."

"Nope," Lucy grinned, unrepentant. "How about we meet at the diner for lunch at noon, when Eulie locks up for an hour. You can talk to Maxie about a job." And she could find out why Buddy had been on Al Pike's list of men to question about Cecile's murder. "And here's a thought: Dallas is practically on the way to Palo Pinto, so I can drop you at home tomorrow to pick up your own car. And check to be sure everything's okay at the house."

"You mean in case Barry, Hal, and Jessup wrecked the place in the three days we've been gone?"

"Exactly."

~

EULIE HAD COMPANY at the library. A girl of ten or twelve sat a near the check-out desk, writing with painstaking care in a school journal with a fountain pen. Perhaps the child would help to break through Eulie's icy reserve? Lucy pulled her pen case from her bag and extracted the Sheaffer Karen had given her on her sixteenth birthday. The same pen the child was using. She held her own up and smiled at the girl.

"That's a great pen. And I can see you're taking really good care of yours, so it should last a long time."

"Yours is real pretty. Is it old?"

"Cassandra. Don't talk to strangers."

The child dropped her eyes. "Yes, Aunt Eulie."

"Oh, I'm hardly a stranger, Eulie." Lucy's friendly tone belied the rage burning the back of her throat. "I've known you since we were kids." She studied the child, who'd returned to her work. The lack of new writing, however, indicated she was following the adult conversation closely. "And unless I miss my guess, this must be your sister Pam's daughter." She should have noticed the resemblance immediately.

"You knew my mom?"

"Cassandra!"

"But, Aunt Eulie, she knew my mom!"

Lucy recognized the look, the desperation, and her heart broke. How long had Pam been dead? Ignoring Eulie's outrage, she pulled up a chair, sat beside Cassandra, and introduced herself.

"I didn't know your mother well. She was a year older than me. But shall I tell you what I remember about her?"

"Yes, please."

"The first thing is that she was very beautiful. Just like you." Lucy tucked a lock of corn-silk hair behind the girl's ear. "And even though she was beautiful and popular, which can make people a little spoiled or self-centered—you know what that means?" Cassandra nodded. "Well, your mom was neither of those things. She was kind to everyone, even people she didn't know very well."

"Like you?"

Lucy swallowed. Hard. Not all the residents of Dobbs Hollow deserved to be tarred with the same brush, and she'd do well to remember it.

"Exactly like me. And she was smart, too. In tenth grade, she won the state spelling bee. I was so impressed. Some people teased her about it, though. And you know what she did? She said she had aspirations. And then she spelled aspirations for them."

"My daddy says next to me my mom was the best thing that ever happened to him and that he'll love her forever."

"I'm sure that's true, honey. The nice thing about love is the more you give, the more you have. So you love your daddy and you love your Aunt Eulie, and if you meet some-one else—like if your Aunt Eulie gets married"—*or your father does*—"you'll have plenty of love left for them, too."

"My daddy says that, too."

"He sounds like a very smart man." Lucy glanced over at Eulie, whose expression had softened slightly.

"Pam married a man she met at college in Houston. You wouldn't have known him. She passed two years ago. Breast cancer."

"I'm sorry to hear it."

Eulie shrugged, then gestured to the lab. "You should get on with your 'research.'" The bitch was back. Lucy said good-bye to the child and headed for the glassed-in enclosure.

Lucy couldn't find much information about Palo Pinto in the *Dobbs Digest*. Palo Pinto came up a few times when the two towns had either cooperated or competed. One head-line blared, Communities Unite to Hold off Developers. The story featured not only Dobbs Hollow and Palo Pinto, along with several other small towns in the northern part of the state, but also the as-yet-unknown Andrew Dobbs, who decried State Senator Sheldon Byrnes's efforts to keep a pair of discount mall chains from taking over rural land.

Lucy put a question mark next to Sheldon Byrnes's name on one of the pages she'd printed out. He'd made the papers frequently in the two years before Cecile had arrived in Dobbs Hollow. His high profile might be irrelevant, but if Cecile had been politically aware, one of his rallies might have enticed her to Dobbs Hollow.

She was slipping the spool of film into its box when she heard the lab door open. Jed Martin slid a chair far too close to her and sprawled in it, one of his legs touching hers. *Great. Not likely to get close to Eulie with Jed in the way.*

"Long time no see. I heard you'd come home."

Lucy deliberately scooted her chair away. "I imagine everyone's heard."

"I wanted to be one of the first to welcome you home." He laid a hand on her knee and goose bumps of disgust crawled up her thighs beneath her jeans.

"Jed?" She lifted his hand, using her thumb and forefinger as if she were picking up a particularly distasteful piece of garbage. "Did you know there are twenty-seven bones in the human hand?" Shifting the position of her hand, she applied a little pressure to his ring finger and he paled. "I can break every one of them in under a minute."

"Shit!" He stuck both hands protectively under his armpits. "You didn't used to be so picky."

"You know nothing about me. You never did and you never will."

"Oh, I didn't have personal experience of your many charms, but that doesn't mean they escaped my attention."

"I have no idea what you're talking about." But she had a sick feeling she did.

"Look what happened to your momma when she got too big for her britches." He paused, letting his gaze roam over her. "Wouldn't want to see history repeat itself."

Lucy tensed, forcing herself to remain calm, not to lunge at Jed. God, but she wanted to hurt him. Physically. She had to get a grip before she could question him, but the threat had shot him right to the top of her personal to-do list. Did he really have firsthand knowledge of what had happened to Cecile, or was he merely taking potshots?

"I suggest you leave. Now. Before I show you once and for all how much stronger I am than my mother was."

His mouth tightened, and Lucy thought, had they not been in the library with Eulie watching avidly through the glass, he might have spat.

"I hear you've taken up with the new police chief. No matter what a prude you pretend to be now, you'll only fool him for so long. You don't have friends here in Dobbs Hollow the way you do in the big city."

Jed stormed from the microfiche lab and Lucy watched as he brushed past Eulie without stopping on his way out of the library. An adrenaline rush composed of equal parts fear, relief, and fury left Lucy trembling as she stared after him. She'd expected people to be threatened by her return, but Jed's attack, so publicly confrontational, had thrown her.

Her concentration shot, she stuffed her printouts into her bag. She had more than an hour before her lunch with Tim, but perhaps she could spend a little more time with Maxie.

"Miz Sadler?"

She was in no mood to talk to Cassandra, but she forced away her own concerns. "What's up?"

"Aunt Eulie says you're a writer, but your books are too grown up for me."

"She's right, sweetie. They'd probably give you nightmares. Heck, they give me nightmares."

"I'm going to be a writer when I grow up."

Lucy smiled, remembering how often she'd heard similar statements from Tim as a child, each time with a different career in mind.

"Well, I can see you're off to a good start."

"Could we talk again sometime?"

"Of course. You just check with your Aunt Eulie. I'll be here a couple of days a week."

Eulie stopped her on her way out. Lucy braced herself

for another attack and was unprepared when the woman thanked her for her kindness to Cassandra.

"No thanks necessary. She's a lovely child."

"She is." Eulie shifted, took a deep breath. "About Jed. He always was an ass."

The statement startled Lucy into a laugh. "It's true what they say: hindsight really is twenty-twenty."

She waved at Eulie and Cassandra on her way out the door. Maybe she *would* get up the nerve to ask Eulie about the rumors from high school and whether they were still floating around. Wouldn't it burn Jed's ass to know that Lucy's first real bonding moment with one of her suspects had come because of his behavior?

Lucy pushed open the door of the diner, glancing down at the hinge she and Tim had installed. Still working. Now that she knew Ethan better, she couldn't help wondering what he would have done if there hadn't been a hinge to fix. Certainly, he was the kind of man who would have found a way to get her to comply with his plan. The memory of their shared intimacy flooded through her, heating her blood all over again.

She looked toward the back stall, and all the heat she'd been feeling fled. Ethan was there, but he shared a table with Billy Pike. Acidic bile rose to the back of her throat and set her stomach on fire. Seeming totally engrossed in his conversation with Ethan, Pike barely glanced in her direction, so she settled into a booth halfway down the aisle and pulled a pad from her bag.

A chubby, teenage waitress stopped by the table to take her order.

"I'm meeting my brother here in a bit. Is it okay if I just get an iced tea for now and work for a while?"

"No problem," the girl said with a smile. "You do your thing. I've never known a real writer before."

If Lucy hadn't been so tense, she would have laughed at the comment. What made a "real writer" anyway?

The waitress brought her the tea, and as she sipped at it she tapped her pen against her pad, considering strategy for her time in Palo Pinto. She already planned to use the newspaper there for more than its morgue; she'd been successful in the past placing ads asking for information. Some achieved results long after she'd left town.

Ad copy, however, presented a challenge, as a simple request rarely sufficed. She had to offer enough of a reward to entice the knowledgeable to reveal their secrets without drawing attention from greedy fabricators. Although focused on the page before her, Lucy kept a thread of attention on the table in the back, glancing up as often as she could without being obvious. When Pike rose, she ignored his approach, keeping her eyes fixed on her notes until he paused next to her.

Still, she kept her eyes trained on the paper until he spoke.

"How's the investigation coming?"

"Well as can be expected, I suppose. Things can be slow in the beginning." She finally met his eyes. "But they do tend to pick up speed."

"Just remember you're not an officer of the law. You're a writer. You go ahead and write, but leave the real investigating to the pros."

"I'll do what I think is necessary. But don't worry, I promise not to give you an excuse to arrest me."

He sighed. "You need to quit being so paranoid, Lucy. No one's out to get you. Whoever killed your momma is long gone."

"Whatever you say."

Shaking his head, Pike walked away from the table. When the door closed behind him, Ethan beckoned.

"Figured you'd want to be farther from the door," he said as she laid her things on the table.

"But you won't give up your seat against the wall."

"Not on a bet." He winked. "'Course, you could come over and sit beside me."

"Not on a bet." But she couldn't prevent a grin, no matter how severe she tried to keep her tone.

"Can't blame a guy for trying. You and the sheriff seemed to be getting along better than I'd have expected."

Lucy snorted. "It's an act, believe me. He probably hopes to keep track of what I find out."

"You think *he* killed your mother?"

"No. I went to school with him and Drew Dobbs. I admit I hate them both, but I know where they were that day."

"So why would he care about your investigation?"

"I don't know. He probably sees his daddy's lack of action as a stain on the family's nonexistent honor. Or he's covering for someone."

"He was what, eighteen? Awfully young to turn a blind eye to murder."

"Maybe, maybe not. He was already a thug and a criminal himself, even if he didn't kill anyone."

"A criminal?"

Dammit, she should have known Ethan wouldn't miss that. She hadn't intended to let it slip out, but his easy manner invited confidences.

"Long story," she said, laughing it off with difficulty. "I didn't realize the two of *you* were so close."

"Nor did I. But Pike's evidently concerned about Renee Josephs. She was killed in Dobbs Hollow proper, but the lake's customarily not overseen by the DHPD. Because more of it falls under county supervision, and because she wasn't a Hollow resident, he wants the sheriff's department kept up to date on our progress."

"That doesn't seem odd to you?"

"Lots of things seem odd to me down here. As TJ reminded me just the other day, despite being DHPD's chief of police, I'm not really a country boy. I'm accustomed to an urban police force with a whole different MO. Maybe it's completely normal for the county to be kept in the loop on town investigations. Especially investigations of this magnitude.

"But, of course, if the sheriff's department is headed by a criminal, that changes things." He paused, waiting.

Tim chose that moment to appear, and Lucy hid a sigh of relief as she waved him over. He slid in next to Ethan, boxing the other man into the booth. Unable to call him on the transparent ploy, she gritted her teeth and smiled sweetly.

"Did you get in touch with the boys and warn them to tidy the place up before we got there?"

"I tried, but the phone was out of order because they burned the house down."

Lucy had to laugh. "Fine. I worry too much. Did you talk to them?"

"Yeah. I told them I thought we'd be there around noon."

"You're going home?" Ethan's neutral tone revealed nothing of his feelings. Would he care if she left? Or would he be relieved?

"I'm dropping Tim in Dallas. I'm going on to Palo Pinto."

"How long will you be gone?" Still that distance. Was he punishing her for refusing to tell him about her history with Billy? She had the childish urge to kick him under the table, hard, just to get a reaction. She restrained it by reminding herself that she didn't trust him, that he'd been hired by Mayor Dobbs, and that he had admitted to having secrets of his own.

"Depends on what I find out. I'm booked into a motel for tomorrow night, but I can extend it if I need to."

The young waitress stopped by to take their orders, and Ethan teased her gently. The girl's crush practically screamed in her blush. Lucy could sympathize. Her mind drifted back to the previous night, and it took an act of will to subdue the heat in her own skin. She dropped her hands into her lap, twisting her fingers together.

"Any progress in your investigation?" she asked in order to distract herself.

"Not yet."

"Maxie's here." Tim jumped up. "I'm going to go ask her about that job." With a little bob of the head in Ethan's direction, he made his escape.

"He doesn't much care for your work, does he?"

"He doesn't understand it. He can't see what compels me to tell depressing stories, much less why people read them." She took a deep breath. She rarely tried to explain what compelled her to tell the stories she told, but it was something she could give Ethan, even if he never grasped how unusual it made him. "Here's the thing: the newspapers, the television shows, they're all about the killer. Take Craig Paxton. His twisted psyche was analyzed over and over. There were dozens of explanations of how and why he rationalized his bloodlust by pretending to believe those poor girls' fathers needed to be punished."

"You think it was an act?"

"I don't care whether it was an act, which is exactly my point. All that time and energy, all that ink and air devoted to a man whose every act was destructive. It's criminal in and of itself. He doesn't deserve it. How do you think the friends and families of his victims felt when, every time they opened a paper or flipped a channel, they were confronted by another talking head spouting off about him? He killed those girls, but the media machine erased them."

"So you fix it."

"I can't fix it. All I can do is create a tiny bit of balance, a little resistance."

"Is that what you're doing for your mother?"

"You don't think she deserves it?" Her muscles clenched, but Ethan merely shook his head in patient resignation at her defensiveness.

"That's not what I said. But looking for her killer is fundamentally different from the work you've done before."

She pressed her fingers to her temples. "It is and it isn't.

I can't tell her story without knowing the end, especially if she was more than merely a randomly chosen, convenient target for a killer."

"Because if the murder was planned, something in her life triggered it."

"Exactly." She looked up at him, hoping the inquisition had reached its end.

"What makes you believe the killing wasn't random?"

The throbbing behind her eyes increased. He kept pushing for more than she wanted to reveal. Guilt swamped her, tried to suck her under. But she couldn't admit the part her own actions might have played. Not here. Not now. She shoved the thoughts away.

"He killed her at home." She might have left it at that if Ethan had let her, but he didn't, simply waited for her to continue. "She never brought men home. A couple of nights a week she'd go out, and we wouldn't see her until the next day. Occasionally, she'd go out and not come back for two days. But that wasn't often. In any case, she never, never brought anyone into our house. She was careful with us, if not with herself." She could feel the familiar ball of pain, anger, and frustration clogging her throat and coughed to clear it.

"He stabbed her to death—a personal act in its own right—in her home in the middle of the afternoon while her kids were out. Nothing in that says random to me."

"No, it doesn't. So, tomorrow you head for Palo Pinto. Any idea what you might find there?"

"Maybe nothing. But Cecile grew up there. The town is so small, it's still unincorporated—fewer than a thousand people live there. Someone has to remember her."

"Be careful." He reached out and ran a long finger across the back of her hand where it lay on the table. She felt the heat of it right through her body and withdrew her hands to twist them together in her lap. "Call if you run into trouble."

"You have a murder to investigate."

"I'm not convinced my case isn't tied to yours. The timing, the victim's physical appearance, the wounds . . . all of it reeks of careful planning, not coincidence."

"They look alike, I'll give you that. But knives are common around here, and there are so many differences: Renee was outside, far from home; she was younger than Cecile, with no children; she died of strangulation, not multiple stab wounds.

"Nothing's going to happen to me, unless someone comes back with more bricks or paint bombs while I'm gone."

"Did it occur to you to take the other night as a warning? To consider that maybe whoever did it hoped you'd take off before he had to go further?"

"Of course it occurred to me."

"And Renee Josephs? Did it occur to you that she might be another warning?"

"If he wanted to hurt me, he could have come after me. He didn't need to go for a substitute first." She tossed the words out, but gauged his reaction carefully. *Loosen up, Lucy. Why do you always have to test people?*

"You've spent enough time around both cops and killers to know that's not true. Renee Josephs didn't come to town brandishing permits for two pistols and a rifle. She didn't carry Mace, and she hadn't had extensive self-defense training, which I'd wager you have."

"You'd be right. I don't take chances."

He ran his hand through his hair, leaving long spikes standing up. The light glinted off a few silver strands she hadn't noticed before. "Yeah, you do, but that's not the point. This guy may have used Renee's murder as a practice run because he found you too intimidating for a first victim. Or maybe he meant her as a warning. Or maybe even just as a diversion. Dobbs Hollow's police department is small. If we're all tied up investigating yesterday's murder, we won't have time to keep an eye on you or dig into a case seventeen years cold."

# CHAPTER SEVEN

My mother hated religion, called it the ultimate hypoc-
risy of men, but she took us to church every Sunday.
"Because they don't want us there," she said when I
asked her why we had to go. For years, that made no
sense to me.

FROM *A BAD DAY TO DIE*
BY LUCY SADLER CALDWELL [DRAFT]

ETHAN RUBBED ABSENTLY at his throbbing knee. He'd
learned the language of his stitched and pinned physiology
over time; this particular ache signified nothing more serious
than a shift in the weather. Still, he could have done without
the reminder of his own weakness. For the first time in years,
he needed to be strong.

He had kept Keith and TJ on the ViCAP crimes, and the
results lay stacked and centered on his desk, each file printed
and given its own folder, though the cases were for the most
part outside his jurisdiction. What would Billy Pike think
of the folders should he decide once again to make free with
Ethan's office?

Seven files. Seven women taken from places they felt
safe — one even from a church parking lot — repeatedly bru-
talized, and then discarded. Every report mentioned hazy
memories, which meant drugs, and one of the victims had a
Taser burn among her many wounds. Unlike Renee Josephs,
these women had lived, though he suspected they might not
have considered that a favor. Had their abductor lived nearby?
Did he get a charge out of watching them attempt to put their
lives back together?

Could he be a doctor? It would provide him easy access
to drugs. Ethan pulled a pad over and made a note. The new

hospital was five years old; where had rape victims gone for help before that? Had they all visited the same clinic or been part of the same recovery group?

And if he wasn't a doctor, who else would see rape victims? Counselors, nurses, cops . . . he needed to get hold of the names of everyone who'd come into contact with the women after their rapes.

He pulled the folders on the two cases that had fallen, at least partially, under the jurisdiction of the Adams County Sheriff's Department. The files were thick. Witness statements, interviews with friends and family, research into every aspect of the women's lives.

He couldn't help comparing the mass of paperwork, the heft of the investigations, to the barrenness of Cecile Sadler's file. Pike and his predecessor, Emmet Tucker, had done everything possible before letting the two rape cases go cold.

He opened the folder for the most recent case and lifted a printout of a photograph of a twenty-eight-year-old mother of two. Under the swelling and bruising, she had a kind of cheerleader's prettiness, with a pert nose and high cheekbones. How much of that prettiness remained now, two years after her abduction from the parking lot of her local supermarket?

He'd just started delving into the investigative details when a tap sounded at the door.

"Come."

TJ entered, more papers in hand. "ME's findings," she explained, handing them over. "Keith watched. I didn't." Between them, Ethan trusted Keith Arlen and Bob O'Reilly to uncover any secrets the body might have. He'd been to plenty of autopsies, but whatever vessel had cracked inside him at the sight of that long fall of blonde hair forming a bloody conduit into the lake had prevented him from attending this one. Renee didn't resemble Lucy in any real way, but he hadn't been able to bring himself to witness the Y incision, the removal of her skullcap, the many indignities both large and small that proved the woman she had once been was no more.

Lucy wouldn't thank him for his concern, and he didn't understand it himself. They'd shared a couple of meals and a single, scorching kiss. Nothing, really, in the grand scheme of things. He'd spent a hell of a lot more time with other women and felt no connection to them whatsoever. Aware of TJ's curious stare, he picked up the toxicology report.

O'Reilly had pushed the lab hard. Or maybe things move faster out in the sticks, where the lab's not overburdened with hundreds of potential homicides. In addition to being strangled with the type of rope available in any hardware store, Renee Josephs had been drugged, and heavily, with GHB. Her murderer, however, had left no trace of himself on her body.

"Thoughts?" Ethan gestured for TJ, still standing in front of his desk, to take a seat.

"He's done this, or something similar, before. Maybe a lot of times."

"Agreed."

"But the cases you had us pull, there are major differences. First off, their rapist didn't kill them. Second, he used chloroform, not GHB."

"GHB is easier to get, which is why it's so popular as a date-rape drug. And only one woman remembered the chloroform. Maybe he realized it was more tightly controlled and could lead us to him more easily. Then, too, we do have another group of possibles to account for."

"The missing women." TJ frowned. "I've been filling out requests for information all morning, but the results will take time to come in. I printed what I could get through the system, and drove around to other stations to get more, but some of these files are old. They've been relegated so far back that even going to the station houses and departments involved won't bring a result. We just have to wait.

"Keith went to talk to Rick Jackson, Beverly's husband. Guy gave up last year and had her declared dead so he could remarry. She had pretty good life insurance, so Charlie Hobart, who sat in that seat before you, took a long look at Rick when she went missing, but he didn't find anything."

TJ dug into the omnipresent tote bag hanging from her shoulder and pulled out a few files. And then more. And more. Christ, what a lot of missing women. He'd never worked missing persons in Houston, but he bet the guys who did started every day with stacks of files. As depressing as Homicide had gotten at times, he wondered now whether looking for all those people erased from their homes, their lives, their families wouldn't be worse.

"I don't have a lot on most of these cases yet. But Renee's different from them, too. If the same guy took them, why'd he suddenly decide he wants his victims found?"

"Can't say." But he told her his theory about the man wanting to watch his victims struggle with re-assimilation. "Let's say he has to kill a couple of them—he's left semen on them, or there's some way to connect them to him—and once he's done that, he realizes he enjoys the murder part as much or more than the rape. Murder's a bigger short-term thrill, but it doesn't have that long-term benefit of watching the women struggle with life after the attack."

"That seems like a stretch."

"Yeah," Ethan nodded. "I just can't figure this guy. These guys. If the missing women are part of the pattern, then at least sometimes when he kills, he hides the bodies. Why would he suddenly deviate from that?"

"Lucy said he thought of Renee as a billboard. Maybe he went for the rape and murder for the big high, then left the victim to be found so he could terrorize a whole community and watch them dance to his tune?"

Ethan sighed. "Christ. What a mess."

He spent the rest of the afternoon with the cold files,

making notes, and adding to them as TJ brought in more information. Keith returned from his meeting with Rick Jackson sweaty and disheartened. The AC in the Crown Vic had broken, and Jackson had given him little to go on.

"The man was certain right away that his wife had been abducted," he told Ethan, "but he said no one would listen. They had a kid, a three-year-old girl, who'd been diagnosed with autism less than a year before. He pointed to the daughter as a reason Beverly would never leave home; others said it's what drove her away.

"Jackson also said his wife had filed a police report about a month before her disappearance. She was convinced someone was watching her, thought it had to do with her community activism on behalf of autistic kids."

"I saw that in her file."

"Well, Hobart told her there wasn't much he could do about it. And, to be fair to the guy, there really wasn't. He increased drive-by patrols around her house and sent an officer to one of the meetings with her, but no one seemed out of place or overly aggressive."

So they'd let it go. They would have had to. Could Beverly Jackson's stalker have abducted her, or had the woman merely felt unsettled in her new role as community leader? That had been Hobart's take. Sick kid, mother not used to being in the public eye . . . to him, they were the ingredients for a nervous breakdown.

"Who else do we have available to actually talk to?" Ethan flipped through the stack.

"I've got a buddy in the Freestone Sheriff's Department," Keith replied. "I can see if he will run out with me to visit the Merrimans or the Axelrods. He's been with the department going on eight years, so he might even have worked the Axelrod case."

Ethan pulled out the files on Julia Merriman—sixteen, brown hair, brown eyes, disappeared in September of 2004 — and Kathy Axelrod — twenty-seven, blonde hair, green eyes, missing for two years — and handed them over.

"Get to it. Check if their positions had changed at all in their communities, like Beverly's had. Did the kid just make cheerleader? Stuff like that. And then see if they mentioned anyone watching them, even if they never reported it. If your friend can't make it happen, find someone who can.

"I'd go with you if I could, but Sarah Josephs, Renee's mother, called. She wants to come in and talk to me."

"No problem, I'm on it." Keith practically saluted as he left, which made Ethan, only a few years his senior, feel like a grandfather. Or maybe that was nothing more than the dull ache of his shoulder and knee, which begged for the relief of pain pills. Instead of taking one, Ethan levered himself out of his chair and began to limp around the office, rolling his shoulders back and forth, forcing the muscles, tendons and ligaments to cooperate.

⌒

Tim kept up a steady stream of chatter all the way to Dallas, but once Lucy dropped him off, her mind returned to Ethan's list of possible connections between herself and Renee's murderer. He'd missed one, or deliberately left it off. It annoyed her that she couldn't decide which. If Cecile's murder had given her killer a thrill, a release beyond what he'd intended in killing her, Lucy's resemblance to her mother could have triggered a craving to repeat the experience.

Renee Josephs had been raped. The case file on Cecile didn't mention sexual assault, and the medical examiner hadn't put anything in the autopsy report, but that didn't mean Cecile hadn't been raped. Al Pike would have assumed any sexual contact — no matter how close to the time of death — had been consensual. DNA profiling hadn't been easily accessible at the time, anyway; even paternity testing had only just become well accepted. Evidence of sexual assault might have been collected in Dallas or Houston in 1994, but not in Dobbs Hollow.

When Lucy had opened the front door that day, she'd found Cecile face down, blood all around her. A few hairs caught in her fingers gave evidence of a vain attempt to fight off her attacker.

Years later, experience studying crime scenes and spatter patterns had taught her to recognize the flat, irregularly shaped patch of red next to Cecile's right elbow as a shoe print. The killer had braced himself with his right foot, forcing his left knee into her spine as he pulled her head up to cut her throat.

By then, Cecile would have almost bled out. She would have been too weak to fight off her assailant even had he not tackled her from behind. She'd probably been heading for the knife block to defend herself, but the blood staining the olive carpet and matching easy chair told a tale of violence to which the pools and puddles in the kitchen were only the finale.

Lucy shuddered, the picture in her mind almost obscuring the road in front of her. She could imagine Cecile's struggle to survive so clearly. She'd dreamt it for the first two years of living in Dallas, waking every night screaming in terror as the faceless figure raised a bloody knife over her own body rather than her mother's. Years of therapy and stability in Todd and Karen's care had allowed her to live with the memories, but they never faded.

A horn blared behind her, and Lucy realized she'd slowed almost to a crawl. She shoved the mental pictures away and returned her attention to the road, thankful Route 180 wasn't more heavily trafficked.

The motel in Mineral Wells, the largest town in Palo Pinto County, was a nationwide chain, with all the attendant amenities, including wireless Internet. Lucy logged on and sent an e-mail to Tim to let him know she'd arrived. He planned to spend a few days in Dallas before returning to Dobbs Hollow, but had been adamant that she keep in touch so he would know she was safe.

As well as being far bigger than Palo Pinto Township, Mineral Wells was home to the local county newspaper. Lucy looked up the address and, finding it only a few blocks from her hotel, walked over to place her ad.

Palo Pinto itself lay just over ten miles west, so once she'd paid for the classified ad to run for two weeks, she climbed back into her car. Palo Pinto was lovely, with meticulously maintained historic buildings, but it was tiny, smaller even than Dobbs Hollow. Her research the previous day had told her as much. The town didn't even have its own high school. Palo Pinto students went to school in Mineral Wells. What would it have been like for Cecile, seventeen years old and pregnant in such a place? And yet she had stayed until she reached twenty-one. Or had she? Might she have left when she found out about the baby?

Lucy parked in front of the pioneer museum, which, she noticed with amusement, occupied the former Palo Pinto jail, and wandered around until she found a small diner with a bright pink sign reading "Suzette's Kitchen." Cafés, diners, soda shops, pizza parlors—in every small town the best sources of information could be found wherever people congregated to eat. With a little luck, Palo Pinto wouldn't prove the exception.

The restaurant sparkled. Each booth and linoleum-topped table sported an individual jukebox and an old-fashioned, glass-and-chrome straw dispenser. The black and white floor tiles had been scrubbed within an inch of their lives, though no amount of detergent or elbow grease could remove the years of wear.

Each of the four men in the booth in the back corner probably had as many years on him as the tiles did, Lucy thought. They'd also obviously missed the new prohibition against smoking in restaurants; a gray haze hung over their table and the smell of tobacco wafted toward her, circulated by the lazily turning ceiling fans. In other parts of the country, she'd peg them for farmers, their skin leather-tough and dark, but here they were more likely ranchers. They'd have turned their land over to their children by now, whether of their own volition or not, and probably spent a good many hours a day smoking in Suzette's Kitchen.

The woman who pushed through the swinging door from the kitchen didn't look much like a Suzette, but she seemed friendly enough. She also had some of the biggest hair Lucy had ever seen.

"Sit yourself anywhere," she called, waving a many-ringed hand tipped with Pepto-Bismol-pink fingernails vaguely around the room. "There're menus on the table. I'll be over in a sec." Picking up a big tub of dirty dishes, she backed through the door from which she'd emerged.

Lucy dropped her purse on the table next to the four men and approached them.

"Hi y'all," she said with her friendliest smile. "Would you mind if I asked a question or two?"

"Not at all," said one from the back corner. "Harvey, pull up a chair for the pretty lady."

"Oh, I can do that." Lucy retrieved her purse, then dragged a chair over and sat at the end of the table. The men introduced themselves as Gus—the leader, and oldest of the lot, who had ordered Harvey to get her a chair—Harvey, Bertram, and John.

"What can we do for you?" asked Harvey.

"Here's the thing: my mother was from Palo Pinto, and I'm trying to find any family I might have left."

"Who're your people?" asked Gus.

"Her name was Cecile Sadler." She looked from face to face,

ready to defend against any censure she might find, but the men barely reacted at all.

"Cece," John said slowly, a frown further creasing his already wrinkled face. "I think Ronnie knew her." He leaned out of the booth to shout toward the kitchen. "Ronnie!"

"Hold your horses," said the woman who'd greeted Lucy when she'd arrived. "I'm coming."

"You were friendly with Cece Sadler, weren't you?"

"Heavens, John, where'd you dig that name up? I haven't thought about Cece in years."

"This here's her daughter."

Lucy introduced herself, and Ronnie examined her closely.

"You surely do have the look of her. I was sorry to hear she'd gotten herself killed."

Lucy's first impulse, which she quashed, was to correct the woman. Cecile hadn't "gotten herself" anything. But this woman had been her mother's friend. The first person who'd known Cecile as a child.

Her stomach churning, she forced a smile. "Is any of her family left in the area? I'm trying to find them. And her friends. I would love to hear anything you remember about her. She never talked much about her childhood to us, so I'm pretty much starting out at square one."

"Her family . . . well, there's no one left as you'd be able to talk to. Cece's daddy—your granddaddy—was a preacher, you know."

Lucy shook her head.

"No? Well, I guess if I had Hiram Sadler for a daddy, I wouldn't be running around announcing it to the world, either. And Cece was a typical preacher's kid. When you came along, your granddaddy wasn't half furious. He like to have kicked Cece out, but she had nowhere to go, and sending her away would have reflected poorly on him."

"What about my grandmother?"

"She was frail, sickly, always up in her bedroom with some kind of nervous disorder. You know the type. She wasn't about to stand up to her husband." Ronnie's snort left no question about her opinion of such a woman.

"Are they still here in town?"

"Oh, heavens, no. Your granddaddy, he died of heart failure, and Evelyn went to live with her sister in Kansas. That was when Cece left Palo Pinto." The waitress pulled over another chair and sank into it with a sigh.

"Did you know my father?" She hadn't even realized she was going to ask until the words were out.

"Honey, no one knew who your daddy was," Ronnie said kindly. "And believe me, we all wanted to, not the least your granddaddy. Cece was crazy popular. A cheerleader, the whole nine yards. He could have been anyone, but Cece always said she wouldn't be stuck here, so she wasn't likely to hook up with a man who'd tie her to this place. She'd have seen him, whoever he was, as a ticket out."

"But he didn't marry her when she got pregnant."

"No, he didn't. If you want my opinion, he was already married. And I wasn't the only one who thought so."

"Which would have made him an even better ticket out. She wouldn't have had to worry about a husband; she could just have taken his money and gotten a new start." Lucy had never had any illusions about her mother, but the more she discovered about Cecile, the harder it was to remember the mother who'd loved her. Maybe it was time to give up, to keep the memories of Cecile singing Timmy to sleep or hugging them both before school, and try to forget the rest.

"That's the way most of us thought at the time." Despite her words, Ronnie didn't seem to disapprove of Cecile's behavior. Perhaps Hiram had been such a tyrant, no one blamed Cecile for getting pregnant? Or maybe Ronnie just wished she'd had a way out of Palo Pinto herself.

"But then why wait until her father died to cash in?"

"She needed a place to stay until she was old enough to go out on her own. Palo Pinto might not have been her favorite place in the world, but it was safe. And she had friends here, people she could leave you with when she needed. But your granddaddy, he left everything, even his house, to the church, so once he passed she had no place to stay. Evelyn could have homesteaded the place, lived there till she died, but she had no income. She'd have taken your momma to Kansas with her, I'm sure, but Cece, she took off in the middle of the night, and none of us heard word one about her until we saw the news about her murder."

"You don't have any idea why she would have chosen Dobbs Hollow to move to, do you?"

Ronnie raised her manicured eyebrows at the four men, but they all shook their heads. "Not a clue, honey. But I wasn't so close to her, either. You want details, you need to talk to Gina Woodward. Back then she was Gina Malloy, and she was Cece's best friend."

"She still lives here? In Palo Pinto?" Lucy's heart thudded. She was so close to her mother now.

"Well, not here in town, but near enough. She and her husband, Mark, live in Mineral Wells. He owns a movie-rental place there. I don't have her number, but they'll be in the book."

"Wow, thanks, that's great!"

"Any time. Now, you want anything to eat?"

Lucy grinned and ordered a burger, fries, and a Coke. This was another familiar dance for her. She would eat, leave a good tip, and hope word got around town that she was free with her cash and looking for information. The habitual behavior felt cleaner than it often did. Leaving cash for Ronnie would be no hardship; the woman obviously had a difficult life, and she'd taken the time to be kind to a stranger.

# CHAPTER EIGHT

Sociologists will tell you that children believe their home lives to be normal, that an abused child assumes all other children are also abused, and perhaps at some level they are right. But on another level, children feel difference far more acutely than do adults. And they are far quicker to point out any deviation from the norm.

FROM *A BAD DAY TO DIE*
BY LUCY SADLER CALDWELL [DRAFT]

GINA MALLOY WOODWARD had been thrilled to hear from Cecile's daughter, and at nine the next morning, she met Lucy in the hotel lobby. Petite, with pixie-cut auburn hair, she radiated so much energy she exhausted Lucy almost before the first hello.

"Ohmigod, I can't believe it's really you! I looked for you, you know, after Cece died. I even went down to Dobbs Hollow, but you weren't there. You surely do take after her. It's amazing."

"You didn't keep in touch after she left Palo Pinto?"

"No, I didn't have any idea where she went. She didn't tell anyone. She liked to keep secrets. It made her feel powerful, gave her a little control, which, believe you me, she needed."

"Ronnie over at Suzette's mentioned that Cecile was popular with everyone."

"Oh, she was. She could be a little flip, a little hard, a little out for herself, but no one held it against her. It came from having to live with her daddy, and everyone understood that. She never meant to hurt anyone."

Tough, but never mean. Yes, that was Momma. The only difference was that Lucy didn't remember her mother ever having friends in Dobbs Hollow. It must have been terribly lonely for her, especially with a past filled with people like Gina.

"And boys? Did she date?" Lucy practically held her breath.

"Your father, you mean? Not that I knew of. Cece was a bit of a wild child; it was one of the things that made her so appealing. She flirted with all the boys, but no one took it seriously, and Hiram never would have let her date." She rolled her eyes, and Lucy thought thirty years hadn't made much of a change in the teenager who'd been her mother's closest friend.

"But you were her best friend. Surely, she would have told you about him." Frustration bled through despite her attempts to hide it.

"Probably so, if he'd been someone she'd hoped to have a future with. Since she didn't . . ." The woman shrugged.

"A one-night stand?"

"I can't say. Cece liked to party. She worked for the school paper so she could get out of town when a story came up. No matter whether it was a cattlemen's association meeting or a local political shindig she knew nothing about, Cece Sadler was first to request the story just so she'd have an excuse to get out of her house. I should know — I took up photography so I could go with her. And any place she wanted to go, she managed to wrangle an invitation on her own if the paper couldn't get her one."

"You must have been quite the pair." Lucy tried to imagine her mother as bright and vivacious as Gina, and failed. Still, having a happier picture of Cecile lightened her heart some after the previous day's darkness.

"Oh, we thought we were going to take the world by storm." Her vibrant green eyes dimmed. "Poor Cece. She never had a chance, really. But she sure did love you, even if your daddy didn't carry her off on a white horse. I looked after you occasionally before she took you away, you know. She'd tell Hiram she was spending the night with me; it was how she got a couple nights of freedom every month."

"You didn't mind? Being left behind while she ran out?"

"Not really. By the time you came along, I had met Mark; he was in the photography club, which I only joined so I could run off with Cece to what counted for gala events in those days, so in a way she brought us together. You were sort of our practice child. I got to test what it would be like to have my own daughter without having full responsibility for your care, because at the end of the day—or the night— Cece would be back."

"Where did she go when she left me with you?"

"I don't have the foggiest idea. When I read about her murder, I wondered whether she'd gone to Dobbs Hollow those nights. She wouldn't have stayed in Palo Pinto, or even Mineral Wells, because she wouldn't have wanted word getting to Hiram, but Dobbs Hollow's a long ways off and she was always home by dawn. Of course, if your daddy lived there, it might have been worth the drive."

Once, finding out her father lived in Dobbs Hollow would have thrilled her, but in those days, Lucy hadn't realized what lay behind the civilized veneers of so many of the Hollow's citizens.

"Did she even say good-bye?"

"No, but that was Cece. Hiram died at the end of the summer, and I got a Christmas card from her that year saying you were both doing great. No return address. It was postmarked Dallas, but even then I didn't put much faith in that; Cece would have asked a complete stranger to mail letters from the city for her in a heartbeat. Not because she was trying to hide out, but to give us the impression she'd found success out of town."

"I don't suppose you knew my grandmother's maiden name? Ronnie from Suzette's Kitchen told me she had moved to Kansas, and I thought I'd try to track her down."

"Cece didn't talk about family. I have a mess of cousins, and she was jealous of that, I remember, so I always assumed she didn't have any."

Now that she knew where Cecile had been born, finding her birth certificate would be easy. Then she could begin searching for relatives. Not that she held out great hope of them telling her anything. If a seventeen-year-old girl hadn't told her best friend who she'd slept with, she wouldn't have confided in a distant relative.

Gina didn't have much information that would help Lucy find Cecile's killer, but she was a marvelous storyteller, and at the end of their meeting, Lucy had enough details about her mother's childhood to flavor the book beginning to take shape in her mind. She'd been planning to write it in the first person, crafting it around her own recollections of her mother, but talking to Gina gave her a new perspective. Cecile's life had been formed before her children had been born. Could her death, too, be the product of events so far in her past? Could she have landed in Dobbs Hollow not because of something drawing her on, but because of something she was fleeing?

Lucy walked Gina to her car, then checked the prepaid cell phone she'd bought after dropping her brother in Dallas. One of Todd's friends had suggested the practice when she'd needed a way for sources to contact her during her research for the Amicone book. She maintained a post-office box and a professional e-mail address, but she'd been reluctant to give out a phone number, even knowing she could change it. The disposable phones, untraceable and refillable, suited her perfectly. She didn't expect any response from the advertisement she'd placed the day before, since the paper copy of the local weekly wouldn't hit newsstands for another two days, but the clerk had assured her the ad would appear on the website right away. She'd also placed a craigslist ad with the same information before leaving home.

The phone's gray screen informed her she had one text message.

WHORE. I AM WATCHING YOU.

The threat took a moment to register, and if it hadn't been for the first word, Lucy would have laughed it off. But the innocuous dark print on the backlit screen brought to mind the same word scrawled on the paper wrapped around one of the bricks tossed through her window, and smeared in blood across Renee Josephs's pale skin.

She shivered and leaned against a car.

Misled by the massive difference in scale of brutality, she had dismissed Ethan's warning about the connection between the bricks and the body. She tucked the phone into her purse and ran her hands over her arms, rubbing away the goose bumps that had formed there.

Why the petty crime and the text message? If the man knew anything about her, he would know they wouldn't chase her away. They were like the acts of a child, while Renee's murder was that of a full-grown psychopath. She'd told TJ that the man who killed Renee Josephs had used her body as a billboard. What if the message he was sending—with the brick, with the text, with the body—was simply: "Fear me"? What if he got his thrills watching people react to violence and threats?

If so, he would be watching now. She glanced around the parking lot, trying to remain casual. A few people were checking out of the hotel. A family packed bags into a big, red SUV. A couple walked, hand in hand, over away from the parking lot toward the town. No one seemed to be paying her any mind.

*Fear me.* Renee's killer hadn't been a novice. The high level of ritualization, the immaculate scene, both indicated he'd had plenty of practice. Cecile Sadler's killer, on the other hand, had left behind a plethora of evidentiary material, had anyone cared to collect it. One man's learning curve? Or two completely separate individuals?

She removed the phone from her bag once more and stared

at the gray screen. The number had not been blocked. She would give it to Ethan to check, but for the moment she had to assume tracking wouldn't help. It likely belonged to another anonymous prepaid cell.

Ethan would be furious that she'd given out her phone number in the paper, even if the number wasn't a personal one, but she did not fear of his anger. In fact, she looked forward to sparring with him. To seeing him. Which just went to show how screwed up she was. She'd shoved him away, terrified by her own reaction to their kiss, and here she was practically salivating at the thought of seeing him again. He'd been more than understanding about her behavior the first time, but she couldn't expect him to put up with it again.

She could spend the next three hours at the Mineral Wells library looking through old copies of the Mineral Wells Index, the local paper, take another three hours in the car on the drive home figuring out what to do about Ethan, and be back in Dobbs Hollow before dark.

⤳

AN HOUR INTO her drive home, Lucy's personal cell rang. For a completely irrational moment, her heart leapt in anticipation of hearing Ethan's voice, but she didn't recognize the number on the car's Bluetooth display.

"I know this is gonna make your day," TJ said without preamble when Lucy answered, "so I thought I should give you the heads-up before you got home."

Lucy sighed, imagining what vandals might have done to her house while she was away. "What now?"

"Drew is telling people you threatened to shoot him."

Lucy couldn't decide whether to laugh or scream. "What?"

"Yeah. He says he went by your place to welcome you home, and you came after him with a gun."

Perfect. Just perfect. "Oh, for crying out loud."

"Yeah, well, you know Drew. He figures if he can portray you as crazy woman, anything you say later will be tainted."

The past loomed between them suddenly, creating an awkward silence.

"Lucy—"

"No. We're not going there, Tara Jean. It's too late to hold him accountable for what happened in school. In some cases, your only hope is karmic retribution." TJ didn't answer, and Lucy, fearing she wouldn't leave the topic alone, switched gears.

"I can't believe your father let you become a cop in Dobbs Hollow."

Tara laughed. "He didn't have much choice. I did my stint in the academy, then took a position in San Antonio. That was a few years ago, and I met Ethan while he was down from Houston on a case. When I heard he got hired as chief here, I applied and he hired me. Nothing Daddy could do about it. He gets to choose the chief, but the chief chooses his own officers."

Ethan. It always came back to him.

"Do you have any idea how your father happened to hire him?"

"No." Static crackled on the line as both women considered the same man. "Ethan's a good guy, Lucy. His service record is pretty much impeccable. I wondered myself why my daddy would hire someone like him over another Al or Billy Pike, but he did. And Ethan took me on, which means he's not just another one of the Dobbs yes-men, hard as that might be to believe."

"I'm sorry, Tara—TJ—but it is hard to believe. This town . . ."

"It's changed. You gotta let the past go. Not all of it, and some of it won't let go of you, I know that, but things do change. The Hollow's grown too big for one man to control, and much as it pains him, I guess even the mayor finally had to admit that."

"If you say so."

"Even if you can't accept the rest of it, accept that Ethan's on your side and that he'll do the right thing."

"You sound very certain."

"I am. I've worked with the guy for six months. He's moody as all hell, but he's rock solid, too. I'm just thankful we got him down here before Renee Josephs's murder. I'd hate to imagine what a mess Al Pike or Charlie Hobart would have made of a case like this one."

"Have you found anything new?"

"Nope. Ethan has me looking into like crimes, but so far there's not a lot. He said he told you about the missing women and the rapes?"

"Yes."

"When I first heard about the pattern—the beatings and accusations—I thought . . ." Even over the static-filled cell connection, Lucy could hear Tara swallow.

"Don't. If you thought about it, then you checked, right? I know you too well to think you wouldn't."

"Yeah, I checked. There were only a few dates I could be a hundred percent sure of, but if we're assuming the rapes were all committed by the same guy, then . . ."

"Then a single alibi rules out a suspect. I do wonder, though, whether we're really looking at the work of one man, or whether Renee is a completely different case, unrelated to the rapist or the abductor. You said Ethan had you going through the ViCAP files?"

"Yes."

"Did any of the women report being stalked before the rapes? Or before they went missing?"

"Yes! Three of the seven rape victims reported having received phone calls or letters beforehand, but none of them took the threats seriously enough to report them until after they were raped. Then, of course, they felt guilty, as if they somehow deserved what happened to them because they didn't go to the police when the phone calls started. We haven't gone through all the missing women's files yet, but so far two had been to the police in the weeks before they vanished and filed complaints about receiving threatening letters, and another two told family or friends. How did you know?"

*Fear me.* "It came to me in Palo Pinto, what Renee's killer might have meant to broadcast. Not his opinion of Renee, but his ability to do what he wants, to whomever he wants, whenever he feels like it. Writing on her was his way of saying that the truth of what you are doesn't make any difference; all that matters to whether you live or die is what he thinks. If he gets off on watching people run scared, I'd be surprised if he hadn't stalked at least one of his victims, terrorized her before he took her."

"Have you talked to Ethan about this? He's thinking along much the same lines."

"Not yet. I've only just been working it out in my own head."

"You should call him."

"I will. There are other things I need to talk to him about as well. I'm on my way home now, actually." She checked the dashboard clock. "I should be there in about an hour. Will you be around?"

"I'm on patrol until midnight. Ethan will probably be at the station, though. You should stop by on your way home."

"I think I'll hit the house first. Shower, maybe grab a bite to eat." Figure out what the hell to say to Ethan.

"If I see him, I'll tell him you'll be by later."

"That would be great. Thanks."

An hour later, however, she pulled up in front of her house with no clearer idea how to deal with Ethan. She would have to tell him about the text, which would infuriate him. And she'd have to tell him about her theory of the case, which—according to Tara—would intrigue him. But she'd also have to be alone with him for the first time since the kiss they'd shared that had shattered everything she thought she knew about herself and her own reactions.

Which was precisely the problem. She preferred situations where she knew exactly what would happen, where she could control the outcome. Getting involved with Ethan would be like being sucked into a riptide—no matter how hard she swam, her strokes wouldn't alter the direction. She might find herself cast up on a remote but beautiful island or she might end up dead on the rocks.

The headlights illuminated the white siding of the house, clean and fresh, as if red paint had never dripped down it. But Lucy remembered, and she passed by the house once, examining it from three sides as she did for any signs of unwelcome visitors. There were none, so she pulled into the driveway. From the back seat, she lifted a heavy-duty flashlight, and with that in one hand and her Glock in the other, she made a quick, efficient circuit all the way around the property.

So far, so good. With a last glance around, she set the flashlight back in the car, grabbed her overnight bag from the trunk, and unlocked the front door. Holding the bag in front of her body and the gun close to her side as she entered, she locked the door behind her immediately. Then she laid the bag next to the door and walked through the entire house, snapping on lights in each room.

Nothing. Letting out a breath she hadn't even realized she was holding, she laid the gun down on the desk and got a glass of water from the kitchen. Next came the ritual turning off all the lights she'd just turned on, save only the living room and the bedroom and bathroom for her shower. The shower revived her, the hot water relaxing her stiff muscles, and a peanut-butter–and-jelly sandwich filled the hole in her stomach, but neither helped her decide what to do about Ethan. Nor did spending an extra twenty minutes deciding which of the few clothes she'd brought she should wear to their meeting. When she could put off leaving no longer, she locked the house and checked the exterior one last time. Tote bag on her shoulder, she slid into the driver's seat of the Rover and pushed the key into the ignition.

A second too late, the sound registered. She was already rolling from the car when she felt the rattler's fangs sink into her calf.

"Fuck!" The scream, like the roll to safety behind the car with her gun drawn, was instinctive. Her leg was on fire, the pain spreading in a circle around the periphery of the bite on the surface and streaking up her leg like an arrow. Thank God the damned thing hadn't gotten her in the thigh. Eyeing the area around her as well as she could, she stumbled back into the house, slammed all the locks shut behind her, and called 911.

"Ambulance is on the way, sugar," the dispatcher assured her. "You hang tight. It was your leg, right?"

"Y-yes." Lucy's teeth were chattering.

"Are you wearing pants?"

"Mmm-hmm." Her nicest jeans. The ones that made her feel almost pretty. The ones she'd picked out because she was going to see Ethan.

"If you can get them off, you should. Snakebites swell like crazy, and if the cloth is too tight, you'll damage the skin and muscle. Can you take them off?"

Lucy looked down at where the bulge of her calf was already distorting the line of her jeans. "I can try."

"Good girl. You do that, and I'll be right here."

Lucy's fingers didn't seem to be functioning properly, and it took forever to get the button undone and the fly down. By the time she'd peeled the jeans off, sweat dampened her shirt, and droplets made

their way down her face.

"Th-they're off," she said to the woman on the phone.

"Okay. Do you have a bandage or bandana or belt? They'd like you to put on a tourniquet. Not too tight, mind you, a few inches above the bite. Can you do that without moving around too much? If not, it's not so important. It's more important to stay still and keep your leg down below your heart. Sit down, but don't lie down."

"Okay."

"Do you have a tourniquet nearby?"

"No."

"Well, that's all right. Just stay still. The EMTs are going to bring the antivenin, but I've also dispatched the Dobbs Hollow Police. They'll be able to take care of you in the meantime."

"Okay."

"You stay on the line with me until they get there, okay?"

"Okay."

"Can you say something else? Tell me a little bit about the situation. I want you to keep talking to me."

"Okay." Oh, right, she wanted more than that. The wrenching pain had surrounded Lucy's whole left leg and every beat of her heart felt as if it overstretched veins too thin to hold her blood. She whimpered, then concentrated on the phone in her hand.

"I was getting into my car, and the snake must have been under the driver's seat. I heard it, but I didn't move fast enough to get out of the way." She paused. "Or stay still long enough for it to settle down and get out without biting me."

"It was inside your car?"

"Y-yes."

"How long had it been since you'd last used the vehicle?"

"An hour? M-maybe an h-hour and a h-half?" Lucy tried the control the shaking in her body, but it refused to obey her commands. Her leg was on fire, but her skin felt cold, overly sensitive to the slight breeze from the ceiling fan.

Someone rang the bell.

"The police have arrived," the dispatcher said. "Is your door locked?"

"Y-yes."

"Okay. Can you get up to let them in?"

"I can get it."

"All right, then. You do that. I am going to stay on the line, so you let me know when they're inside."

Lucy checked the monitor and saw Ethan standing outside. Moving as carefully as she could so as not to put any pressure on the envenomed leg, she limped over and let him in. She handed him the phone. "Nine-one-one operator," she explained, heading back to the couch.

"Chief Donovan here," he said into the receiver. Then, "Oh hi, Marie. Yeah, we've got it. How far out are they? Okay. Tell them pedal to the metal, okay?"

He flipped the phone closed and came to sit next to her. "How come you didn't call me?"

"The dispatcher s-said she already had. And she w-wouldn't let me off the phone."

Ethan smiled, but his eyes remained shadowed. "That's her job. Keep you awake and talking. How long has it been since the bite?"

"N-not long. Five minutes? Maybe ten. Not more."

"Good. Let me have a look at it." He knelt on the floor and examined her left calf, his hand busy stroking her right one the whole time.

"How bad's the pain?" he asked, looking up at her.

"It hurts." She tried to smile, then went for an Indiana Jones joke: "Why did it have to be a snake? I hate snakes."

When he grinned up at her, everything inside her suddenly collapsed, and she burst into tears. In a split second, Ethan was back on the couch, his arms around her.

"Shhhh," he said, sliding his fingers up through her hair and gently massaging her scalp. "It's gonna be okay, sweetheart. The ambulance is on the way. And I've seen a lot of snake bites. Yours doesn't look all that bad. I know it hurts like the devil, but you're going to live. I promise."

She shuddered, unable to stanch the tears, and he lifted her slightly and settled her in his lap, her legs straight out on the couch.

"You'll be okay," he promised, tucking her face into the hollow of his neck. "The best thing you can do is keep the leg still and try to relax. The slower your heart beats, the less the poison will spread."

"I thought you said it didn't look bad?"

His fingers continued their gentle massage, and despite the pain, Lucy felt herself calming.

"It doesn't. But snake-wrangling is best left to experts. How'd you get bit?"

"It was in my car," Lucy murmured into his neck. He smelled of soap with a hint of spice, and sweat with a bitter undertone. Fear? Had he been frightened for her? She slid her arms around him and hung on, giving comfort and taking it at the same time.

"It must have been under the driver's seat. I heard it, but didn't register what the sound meant. Then I felt movement and jumped out, but obviously not fast enough."

"Took balls to put it there. You could have caught him at any moment."

"He probably thought I was in for the night. If he was watching, he would have seen me turn off most of the lights when I went up to take a shower."

"So you took a shower, then what?"

"I made myself a sandwich. And then I was coming to see you."

"Without pants?" he teased, and Lucy actually laughed.

"Jerk. The nine-one-one operator told me to take them off."

"Damn. Here I thought I'd succeeded in charming the pants off you. But at least you were on your way to see me, so I take that as progress." He pressed a light kiss to her forehead, and Lucy felt it all the way to her toes. Before she had time to respond, however, he changed the subject.

"So did you find anything useful in Palo Pinto?"

"Yes and no. I met my mother's best friend from high school."

"Wow. What was that like?"

"I'm not really sure. I haven't processed it yet. I tend to . . ."

"You tend to what? Finish it. By now you should know you can trust me."

"I do." And she did. When had that happened?

"Then tell me."

"I guess I'm not very comfortable with emotional situations. So when I encounter them, I—I tend to keep things in a bit of a box until I can sort through what they mean to me."

Ethan was silent a long time. Did he realize she had been talking about more than just Gina, that their relationship, whatever it was and wherever it might be going, constituted another situation that would take her a while to process?

"That must make life complicated," he said, just as Lucy heard sirens.

She shrugged. "I wish I could be different, but I can't."

He tilted her chin up and looked her directly in the eye. "If you want to change, sweetheart, you can change. I've never met anyone more determined. And this, well, I'd be happy to help." His tone was unbearably gentle, and Lucy felt tears clog the back of her throat once more. But Ethan slid her off his lap and went to the door to greet the paramedics.

# CHAPTER NINE

Momma used to tell me, "Better safe than sorry." She also warned me never to trust a man. Like so many people, however, she was better at giving advice than at taking it.

FROM *A BAD DAY TO DIE*

BY LUCY SADLER CALDWELL [DRAFT]

ETHAN LISTENED TO the paramedic question Lucy about the size of the snake and other factors affecting the bite with half an ear. Simply maintaining his customary control consumed the remainder of his energy. He hung on to Lucy's hand as the ambulance bounced and jerked over the pitted, potholed road, and for the life of him he couldn't have said which of them the touch was meant to reassure. For her part, Lucy didn't seem any more anxious to let go than he was. Even as her mind turned back to practical matters, her long, slim fingers remained entwined with his.

"If they're going to keep me overnight," she said, "I'm going to need some things from the house."

"No problem. Once we get you settled in, I'll have TJ pick up whatever you need." She wouldn't want anyone else in her home.

"A change of clothes, my computer, and my tote bag should do the trick."

"Hospitals aren't designed to be the easiest places to work, you know. Not like they give you a desk and an ergonomic chair or anything."

"What else am I supposed to do?"

"You could rest."

Her eyebrows went up and her lips twisted down. "Right.

Like I am going to sleep in a public hospital when someone just put a damned rattlesnake in my car."

Ethan rubbed his thumb across the back of her hand, feeling the small bones and veins beneath the soft skin. She was fragile, despite her toughness. Of course, she'd never admit it. "You'll be in a private room. And you won't be alone." He'd be with her every second. "No one will be able to get to you."

"I won't be able to sleep anyway. I might as well work."

"Okay." He certainly wasn't about to stress her out with an argument. When the docs shot her full of pain medication, she'd go to sleep.

At the hospital, the EMTs rolled Lucy into an exam room, and Ethan followed over the protests of the battle-axe manning the intake station. She came after him, but he dug his badge from his back pocket and shoved it in her face, too impatient and worried to be polite.

"Where she goes, I go," he said to the woman. She glared at him but backed off and let him enter the curtained room where Lucy was being transferred from gurney to bed. Moments later, a harried-looking doctor came in, introduced himself, and asked Lucy to remove the sheet covering her leg. He paid Ethan no mind at all.

After prodding at the wound, which made Lucy hiss in pain and Ethan clench his fists to stop from strangling the guy, the doctor proclaimed the venom level low.

"Doesn't look as if he got you too badly." The doctor checked the chart that, Ethan assumed, contained the notes from the EMTs. "We have to wait to get the blood test results back, but you should be out of here tomorrow. We'll move you upstairs for tonight as soon as Myrna finds you a bed."

"She's under police protection," said Ethan. "She'll have someone with her at all times and needs her own room."

"As it happens," the doctor said with a sniff, "when this place was built, they made all the rooms singles. So you don't need to worry about the attention your girlfriend will get."

"She's not my girlfriend. She's the victim of a crime." Shit. Could he sound any more defensive? But "girlfriend" sounded so damned high school, and it didn't touch whatever it was he was beginning to feel for Lucy.

The doctor shrugged. "Fine. Your victim, my patient. She'll be moved up to the third floor as soon as Myrna gets it organized." He fiddled with Lucy's IV. "Now. Do you have any allergies?"

Lucy shook her head.

"Good. We'll put you on an antibiotic as well, to counteract infection in the punctures. I'm on all night, so I'll be checking your levels periodically. Once you're in your own room, you'll be on a morphine pump for the night. It will allow you to dose yourself—within reason, of course—for the pain."

"Don't bother," Lucy said. "I'm not planning on using it."

"Bother," Ethan said. She glared. "You don't have to use it. But pain builds up. Trust me."

Her eyes went to his shoulder, then his knee, and she nodded.

The doctor snorted and muttered under his breath, then left the room.

"Thanks for coming with me," Lucy said. She gave him a half-hearted smile. "I'm not a fan of hospitals. I can't imagine you are, either."

"Not so much, no."

A young attendant came in before Ethan could say anything else.

"We're going to move you upstairs now," he said. He snapped the brakes off the bed and began to roll her away. Ethan followed, alert to everything and everyone that crossed her path. It was unlikely anyone would try to get to her in such a public place, but nothing about this situation conformed to textbook procedures. First, a brick through the window, then the violent and ritualistic murder of someone unrelated to Lucy, then a snake that could have been deadly?

It was almost as if three separate people had committed the crimes.

"What else happened in Palo Pinto?" he asked as soon as the attendant left them alone in Lucy's new room.

Her blue eyes went wary. "What do you mean?"

"You weren't coming to see me to tell me about your mother's friend. And much as I'd like to believe you just couldn't stay away, well, that's not your style. So you found information important to the case, or something happened."

"Okay, yeah." She shifted in the bed and wouldn't meet his gaze. "I put an ad in the local paper. Online, too. Asking for information about my mother. And I left a phone number. The number of a burn phone I bought for this case, not my personal cell."

Ethan's gut tightened. "And?"

"He texted me. Or someone did. When TJ brings my stuff, the phone will be in my tote. I am sure he texted from a burn phone of his own, but it's at least worth the effort to see where the number leads."

"Hell yes, it's worth the effort. What did it say? And why didn't you call me as soon as you got it?"

"It said he was watching me. He . . ." She swallowed, and Ethan braced himself. "He called me a whore."

"Dammit, Lucy." Ethan wanted to hit something. "Whore" in red paint on paper wrapped around a brick, "whore" written in blood across a dead woman's abdomen, "whore" muttered over and over by a serial rapist, and now "whore" again, in Lucy's text message. Would he find it in her car somewhere, placed there with the snake, once he'd had the Rover towed in for fingerprinting?

"I know. But it gave me an idea about the killer's message." She explained her theory about the killer wanting people to fear him. "TJ said you were thinking along the same lines."

"I am. Let me call her and get her to pick up your stuff. You said you wanted clothes, your computer, and your tote bag?"

"Yeah. It has my phones and my notes from the trip in it, and I want to enter them while they're still fresh in my mind."

Ethan called TJ and explained the situation.

"I'll be there in forty-five," she said. "I'll have to break a window, though, unless you left the door unlocked."

"No, it's locked. Do what you have to. Then call a glazier. I want it boarded the instant you're done and fixed properly ASAP."

"Boards are in the garage," Lucy said.

"Got it," TJ replied. "I'll ask Scott to put the boards up while I hit the hospital. I saw him signing out not too long ago, and he said he was only planning on drinking beer in front of the television."

"Good. I'll pay him overtime out of my own pocket." He flipped his phone closed and examined Lucy, whose fair skin had acquired a decidedly olive tint. From more than just the fluorescent lights and the reflection of the pale green walls.

"Pain?"

She nodded. "I thought it would get better. Or at least stay the same. But it seems to be building."

"It happens that way." He sat down on the edge of the bed and pushed her hair away from her face. "Hit the pump."

"I have work to do."

"And you can't do it if you're in pain. You don't want to sleep. You don't want to lose control. I get that. Believe me, no one understands it better than I do. But TJ won't be here for almost an hour, and if you relax now, you'll be in better shape when she brings your stuff."

"Forty-five minutes?"

"Yeah. So take a dose and close your eyes. I'll be here. Nothing will happen. I promise."

The pain had to be bad, since she didn't argue further.

"Thanks," she whispered. In minutes, she was asleep.

For the next half hour, Ethan paced the room, trying to work out what could possibly be going on. When TJ arrived,

Ethan pulled her out of the room so as not to disturb the still-sleeping Lucy.

"She's going to be okay?"

"Yeah. But I'd for damn sure like to know how a four-foot rattler got into her car. You're having it impounded?"

"It's done. The print guys are working it over now, though I'd hardly handle a snake like that without gloves, so they probably won't find anything."

"No. We need a break."

"Ethan, you might want to talk to Scott Allenby about the rattler. Just . . . go easy on him."

"You think he knows something? And you left him at Lucy's?"

"No, I don't think he knows anything. But his brother might. Eric was forever terrorizing the girls in school with snakes, toads, spiders . . . any creepy-crawly thing he could find. I'm not saying he did this, but he's not afraid of anything that lives in the woods, and he might have been willing to catch a rattler if someone asked him to."

"Shit. Have I ever met Eric?"

"He's kind of a skinnier, scrawnier version of Scott. He works five nights a week as a security guard over at Farmer's Feed Plant."

"Oh, yeah." An image took form in Ethan's mind. He'd met the man once, maybe twice. Nothing remarkable about him at all.

"Okay. I'll see what I can find out. In the meantime, check and see whether you can find any snake owners or dealers locally. If you don't mind putting in the overtime, check websites, too, and see if anyone has shipped any vipers to our area. If a guy has one, he may have more, so keep the search general."

"Will do."

Ethan took the bag TJ had brought for Lucy and slipped back into the room. In the brief time he'd been outside, she'd woken up and was struggling to raise herself higher on the pillows. He dropped the bag into a chair and went to help her.

"Was that TJ?" she asked, her voice muzzy with sleep.

"Yeah. She brought your things. But there's no need to get up yet. Why don't you go back to sleep for a while?"

"No, I'm fine. Can you get my laptop?"

He did as she requested. But instead of returning to the chair, he nudged her over so he could sit on the bed beside her. She was trying to withdraw, he could feel it, and he wouldn't let her get away.

~

PANIC WELLED INSIDE Lucy for a minute when Ethan slid his long body onto the bed beside her. He was always so close, always invading her carefully cultivated personal space. But she had to admit, his warmth was welcome. Despite the pain-killers, her body throbbed oddly and her skin still felt chilled. He slipped one arm around her shoulders, tugging her even closer, then glanced down at the program she'd opened on the computer.

"I've never seen anything like that. Do you use it for your writing?"

She considered lying. It would have been easier. But Ethan deserved better.

"It's in development, as yet unnamed, but I call it DJ."

"DJ?"

"It's the brainchild of a friend, a computer programmer who used to work in law enforcement. He could follow details in his head that no one else could—give him eight suspects, twelve crimes, and he'd manage to track where each guy was on each night, separate them by all kind of characteristics. Since I do a lot of timelines and picayune detail for the books, I once joked that I needed a 'digital Jake.' He said I could beta test the one he was writing as long as I uploaded notes on features and bugs to the server while I was using it."

"So how does it work?"

He pressed closer still, eyes fixed to the screen, and she felt the heat of his body all along the side of her own. It would be so easy to turn into that warmth, to surrender to the promise of comfort and security, as well as to the spice of excitement, but she couldn't afford to let herself do so. She focused on the laptop instead.

"There are sections. This card, for example, is in the victim biography section. I'd put everything I can find out about my mother here. Not about the murder—that's an event, and goes on a different form—but about her. The straight facts you can get off a driver's license, and the not-so-obvious. There are places for friends, enemies, and acquaintances. There's a spot to list a person's frequent activities—does she go to the gym three times a week? Get her nails done on Mondays? You don't have to fill everything in, but there are spaces for whatever you can get. There's even a section for free-association notes. Jake calls it 'intuition entry.' Then there are tags. For Cecile, I have dozens, everything from 'prostitute' to 'mother' to 'outsider.' My mother's father was a preacher. I discovered that in Palo Pinto, and once I enter it, the program will look for significant religious background in other victims, as well.

"There are other kinds of biography cards. Suspects, random people who turn up in the investigation who are hard to keep track of but you don't want to forget. People you have no good reason to suspect but just feel hinky about. You can put in cards for anyone you want. Of course, you're not going to have as much data on them, but you add them anyway. The program looks for links between them and victims, as well as between victims and each other. Let's say all your victims have a three somewhere in either their birthdays or their addresses. You probably wouldn't notice—and it might mean nothing at all—but DJ will flag the recurrent number as interesting.

"There's also the event section." Switching screens, Lucy brought up the page for her mother's murder. "The first thing the program wants to know is as close to the exact time of the event as possible. Sometimes, you have nothing to go on for timing, so the event ends up outside the case timeline. My mother was killed between two and three that afternoon. Then the program asks where everyone else with a card for this case was at that time. I'm working on filling that in at the moment, because it's the easiest way to eliminate people."

"There's an 'intuition' box for events, too? And tags?"

"Sure. Along with crime-scene photos and a card for each of the places involved, like if the victim was killed in one spot and dumped in another. Jake is always looking for patterns, and he says intuition is usually your brain trying to tell you that it sees a pattern you can't consciously access. The program actually keeps a list of tags you've already used, to prompt you in case one is relevant to a new person, place, event, or item. Those are the other classes of information—places and items. And they're all tied together. So if you have a series of murders, many of which take place in cars—which could be both places and items—the computer tries to find that connection. An item could be a piece of music that's always playing at a crime scene, too, or a scent you notice in the air. There's also a journal feature, where you can record anything you want. The computer won't bother to use the journal information unless you specifically tell it to sync journal data with the case file."

"This Jake sounds like a smart guy. You talk to him often?" Ethan's voice was cool, and when Lucy glanced at his face, she saw he wore his cop's mask. He couldn't possibly be jealous, could he? No, more likely he found something about Jake suspicious. The application embodied the obsessive attention to detail that had made Jacob Nolan a great agent, if sometimes a less-than-perfect friend; Ethan probably couldn't imagine why anyone would put so much effort into a project that would bring little in the way of financial reward. Police departments everywhere were strapped for cash—even if they wanted to run a program like DJ, they couldn't pay enough for it to make it a cash cow for Jake. But she wasn't going to second-guess the man. He had his own reasons for everything he did, and he'd been nothing but good to her.

"Nobody talks to Jake," she answered carefully. Jake had never asked her to hide her use of the DJ program, but neither had he ever given her permission to talk about it. He'd never mentioned any other testers.

"He left the FBI two years ago and fell off the face of the earth. I know he's out there because he updates the software periodically. I log in, and the interface has changed or there's an update notice. Other people get the occasional postcard from him, but there's never a return address and the postmarks are all different. I don't have an e-mail address or anything for him. I maintain a backup copy of my DJ records on my own computer in case he decides to pull the application, but all the number crunching is done on a server elsewhere. If I tried to log in one day and the site was gone, I'd have no way to contact him."

Ethan remained stiff, though she thought the lines bracketing his sculpted lips eased a bit. Could he imagine that she would leak details of his case to Jake? Was that what was behind the questions?

"But you trust him?"

"Yes." For the most part. In every way that mattered, she trusted Jacob Nolan implicitly, but she wasn't entirely sure he didn't log into the DJ server at night and read up on her activities, which was why her more personal observations remained unrecorded.

"Okay, then."

He watched as Lucy entered all the information she'd

learned, and all her suspicions. Except to contribute a bit of advice here and there, he didn't speak until she was done.

"You need another spot on those forms," he offered at last. "Might be a recommendation to make to your friend."

"What's that?"

"You have a box to put where information comes from, to create a link. Like you linked the information you got from this Gina Woodward back to her."

"Yes."

"But it only goes back one generation. Hearsay evidence isn't admissible in court, but gossip is the lifeblood of an investigation. You don't just want to know who gave you the information, you want to know who told her, and back on up the food chain as far as you can go. Your friend, Jake, he's FBI. If he's a profiler, he may be dealing with different kinds of cases. But if this program is meant to help us regular Joes, we need that data.

"For example"—he tapped the timeline at the bottom of the screen to indicate Cecile's murder, and Lucy pulled up the event card—"I see you've entered all the information from her case file. And you've attributed it to that file."

"Of course."

"But nowhere does it say how you got your hands on that file. I assume you have a screen in there with my name on it?"

Lucy felt her face redden, but Ethan merely smiled and leaned over to press a kiss to her forehead. Then he let her go as if the gesture meant nothing at all. And maybe, to him, it didn't. Hadn't he denied any relationship between them when the doctor had assumed one? Maybe he kissed women all the time, and every one of them felt the same shock of fire slamming from his lips all the way down her body. She'd never run across a man like Ethan Donovan.

"You wouldn't be much of an investigator—or a writer— if you didn't. But back to business. On the card identifying the case file as an 'item,' you've probably listed me as a source.

But in a bigger department, I wouldn't be the one who pulled the file from records. You would want to be able to mark down every person who'd handled it, on the off-chance someone was cherry-picking information to give you. Or in case all the leads you had that seemed to come from different sources could be traced to one or two individuals."

"Gotcha. I'll make a note for Jake." She'd also add more details to the intuition section of Ethan's card, which was beginning to weigh rather heavily in his favor. For that, however, she'd wait until he was gone.

"And what about the word 'whore'? I notice you put in the events where it's appeared, but shouldn't there be a way to highlight it? Especially now, after the text message?"

"That's exactly the kind of thing the program will pick up. But, yeah, I'll put it in, too."

"The program can't protect you, Lucy."

"Of course not."

He gently closed the lid and set the laptop on the table next to the bed. "You need to be more careful." He shifted on the bed until her head lay in the hollow of his shoulder. Beneath her ear, she could hear his heart pumping blood, pumping life through his body, its beat solid and stable like the man himself. So what did he want with her?

She didn't even realize she'd asked the question aloud until he answered it.

"At the moment, I just want to know you're safe."

"Why?"

"Does there have to be a why?"

It wasn't the answer she'd hoped for, but since she refused to acknowledge what, exactly, that answer might be, she also refused to acknowledge the niggle of disappointment that wormed through her.

# CHAPTER TEN

Word around town had it that Cecile Sadler was easy. None of the people making that claim, however, actually lived with her. As I grew up, I had a hard time imagining how a woman as tough as Momma could have ended the way she did.

FROM *A BAD DAY TO DIE*

BY LUCY SADLER CALDWELL [DRAFT]

LUCY KNEW SHE should pull away, push Ethan out of the hospital bed and back to his chair. Despite his protestations the other night, he had to have been put off by her behavior. Though she trusted him with most of her secrets, and certainly with her safety, he obviously didn't feel the same. Until he could be completely open, she had to remember to keep her distance.

But, dammit, she didn't want to. The solid beat of his heart beneath her ear and the warm strength of his arms combined to make her feel more secure than she had in all the months since Todd's death. Fair was fair, however. She wouldn't offer him false hope.

"I can't do this," she said, shifting away from him and reaching for the laptop. He accepted the move with grace, helping her to get the computer and removing the arm he had laid across her shoulders.

"So what has your fancy program come up with?"

"Nothing yet. But as you saw, I've barely begun entering information. I was hoping I could convince you to share what you'd found out about the girl by the lake, in case her murder does tie in with my mother's."

"You admit it's a possibility, then?"

"I never said it wasn't. They don't feel the same, but there is a peculiar kind of symmetry. If nothing else, the timing's awfully coincidental."

"And the other anomalies in the area? The rapes and disappearances? I suppose you want access to those files, too?"

"I'm not naive, Ethan. I realize you can't just open your files to me. I'll take whatever I can get."

"But you believe it all ties together."

"I'm not sure. But I think it would be a mistake to dismiss the possibility."

He studied her in silence for a long moment. She wished she could read the thoughts behind those glade-green eyes, but the mask he wore was impenetrable.

"As it happens," he said finally, "I agree with you. The sheer number of cases in one area argues for more than mere coincidence. So I'll make you a deal."

"A deal?"

"Yeah. I want access to that program."

"I can't—"

He held up a hand, anticipating her protest. "I understand it's not yours to share. So, here's my proposal. I'll give you the data to enter, which will allow you access to the files you want. In return, you share anything you—or the computer—come up with, whether it has anything to do with my cases, your mother, whatever. And you don't make a move without telling me."

"It sounds as if I give up a lot more than you do in this deal."

"You get more. I could do what that computer does. It would take me a huge number of man-hours, but I could do it."

"Okay, I'll give you that. But what does telling you everything I do have to do with the investigation?"

He smiled, a crooked, wolfish grin that banished the chill of separation. "Oh, that's not about police work. That's personal."

Her heart gave a reluctant thump. "I can take care of myself, Ethan."

"I know." He stroked her cheek with one calloused finger, and his eyes darkened. "But just because you can do it alone, doesn't mean you have to. I want to help. And if I have to bribe you to get my way, well, I guess I'm not so devoted to the law after all."

Her mouth went dry. "Ethan—"

"Shhh." He leaned forward and pressed a soft, almost teasing kiss to her lips. "Just say yes. It's easy. One little syllable."

She pulled back slightly from the temptation of those incongruously soft and gentle lips and shook her head to clear it. "How will you get permission for me to see the files?"

"You're too accustomed to thinking of this as the Dobbs family's private fiefdom. I'm the chief of police. If I want to bring in a professional consultant, I can. I'll have June Gibb, the town's legal advisor, draw up papers dictating the restrictions and regulations tomorrow, and once you're out of here, you can come in and sign them."

He leaned back, arms crossed over his chest, and waited for her answer.

She couldn't quite meet his eyes when she gave it to him. "Okay, then."

⌒

Sitting in the dark, kicked back in a recliner, the Commander let the burn of whiskey down his throat combat the anger boiling there. He pulled a disposable cell from inside the chimney where it was taped and texted Drew Dobbs. The text contained only the number one. It was their signal. Drew would call him back as soon as he could get away.

The cell rang four minutes later.

"I know why you're calling, and I didn't do it." The man was such a sniveling, pathetic brat. He needed a lesson.

"You will address me properly."

A long pause. Every fucking time, the idiot thought he would get away with not using the

Commander's appropriate title.

"Yes, master."

"Better. You didn't put that snake in her car?"

"Hell, no! I can't afford to have her point the finger at me. I want her to go away quietly."

"You didn't care how we got rid of her not so very long ago. What's changed?"

Another protracted silence, which meant the fool's divided loyalties were acting up again. Perhaps his usefulness was coming to an end.

"A man can only serve one master. Your father does not control you anymore."

"My father is looking out for my career. He says she has too many friends on the police force and even in the FBI from writing her books who'd come around if anything happened to her. He's also . . ."

"Yes?"

"He's worried about the dead girl. Renee. You did that, didn't you?"

"Do you really want to know?"

"No. I don't. I thought . . . I thought you were over the girls. At least, alone."

"I only did it to protect you," the Commander said sooth-ingly. "You had dozens of witnesses to alibi you. I don't want you to fall under any scrutiny. I had to do it without you."

"You could have just killed her. I heard she was raped."

The Commander smiled and sipped his whiskey. Hell, yeah, she'd been raped. And she'd wept her way through it, just like they all did. Just like Drew himself the first time he'd been sub-mitted, even though he'd professed his love only a week earlier.

"You know I don't have any feelings for them. They're nothing more than fun and games. What we have is all that matters."

"Then why—?"

"Do not question me!"

"No. I didn't mean—"

"No, what?"

"No, master."

⌒

EARLY THE NEXT morning, the doctor told Lucy she could go home. He gave her crutches to use, since walking on the bitten leg was still painful, and told her not to soak the leg until the wounds had completely healed. Since both Ethan and Lucy had arrived by ambulance, he called a cab to take them back to her house. Once there, he searched the place thoroughly for any booby traps, living or not.

And then he was stuck. He couldn't leave her alone, but he couldn't defer his duty to Renee Josephs and the other victims they'd uncovered any longer, either.

"Go," Lucy said from the couch where he'd seated her. "I know you have a ton of work to do."

"I don't like to leave you," he admitted.

She snorted. "Get. I'll be fine."

"I'll call. And come and get you once I have approval for you to be a consultant. Okay?"

"Sure."

But the promise of a coming visit wasn't enough, and he sat beside her the way he'd first sat on the edge of the hospital bed and cupped her cheek with his palm. Slowly, cautious of both her leg and her emotions, he drew her forward and pressed a lingering kiss to her lips.

"Ethan—" she said on a breathy whisper when he pulled away.

"I know, sugar. You need time. I got it."

But on the way out, he couldn't resist looking back, and

the slightly dazed expression in her eyes, along with the way her fingers were pressed against those soft lips, sent a curl of satisfied heat through his belly.

AT THE STATION, he called the town's legal advisor and explained his needs. She said she'd be by in an hour with the necessary paperwork, which eased a little of his tension. If he could get Lucy on the payroll, he'd be able to keep an eye on her. Picking up his second cup of coffee, he settled behind his desk to review the information TJ had gathered for him.

No known snake aficionados in the area. Of course not; that would be too easy. She'd found a couple places online that sold the deadly critters. Ethan shook his head over that—who wanted a rattler as a pet?—and promised to check into whether anyone local had bought one. The last line of her note was clearly worded to sound innocuous to anyone who might see it.

Don't forget to ask Scott about Eric.

Ethan rubbed absently at his knee, then elected to call TJ and get as many details as he could before approaching Scott about his brother.

"Got a minute?" he asked when she picked up.

"Sure. Is Lucy okay?"

"Yeah, she is. I wanted to ask you about Eric Allenby. Before I hit up one of my officers with questions, I need background beyond 'he liked slimy things when we were kids.' What can you tell me about him? Who does he hang around with?"

"Jeez, I don't know. He dated Amy Callahan for a while, but she couldn't handle his hours. He works four a.m. to ten a.m. five mornings a week. Plus, he's really outdoorsy. He always wanted to take Amy camping and fishing and rafting and stuff."

All those women raped out in the woods. Suddenly, Eric Allenby shot right to the top of Ethan's short list. Could he have wanted to take his date to the same spots where he had held his victims? Other rapists and murderers had succumbed to that compulsion. Ethan needed to talk to Amy. He scribbled her name on the pad in front of him, then returned to the conversation with TJ.

"So Eric's a part-timer. Does he do anything else for money?"

"Odd jobs when he feels like it, and I remember Amy saying he took extra shifts at work when anyone wanted time off, and the late-night thing pays pretty well, since it's hard to find anyone willing to do it. But the Allenby boys are pretty well-off. Their parents died in a small-plane crash when they were kids and left them sizable trusts from their life insurance. It's not that they don't need to work, but they can afford not to make a huge amount at it."

"Gotcha. Aside from Amy, anyone else he might count among his friends?"

"Jed Martin. Bob Redmond. Richie Mack. Chuck Hemming. I can't say whether he's close to any of them, but he and Amy used to double date with Jed Martin and whichever girl he was currently sporting on his arm."

Ethan added these names to the list and circled Jed Martin's a couple of times, frustrated by his neophyte status in the town. His first suspect in a relatively small crime maintained a years-long friendship with his first suspect in a murder. Coincidence? Fact of life in a small town? Or more? And the other men on TJ's list belonged to Jed Martin's crew, too. In fact, two of them had apparently been playing poker with him the night Renee Josephs had been murdered.

Bob Redmond owned Redmond's Hardware and Housewares and came across as a decent enough sort of guy, if a bit brusque. You could get him going if you asked about plumbing supplies or do-it-yourself projects, but he didn't have a truly social bone in his body. His wife, Sally, took care of the housewares half of the business and smoothed any feathers her husband's attitude might have ruffled. A vibrant, happy creature, she seemed a peculiar mate for the sober Bob.

Richie Mack, on the other hand, was a tweaker. Ethan couldn't prove the man sold meth, but he knew it to be true. He'd been arrested twice for possession, had lost his license after a DUI, and now hung around Rosalita's, playing pool and drinking, and occasionally working for Brad at the Gas 'n' Go either cleaning up the shop or filling in behind the counter in the snack shop. Ethan circled his name, too. Ethan didn't imagine Richie would go within a hundred feet of a snake, but addicts had peculiar ideas.

Ethan had vaguely recognized Chuck Hemming's name when Jed had mentioned him, but he hadn't had a chance to question him yet, so he asked TJ what she knew.

"Chuck's a manager over at the plant. He lives in Palestine these days, but we all went to school together, and he's still buds with Jed and Eric."

"Gotcha."

The plant again. He wondered whether Lucy's fancy program would be able to link the plant to anyone else, and whether—given how many people it employed—there would be any significance to the connection.

Which, of course, brought him back to thinking about Lucy and the memory of their shared kiss and the softness of her body against his in the hospital bed. So she had trouble coming to grips with her emotions. He'd been called stubborn more than once; he was willing to wait her out.

Lucy woke when her computer fell from her lap with a thud. Damn. Instead of working, she'd fallen asleep on the couch. The punctures in her leg pulled slightly when she stretched, but the pain had diminished a great deal while she slept.

She made a pot of coffee and settled on the couch with the biggest mug she could find to clear her head of the painkillers so she could finish entering all the information she'd gathered the day before. She hadn't had time or energy at the hospital, and she hadn't wanted to show Ethan the things she was writing about him. Most of the information she had now wasn't relevant to the case in any way she could tell, but it would end up helping her with the book. After all, she planned to write about her mother's life, not just her death, and the stories Gina Malloy Woodward had told revealed sides to Cecile Lucy had never imagined.

When she looked up from making notes, it was almost two in the afternoon. Maybe she'd take a cab down to the police station and see whether Ethan had the consultant's forms for her to sign. He hadn't called, but perhaps he'd been too busy.

Back in her bedroom, she carefully covered the snake bite with the two-inch-square waterproof bandage they'd given her at the hospital to keep the wound dry while showering. She dressed in a khaki skort, a white T-shirt, and a pair of running shoes, then swapped out the waterproof bandage for a breathable one. If she paid a tad more attention than usual to her makeup, it was only because she looked so pale from the long night in the hospital, not because she wanted to impress anyone in particular. She'd already put her notebook and the novel she was reading into her satchel and set the crutches by the front door when she remembered she'd promised to call Ethan to let him know if she left the house.

He answered on the first ring.

"I'll be back in the office in about an hour," he said. "How are you planning on getting to town?"

"Cab."

"I'll send TJ for you."

"No, Ethan." His name on her tongue tasted dark and sweet with intimacy and just using it sent a shiver through her. How had she come to this? "Really, I'm not the department charity. You have work to do. I'll call a cab."

"Yeah, okay. That should be safe enough. Stay inside until they get there, though, okay?"

"I will. Don't worry."

"Can't help it. But we'll leave that for later."

⌒

WHEN LUCY ARRIVED at the station, Ethan wasn't in. Marge Bollingham, the dispatcher, had the consultant papers ready for Lucy to sign, and she did, noticing that the department had indemnified themselves against any injury she might suffer as a result of her position. She was signing the final page, with Marge witnessing, when her cell rang. It was her personal cell, not the prepaid one, and the caller ID read "Ethan." She'd programmed his numbers in before leaving for Palo Pinto, though she hadn't bothered to examine the impulse too closely.

"Where are you?" he asked when she picked up.

"At the station, signing the release forms."

"Great. If you wait there for me, I'll pick you up. I'm picking up your car now."

"I can have it back already? That's great! I expected I'd have to rent one."

"Nope. Unfortunately, we didn't find anything. Your fingerprints, Brad's—from when I had him change your tires—and an unknown set that's probably Tim's, since it appears all over both the passenger and driver's side. There's nothing unusual in the pattern of prints, nothing that shows where someone might have put the snake in. The lock was popped with a slim jim."

"Lovely." Lucy could only imagine how long it was going to take to get all the fingerprint powder out of the Rover.

"I'll be there in five," Ethan said. "Go on in and use my office if you want to. There are files in there I'd like you to take a look at anyway. If TJ's there, she can show them to you."

"She just got here."

"Excellent. See you in a few."

When Ethan entered the office, where she and TJ were sifting through files, Lucy had to twist her hands together to stop herself from reaching out to brush away the lines of weariness in his face.

"Long day?"

"You could say that. I ran over to Palestine for a conversation with a family whose nineteen-year-old daughter went missing a couple years ago." He pulled out a file and laid it on the desk. "And while I was there, I had a little conversation with Jed Martin about snakes, his memories of high school, and his buddy Eric Allenby.

"No sooner did I leave the car lot than I got a call from His Honor the mayor, wondering what the fuck I was doing out of town harassing upstanding citizens when we had problems right here at home with a dead woman who might ruin his son's political aspirations if I didn't get in gear and solve her murder."

"Joy," said TJ.

"What were you saying about this not being his own private fiefdom?"

"I didn't say he was aware of that fact."

The comment startled a laugh out of Lucy. "Touché."

"So, I copied the files for you to start with." He laid a hand on the stack on his desk. "You can take this stuff home if you like. I'll stop by later on and see how it's going. For the moment, I want to wait for Keith. He called in and should be back soon with more on the two Freestone victims."

Lucy packed the papers he had for her into her tote, and he walked her out front where he'd parked her Range Rover in one of the reserved slots. It sparkled in the sun, and through the window she could see the leather seats gleaming.

"What did you do?"

"Had it detailed. Only way to get rid of the fingerprint powder, I'm afraid. Otherwise, you'd have been tracking the stuff around for weeks. Believe me, I know."

Her throat tightened at the unexpected kindness. "I could've done that. But I appreciate it."

"Sure thing. Now go home and get the weight off that leg."

With a quick nod, Lucy climbed carefully into her car and drove off.

⌐

JED SPUN AROUND in the ergonomic chair in the glass cage of his office. What the hell had Eric been thinking? True, Jed hadn't bothered to tell him about the paper the cops had found in the woods. He should have searched the girl before he brought her out to play. But even without knowledge of the evidence, Eric should have avoided anything that would bring scrutiny to bear on them. And that snake, it was vintage Eric. Not that Ethan Donovan should recognize such a thing—one of the purposes of hiring an outsider was to keep him an outsider.

Not everyone had been pleased when Dobbs had hired Donovan, but Jed had a great deal of respect for the mayor's foresight. Rather than promoting the likes of Ellen Wilson's nephew, Johnny—chief deputy with the Adams County Sheriff's Department, who'd grown up in the

Hollow — Dobbs had chosen a city boy who would likely never get a handle on the slippery relationships between locals. Jed only wished he knew what Dobbs had to hide, because he'd love to tap that well. He lived nicely on what he made from the dealership and his other activities, but a little backup never hurt.

On the showroom floor, one of the salesmen was showing off an F-250 to a guy who wouldn't buy it. If he bought anything at all, it would be a used piece of crap Jed would hardly make a dime on. The economy was in the toilet.

In frustration, he locked the door to the office from his desk with his favorite new toy, a remote control lock, and pulled a disposable cell from under the false bottom of a desk drawer.

Eric picked up on the third ring.

"We need to talk," Jed said. "Is it safe?"

"Would I even be answering if it wasn't?"

"Yeah, okay. It's about Chuck and Richie."

"Richie's a problem. All fucking tweakers are problems. Too bad you can't run a business without them."

"Yeah, but he's been buying elsewhere, which means his loyalty's no longer guaranteed."

"I have an idea about that. Might kill a couple of birds with one stone." Eric laughed, and the sound sent a chill up Jed's spine. Shit. He'd always known his partner was half-insane.

"What's up with Chuck? He can't have figured anything out. If the man had a single live brain cell, it died of loneliness years ago."

"He's still stewing over that incident in high school when we drove out to Cecile's house." And hadn't that been fun. She'd mocked them, told them to take their spare change and their tiny cocks and run home to their mommas. Jed had wanted to kill her that night, but too many people knew where they were and what they were doing.

But once Cecile was dead, she'd ceased to matter. Jed had always assumed the others felt the same way.

"He's getting increasingly impatient to have what he sees as his revenge on Lucy, and since he thinks of us as bonded over the incident, he's becoming a flat-out nuisance."

"If we do it right, we can use him as a scapegoat. He has no social life. Every night he goes home after work and drinks until he passes out. He won't have an alibi."

"An alibi for what?"

Eric told him.

AT SEVEN, ETHAN gave up trying to concentrate on the files on the desk in front of him. His head ached and his knee throbbed. And his stomach rumbled. Time to go see what Lucy's fancy program had come up with, because nothing in the files seemed clear to him. Keith had gotten nothing new from his trip to Freestone. Two women gone, just disappeared, and one barely more than a child.

He drove to his favorite Mexican restaurant, picked up burritos, queso, and guacamole, and headed over to Lucy's, figuring she wouldn't have eaten, either. When he got there, he pulled his truck around the back. No need for the gossips to make something out of nothing. And if what he felt wasn't precisely nothing, well, he wasn't sure precisely what it was, either. He rang the doorbell by the back door and waited under the glare of the security lights for Lucy to let him in.

"That smells heavenly," she said when she let him in. "How did you know I hadn't eaten?"

"Wild guess."

Her slow smile smoothed his aches, and he caught himself wondering what it would be like to have that expression greet him at the end of every day. He shut the thought away before it could show on his face.

"I'm afraid the kitchen table is my work area at the

moment," she said, gesturing to the stacks of papers covering the surface, "so we'll have to eat in the living room. Can I get you a beer to go with that, or are you technically still on duty?"

"Nope, I'm free. And I'll take whatever you've got."

Lucy pulled a couple of Modelos out of the fridge and led the way into the living room. He had to force himself not to chastise her for ignoring her crutches, and once she'd sunk onto the couch, he couldn't refrain from asking about them.

"My leg hardly hurts at all, actually. The doctor said it would heal fairly quickly. I have to keep taking the antibiotics all week, but I think I'm done with the crutches."

He plunked down next to her and parceled out the burritos, chips, guacamole, and salsa he'd brought. "Just don't be a hero."

"Yes, sir." She gave him a mock salute, and he laughed.

⌒

ETHAN'S LAUGHTER WARMED her more than the scent of spicy food or the rich fizz of the Mexican beer, and Lucy felt herself relaxing, the stress she habitually carried draining out of her muscles, only to be replaced by tension of an entirely different kind. Unsure of herself, she concentrated on eating. When the food was gone and she could ignore him no longer, she glanced up.

"Thank you," she said. "The car, the food, the files . . ." Most men would have waved away her gratitude, but Ethan did not. He merely caught her eyes with his own, which seemed to grow darker as he held her gaze. She could not look away, and when he leaned toward her, she met him halfway.

His lips were hot, but surprisingly soft on her own. They teased and tempted, incited and seduced, and Lucy's entire awareness narrowed to the single spot at which she and Ethan were joined. She moved closer, cradling his rough, stubbled jaw in her hands, and expected him to follow suit. Craved the feeling of his palms against her skin.

But he did not, and after a moment, Lucy pulled away, only to find his hands fisted in the cushions of the couch.

"I didn't want to frighten you," he said, following the direction of her glance. "Last time . . . last time, I got the feeling things moved too fast. I was trying to slow down."

Lucy's eyes stung, and she blinked away the tears trying to form there.

"I'm not afraid of you, Ethan."

"No?"

She shook her head, and he grinned at her. "Thank God." He reached for her, and she practically threw herself into his arms, but before he could kiss her again his phone rang.

He dropped his head back and banged it twice on the back of the sofa. "I have to get that. I'm not on duty, but with this case I'm never really off, either."

"I know. Next time."

"I'll hold you to that."

Lucy almost didn't recognize the little thrill that went through her at the promise. Joy. How long had it been since she'd felt that tingle of anticipation, that indescribable tickle of elation? Certainly, no man had ever inspired it in her before. No, it had been reserved for book contracts and graduations. For a moment, the strength and unexpectedness of it actually did scare her.

Especially with this man, who still held secrets. Of course, she had her own. It was time to share them if she expected him to trust her as she'd learned to trust him.

"I have to go in," Ethan said when he hung up. "They caught the Archer Apartments peeper. I doubt he's connected to the murder, but I want to be the one to interview him. Besides, patrol brought him in, and the only other detective I have is Keith, and he just got off duty, too."

"I understand." And she did. Didn't mean she wasn't

fiercely disappointed, or a little tiny bit relieved. She walked him to the door, where he pulled her close for another brief, mind-numbing kiss before letting her go.

⌒

JIM RANDOLPH'S MOTHER caught Ethan the moment he entered the station.

"Chief Donovan, there has to be some mistake," she said before he could even greet her. "I promise you, Jim's a good boy. He's never been in any trouble at all."

Right. Ethan knew sexual predators as well as any cop. If her good boy was peeping into windows at nineteen, he'd likely be committing sexual assault by the time he was legal to drink. But he couldn't very well tell that to the kid's mother.

"Mrs. Randolph, why don't you sit with Officer Wilkes and go over everything you remember happening tonight while I have a little chat with Jim. Is that all right?"

The woman nodded, sniffing back tears, and Cal Wilkes led her away.

Ethan slipped into the interview room where Scott Allenby was questioning the boy.

Jim had the physique of a health nut but the flitting eyes of a habitual drug user. And, at nineteen, he still had bad acne. Possibly, he suffered from a genetic curse of overactive sebaceous glands. More likely, he used steroids.

"Has he been informed of his rights?" Ethan asked Scott.

"Yes, sir."

"I don't see a lawyer."

"He doesn't think he needs one at the moment."

"Hmm." Ethan pulled out a chair and sat next to Scott, across from Jim. "So, Jim—it is Jim, right? Not Jimmy or James?" The kid nodded. "Good. So, Jim, tell me about what happened tonight."

"Huh?" Clearly, not what the kid had expected. Ethan just leaned back in his chair and waited.

"Well, uh, I went out for a while, to, you know, get out of the apartment. My mom made cabbage for dinner, and the place stank. So I wandered around, and then, like, I saw a light from this one window, and I got curious, so I looked in, and then this guy"—he gestured to Scott—"he grabs me and hauls me in here. I didn't do anything."

"You must have been more than curious. That window was in a third-floor apartment. Officer Allenby found you halfway up a tree."

"Yeah, well, I was bored."

"Not going to cut it, Jim. We've had reports of someone matching your description peering in windows at the apartment complex for at the last three weeks—coincidentally, exactly the same length of time you've been home from college."

Jim shrugged. "Like you said. Coincidental."

"I don't think so. I think if we put you in a lineup, people will be able to ID you. And I think your prints will match the ones we found on two victims' windows."

"Look, those chicks shouldn't have left their blinds open. They wanted me to look!"

"I see."

"I'm stuck here all summer long, and my mother can't afford high-speed Internet, so I can't even get online. I don't even have a car, and there's nothing to do in this Podunk town. I gotta have entertainment. I'm not hurting anyone."

"So tell me, Jim, you ever seen anyone else out and about when you're . . . doing your thing?"

"Huh?"

"You know, a guy who might be doing the same thing you were doing? Someone else . . . bored?"

"No. I never saw anyone." Unfortunately, Ethan believed him. And the reports of peeping on the night Renee had been killed gave Jim an alibi. Good for Jim, bad for Ethan. True, the boy might have gotten a friend to drive him out to the bar where Renee worked after his evening activities, but Ethan doubted it. Plus, instinct said little Jim hadn't gone beyond the peeping stage yet, though he soon might, and the man who'd killed Renee had considerably more experience.

THE COMMANDER TRACKED Drew Dobbs through the night scope attached to his favorite rifle as he let himself in through the construction site's gate, his movements jerky and agitated. Normal excitement over the evening's potential, or did Drew sense he'd become prey as well as predator?

Drew reached into the backpack he'd brought with him and pulled out night-vision goggles. Strapping them on, he peered around the site. He didn't call out—he knew better than to alert anyone to his presence—but he clearly wished he could.

The Commander gave Dobbs points for having put on latex gloves before getting out of his car. Under other circumstances, no one would ever associate him with the place, because nothing would be left to show he'd visited other than normal detritus: a few hairs that could be explained by secondary transfer, a shoeprint in the clay soil that might belong to anyone. Of course, tonight such precautions were unnecessary, but Drew had no way of knowing that.

Dobbs pulled his cell phone from his pocket and glared at the screen as if willing a message from his partner to appear. The Commander almost laughed. The only message he'd be getting tonight would signal the dissolution of the partnership.

Dobbs took up a position by the gate, just as the Commander had known he would, just where he was most vulnerable. The Commander sighted down the scope again, sucked in a deep breath, let it out slowly, and squeezed the trigger.

He could have gone for the head shot, but he was no glory hound. The bullet went in an inch to the left of Dobbs's sternum. The big rifle barely bucked at all, and the shooter never lost sight of the target, watching as the man crumpled slowly to the ground, a look of complete surprise on his face.

Man, what a thrill! He only wished he could have done Dobbs in close rather than from afar. But he couldn't afford to take that kind of chance. His thoughts turned almost immediately to his next target. When he killed her, and he would, it would be up close and personal.

# CHAPTER ELEVEN

Regardless of a parent's capabilities, a child's natural instinct when in pain is to cry out for her mother.

FROM *A BAD DAY TO DIE*

BY LUCY SADLER CALDWELL [DRAFT]

THE STATION LINE rang at seven-thirty and Marge picked it up with a cheery expression that quickly turned grim. Ethan couldn't hear her, but she hung up quickly and turned to TJ. Ethan rose from his desk and hurried toward them.

"Ohmigod, Tara Jean," Marge said, "you need to go home right now. Your brother's been shot."

Ethan remembered the words TJ had said to him the day Lucy came to town. If he had a heart, she'd probably put a stake through it. And then there was Tim's shaky phone call after Drew visited their house: He scared her. And Lucy's not scared of anything.

"Where?" Ethan barked at Marge. "When?"

"I don't know when! That was Sue, from the sheriff's office. She said a construction worker found him this morning at the Belle Pointe development." She switched her attention back to TJ. "Sheriff's there now, but I don't know if they've called your daddy. He'll need you."

"I'm going. Ethan?"

"Yeah. Marge, call Keith and get him in here. I'll call in later. You can reach me on my cell." If she chose to interpret his statement to mean he'd be with TJ, he wouldn't argue. But he had no intention of spending time with the mayor; he needed to get to Lucy before Pike did.

On the way over to Lucy's, he made two calls. The first, to tell her he had something urgent to discuss with her, the second, to call in a favor.

"What's going on?" Lucy asked, meeting him at the door, her fingers busy braiding damp hair into a long queue. She'd clearly just come from the shower, and he forced his mind away from the picture of the water sluicing over her naked body.

Back to business. Lucy had asked him what he'd discovered when he'd called, but he had refused to explain. Regardless of his attraction to her, regardless of the fact that he trusted her almost completely, he needed to see her reaction when she heard about Drew. She invited him in, and he followed her into the kitchen, where she poured coffee for both of them.

"I think we'd better sit down for this one," he said, when she leaned back against the stove and raised her eyebrows expectantly.

"Oooo-kay."

He trailed her into the living room, and they sat on the couch. She put her coffee on the table and he followed suit.

"Drew Dobbs is dead."

Her eyes widened and her face paled. She could have faked one, but not the other. Ethan tried not to acknowledge his own relief. If he let it show, she would know that he hadn't had complete faith in her and it would hurt her, which was the last thing on earth he wanted to do.

"H-how?" Her huge, blue eyes were fixed on him. It cast him back to the way Renee's mother had avoided looking at him—she'd wanted to hear nothing; Lucy wanted everything.

"I don't have many details. It's not my case. He was found this morning at the Belle Pointe development site, shot to death, which makes it Sheriff Pike's jurisdiction. Marge told TJ, and I just happened to be there."

Lucy nodded slowly. "And Drew told everyone who would listen that I threatened to shoot him."

"He did."

"Goddammit. Even dead, that man is intent on ruining my life."

"What did he do to you?"

She shook her head. "Old news. I've only seen him that one time since he came back, and we hardly spoke at all."

"But your opinion of him is well known."

She didn't reply to the implicit question. "Drew and Billy Pike were best friends. They probably still are."

"That's been my impression."

"So he'll be on his way over here." Her hands twisted in her lap, and Ethan could see them shaking. If she hadn't killed Drew—and he would swear she hadn't—what could she possibly have to fear from the sheriff?

"I'm sure he will once the scene is under control. I hope you don't mind, but I called a lawyer for you. He's damned good. The kind of guy no one wants to go up against in a courtroom. He's in Houston, so he could be here in a few hours, but he felt he might cause more problems by showing up before you're officially a suspect. He said to cooperate until you think it's time to stop, then call him." He handed her the business card he'd carried in his wallet for years.

<hr>

Lucy knew she should protest. She had always taken responsibility for her own life, faced down anything that got in her way. But Ethan's assistance didn't irritate her. It didn't feel like interference; it felt like . . . caring. Not that she was even close to ready for that, but she couldn't get angry about it, either.

"Why would you call a lawyer for me?" He couldn't possibly believe she'd killed Drew, could he? He was sitting close to her on the couch, and she pulled slightly away, trying to evaluate his expression.

"You've seen the justice system at work. Small town, big city. Some things remain the same, and one is that when a big shot—

or a relative big shot—is killed, there's a whole lot of pressure to close the case. First Renee, a beautiful young girl, now Drew, a promising politician. It would create a splash even in Houston, let alone in Dobbs Hollow. People are going to be freaking out. They're going to be calling the station, asking what the hell we're doing to keep them safe.

"So there'll be that kind of pressure. And then, too, I suspect the mayor will want your head on a platter. He knows you and his son don't get along, even if he doesn't know why."

The explanation had validity, and she relaxed, let herself lean toward him again. "I see your point. I wish we knew more about what had happened. Why would anyone want to kill Drew, of all people? I had my own problems with him, it's true, but I would have guessed everyone around here considered him golden."

"TJ went on to the mayor's house. With any luck, the sheriff's department will keep the family informed, and we can find out that way. But I am hoping that when Pike comes by here, he'll let a few things slip as well. It's hard to perform an interrogation without giving away any information."

"You believe Drew's death is related to Renee's?"

"I do. We just don't have premeditated murders here. I looked into the records when I got hired. We have domestics that escalate too far, the occasional drug deal gone bad, armed robberies where someone dies, but nothing like Renee's murder. We don't know enough about Drew's death to judge—maybe it belongs in the drug-deal category—but the timing . . . I don't believe it."

"Maybe Drew killed Renee and someone avenged her."

"Do you see him as a killer?"

The question surprised her. She hadn't really thought about her words before speaking. She chose her next words carefully.

"Except for a few words the other day, I haven't seen or spoken to Drew Dobbs in almost twenty years. He was a creep in high school, and unbearable when he came over here, but I don't know whether he'd have the stomach for murder. At least, not one like Renee's. If he were going to kill someone, I'd peg him for the 'shoot you in the back' type."

Ethan started to speak, and she braced herself to answer the inevitable question of why she should feel so strongly about a man she hadn't seen in years, but the doorbell interrupted him. Lucy checked the security monitor and saw Billy Pike and two deputies standing outside.

"Well, this should be fun."

Ethan moved to stand behind her as she opened the door.

"Chief Donovan. What a surprise to find you here." Lucy didn't miss the fact that Pike addressed Ethan first. "Miz Caldwell—it is Caldwell these days, isn't it?—we need to have a chat." The words clearly indicated that this was official business and Ethan should leave, but he merely took up a position leaning against the wall while Lucy offered Pike and his deputies seats. The two deputies took the couch, while Pike and Lucy each took an armchair. For the moment, Pike was playing it cordial.

"You know why I am here, Miz Caldwell?"

"I assume it has to do with Drew's death." She kept her voice cool and even.

"Murder. Drew Dobbs was murdered." He paused. "You don't want to know when? Or how?"

"I know he was shot. I know he was found this morning."

"And how is that?"

She shrugged. "I'm consulting with the Dobbs Hollow PD, and Ethan told me this morning when he came over."

"Consulting on what?" Pike addressed the question to Ethan.

"A series of possibly related cases."

"Cases of . . . ?"

"Rapes. Missing people."

"I see. And all these are Hollow cases?"

"Nope." Lucy almost laughed. Ethan did monosyllabic very well.

"Some of them are Adams County cases?"

"Yup."

"And yet you didn't feel the need to inform my department that you were reopening them?"

"Nope."

"And why is that?"

"Because I'm not. Reopening them, that is. I asked for the files so I could have a look at them, and no one seemed to feel I needed to put that request through you; I just sent one of my officers over to your property clerk. Right now, all I'm doing is trying to decide whether Renee Josephs's death is part of a pattern. If it is, then I'll request all the evidence as well as the case files, and reopen the cases that fit the pattern."

Lucy watched Billy fume and tried not to let her satisfaction show.

His jaw clenching and unclenching, Pike switched his attention back to her. "You want to tell me where you were last night, Miz Caldwell?"

"Right here. Working on my book."

"And was anyone with you?" The innuendo was unmistakable.

"Nope," she said, slathering her response with cheer.

"Well, now, that's a problem. Because Drew Dobbs was shot last night around three a.m., and everyone in town knows you threatened to kill him."

"Oh, please. First of all, just ask the chief: before I had my security system installed, I met everyone at the door with a gun, not only Drew."

"Absolutely true," Ethan commented.

"Second, I asked him to leave, and he seemed as if he was going to stick around. I didn't threaten him, I merely used the shotgun for emphasis to prove I was serious about him going.

"And third, if I had planned to kill the man, I certainly

wouldn't have made my dislike of him so obvious." None of which would make a damn bit of difference if Billy Pike decided to arrest her. She crossed her legs, tapping her toes to prevent Pike from seeing the slight tremor of nerves.

"You have a rifle, Miz Caldwell?"

"Nope."

"That's not what Drew said. He told people you threatened him with one."

Lucy nodded at the fireplace mantle where the Remington lay. "Amateur mistake. That's a shotgun, not a rifle. He was shot with a rifle? From what kind of distance?"

"That's none of your concern."

A pounding on the front door shook the house. "Open this door right now," shouted an all-too-familiar voice. With a deep breath she did her best to hide, Lucy rose and walked over to let the mayor in. Behind her, she felt Ethan straighten from his nonchalant pose against the wall, ready to defend her if necessary. The knowledge sent a frisson of pure, feminine awareness through her.

"You little bitch," Dobbs howled the minute the door opened. "You killed my son! My son!"

"No, I—" Despite her determination, she backed up two steps, encountering the solid wall of Ethan's body. His hands went briefly to her shoulders, steadying her, then dropped before the support could draw attention to the fact that he was no longer entirely impartial.

But the mayor had turned his attention to Pike. "Why the hell isn't she in custody? And what is he doing here?" He nodded at Ethan.

"We're trying to work through a few things," said Pike. "Don't worry, we'll have Drew's killer locked up in no time."

Dobbs leaned forward, his fleshy jowls close to Lucy's face. "You're just like your mother. Both of you—"

"Daddy." TJ, who'd followed the mayor into the house, tugged ineffectually at his hand. "Come on home. You need to rest."

He turned on her. "Get the hell away from me. My son is dead. I don't have any reason to rest. Everything I hoped for, everything I loved is gone!"

Lucy's heart ached for TJ. Cecile hadn't been a prize, but she'd loved both her children to the best of her ability.

"I didn't kill Drew." Lucy couldn't—wouldn't—lie about being sad he was dead, so she said the only thing she could think of. "I'm sorry for your loss. I know the two of you were close."

"Come on, Mayor." Pike threw his arm across Dobbs's stooped shoulders, gesturing to the deputies to come along. "Let's get you home." TJ trailed them out with an apologetic glance at Lucy.

Lucy locked the door behind them, then laid her forehead against the wood with a deep sigh. Ethan's hands came down on her shoulders and began to knead them gently. For a moment, too worn out to move, she let him, but then she shrugged him off and went to sit on the sofa.

"Well, that was enlightening," Ethan said, joining her. He slid one hand over hers and captured her fingers with his. The casual touch calmed a tension she hadn't even realized she felt.

"Really? How so?"

"To start with, Drew Dobbs told everyone you'd threatened him with a rifle. Not a gun, but a rifle. Which happens to be what he was killed with."

"Yeah, but I don't have one. And even if I did, they could do a ballistics match and prove my weapon didn't fire the bullet that killed him."

"If they found the bullet. But you're assuming a frame. I'm not. A real, competent frame is hard. Way beyond most people's skills. Further discrediting of an already disreputable subject, on the other hand, is easy. If someone wants to make your job here considerably harder, they only need to plant the seeds of doubt or water the seedlings already growing. And if Drew's death makes someone angry enough, scared enough to hurt or kill you, that would serve as a bonus."

"Wow, and I thought I was cynical."

"I'm not cynical. I just have a very bad feeling about what's happening around here. The sooner we solve our cases, the better."

"Then we should get to work."

"Let me text TJ and tell her to drop by here whenever she gets done at the mansion. I can't imagine her father will want her to stick around, but I'd like her to do her best to listen in as long as Pike's there and to talk to Alicia, Drew's wife, too. What the hell was Drew Dobbs, state senator and congressional hopeful, doing at the Belle Pointe construction site at three a.m.?"

⁓

TJ SLID INTO the home of her childhood behind the sheriff, who'd brought her father home in his car, leaving her to follow. It shouldn't have bothered her, being invisible here, any more than her father's words at Lucy's house should have bothered her. She'd always been a disappointment to her father; the insult should have stopped cutting long ago.

"Mayor Dobbs," Billy Pike was saying as TJ shut the massive oak door behind her, "you need to sit back and let me take care of this."

"What have you found out?"

"Yes, Billy," called Alicia Stevens Dobbs, gliding down the curved stairway into the foyer to join them, a glass of amber liquid in hand, "what have you found out?"

"Now, Alicia, it's a little early in the day to be drinking, don't you think?"

"My husband is dead, Billy. A little scotch isn't going to hurt anything. We don't have to concern ourselves with his impeccable reputation anymore."

"Well, then, perhaps you'd like to tell me how he managed

to go out to Belle Pointe last night in the middle of the night without you knowing? Or what might have drawn him there?"

"Obviously that woman called him," shouted Dobbs.

"Did you hear the phone?"

"She probably called his cell!" Watching his florid face flush, TJ wondered whether the mayor might be about to expire right in his own front hall from sheer frustration.

"How did she get that number?" Pike's question was far more reasonable than TJ would have expected. She'd have thought he'd jump right on the "blame Lucy" bandwagon. "Could he have been looking to buy drugs from someone there?"

"Drugs?" Alicia gave an inelegant snort. "I wish. I can't tell you how often I wished the man would at least take a Viagra or two. But he refused to 'pollute the temple of his body.' It could have used a little pollution, if you ask me."

Viagra? TJ almost choked, amusement bubbling up despite—or perhaps because of?—the shock still swamping her. The mayor's face reddened even further, and despite her desire to remain under the radar, TJ stepped forward.

"Maybe we should go into the library and sit down? It's been a bad morning, and I imagine it isn't going to get any better, so let's everyone take it easy." She touched her father's arm. He shook her off, but followed Alicia into the den.

Alicia didn't seem anxious to play hostess, so TJ—playing up her family role in the hope that everyone could forget she was a cop—asked if she could get anyone a drink. Pike requested iced tea. The mayor decided to join Alicia and got up to make himself a gin and tonic.

When TJ returned with Pike's tea and her own diet soda, along with a tray of cookies she'd finagled out of Maria, who'd cooked for the family for more than thirty years, the atmosphere in the den had calmed considerably. She handed Pike his drink and sat on the leather couch next to Alicia, laying the cookies on the coffee table.

An uncomfortable silence settled over the room, only to be broken by the strident ring of Pike's cell. He excused himself and walked out into the foyer to take the call, but even the mostly closed door between the rooms couldn't dull the shout that followed.

"You found what?" He paused. "Where?"

TJ fidgeted in her chair, sipping her diet soda and wishing she knew what the person on the other end of the line was saying.

"Is O'Reilly still there? Well, get him to the second one as soon as possible. We need to know who she is and when she died!"

Which could mean only one thing. Another dead body. Suddenly, TJ couldn't wait to get out of the mansion and talk to Ethan. But thunder rumbled in the distance, and the urgency in Pike's voice increased. "Just do it, dammit! Increase the fucking perimeter and tarp the scene until he gets there!"

DESPITE THE AIR-CONDITIONING at the plant, sweat rolled down Eric Allenby's face as he walked his last rounds for the day. His brother's call had shaken him deeply. How could Drew be dead? He and Eric had been doing business for years, whenever the stress had gotten to Drew and he'd needed to take the edge off, or when he'd needed to psych himself up for some big political shindig. In fact, he'd stopped by Eric's trailer a couple of tweeks before, when he'd returned from Austin once the legislative session had ended. They'd been friends since high school, so no one considered it odd that Dobbs would stop by to see him, even though they no longer traveled in the same social circles.

And why Belle Pointe? Christ, he could have been out there last night himself. He often slipped away from the plant at night to do a deal in Belle Pointe. Scott hadn't been able to tell him much, just that Dobbs had been shot at the construction site during the night. Any further details were still controlled by the sheriff's department. Frantic, he tried to imagine if there could be anything at the site connected to him. The biggest problem, and the one that had the coffee he'd drunk churning in his gut, was the woman he'd buried there mere days earlier.

He had to call Jed, and do it soon. If the cops didn't find that woman, there was no reason to worry, but depending on where, exactly, Drew had been shot, the sheriff's men might practically trip over the damned hole. And it was the sheriff's jurisdiction, too, which meant Eric couldn't count on his brother to know all the details of the investigation. Not that they were close enough for him to ask anyway, but Scott was such a fucking sucker, all Eric had to do let on that he wanted to spend time with "big brother" and Scott would happily chat with him.

Like this morning. Scott had called to warn him so he wouldn't have to hear the news through the gossip mill, because Scott knew how upset Eric would be that one of his friends had been killed. Right. The minute Eric was in his car, he pulled a TracFone from his pocket and dialed the only number in memory, another prepaid wireless. Jed picked up on the second ring.

"Are you at home?" Eric asked.

"Yeah. Haven't left for work yet. I saw the news. First that girl, now Dobbs. Who the hell is hunting in our woods?"

"Worse than that, they found him at Belle Pointe. The last time we were out, that's where I dumped the refuse." Even on the TracFone, Eric wasn't about to give details.

"What? Why?"

"Shit, it's easy. I've even used their Dumpsters a couple times. Loaded garbage bags and dropped 'em in when I knew pickup was the next day. Once, when they left a wet foundation, I put some trash in there and smoothed it out. All the woodland over there by the development is zoned greenbelt. No one was supposed to touch it. It should have been safe."

"That's just fucking perfect. Have you heard anything else?"

"No."

"Hell. Well, there's one obvious candidate for the killer. Maybe they'll go after her and won't look too hard for anyone else."

"You're talking about Lucy?"

"Yeah. Drew told everyone she threatened him, right? So maybe she finally went through with it."

"You don't believe that."

"Doesn't matter to me one way or the other. As long as they don't find the . . . trash . . .we're solid.

LUCY HAD LAID out all the papers Ethan had given her on the kitchen table and set up her computer to enter the information from the files, but she couldn't concentrate. Her mind kept flicking back to the hint of evaluation she'd seen in Ethan's eyes when he'd told her about Drew's murder.

As he read off details to her, she entered them into the computer, but her eyes constantly strayed from the screen to his sharp, strong profile. She had to tell him about her past with Pike and Drew. It was only fair.

But how? She couldn't simply blurt it out. He would go ballistic. He'd proved himself protective already, and she wouldn't endanger him by sending him off on a fool's errand on her behalf. But he had to know. She would simply have to muddle through. Gritting her teeth, she touched the back of his hand.

"Ethan?"

"Hmm?" He looked up from the file he'd been studying, raking one long-fingered hand through his hair, leaving it as furrowed as his brow. And suddenly the memory came, unbidden and unforeseen, of her mother sitting in the same position, her expression that same blend of distraction and determination.

I've had enough of this town, baby. I'm gonna get us the money, and we're going away, where no one can hurt us, where you and Timmy can grow up clean.

"What is it?" Ethan asked.

And everything else went out of her head as she was sucked into the memory. "She had a plan. How could I have forgotten? Right before her death, she told me she was going to get the money to move us out of town."

"Alcoholics often have ambitions they can't fulfill."

"I know. Which is probably why I'd just put this one out of my head." Plus, her own problems had blinded her to her mother's ramblings at the time. "But looking back, it doesn't feel the same as one of her grand schemes. The way she said it . . . as if the whole thing was a matter of fact. We were going to have enough money to leave Dobbs Hollow and go somewhere to start over."

"Blackmail?"

"Given her profession, it seems likely."

Ethan's phone rang, and Lucy listened while he arranged with TJ to meet them at the Joint for lunch so she could fill them in on what she'd learned at the Dobbs home.

"It would have to be someone with a lot to lose," he said when they'd settled into his truck for the drive to the restaurant and got back to the discussion of Cecile's blackmail. "True, twenty years ago seeing a prostitute was a good deal more embarrassing, but it takes a cold-blooded man to kill a woman rather than paying her off. Especially if she planned to use the payoff to get out of Dodge."

"Which puts Andrew Dobbs, Senior, at the top of the list,"

Lucy said. "I've never considered him a suspect because the legislature was in session, so he should have been in Austin when she was murdered. Of course, there's no saying he couldn't have driven home, killed her, and headed back. But still, Maxie indicated that Dobbs's . . . relationship . . . with my mother was well-known, or at least much gossiped over. So her threat would be pretty pointless—she'd only be confirming the rumors."

"Questions on top of questions," Ethan muttered, his truck bumping along into the dirt lot beside Edgar's Bar and Burger Joint. "A couple of answers would be nice."

They had their pick of the picnic tables, so they chose one toward the back of the restaurant. Ethan, naturally, sat with his back to the wall, which left Lucy the options of sitting with hers to the door or taking the spot next to him. Both made her feel vulnerable in different ways, so she elected to sit across from him.

A pretty woman with long brown hair liberally streaked with gray wrapped in a coronet on top of her head came over.

"Hey, Megan," said Ethan. "Have you met Lucy yet?"

"No, but I was hoping I might have a word with you?" She addressed the question to Lucy. "It's, um, about your mother."

Lucy was taken aback. "Oh. Sure. Do you want to talk in private?"

The woman looked around the mostly empty restaurant. "It doesn't matter."

"Then, please, sit down." Ethan patted the bench next him, and she lowered herself slowly, as if using the time to compose her thoughts.

"I heard about your plans when you came back to town, and I saw you when you were in the other day. I was going to approach you then, but I had to talk to Josh first, ask him if it was okay. We're engaged, you see, and we're in a bit of a tenuous position here in town, so I can't do anything that might disrupt the situation further without his approval."

"Of course." Black ex-con engaged to white woman in a small southern town. Lucy guessed "tenuous" didn't begin to describe their situation.

"But Josh says it can't hurt, and you should hear at least one nice thing about your mother."

"I'd like that."

The woman rested her forearms on the table, twisting her fingers together for a long moment before she spoke. Lucy clamped down on her own desire to reach across the table and shake loose whatever information the woman held. "I know people said your momma was always going off with different men, and maybe she was. But she went off with my brother, too, the last couple years of her life, and it wasn't for sex." The woman blushed. "A few times a month, Brian would pick her up at Rosalita's. He'd buy her a few drinks, then they'd go check into a motel. Everyone knew it, which is the way he wanted it. She was his beard. He told me once she was a great poker player, and they'd spend hours in that hotel room playing cards.

"He paid her for her time, but he told me she probably would have done it for the thrill of helping him put one over on the fine residents of Dobbs Hollow. He liked Cecile, enjoyed her company. He said she understood him, that she knew what it was like to do stupid things because you let your heart rule your head.

"Anyway, I just thought you should hear another side to what you're like to be getting from most people around here. It would be nice if Brian's name didn't end up in your book, but I'll understand if you can't make that promise. That's why I had to talk to Josh."

"If it turns out that I want to tell that story because it's a facet of her life and lifestyle, I will change enough details to hide his identity. I take it Brian doesn't live in the area anymore?"

Megan's brown eyes darkened. "He died in 2000. AIDS.

Of course, we didn't call it that around here. We called it cancer."

"I'm sorry. And sorrier still that he couldn't be himself."

"Me, too." After a moment, she shook off the melancholy and rose. "I'd better get back to work. Can I bring y'all anything just now?" They requested iced tea but declined to order food until TJ arrived.

When Megan had dropped off their drinks, Lucy leaned across the table and asked Ethan what he knew about her family.

"You mean, do I think Brian Matheson killed Cecile because she was blackmailing him with the secret of his homosexuality?"

"Exactly."

"No. The family is solidly middle class. Meg's parents are still alive. They're horrified by her choice of a husband, but doing their best to overcome the feeling.

"I expect Brian kept his sexuality a secret so as not to disappoint them. But even if Cecile had threatened him, I doubt he could have come up with the funds for her escape. Paying a woman to go out with you a few times a month is doable; paying to relocate a whole family is a different ball-game entirely."

"Which brings us back to the Dobbs family."

As if on cue, TJ ducked into the restaurant. Behind her, lightning flared, and hail began to patter on the Joint's tin roof. "It's going to be an ugly storm," Ethan remarked, rubbing his knee. "Been building for days."

"And it's going to destroy the sheriff's new crime scene." TJ dropped onto the bench next to Ethan and pulled off her hat, shaking off the hail. Outside, the staccato thump of hail stopped as abruptly as it had begun. Thunder rumbled, and rain began to fall.

"Another scene? Was the construction site a dump, then?" Ethan asked Lucy's question before she could get it out.

"Let's order first," TJ suggested. "It's a long story." After ordering, they all leaned in to hear what TJ had learned. Lucy watched her friend carefully, but TJ kept any emotions she might have well hidden.

"I'm pretty sure Billy said 'she' when he referred to the second body," TJ said when she'd caught them up on the situation, "and when Billy came back into the living room, he really went after Alicia. He pushed her hard on whether Drew might have been having an affair, what kind of relationships he had with women, things like that. And, given her Viagra comment, I can only assume their sex life wasn't much fun."

"Jesus, TJ," Ethan said quietly. He laid a hand over both of hers, which were locked together on the table. "You're not saying he could be our rapist, are you?"

Her eyes shifted away, and Lucy—seeing how torn she was—interrupted.

"Have you forgotten that Drew was Tara Jean's brother, Ethan? Give her a break." TJ seemed poised to speak, but Lucy rushed on. "Besides, before we can speculate on anything like that, we need to know about the condition or staging of the woman's body." She turned back to TJ, giving her the out. "Did you hear anything about that? Did this woman have anything in common with Renee Josephs?"

TJ winced. "I couldn't tell. From what Pike said on the phone, and from what he asked us, my guess is she's been dead awhile. And buried. He kept harping on the condition of Drew's hands—whether Alicia noticed if he came home dirty, that kind of thing. Plus, whoever she was, she wasn't easily identifiable. Or at least none of the deputies on scene recognized her. I could tell that much just from the questions." She visibly braced herself. "In answer to your question, Ethan: no, I don't suspect Drew in all the ViCAP cases. Not because I don't think he was perfectly capable of forcing a woman, but because he had fund-raisers or other political events that give him an ironclad alibi for a couple of them. Of course, if we're looking at more than one rapist, the situation changes. He certainly won't have an alibi for every one of the nights—or afternoons—in question."

"You checked your own brother's alibi?" Ethan's puzzled question prevented Lucy from asking her own. TJ had admitted checking Billy Pike's whereabouts during some of the cases; Lucy hadn't realized she'd also scrutinized her brother's activities.

"That a problem?" TJ asked in prickly tone.

"Not at all," said Ethan, ignoring her defensiveness. "I knew you were thorough when I hired you." Lucy saw TJ's muscles relax and could have leaned across the table to kiss Ethan for so handily putting her at ease. Instead, she toyed with her napkin and looked at anything but him.

"What the hell is going on in this county?" Ethan asked. "One college student, upstanding, pretty, clean-living as far as we can tell, is murdered in a ritualistic fashion that would indicate a serial killer at work. An up-and-coming politician who comes from one of the town's top families is shot to death with a long-range rifle. Nothing ritualistic about that that we know of, but both he and Renee are left out in the open, where anyone can find them. Another victim, a woman not recognized by the locals, is also killed—we don't know yet how—but this one is buried. Bears no relationship in MO or pattern to the other killings."

"People are going to lose their minds when it becomes public," TJ said gloomily. "The only positive thing about the mystery woman and Drew being the sheriff's cases is that leaks may be kept to a minimum."

"You saying our department has a leak problem?"

"I'm saying our department has Marge."

Ethan sighed. "Point taken."

"Look," Lucy said, determined to get them back on track, "if we assume for the moment that the ViCAP pattern cases are related, then TJ's research shows they can't be laid at

Drew's door. So where does this mystery woman fit in? Can we put her aside until we get more details?"

"I think we'll have to," TJ agreed. "And given that it's the sheriff's case, who knows when that will be? But I had an idea on the way over here: remember how you said the rapist got off on watching the women he'd raped recover? And that Renee was meant to scare the town? Maybe he figures Drew's important and therefore a more terrifying object lesson."

Lucy started to speak, but under the table Ethan tapped her foot gently with his own and then stood.

"Rita, Tom," he said to the couple approaching the table. "What can I do for you?"

"You can get out there and find out who's killing the citizens of our town!" The woman, Rita, glared at Lucy with poison in her eyes, and then turned her wrath on TJ. "And you, Tara Jean. Drew was your own brother, and here you sit doing absolutely nothing!"

"Rita," the man tried to pull her away.

"Mrs. Calloway," TJ said, rising. "Believe me, if there were anything I could do at the moment, I would be doing it. As you say, Drew was my brother. But right now, his case is in Sheriff Pike's hands."

"And that means you have to sit down with the likes of her? Why, everyone knows she threatened Drew. She probably killed him."

"Rita!" Again, the man—her husband?—tugged on her arm.

Lucy saw Ethan give TJ a subtle shake of the head, telling her to leave the subject alone. "Rita," he said kindly, "I know you're afraid. I understand that. As TJ said, Drew's murder is the sheriff's case. Renee Josephs's murder is mine, and I am doing the very best that I can to find out anything about it. You never met the girl, did you?"

"N—no." Rita seemed taken aback to have the questioning

turned on her. Lucy dabbed her lips with a napkin to hide her grin at Ethan's tactic.

"And you haven't heard anything? Any gossip, any news about strangers in town?"

"I'm not a gossip!"

"I certainly never meant to imply that you were. But the citizens of this town are the police force's best source of information."

"Well, I don't know anything. Except that all this started when she got here." That poisonous glare returned to Lucy.

"I understand," Ethan said. "And Miss Caldwell is cooperating fully with our investigation."

Rita's lips twisted into a grimace. "I'm sure." She took her husband's arm. "Come on, Tom, let's go somewhere else."

"Who was she?" Lucy asked as soon as the couple was out of earshot. "I don't even remember anyone named Rita."

"You wouldn't. She's Marge Bollingham's second cousin. She didn't even move here until you'd left town."

"Lovely. I can't wait to get out of this town."

"I'd tell you to go right now, but I know you wouldn't listen," Ethan said.

"Damn straight."

Ethan's phone rang at almost the same moment Lucy heard the storm sirens go off outside.

"Yeah," he said. "I'm on my way. TJ, too." He dropped money on the table to pay their bill. "Duty calls. It's all hands on deck until the storm slacks off a bit. I'll drop you off at home and come by as soon as I can get away."

# CHAPTER TWELVE

We breathed alcohol and smoke and innuendo from
the day we were born. But Momma didn't mean for
us to suffer, and she never abused us either physically
or verbally.

FROM *A BAD DAY TO DIE*

BY LUCY SADLER CALDWELL [DRAFT]

LUCY HAD BEEN working for three hours when the lights
in her house began to flicker. Within minutes, they died
completely. Damn. She had maybe an hour of battery life
on her computer, but with the Internet connection down,
she couldn't access the server to upload her information,
and she hadn't thought about buying storm lanterns or
flashlights when she moved back to the Hollow.

Hooking up a spare drive to her computer since her
wireless backup relied on electricity, she copied over all the
information she'd entered. How long would it take them
to get the power back on? She prowled the house, anxious.
With the plywood over the front window, she couldn't see
out, and even the gray half-light of the stormy sky couldn't
make its way into the living room.

Maybe she should have gone to the library after all. It
was closer to town and doubtless on a generator if not on a
different part of the electrical grid altogether. Here, she felt
vulnerable, not a sensation she enjoyed.

Her disposable cell phone buzzed from inside her bag,
indicating a text message. She dug it out and flipped it open.
ARE YOU ALONE IN THE DARK?
Shit. Lucy's lizard brain screamed for flight—notsafenot-
safenotsafe—but for all she knew, that's exactly what he,
whoever he was, wanted. She dropped the phone back into

her purse and pulled out the revolver she carried in a specially constructed side compartment. Her eyes were adjusting slowly to seeing with only the faint illumination seeping in from windows in other parts of the house, so she dragged a chair into the corner and set up a guard station where her back was protected.

She wanted desperately to call Ethan, even if only to hear his voice. But he'd promised to come over as soon as he could, and she knew he'd stick to his word. She was safe in her corner. She could wait this guy out. And if he showed up, she could put a bullet through him without any hesitation at all.

Still, she wished Ethan were there.

Rain clattered on the roof and spattered against the windows, punctuated by the occasional rumble and crack of thunder. Her watch ticked off the seconds. Hundreds, thousands of seconds passed before she heard the low thrum of a Hemi engine beneath the myriad sounds of the storm. Closer and closer it came, dying at last directly in front of her house.

Her phone rang again. Without taking her eyes off the door, she flipped open the cover.

"Your house is dark," Ethan said, "which means your security cameras probably aren't working. Since I have no desire to face the business end of your shotgun, I figured I'd call before knocking on the door."

The shakiness of her own laugh surprised her. "Probably a good decision. I'll let you in."

"I'll drive around to the kitchen door. I'm soaked, and I don't want to drip on your carpet."

The engine outside came to life again, and she heard him pull around as she eased out of her chair. The tension had stiffened every joint and muscle in her body. *Oh, Momma, telling your story is making me old.*

"I thought you couldn't get away from the station," she called out as Ethan dashed up to the door, two battery-operated storm lanterns in hand. Even as she spoke, she realized how ungracious she sounded. But Ethan just grinned at her, his heavy beard shadow and dripping black hair giving the expression a faintly piratical cast. She could almost imagine a sword in place of the pistol hanging from the duty belt that encircled his lean hips.

"You have a real problem with saying thank you, you know? We're going to have to work on that."

A blush crept over her face. "Thanks for bringing lights."

"I'd have been here sooner if it had occurred to me you wouldn't have them. Everything's back on in town, but it can take them a while to restore power to the outlying areas like this."

"Some things never change." She set the lanterns down and turned to him. "Something happened earlier," she said.

"What do you mean something happened?" Immediately, his hands were on her arms, his eyes sweeping over her, looking for damage.

"I'm not hurt. Really. It was just another threat." Lucy showed him the text message.

"Dammit, Lucy, we had a deal! Why didn't you call me right away?" He shoved his chair away from her and stalked out of the kitchen. She caught up with him pacing in the dark living room.

"Ethan—"

"Don't. Look, I know you're not used to asking for help. I get that. I do. But aside from your mother's murder, we have Renee's, Drew's, and the other woman they found out in the woods. We also have a slew of other missing women, some or all of whom may be dead.

"If even a few of those cases are related, we have a monster on our hands, and he's obviously fixated on you. Even if you don't give a damn about your own safety, consider cooperating for the sake of the other women he may go on to later.

Or consider it for Tim's sake. If this guy kills you, who's left to take care of him?"

Lucy dropped to the sofa. "That's low. Using my brother to manipulate me."

"I know it is." Ethan took off his duty belt and laid it on the coffee table, then sat beside her. She could feel the heat of his body reaching out, drawing her in despite the fact that not even the coarse black hairs on his arms touched her skin. "But here's the thing: your only goal is to find your mother's killer. I want that, too. But I have other, equally important priorities, and one of them is being certain nothing happens to you. If that means reminding you that Tim relies on you, so be it."

"Don't lecture me about Tim. There hasn't been a day in his life I haven't put him first. Not since the minute my mother brought him home from the hospital." Lucy rubbed her temples. "He was precious. Perfect. She'd even given up drinking—at least mostly—during her pregnancy. For a couple of years, right before and right after he was born, things were better than I ever remember."

"And then?"

"She got lost again. She turned Timmy over to me and gave up."

"Not entirely. You said she had a plan to get all of you a new start."

It was as good an opening as any, and the duty belt had given Lucy an idea.

"Do you trust me?" she asked.

⌒

ETHAN WATCHED HER carefully. Now they were getting to it. Everything inside him told him she'd finally begun to take down the wall he'd been trying to scale since the day they'd met. "Haven't we gotten beyond that? Of course I trust you."

She let her gaze slide deliberately to the cuffs clipped to the belt and linger there. Her meaning was clear, but her breathing was shallow and a bit ragged.

If she didn't relax, she might break, so he went for a little humor. "I wouldn't have figured you for the type."

A blush burned into her cheeks. "I'm not talking about sex."

"Naturally." He winked at her to take the sting from the word. "But you do want me to let you hook me up." It wasn't a question, but she nodded nonetheless. "Why?"

"Because I have a story to tell you, and I don't want you to storm out in the middle. You need to hear all of it. All the way through to the end."

"And my word's not good enough? Now who has trust issues?"

"I don't think it's fair to ask you to give your word blindly." She couldn't look him in the eye, and she was practically hyperventilating. Whatever this was, she needed to deal with it.

"Okay, then." He unclipped the cuffs. "What were you planning to shackle me to?"

"I hadn't gotten that far." Lucy looked around, examining the dimly lit outlines of the furniture. The sofa had thickly upholstered arms, as did the armchairs.

"Maybe we should go with the tried and true," Ethan suggested. "Surely there's a way to hook me up to your bed? If not, we can go to my place—my bed has a plain steel frame that would do nicely."

"Mine will work." Slowly, and with obvious reluctance, she rose from the couch.

Ethan followed her up the stairs, cuffs in hand. "You look as if you're going to the gallows," he said as she paused in the doorway to her bedroom. "We don't have to do this."

"Yes, we do." She gestured toward the bed.

Ethan took his time. Whatever Lucy felt compelled to tell him, he suspected he wanted to hear it almost as little as she wanted to say it. He settled on the edge of the bed, then leaned down and pulled off his boots. Lucy, meanwhile, sat cross-legged at the foot of the bed, watching him with wide, shadowed eyes.

When he had laid his boots next to each other beneath her nightstand, he patted the coverlet next to him. She shook her head.

"Uh-uh, honey," he said. "We can do part of this your way, but not all. You did say you weren't afraid of me, remember?"

He saw the memory flare even in the dusk-dark room and allowed himself a frisson of satisfaction. The sensation grew when she scooted up next to him. He slid a hand behind her neck and drew her closer still, ignoring her faint resistance. Her palms rested against his chest, but she did not push him away. He held her gaze with his own as he lowered his head.

At the last second, when he could taste her breath, she pulled back. Not far, but just enough for him to see the conflict twisting her features.

"We should wait."

"I won't listen nearly as well if we do," he teased. Christ, but the woman drove him crazy. She was practically vibrating with tension. A physical release would be good for both of them and, though a simple kiss wouldn't do the trick for him by a long shot, it was a good start.

"Once you hear what I have to say, you may not be so eager."

"If you studied regular men as closely as you do criminals, you'd realize how truly unlikely that was. I've wanted you since the moment you stalked into my office, accused me of being one of Dobbs's lackeys, and announced your plan to do my job for me."

"That's not what I said!"

"No?"

Her full lips twisted into a rueful grin. "Okay, I can see

how it might have sounded. In which case, you must have very peculiar taste in women."

"I guess I must." But the moment was gone, so he snapped one of the cuffs to a rail in the headboard and the other to his left wrist, propped himself up against the pillows, and readied himself for whatever Lucy might have to tell him.

# CHAPTER THIRTEEN

My memories of that day are painted in shades of red from a deep, almost black burgundy to a bright and reflective vermilion. And no matter the shade, no matter the hue, the tints all taste of copper.



"I'VE NEVER TOLD this story," Lucy began, crossing her legs Indian-style on the bed and carefully avoiding Ethan's all-too-penetrating gaze. "I hoped I'd never have to. But there are people who know it. TJ. Drew Dobbs. Billy Pike. Maybe more. And sooner or later, if you're right about this coming to a trial, I may have to tell it to your lawyer friend, because it absolutely gives me motive in Drew's murder." She was babbling, she knew, but it was so hard to admit her own stupidity, her cowardice, her guilt, especially to a man who probably had no experience with such weaknesses.

"When I was fifteen, I had a terrible crush on a boy two years older than me. Pete O'Connell. He was a quiet kid, kind of a nerd. I thought I hid my feelings pretty well, so I was shocked when I opened my locker one morning before school and found a note from him. I couldn't help wondering whether anyone had seen him pushing it through the slats and thinking about how my status might change if they had. Pretty pathetic, really, considering Pete wasn't much further up on the food chain, socially speaking, than I was."

"When you're in the gutter, even the curb looks miles high," Ethan said, his rough voice drawing her attention. He'd clenched one hand around the iron rail to which it was shackled, while the other twisted in her sheets. His muscles bunched and his face had shuttered. He obviously knew the story wouldn't end well.

"That's pretty much the sum of it. Pete's note asked me to meet him after school in room two fifty-two. Everyone knew about that room. It had a broken lock, so kids met there when the teachers had locked up all the other rooms. One always had to do guard duty while others were using the space. When I arrived that afternoon, Drew Dobbs was standing in front of the door. I should have known right then something was wrong. Even if the note hadn't tipped me off, I should have realized Pete didn't have the kind of status required to make Drew stand guard for him.

"But I was stupid. I didn't pay attention to any of that."

"For God's sake, Lucy, you were a fifteen-year-old girl who thought she was going to meet the boy of her dreams. Cut yourself a little slack."

"I can't. Those kids made my life miserable. I should have realized immediately things couldn't change that quickly. But I didn't. I went on into the room. But Pete wasn't there. Instead, it was a friend of Drew's. Another senior." Lucy could hear her own voice as if from far away. Aside from a faintly hollow echo, it held no inflection, and she found herself obscurely proud of the fact.

"Senior year was American lit at Dobbs Hollow High School, and they'd been reading *The Scarlet Letter*. I don't know which of them came up with it, but between them, Drew and Billy conceived the idea that I needed to be marked."

"Pike?" The bed rocked as Ethan lunged forward and was jerked back by the handcuffs. "Goddammit, Lucy, let me loose. I'm going to kill him."

"No, you're not."

"He hurt you!"

Yanked out of her reverie to the present, Lucy suddenly considered where Ethan's mind might have gone. "No," she said, laying a hand on his knee. "No, not the way you're thinking, and not as badly as you imagine. I swear." He stared at her, and she met his gaze steadily until the fury began to fade from his eyes.

"Okay, I admit, you were probably right to lock me up. But now I need you to take the cuffs off. I won't run out on you, but I can't listen to the rest this way."

Lucy retrieved the key from the bedside table and twisted it in the lock, releasing Ethan's wrist. Expecting he would want to rise, she started to back away, but he grabbed her before she was out of reach and hauled her close. He arranged her against him as if she had no will of her own. And perhaps she didn't, because she let him pull her down, tangle his long legs with hers, and tuck her head into the hollow of his shoulder. His arms came tight around her. The sensation might have been smothering, probably should have been, but it wasn't. Rather, she felt secure, surrounded by sinew and muscle, heat and skin and breath, as if each of his exhalations infused her with his strength.

Ethan rubbed his stubbled chin on the top of her head. "Ready when you are, sugar."

She reorganized her scattered thoughts and picked up the story where she'd left off. "Once I was in the room, they pushed me to the floor. Drew sat on my legs and Billy shoved gym socks in my mouth and slapped on a piece duct tape, pulled out a switchblade, and explained the whole Scarlet Letter thing. He always did like to hear himself talk."

Lucy felt Ethan's breathing go ragged and his muscles clench, but she couldn't bring herself to look him in the eye. Instead, she focused on a bit of gray lint caught in the seam of his shirt as she continued.

"They'd decided to go with a W rather than an A. I guess "adulterer" was too hard a word for them. Anyway, Billy was sitting on my stomach, so my arms were trapped, but when he'd only managed to make two cuts, the door rattled. Both of them lost their concentration for a sec and Drew jumped up to grab the handle and hold it shut. I got the best leverage I could, dumped Billy on his ass, then kicked him in the nuts and took off. Drew was so shocked, he didn't even really try to stop me.

"I was bleeding pretty badly, though, and Billy had cut right through my shirt. I couldn't go home in that condition. I had gym clothes in my locker, so I headed there, figuring they wouldn't be apt to come after me in the halls. I'd gone into the girls' bathroom to change and mop up when I ran into Tara Jean. She waited for me, made conversation, and then went all the way home with me."

"She knew?"

"I didn't realize that until I came back. I just assumed she thought I wouldn't be safe walking alone, whereas no one would touch her, not with the wrath of the Dobbs family likely to descend on them. So she walked me home, then called their maid to come get her. I should have known she'd grow up to be a cop; 'protect and serve' is evidently in her blood."

"What happened after that?"

"I couldn't hide the fact that I'd been injured from my mother, so I told her I'd gotten in a fight. It was close enough to the truth."

"Why didn't you tell anyone what had really happened?"

"What would have been the point? Billy's father was the chief of police. Drew's family was the second richest in Dobbs Hollow next to the Farmers. Making a fuss would have hurt us, not them.

"But even without details, my mother knew the fight had to do with her, and that's when she told me we could leave town, start over. The next day, she was murdered." Possibly—probably—because she'd tried to extort money from the wrong man. Money she wanted quickly because her daughter had gotten into trouble.

"Jesus. But you said you knew where Drew and Billy were that afternoon, so they couldn't have done it themselves."

"Yes. It seemed as if everywhere I turned the next day, one or the other was passing me in the hall, chatting outside my classroom, whatever. Maybe it had always been that way and I'd never noticed, but I don't think so. I think it was terrorism, plain and simple. But either way, they weren't playing hooky.

"My mother had given me cab fare to get to the babysitter's from school. Usually, I'd walk, but she knew I wasn't feeling well. She might even have known I was afraid, though she didn't say so."

Ethan's hand stroked her hair, his touch soothing. "What about Al Pike or Mayor Dobbs? Maybe their kids told them what happened and one of them decided to keep your mother quiet."

"Dobbs should have been in Austin. The legislature was in session, and he usually stayed away as much as possible while that was going on. It's possible he came home for the day, though. I haven't been able to find out. Al Pike . . . I'd love to find a way to hang my mother's murder on him, especially after hearing they had an affair, but I doubt he did it. He was in the station all day, according to everything I've managed to get my hands on. It's not much, just what the local papers said at the time."

"I'll look at the logs."

"I'd appreciate that."

"I can't help wondering whether Drew and Pike are worried about you coming forward with this now. What with all the scandals in politics lately, your arrival at the very moment Drew was getting ready to move his career forward must have horrified him. No wonder he wanted to discredit you."

"I have no evidence. I never did. I mean, when it first happened I could show that someone attacked me, but now I can't even really prove that." Lucy shrugged.

"And you've never mentioned this to anyone?"

"No. I knew where my mother kept her emergency cash. When I found her that afternoon . . ." Her throat dried up, and she swallowed several times. Ethan's fingers slid to the back of her neck and made small, soothing circles.

"When I saw her, all I could think about was getting out before whoever had done it came back to finish the job. I took the five hundred dollars from the box inside the chimney, grabbed Timmy, and headed back to the babysitter's. I told her my mother wasn't home and asked her to drive us to town so we could wait for her at the library. Once she'd driven off, I headed for the bus station and got tickets on that night's bus to Houston. After two nights there, we took another bus, this time to Dallas."

"Where you met Caldwell." Ethan's fingers had moved from her neck to her spine, slowly slipping up and down, pressing here and there to release the knots of tension.

"Todd knew I'd been hurt because by then infection had taken hold. I had been afraid to go to a hospital, and Timmy and I weren't exactly living clean. He assumed I'd been attacked on the streets, though, and I let him believe it. It was almost three years before I trusted him enough to tell him the truth about my mother.

"He and Karen had been nothing but good to us. It must have hurt them to know I'd kept such a big secret, but he never blamed me for it. He asked whether I wanted him to investigate the murder, and I said no."

"You were afraid whoever did it would find it curious that a Dallas cop would ask about a small-town prostitute's murder and come looking for you?"

"Me? No, by then I could take care of myself. But Timmy was just a toddler, and Karen was already sick. We needed Todd to be safe much more than my mother needed justice."

"And you decided to pursue this now because you figure Tim's finally old enough to take care of himself."

His surety astounded her. She doubted even Tim realized she'd been waiting until he could survive without her before venturing back to Dobbs Hollow.

"But sugar, the W, the fact that they wanted to cut you that particular way . . . why didn't you say anything sooner? That damned word is all over every incident that's happened since you got here."

"I know." She tried to pull away, but he wouldn't let her. There was no anger in his hold, but his arms flexed ever so slightly to keep her in place.

"I get that you didn't trust me at first. Really, I do. Now I even understand why. But this is important."

Lucy sighed. "The thing is, Drew was at a fundraiser the night Renee was killed. And when you gave TJ the ViCAP list, she checked Billy's alibis and told me he's solid for some of them, so I had to put it aside, to admit that what they did to me might make me jump to conclusions about their guilt in other instances."

"So that's why she happened to know about her brother's alibis."

"Yes."

Ethan set her slightly away from him and tipped his head down to stare directly into her eyes.

"What if we take Renee out of the equation? Have you considered that? Considered that Pike might be behind everything that's happened since you got here?"

"I did. But when you told me about the pattern, about the fact that the rapist always calls the women whores, it seemed so much more likely that it was all one person . . . and Billy has alibis."

Ethan shook his head. "Not good enough. As a high school senior, he was a criminal. You told me so yourself. People don't change that much."

"At fifteen, I was a coward, so I guess you're right."

"What are you talking about?"

"You were right. I should have spoken up. I should have confronted them. But I didn't. I went home to my alcoholic mother who I knew was incapable of doing anything rational, and I told her just enough about what had happened to get her killed."

"Christ, Lucy, you can't possibly blame yourself for that."

"Why not? It was the next day, Ethan. Not even twenty-four hours later. You tell me that's a coincidence." She could feel tears pressing against the back of her eyes, and she blinked furiously.

"Lucy, sweetheart, you don't know what it is. Your mom, she lived on the fringe and that's not a safe place. You know that."

"I can't help it, Ethan. Logic doesn't help the way I feel."

He pulled her close again and tucked her against him. His heart beating beneath her ear was comforting, and she felt the tears slowly recede.

"So I guess this is more of that emotional stuff you're not so good at processing," he said at last.

"'Fraid so."

"But surely the men you've dated have asked about the scars. What did you tell them?"

"How do you know I have scars at all? Maybe I had plastic surgery. Got rid of them."

"Not a chance."

Like his understanding of her reasons for waiting to investigate her mother's murder, his recognition that she would never remove the scars touched her deeply. Todd had offered to pay for surgery, and her first lover, Sean, had even found her a doctor, so certain had he been that she'd go along with his plan for her to have the scars removed. But they were part of her. They marked her for who and what she was, a survivor and a crusader, and kept her on track. At times, she even found herself fingering the welts as if for luck when she needed direction.

"So what did you tell them?"

"That I'd been injured in an accident."

Ethan's fingers wrapped into her hair and tugged, so she

tilted her head back to look him in the face. "That's it? An accident? For crying out loud, Lucy. I've seen knife scars. I have a couple myself. They're not exactly inconspicuous. None of these bozos asked for more details?"

"It's not like there have been all that many. One accepted the explanation because he much preferred talking about himself to talking about me. The other didn't want details because he was a trifle squeamish."

Ethan chuckled, the sound a deep rumble beneath her ear.

"Sweetheart, you've been dating the wrong men." The words whispered across her skin as he lifted her and twisted slightly so they lay face to face on the bed. She started to reply, to protest, to say anything at all, and he took immediate advantage, covering her lips with his own. His tongue tangled with hers in a muscled velvet dance and her whole body caught fire.

Reason cried a faint protest in the back of her mind, but passion silenced it. He knew the truth now, had seen her faults and failings, and still wanted her. Nothing was as seductive as that. His hand slid up and down her side, molding her curves, setting her nerves to tingling and chasing all thought from her head.

He sat up suddenly and reached for the buttons of his shirt. Lucy sat, frozen, unable to take her eyes from the movement of his fingers. He yanked the material from his jeans and pulled it off entirely, exposing a smooth, muscled chest liberally sprinkled with coarse black hairs. But it was his left shoulder that drew her attention, and involuntarily she reached out to touch it.

"Switchblade," he said when her fingers ran over the knot of scar tissue. "Addict didn't feel like turning over his stash. He and a couple of his pals were real vehement about it. I bet yours is a lot prettier."

He slid long, calloused fingers beneath her T-shirt and fluttered them across the skin of her stomach, her sides, her back, assiduously avoiding her breasts, which ached for his touch.

But he didn't pull the tee off immediately. Instead, he bunched the cloth in one hand and pulled her forward to kiss her again. This time, he began with her lips but moved on, brushing his lips across the tip of her nose, across each cheek, across her chin, across her neck. He tasted her there, in the hollow of her clavicle, where sweat had begun to gather, and she shivered.

With a quick yank, he had the tee over her head and off. In the soft, stormy afternoon light, he examined her, the touch of his gaze a tangible thing, creating goose bumps on her skin. With two fingers he traced the lines of her scar to the point at which they intersected, then leaned forward and pressed his mouth against the spot.

"V is for victory," he said.

"No."

"Oh, yeah. Sugar, you won that day. You kicked ass, along with other parts of Billy's anatomy, and don't you forget it. You are amazing."

She felt a blush creeping up her face and leaned forward to kiss him rather than responding verbally. Their lips met and his hands slid over her, still avoiding her breasts. She bit his lip, and he laughed. When at last his thumbs slid across her pebbled nipples, shocks ran straight through her body, and she almost sobbed aloud. She reached for the button on his jeans, and within moments they were both naked on the bed, all humor abandoned, exploring with eyes, hands, mouths.

And still, he took his time, even when she would have rushed. His erection jutted up, rock hard, and she traced it with the tips of her fingers, loving the feel of silky skin stretched over steel. So much of his body was like that, taut muscle lying under satin, lightly dusted here and there with crisp, prickling hair.

His own hands had covered every inch of her, and now his long fingers darted into the curls at the apex of her thighs. This time she did cry out, overtaken by sensation. Damp heat flooded her, but it brought no shame, none of the awkwardness she usually experienced at the evidence of her own desire. She arched closer to him, simultaneously tightening her grip until he, too, let out a guttural moan.

He pulled away just long enough to dig his wallet from his jeans pocket and extract a packet from inside it. In seconds, he had the condom out and on, and he was inside her, filling her senses as he filled her body. His scent, his taste, set her heart pounding. And yet . . .

And yet, there was the part of her that always remained separate, that dreaded the coming minutes, the race to the finish, the inability to reach the same peak everyone else seemed to find so effortlessly. Her body met his rhythm, and she tried to shut away the worries, but—as always— the more she tried to suppress them, the more present they became.

And the worst of it was that Ethan noticed. He slowed, then rolled until she was atop him. She tried to take charge of their movements, but he held her still, big hands tightening on her hips.

"What's wrong?"

"Nothing." But she couldn't meet his eyes. "I . . . this isn't my favorite position."

"That's a start." He reached up and pushed her hair away from her face, then ran a thumb across her lips. She felt her lower body clench involuntarily. "What do you like?"

"I don't know. I mean . . . I just feel . . . exposed this way."

"Ah." He studied her, and she wondered whether he was reconsidering getting involved with a woman so clearly damaged. When he slowly pulled out of her body, she wanted to clutch at him, but she didn't.

"Flip over, sugar," he said, his hands settling her where he wanted her. He knelt between her legs and then pulled her back so she rested on her knees and forearms. Talk about feeling exposed! Her face burned and she was fiercely glad he couldn't see it. But then he nudged his way inside her and all embarrassment fled. This was what she had been missing. Somehow, here in front of him she had control that she didn't have above or below. His hands were on her hips again, but she didn't need or want his direction. She set the pace, fast and hard, and he let her, remaining virtually still.

Faster and faster she thrust against his body. Close, release was so close. And then his arm snaked around her waist and his hand dipped down, and his finger found her core and her whole body convulsed and she lost the rhythm, but it didn't matter because he'd taken over and they were falling together.

∿

ETHAN THOUGHT HE might be about to have a stroke. He could barely breathe, and sweat dripped down the back of his neck. Who knew sex could be like that? Not that he didn't enjoy sex, because he did. Hell, even bad sex was good sex, when it came right down to it, but what had just happened went way beyond anything he'd experienced before. He slid out of the bed to dispose of the condom and clean up. When he came back with a warm washcloth for Lucy, he found her curled up on her side, her back facing him, fast asleep.

Each knob of her spine was clearly articulated. The eroticism of the pose brought parts of his exhausted body to abrupt attention, but the vulnerability took his breath away. It spoke of complete trust, which he had done nothing to deserve. He had nothing to offer her.

Ethan couldn't leave Dobbs Hollow, and Lucy couldn't stay.

He crept toward the bed, determined to let her sleep, but his plan was thwarted by a sudden thump that faintly shook the walls. He scrambled for the bedside table, cursing when he remembered leaving his gun downstairs. Lucy, who'd shot straight up in bed, echoed his sentiments, then relaxed.

"It's the compressor. For the air conditioner. The electricity must have come back on."

"Christ," Ethan said, lowering himself to the edge of the bed, "that's a hell of a way to get your adrenaline flowing."

"No kidding."

He stood and stepped into his boxers and jeans. "I'm going down to get my gear. Then we need to talk." And he dreaded it. She'd told him of her bravery; now he would have to admit his own cowardice.

"I guess I should get dressed, then."

Lights blazed downstairs. Out of habit, he checked the cell in its belt holster to be certain he hadn't missed anything, but no one had called. Thank God. He was pretty sure he'd reached his limit. His head pounded and his knee ached in a psychosomatic reaction that nonetheless had him desperate for a painkiller.

He decided to grab a glass of water before heading back to Lucy, so he slung the duty belt around his jeans and walked into the kitchen. He'd just filled the glass when a tremendous crash shook the house. Wood splintered and he heard Lucy shout even as he stumbled from the kitchen.

Into complete chaos.

An old, beater pickup truck had crashed through the boarded-over front window of the house. It rocked there, tilted over on one side for interminable seconds, then slammed down onto all four tires. Dust rose in a massive cloud, and Ethan choked. Squinting against the particles hanging in the air, he could see a man slumped over the steering wheel, unconscious or dead. Or faking it.

"Ethan? Are you okay?" He looked up to see Lucy coming down the stairs. Her eyes were fixed on him, and her feet were bare.

"Stay there. I'm fine. You?"

"Fine. What happened?"

A quick, visual once-over told him she was uninjured and that she'd taken his advice to stay upstairs.

"Hell if I know." He picked his way toward the truck cautiously, gun drawn. When he reached the driver's side window, he put the gun away. Whatever else the guy might be, he wasn't faking his injuries. Blood had crusted on the side of his face; he'd been dead before the crash. A branch had been wedged beneath the driver's seat, forcing the gas pedal to the floor. It had obviously come loose in the crash. Ethan reached through the window, slid the truck into park, touching the gearshift as little as possible, and switched off the ignition.

Silence filled the room. Far away, Ethan heard the sound of a small engine receding. Motorcycle or ATV, he thought, the getaway vehicle for whoever had set this up. A creak jerked his attention to the stairs, but it was just Lucy venturing down once again.

He twisted his head to get a better view of the driver, and recognized him as Richie Mack. And wasn't that the topper to the evening. Richie, who was on his list of people to talk to about Eric Allenby and snakes and other creepy things, and who was a known associate and long-time friend of Jed Martin, originator of the chores list found near Renee's body. And a tweaker. A man with loose lips who wouldn't be missed, except as a source of cash to his meth dealer.

"Do you think he was drunk," Lucy asked, making her way toward him through the wreckage, "or high?"

"No. He was dead."

"You mean . . . before?"

"That's what I mean."

"I don't understand what's going on here." She was shaking, and Ethan stepped around the rubble, watching where he put his bare feet, to pull her into an embrace.

"We'll figure it out. We just have to take it one step at a time." He gestured at the truck. "Do you recognize him?"

Lucy pulled out of his arms and squinted through the passenger side window. "No. He looks vaguely familiar, like I might have seen him around when I was a kid, but I can't think of his name."

"Richie Mack. Does that ring a bell?"

"Oh, yeah. He was on the football team. He's lost a lot of weight since then."

"Meth."

"That'll do it."

"Yeah. Can you think of anything he might personally have against you? He wasn't connected in any way to what happened to you in high school?"

"No. That was just Drew and Billy. Billy was friends with Richie, but not the same way he and Drew were. The thing I remember most about Richie was that he and three of his football buddies—Chuck Hemming, Jed Martin, Eric Allenby—tried to cause trouble for my mother one night. It was a few weeks before she died. I don't know what was said, but I peeked out the window and saw them pull up in Jed's car. Saw my mother shoo them away, too."

Yet another connection to both Eric and Jed, who'd raised Ethan's curiosity already. He had a pretty good idea how that particular conversation had progressed. But could anyone still hold a grudge so long after the fact? No longer teenaged boys with bruised egos, these were grown men.

Of course, that hadn't been true at the time of Cecile's murder.

Lucy looked around at the destruction of what had once been her home.

"It's like the past lives on right here in this house. All I have to do is set foot here, and the ghosts all come back." She gestured at the enormous hole where the truck had come through the wall. "But I guess I don't have to worry about that anymore."

Ethan heard the shakiness behind the attempt at humor and drew her attention away from the destruction, back to the case. She would feel safe there, on professional footing. They were alike that way.

"Do you remember seeing them at school the day your mother died?"

"I thought about it then, and I can't swear to any of them except Chuck. He was getting an award. But he and Richie were always joined at the hip. Eric is a couple years younger, so he couldn't always get away when they did, and I never had that much contact with Jed, so it's hard for me to remember. But they were friends. Why would one of them do . . . this . . . to him?"

"Nothing makes sense to me. Just try to remember what you can from the day your mother died and whether you saw them while I call this in," Ethan directed.

"Of course." With a wan grin, she rubbed a hand across his chest. "I suppose I'd better get the rest of your clothes, too." Despite the situation, Ethan felt an echoing smile tug at his own lips.

"That would probably be a good idea."

She climbed the stairs and Ethan, forcing his eyes away from the seductive sway of her rear end and back to the task at hand, called the station. Still bootless, he made his way around the front of the cab and read off the truck's plate to Marge. "Tell Scott to find the RO. Mack doesn't have a license, so I doubt it's his. Who else is on tonight?"

"Ed and Dan are in one car, Aaron and Cal are in another. Keith went home. He'd been here forever. TJ and Scott are both in house."

"Send TJ over here, along with Aaron and Cal. And sorry as I am to have to say it, get Keith over here. You'll have to call Bobby O, too. I've got another body for him."

"Scott can access the DMV just as easily in route. Why don't I send him over there?"

Because his brother may be involved in this mess. "Because I need someone coordinating down there, and I trust Scott to get it right. This isn't a car accident. Richie Mack was dead before the truck started. He may have been killed in the truck, he may not have. Either way, we have a lot of work ahead of us, so you'd better put the coffee on." He clicked the phone closed and reflexively checked the time. Not even eight. It felt like midnight.

Lucy came down the stairs. She'd dressed in jeans and sneakers and tied her hair into a high ponytail that made her look about fifteen years old. The age she'd been when all this started. The age at which she was attacked by Billy Pike and Drew Dobbs. Looking at her, he was swept by dual waves of possessiveness and fury. She'd had years to overcome her past, but he hadn't. He and Billy Pike would have a reckoning.

She handed him his clothes, and he sat on the stairs to pull on his socks and boots. He was buttoning his shirt when he heard sirens approaching. He'd meant to tell Marge they weren't necessary, but he'd forgotten. Richie Mack wasn't going anywhere, and he preferred the town kept quiet. Sirens attracted attention, and he'd be getting calls about what had happened. Dobbs Hollow didn't need a newspaper; the grapevine served as the police blotter.

TJ arrived first, as Ethan had expected. He understood the protective instinct better now, having heard their history. The front window was a mangled mess, but the door was still functional, and she chose that entrance, rather than pulling around back as he had. Her blue eyes met his, and he was surprised by the fear he saw there.

"Have you been outside?" she asked.

"No. What's going on?" He strode toward the door.

"When I pulled in, the headlights caught the bed of the truck. There's something in it."

"Shit."

The sun had finally gone down, so although the rain had

almost stopped, the sky was black. He pulled his Maglite from his belt and shone it on the truck's bed. Watery red fluid dripped from the tailgate. Mindful not to step in any of the pooling liquid, he approached the side of the bed and looked down into it. And almost threw up.

The body—for there was no mistaking the fact that what now lay in the truck's bed had once been human—had been dismembered. But before that, it had been . . . skinned. Pieces lay piled around the bed of the truck. He could distinguish at least one arm, two legs and the head, all tissue exposed, occasionally cut down to the bone.

"Holy mother of God," Ethan murmured. He closed his eyes for a minute, then dragged himself back to work. "TJ, call Marge and tell her I want Bobby out here ASAP. This just got a whole lot uglier, and if there is any evidence at all left in that truck after the rain, I don't want to lose it. Do you have an evidence collection kit in your trunk?"

But he didn't hear her reply, because a crash sounded inside the house, and Lucy shrieked.

# CHAPTER FOURTEEN

People say everything looks worse at night. But morning can be equally cruel, pointing out ragged edges
misted over by the shadowy light of evening. And
while darkness may bring fear of the unknown, daylight can gleam from monsters' teeth, showing the truth
to be more frightening than anything the imagination
dreams up.



ETHAN BOLTED FOR the house. He scanned the interior,
his heart settling only when he spied Lucy at the back of
the living room. The table she'd been using as a desk lay
overturned at her feet, and she was scrabbling through the
objects on the floor. Even from the door, Ethan could hear
her breathing, harsh and irregular.

"Lucy?"

She didn't look up. "I can't find my cell phone. I don't have
their numbers anywhere else. I need my cell phone."

"Whose numbers, sugar?" He approached her slowly. She
was obviously terrified and he didn't want to make things
worse.

"The boys. I need their numbers. He's not answering."

He reached her side and leaned down to urge her to stand
and look at him. Her whole body shook and her face was
dead white. Shock. What the hell had happened in the few
seconds he'd been outside?

"Who's not answering, sweetheart?"

"Timmy."

"Why do you need to talk to Tim?"

Rather than replying directly, she reached into the pocket

of her jeans and pulled out her disposable cell. Clicking the message button, she turned it over so he could see the screen. A picture of her brother popped up, with the caption "Time to go home." In the shot, Tim held a basketball and faced another boy, Ethan didn't recognize the background, but assumed the shot had been taken in Dallas. The blur and pixilation suggested it had been taken with the camera's phone from several feet away.

"I can't reach him," Lucy said, her eyes full of tears.

"Let me make a call," he said, pulling her close with one arm while flipping open his own cell phone with the other hand. He hadn't put Artie Buck's number into his contacts, but it remained in his previous calls list.

"Yeah?" The man was short on formality, but Ethan didn't care.

"Artie, this is Ethan Donovan in Dobbs Hollow. I need to ask you a favor. It's for Lucy and Tim." He outlined the situation as quickly as he could and asked Artie to drive out to the Caldwell house and see what he could find out.

"I'm on my way," Buck said. "Lucy's okay, though?"

"She's right here. We'll be waiting for your call." He flipped the phone closed, laid it down on the table, and pulled Lucy tight against him.

"He'll be fine, sweetheart. Artie will take care of him."

"He's all I have, Ethan."

Even muffled against his shirt, Lucy's words stung. Taking her by the shoulders, he set her away from him so he could emphasize his words by fixing her eyes with his own.

"We're going to get him back. We are. But, Lucy, Tim isn't all you have. Not even close. If nothing else, I would have thought what just happened between us ranked me among those people you felt you could count on."

Lucy shifted, looked away from him, then looked back. Her eyes were damp, and her lips trembled, but her chin lifted, and even through his frustration he admired her strength.

"Don't go there. You know it was great. And I'm not discounting it. Not by a long shot. But it's not permanent. One day, you'll be gone."

"Really? That's how you see things? One day, you'll wake up and I will have disappeared?"

"You don't need me," she said, as if that explained everything.

"And you're so sure that's all that ties people together?" He could hear the frustration bleeding into his words, but he couldn't seem to stop it. Dammit, he did need her. He didn't want to, but there it was. And even if he hadn't, there was more to a relationship than that. "Is that what kept your foster parents together for so long?"

"No. Todd and Karen loved each other. What they had was special. But you're not telling me that after one night you suddenly love me, are you?"

Was he? Hell, yes. And not after one night. But his feelings weren't the issue. "Lucy—"

Sirens screamed as the other patrol cars pulled up as close as they could get to the house without destroying the scene, and Lucy fled up the stairs. He almost chased her, but what could he say? Love didn't solve problems, especially if it was one-sided. Lucy of all people should know that.

The squad car with Aaron Barrett and Cal Wilkes pulled up at the same time as Keith's Ford Explorer. They parked behind TJ, to keep the scene as clear as possible.

"Oh, shit," said Keith when he saw the contents of the truck bed. "What the hell is going on around here?"

Both Cal and Aaron looked to be trying to keep from vomiting. Ethan figured this was probably their first murder scene. If they could hold it together, they'd have a good start on anything else the job might throw at them.

"Richie Mack was in the front seat, but he was dead before the crash. You know anything about him that might connect him to a killing like this?"

"Was he . . . ?" Keith gestured to the body in the truck bed. "No. At least as far as I can see, he's all in one piece. He was even belted behind the wheel, though I suspect whoever did this wanted him upright, and wanted to be certain he didn't knock loose the branch holding the accelerator down. Everything else was for effect."

Lucy stepped outside and held Ethan's phone out toward him.

"It's Scott," she said.

Ethan took the phone from her, and she slipped back into the house, a ghost on her own property. "What have you found?" he asked, wishing he could follow her. Keith began snapping pictures of the truck and its gruesome contents.

"Registered owner of the truck is one Juan Ramirez. Long sheet, current address appears to be San Antonio. But I recognize this guy. I've seen him around town, I just can't think of where."

"What's the sheet for?"

"Mostly possession. One weapons charge, one sale of methamphetamines."

Meth. Richie Mack's poison of choice. Ethan wondered if they'd identified the human remains in the back of the truck. Were both Richie and his dealer on someone's hit list?

"Keep on it. Show his picture around. I want to know where he's been, and if he's still there. We have a dead body here that might be him, but no way to tell without waiting for DNA, if his is even on file. If he's alive, who did he lend his truck to?"

He hung up just as the medical examiner's van pulled up.

"You think I need to be busier or something?" O'Reilly joked as he climbed out. "'Cause I was doin' fine without you piling bodies on me. Where you expect me to put them is beyond me. I've never had so many slots filled in the morgue at one time."

"Believe me, Bobby, I wish I didn't have to call you on this one. I've never seen anything like it."

O'Reilly peered into the truck bed. "Well, hell." He

gestured to his assistant for the evening, a young Asian man whose name Ethan couldn't remember for the life of him. "Lay that one out and see if you can determine whether there are any parts missing before you bag him. I'm going inside to check out the other one."

They walked inside, and Ethan found himself pausing to look for Lucy before he followed O'Reilly to the truck. Apparently, she'd gone upstairs or into the kitchen.

"No immediately apparent cause of death," the ME said, drawing his attention. He gently manipulated Richie's head to look for signs of trauma. "If not for the other obvious inconsistencies, my first instinct would be accidental overdose. He's been headed that way for years."

"Yeah, well, I think we can rule that out."

"Not necessarily. Maybe he died, then someone came along and decided to use the body to made a point."

"And that point would be?"

"Not my department. I tell you when and how. Who and why is up to you. That's why they pay you the big bucks."

Ethan snorted.

"Not the fabulous salary, then." When Ethan cocked an eyebrow at him, O'Reilly continued. "As many people in this town gossip about why you took this job as question why it was offered."

"As I've said before, I needed a change of venue, a chance of pace. And until the past few days, I'd gotten it."

"Right about the time your girlfriend moved home. Maybe she's the one should consider a change of venue."

"Bobby . . ."

The older man held up his hands. "Look. I just moved here ten years back. I've got no dog in this fight. But someone just went to a great deal of trouble to destroy her house in a particularly nasty manner. Seems to me she'd be safer if she got the hell out of Dodge."

A creak from the stairs had both men turning. Lucy's voice

when she spoke was perfectly composed, but Ethan noticed how tightly she clutched the cell phone in her left hand. "I'm not going anywhere but the nearest motel."

"We'll talk about it."

"I. Am. Not. Leaving."

"Did I say you were?" Ethan's temper frayed. "For crying out loud, Lucy. Give me a little credit. Maybe, just maybe, I had a few ideas of places that might be safer than a cheap motel with flimsy, hollow-core doors and credit-card locks."

"Oh." She looked suitably chagrined, and Ethan felt his anger drain away, leaving only frustration behind. His head pounded, and he scrubbed a hand across his eyes.

"I can't deal with this right now. I'm going to be tied up here and at the morgue for hours."

"Lucy can come home with me," TJ offered.

Ethan wanted to jump on the suggestion, but forced himself to defer to Lucy. When she agreed, he managed to keep private his sigh of relief. TJ and Lucy went upstairs to pack a bag, and he went back to work.

⌒

Lucy checked out TJ's apartment with interest. She'd imagined a sedate décor, in keeping with her friend's basic blue uniform and unpolished nails, and the exterior of the place had reinforced her expectations. Once inside, though, she realized how wrong she'd been. The walls remained rental white, and the couch that dominated the living room was a deep, chocolate brown, but everywhere splashes of color brightened the space. A Mexican woven throw in reds, yellows, and greens lay over the back of the sofa, and a rag rug covered most of the tile in the tiny kitchen. Miniature pepper plants sat in terra-cotta pots on the coffee table and the dining table, and Art Deco posters hung on the walls.

"Make yourself at home," TJ said, dropping her bag on the couch. "Can I get you a drink?"

"A beer would be great, if you have one."

"Coming right up."

As TJ handed her the bottle, Lucy's phone rang. Her heart leapt when she saw Tim's name.

"I'm coming back," he said, without any greeting at all.

"No, don't. It's not . . ." She couldn't tell him it wasn't safe in Dobbs Hollow, he'd only run faster. "The house isn't livable at the moment. I'm crashing at TJ's. Did Artie find you?"

"Yeah. He told me what happened."

"You should stay with him. It's just for a few days, until we work things out here."

"And what about if it's more than a few days? What about if you don't figure out who's doing this?"

"Then we can renegotiate. But right now, I'd worry a lot less if you were with Artie."

"You're manipulating me."

The same accusation she'd laid at Ethan's door. But she and Tim were bound by blood and love. Whatever she and Ethan had, it was more tenuous. Attraction, certainly, and maybe even respect, but when he'd pushed her buttons, it was about some white-knight complex he had, nothing deeper or more permanent, no matter his protestations to the contrary.

And he hadn't really protested much. He'd looked as if he might, but then her home had filled with cops, and the moment had been lost. And what would she have done had he taken that opportunity to commit himself to her? She'd probably have done exactly what she'd done anyway: run. So, really, she had no right to be upset. Still, she had to shake off an achy melancholy in order to be firm with her brother.

"I'm your sister. I'm allowed to be manipulative when it comes to your safety."

"I'm not a kid, Luce."

"I understand that. Please. For me."

He sighed. "Fine. Just two nights, though," he warned. "And that's counting tonight. So Sunday afternoon I am coming back to Dobbs Hollow, even if I have to stay in a hotel room." Lucy remembered Ethan's comments about flimsy motel doors, and shuddered. She'd get a handle on this before Sunday.

She had to.

"Call first," she said. "I told you we'd renegotiate, and I meant it."

"Maybe. I told the guys what happened and asked them to keep an eye out for anything weird. They wanted to come down to Dobbs Hollow with me and kick some ass, but I explained we didn't know who to go after. I did promise they could help, though. So at least Barry will probably come down with me. Hal and Jessup are both working."

Lucy couldn't help grinning at the thought of a bunch of college boys coming to her rescue. "I guess I'll have to accept that."

When she hung up, her mood had lightened considerably. Just hearing her brother's voice released a huge chunk of the tension she'd carried since receiving the text message at her house.

"He's okay?" TJ asked.

"Yeah. He's going to stay with a friend, our adoptive father's partner, for a couple of days." She quickly texted Ethan to let him know.

"He seems like a good kid."

"He is. I worry about him." Lucy explained about Tim's spinal muscular atrophy. She rarely discussed his condition with anyone, but then, Todd's colleagues in the PD already knew about the diagnosis, and Lucy didn't have many other close friends. Talking to TJ was surprisingly easy.

"So there's nothing to do?"

"Not really. It doesn't bother him much and it doesn't seem

to be getting worse, so with luck he's escaped the worst problems. It would have been far worse if it had shown itself at birth. SMA is the primary genetically based cause of death in infants."

Seeing the horrified expression on TJ's face, Lucy hurried to reassure her. "But Tim's not in that kind of shape. Adult-onset has a much better prognosis."

"No, it's not that. I mean, it is that, but—" TJ shook her head for a minute. "What did you say causes this?"

"It can be a spontaneous genetic mutation, but most of the time it's because a child has two parents who are carriers. Like any recessive genetic trait, it takes both of the genes of the specific pair to be bad for the mutation to show up. Nowadays, many doctors recommend SMA testing if a couple plans a pregnancy because so many of us are carriers. Why?"

"Luce, Billy Pike's family has a history of infant death. His mom miscarried once before he was born. Then he had an older brother who died right about the time Billy was born. And then they had another kid a couple years later who also died. My folks called those deaths 'crib death.' But what if they were more than that?"

Lucy's stomach lurched and acid backed up into her throat. "Al Pike. You think Al was Tim's father." It fit with what Charlene had said about Cecile having an affair with Al Pike, but Lucy had not wanted to delve too deeply into that aspect of her mother's life. Had Cecile tried to blackmail Pike when the baby was born? Could that have been the reason for her murder? But why wait almost three years? Maybe she hadn't needed the money until she was ready to leave town, and then she'd gone to Pike, threatening to expose Tim's parentage?

"Chief Pike wouldn't have killed her over that. I mean, his wife was dead, right? His affair wasn't even adultery. Would anyone care that he'd fathered a child with Cecile?" Lucy would have loved to solve Cecile's death so neatly, but there was simply no evidence, not even any motive.

"I doubt it. He wasn't sheriff, so he didn't have to be elected. And he might not even have been Tim's dad. Seriously. You know the statistics better than I do. How likely is it that another man in town carries a defective gene?"

"Likely. But still . . ." Memories of Billy Pike ran through Lucy's head. His sneering presence in high school, the assault, their encounters since her return. Did he and Tim have any features in common? Both had hazel eyes, but Cecile's eyes had been hazel, as well. Was it really possible that she and Billy could be related, even peripherally? No, surely not.

"I hate the idea that Tim could have Al Pike's blood running through his veins."

"Maybe he doesn't. And even if he does, it's no big deal. You raised him. You and your foster parents. Those influences far outweigh whatever he might have gotten genetically." TJ jumped to her feet and struck a pose. "Look at me! How much Dobbs do you see here?"

Lucy laughed weakly, more because TJ expected it than because she felt anything even bordering on amusement.

"If SMA is so common, do you have to get tested?"

"No, Timmy and I have different fathers. Or, at least, I've always assumed we did." Her stomach lurched again. "I'm almost certainly a carrier, because my mother was, so if I planned to get pregnant, I'd get tested and get my partner tested, too, to be certain. But I can't see me with a kid, can you?"

"Why not?"

Lucy stared at TJ, whose blue eyes reflected genuine curiosity.

"Jeez, TJ! You can't be serious. Look at me. I'm not cut out for motherhood. First, there's the job. I spend hours and hours closeted with my computer, and the rest of the time I'm interviewing criminals and families of victims."

"Maybe you don't have to do that for the rest of your life. I'm just saying, I heard you on the phone with Tim, and I've seen how determined you are to get justice for your mother. Family has meaning for you. I bet you'd be a great mother."

"Yeah, well, I doubt we'll find out how good a bet that is. What about you? You planning on having kids?"

"Me?" TJ laughed. "Please. Talk about the original dysfunctional family. I don't think I have a lot to offer the gene pool. And as for jobs, I can't even keep a cat, let alone a child."

"You're not your family, TJ, as you just pointed out. You should get out of this town. It's poisonous. Why did you come back?"

"You really want to know? It doesn't speak so well for my maturity."

"Out of spite?"

"Pretty much. Though I really do prefer life in a small town to life in a city. I managed fine on the force in San Antonio, but I never really liked living there. Eventually, I suppose, I'll move on. As they used to say in old westerns, 'This town isn't big enough for the both of us,' and the mayor is here to stay."

"Do it sooner rather than later is my advice." Lucy took a slug off the bottle of beer in her hand. "Hey, do you have an Internet connection I could use? I want to upload the work I got done earlier and write up my thoughts on what happened at my place."

"Sure thing. It's wireless. The password is 'morticia,' all lower case."

"Morticia? Like in The Addams Family?"

"Yeah. I loved that show when I was a kid. Still do, really. I always figured if I were home enough to have a pet, I'd get a black cat and name him Gomez."

Laughter bubbled up in Lucy's throat as she pulled her laptop out of its case. "What a great idea for a name! Cats don't need much care, you know. You should get one."

"Maybe I will." TJ gestured to the dining table. "You can set up there, if you like. That's where I usually work."

"Great. Thanks." Lucy popped open her laptop and entered the Digital Jake program so she could upload all the data to the server to begin crunching.

"What's that?" TJ asked, and Lucy found herself explaining the program once more.

"The FBI guy wrote it? The one from the Paxton case?"

"Jake Nolan. Yeah. He's a computer genius. Made a fortune designing a little widget that does predictive analysis based on previous activity. You know, like when you go on a website and it gives you recommendations based on what you've bought before."

"This is a sweet program."

"It is. We can only hope it comes up with a direction for us."

"How long does it take?"

"As long as it takes. I've never actually used it this way. As I said to you before, I'm not an investigator. Jake knew I'd want to look into my mother's murder, so he offered it to me."

"Nice. With any luck, it will come up with a new direction before anything else happens."

"Yeah."

"Look, I've been wearing these clothes for almost twenty-four hours straight, so if you don't mind, I'll leave you to it and go shower."

It had been a long day, starting with Drew Dobbs's murder.

"How are you doing? I know you didn't get along with Drew, but still, he was your brother."

"What bothers me most is that it doesn't bother me. Maybe I'm just too tired today to think about it, what with running all over town from blackout panic. Then again, maybe I stopped considering him my brother a long time ago."

"Well, if you want to talk about it, you know where to find

me." She gestured to the spare room. "It's not such a long walk, either. Thanks so much for allowing me to stay here."

"Happy to have you."

 

Ethan arrived at the station with his head full of death, blood, and horror. He'd seen a lot in his days in Houston, maybe too much, but he'd never come across anything quite as gruesome as the body in the bed of the truck. That it had been delivered to Lucy only added to his stress. And then there had been her rejection of his . . . whatever he'd offered. He shouldn't have yelled at her, but he wanted her to acknowledge him, to lay herself on the line just a little. He cracked his neck, but the pain in his head and shoulders didn't abate.

And, joy of joys, at the station both Mayor Dobbs and Sheriff Pike awaited him inside his office. At the site of Billy Pike's face, rage boiled up, burning away any other feeling. Ethan's fists clenched at his sides, and for a long moment, he savored the purity of the emotion. No confusion, nothing soft: simple, straightforward fury. Billy Pike was going to get what was coming to him.

But not yet. He wanted Pike alone, when they could take their time. For the moment, he had to deal with the man professionally and leave the personal out.

He forced himself to count to ten, then repeat it, while flexing his fingers and damping his anger. When he had full control, he approached the two men.

"Gentlemen. What can I do for you?"

"You can tell us what the hell is going on with the Sadler woman," Dobbs growled. "First you refuse to arrest her for killing my boy, and now I hear she's mixed up in two other murders."

"You'll have to talk to the sheriff here about your son's

murder, Mayor. But if you want my opinion, Lucy had nothing to do with it."

He flicked a glance at Pike. "I understand you discovered a second body in the woods? Close to Drew's?"

"You're well informed," said Pike.

"As are you. And since you both evidently already know what happened tonight, I don't see what else I can do to help you. O'Reilly's office is working overtime on the bodies, and you're taking my time away from looking into leads we might be able to come up with."

"You don't need to look for leads!" The mayor's face had turned bright, apoplectic red. "All you need to do is ask Lucy Sadler who would send her two dead bodies!"

"Believe me, Mayor Dobbs, I have asked her. She doesn't know. If you do, I'd be more than happy to have that information as a place to begin. But there seem to be an abundance of people in this town—this county—who'd like her gone. Just tonight, Rita Calloway—who didn't even live here until a few years back, treated me to her opinion of Lucy's character. It doesn't make the suspect list any shorter."

"Maybe she planned it herself. With the things she's written about, I wouldn't put it past her." This from Pike. "Gave herself the perfect alibi by having you there at the time. Wouldn't that just be great publicity for her book about her mother?"

"Are you working on that case?" The mayor's shout could probably be heard halfway to Dallas.

"That woman died almost twenty years ago! I demand you leave that case alone until you've fixed the problems we have right fucking now!"

"Mayor—"

"Have you ID'd the body in the truck yet?" Pike asked.

"Not definitively. Registration comes back to one Juan Ramirez of San Antonio. Name ring any bells?" Both men shook their heads.

"I figured out where I'd seen him before," said Scott from behind Ethan's back. Thank God. Someone sane.

"Yeah? Where?"

"He's a day laborer. Hangs out in the parking lot of the El Lobo Loco looking for work, and in the bar itself at night."

"Interesting. I've been meaning to stop over there and check it out. Run a search and see what you can dig up on the place, will you? Call outs, ownership, whatever you can find."

"On it." Scott walked back to his desk and began pecking away on his computer.

"Now, if you'll excuse me gentlemen, I have to work."

"You're over your head here, Donovan," Pike said. "Let me send you a few men to help. You've got a dead coed, and now two more dead."

"And you have a dead politician and the body of an as-yet-unidentified female. I'd say you have enough on your plate. If I need help, I can get it from the state or from the Feebies."

"What the hell would the FBI want with any of this?" Was he imagining it, or could that be a note of real panic in Pike's voice?

"I told you before. My consultant is looking into connected cases."

"Your consultant. You mean Lucy Sadler."

"Yes."

"And I told you before, Donovan, that girl is nothing but trouble."

"Don't go there, Sheriff. We'll have a chat about your high school experiences another time. That's a promise."

Pike stared at him for a long time, but Ethan wouldn't back down. His teeth clenched so tightly he could feel the stress all the way up to his temples. Pike looked away first. "No idea what you're talking about, Donovan, but I'm always happy to relive the good old days. As you say, though, you have a lot to do. So the mayor and I will let you get to it."

Ethan ran a hand over the back of his neck and wished

like hell he'd never accepted the position of chief of police. In three months, his contract would be up and there wasn't a chance in hell of Dobbs renewing it at this point, which meant all he'd done was buy himself a year by taking the job.

Of course, a treacherous voice whispered in the back of his mind, if you weren't tied to this town, you might have a future with Lucy. But Lucy hadn't shown any interest in a future. And all the conflicts remained. If he wasn't chief of police in Dobbs Hollow, where no one cared about his disability, what would he do?

He shoved the thought away and went to see what Scott had uncovered about El Lobo Loco. Not much, as it turned out. In the nine years since it had opened, the bar had hosted only a handful of fights requiring police attention, probably because it catered to illegals who preferred to stay under police radar. The owner, one Diego Sanchez, had no record. His driver's license showed an address a few miles outside of town.

Ethan checked his watch. Eleven. Friday nights were apt to be busy at El Lobo Loco. He wondered whether the boss would be in.

"C'mon," he said to Scott. "Let's check it out."

Sanchez was tending bar when they arrived. If having the police in his establishment bothered him, it didn't show. Short, fat, and rapidly losing his hair, he presented as unthreatening a front as Ethan had ever seen. So why did he set the fine hairs on the back of Ethan's neck to bristling? "Sure, I know him," Sanchez said without hesitation when they showed him the enlarged driver's license picture of Juan Ramirez. "He's in here several nights a week, and I see him outside looking for work. I give the guys coffee if they want it. It's a hard life they have."

"You haven't had trouble with anyone in town because of the way you treat the illegal immigrants? No one's made threats?"

"Threats?" He shrugged. "A few folks are upset about the men I serve, sure, but not enough to do anything about it. It's not as if any of them want the work these guys do, after all."

"What else can you tell me about Juan Ramirez?" He'd like to ask whether Sanchez had seen anyone dealing drugs in his bar, but he wasn't ready to antagonize the man. "Any particular group he hangs out with?"

This time Sanchez paused for a split second before answering. Was he just thinking or did he know more than he was willing to say? "Not that I've noticed. Sorry."

"Mmm." Ethan eyed the dozen or so men in the bar, three at the bar, the others at flimsy wooden tables. Unlike the place's owner, its customers were an underfed lot, if muscular from the manual labor they performed. Not one would meet his gaze.

"How about you?" he said to the nearest man at the bar. "You know Juan Ramirez?" The man barely glanced at the picture before shaking his head, still without fully facing Ethan. He'd likely have no better luck with any of the rest of them, so he nodded to Sanchez, and he and Scott headed back to the station. He'd up police presence in the bar for a couple of days, put the pressure on Sanchez. If Sanchez knew anything about Ramirez, he'd talk when business started dropping off from having cops in the bar all the time.

Ethan wanted to call Lucy, to hear her voice, even if all she wanted to do was curse him out for his behavior that afternoon, but he figured she'd probably fallen into bed the minute they'd gotten to TJ's apartment. He drove by there and checked the windows, but there were no lights on. Not like he could have invited himself in even if they'd been up. One more trip, this time past Lucy's house to see whether anyone was hanging around, and he forced himself to head back to his place alone.

WELL, WELL. SOMEONE else was having fun with Lucy Sadler. No skin off his neck, but he'd like to know who. He didn't appreciate interference. He'd thought he put a stop to it when he'd taken Drew out of the picture. Of course, Drew had insisted he hadn't had anything to do with the snake, so the Commander should have recognized another hand in the game. Still, dead men were in a completely different class than rattlers. Especially given what he'd heard about the body in the back of the truck.

How the hell could another man be operating in town without his knowledge? It meant he'd misjudged someone. Because he knew just about everyone in Dobbs Hollow one way or another, and he'd never even considered one of them capable of the kind of violence it would take to dismember a human being.

And then there was the dead Jane Doe. Who the fuck was she? And where had she come from? Renee had been a thing of beauty. Best job he'd done in ages. And she'd riled up the town like crazy. God, what a rush. Way better than those pathetic women he'd had to bury over the years because they didn't survive his games.

And Lucy Sadler would be even better. He just had to be sure no one else got to her first.

# CHAPTER FIFTEEN

My mother moved to Dobbs Hollow when she was twenty-one, with a child and no husband. She hardly lived a perfect life, either before her arrival or after, but she didn't deserve what happened.

FROM *A BAD DAY TO DIE*
BY LUCY SADLER CALDWELL [DRAFT]

TJ MOVED SLOWLY through her morning tai chi routine. Breathe, move, focus, balance. Find your center. Focus. The sun shone through her windows, and she found herself humming slightly despite her knowledge of the grim day ahead. Down the hall, she heard the shower shut off. Lucy, too, was preparing for whatever was to come.

The doorbell rang, surprising her into losing her balance, and she cursed as she tripped, barely managing to catch herself without toppling the floor lamp beside the dining table. She stumbled to the door and peered out the peephole, ready to berate whoever dared show up on her doorstep at eight in the morning.

Of course, that was before she saw him.

Despite the fisheye distortion of the peephole, the man waiting in the hall was almost shockingly handsome. Thick, dark hair sprang back from his face in barely controlled waves. Black stubble covered, but did not mask, a sharply defined jaw and chin. And his body, well, it was a thing of beauty. Even at ease, muscles stood out beneath his black T-shirt and well-worn jeans.

Too bad she had to meet him, whoever he was, in sweatpants and a tank top.

"Yes?" she called through the door.

"My name's Jacob Nolan. I'm looking for Lucy Caldwell."

"ID?"

He held up a badge to the peephole. Lucy had said he'd disappeared, but apparently, he hadn't resigned from the FBI yet. She opened the door.

For a moment, neither of them spoke, and she had the sense he studied her as closely as she did him. Up close, his masculine appeal took on a sharper edge. His eyes were the color of shadows on slate, a dark gray-blue that revealed nothing of what he might be thinking.

And then a shriek had TJ stepping out of the way as Lucy launched herself at Nolan.

"Jake!" Lucy pummeled the broad chest, but not hard. "Where in the hell have you been?"

"Here 'n' there." The man's grin should have been illegal. It lit those stormy eyes and cut deep grooves in his cheeks. "Georgia, mostly, and Louisiana. But I caught your upload last night and decided maybe you could use my help."

"Of course we can! But are you sure you want to come back? You look much better having been away for a while."

"You don't. You look like crap."

"You're such a gentleman." But she smiled, then turned to TJ. "You two met?"

"Not really." She held out a hand to Nolan. "TJ Dobbs."

He took it in his own and a tiny shiver snaked up her spine.

"Jake Nolan."

"Lucy showed me your program. Very impressive."

"Thanks. With a little luck, it will bring answers."

"How did you know where to find me?" Lucy asked.

"I went by the cop shop, and Donovan told me where you were staying."

"He's still there? Doesn't the man ever sleep?"

"Actually, he's right behind me. Got a radio call as we were pulling up." TJ couldn't decide which she found more intriguing, the excited, happy Lucy who'd thrown herself at Jake or the concerned and caring Lucy who worried over Ethan Donovan's lack of sleep. This must be the true Lucy, Lucy when she wasn't searching for her mother's killer. TJ found herself smiling. She hadn't even realized how much she'd worried that, between Drew's actions in high school and her mother's murder, Lucy's emotional life would have been stunted forever.

A knock on the door signaled Ethan's arrival. TJ let him in, then watched in fascination as both he and Lucy tried to avoid looking at each other. Lucy blushed.

"Why don't I get us all coffee," TJ offered. "Then we can figure out what to do next."

She headed for the kitchen, too aware that Jake Nolan followed her. "I'm perfectly capable of fixing coffee myself."

"I know that. I thought they might want a couple of minutes alone."

"And that doesn't bother you?"

"Why should it?"

TJ shrugged. "I'm not clear on your relationship."

"We're friends. Nothing more."

THE MOMENT TJ and Nolan left the room, Ethan pulled Lucy into his arms. She slid her own around his waist and turned her face up to him, waiting for a kiss. He obliged, glad she had forgotten their tiff. Or at least forgiven it.

"I missed you last night." He hardly recognized his own voice, rougher than he'd ever heard it.

"Did you get home at all?"

"For a few hours."

"You should have let me stay at your place."

"I would have. I will if you want to. We didn't exactly part on the best of terms, so it didn't seem appropriate. Besides, there are a few things I should tell you first." After which she might not be so eager to put her safety in his hands.

Sensing his misgivings, she put her hands on his cheeks and held his eyes with her own. "Whatever it is, I promise it's okay."

Before he could reply, TJ and Jake returned to the room, coffee in hand.

"So what did you discover last night?" TJ asked as she put a coffee mug at each place on the small dining table and a bottle of milk and jar of sugar in the center.

"Last night wasn't terribly productive," Ethan admitted, "but I just got off with Scott, and I'd like to discuss what he told me."

"Scott Allenby is one of the DHPD officers," Lucy explained to Jake.

"Last night, Scott and I went to El Lobo Loco because that's where the RO for the truck has been known to hang out. I had Scott work up deep background on the owner, and he turned up several old charges. Nothing stuck, so nothing in his official record, but Scott went the extra mile and called to talk to the local PD where the guy used to live."

"What were they for?"

"Cocaine."

"The owner of El Lobo Loco?" TJ sounded flabbergasted. "He's a good hundred pounds overweight. He was using blow?"

"Selling it. Meanwhile, both Richie Mack and Juan Ramirez were chronic meth abusers. I'd bet good money Sanchez is back in business, using his bar as a cover. If he's not selling meth himself, he's taking a cut of deals that go down under his watch."

"Okay. What does that give us?"

"In itself, not much. But Scott. . ." He sucked in a breath and let it out slowly. Under the table, he felt Lucy's hand touch his thigh in reassurance. He grasped it in his own. "Scott thinks Eric may be dealing drugs."

"Oh shit," said TJ.

"Who's Eric?" asked Jake.

"Eric is Scott's younger brother," Ethan explained. "Scott said he's suspected it for a couple of years, even tried to discreetly search Eric's place when Eric would invite him over, but the brothers aren't close, and he never found anything. Thing is, Eric lives beyond his means, and he's never been fond of rules and regulations."

"We still don't have proof."

"No, we don't, which is why Scott let it go all this time. But once it began to look as if last night's events might be drug-related, he felt honor-bound to admit his suspicions. Of course, hearing his story reminded me that, after the snake incident, TJ mentioned that Eric also has an affinity for creepy-crawly things I asked Scott whether Eric was still handling critters and he said Eric still spends a good deal of time in the woods, so it's possible. But that he didn't believe Eric had any reason to hold a grudge against Lucy or put the snake in her car."

"I'd managed to forget that about him," Lucy said, wrinkling her nose with distaste. "But what could he possibly have against me?"

"Maybe nothing. Right now, we're just playing with a theory. These are the first links we've found."

"Will Scott talk to us honestly about his brother? In more detail?"

Ethan sighed at Jake's question. Some days he really, really hated his job. "Let me call him."

Scott arrived about twenty minutes later. TJ brought him a cup of coffee, and he stared down into the mug as he stirred in sugar. No one spoke, letting him figure out how he wanted to begin.

"Eric was always a weird kid," he said finally. "My parents' death hit him hard. He was only thirteen. We didn't have to move or anything—my aunt and uncle came to live with us so we could stay at the same school, live in the same house—but Eric ran a bit wild. He'd sneak out at night, cut school, cause trouble, get into fights. Normal kid stuff, but taken to extremes. He spent every free moment in the woods, told my aunt he wanted to be a hunting guide when he grew up." Scott fell silent.

"So, he's a loner, then?" Jake asked, and Ethan could practically see the profiling instinct kick in.

"He was." But Scott still didn't look up. "My senior year, his sophomore year, he started hanging with a few of the guys in my class. Mostly Chuck Hemming and Richie Mack. All three played football. Eric sat on the bench, but I guess they liked him anyway. Chuck was okay, but Richie had a few screws loose even then.

"I spent most of that year in and out of hospitals because I had some mysterious disorder they never did figure out. I'd get violently, incredibly sick for two or three days at a time. Dehydrated, the whole deal. My aunt and uncle spent a lot of time taking care of me, and Eric got ignored. I'm pretty sure that's when he fell in with that crowd, got out of control."

"He was your brother, not your son." Lucy reached her free hand across the table and covered one of Scott's. "And you were just a sick teenager. You couldn't control what he did."

"That how you feel about your brother?"

"No." Lucy's half-sad smile twisted Ethan into a knot, and he squeezed her fingers in reassurance. "It's how I try to think of him, though. Some days are harder than others."

Ethan brought the conversation back on track. "You think Richie might have been buying drugs from Eric?"

Scott shrugged. "If you'd asked me last week, I'd have said no. Richie's a tweaker. I figured Eric might be growing weed in the woods and selling it to his buddies, but not cooking meth. No way. On the other hand, most of the meth in this county isn't local. It comes up from Mexico. He could be distributing for someone else."

"So Juan and Richie ended up in the middle of a turf war?"

TJ's brow wrinkled. "Maybe Juan was dealing out of El Lobo Loco, and Eric's supplier decided to make an object lesson of him?"

"It's the only thing that makes sense, the only way Eric could be tied into this. He's not perfect, not by a long shot, but he's no psycho, butchering murderer." Finally, Scott raised his eyes, only to glare around the table as if daring each of them to contradict him. "He enjoys high-end camping and hunting gear, and he's essentially lazy, so he probably thought dealing was easier than getting a better job than that crappy night security position he has, but he'd never kill anyone."

"Assuming a drug-related motive behind Juan and Richie's deaths, though, why deliver them to me?" Lucy pinpointed the exact question that had kept Ethan up most of the night.

"If your major player in the drug game is local, it could be a twofer," suggested Jake. "He could want you out of town for personal reasons. He's got to get rid of a competitor, why not scare off a woman whose investigation might bring his business dealings to the attention of the police?"

"Or maybe more than his business requires protection," said Ethan. "Lucy's investigation might uncover other secrets he's hiding. Or he could have personal reasons for wanting her gone."

"Jed Martin," Lucy said. "I'm not necessarily naming him a killer, or even a dealer, but if you're looking for someone with a connection to Richie Mack who has it in for me, I'd start with Jed."

"Why Jed, in particular? He's no more connected than half a dozen other men. Brad down at the Gas 'n' Go hires— hired—Richie from time to time even knowing what a tweaker he was. He'd be first on my list. He's almost as much of a loner as Eric." This from Scott.

"Yes, but Jed came into the library when I was there one day. He insinuated he had information about my mother's murder, though that might have been bluster. Either way, we had words. I think it's fair to say I humiliated him."

"And—" TJ started to speak, then stopped.

"What is it?"

"Well, I don't suppose I'm spilling secrets to anyone who's lived in this town the past twenty years," she said, "but Jed used to beat Eulie when they were married."

"And he let her go? The usually don't," said Ethan.

"Eulie's family was pretty powerful in town. When it was minor stuff, they let it go. But the day he broke her arm, she moved back in with her folks. She let him pull the whole story about kicking her out because she wasn't a good wife, but it was an open secret that she'd left him."

"So he's a bully," Jake put in. "And Lucy humiliated him, which bullies don't take well."

"Plus, you said your mother had also humiliated him," Ethan said slowly, turning the information over in his mind. "Him, Chuck, and Richie, right?" He deliberately left Eric's name off the list. No need to antagonize or upset Scott any further.

"I don't know that's what she did."

"Oh, believe me, she did. You've never been a teenage boy. I have a damned good idea what brought them to your house that night, and it wasn't conversation. She sent them away, which would have completely pissed them off. And everything I've heard about Martin since I arrived tells me he was the ringleader. Quarterback, football scholarship, came back to town and was immediately accepted back into the fold. He wouldn't have been accustomed to turndowns. Especially not from women he considered well below him.

"The problem is, it's all conjecture. Nothing solid enough to get search warrants, even if we knew exactly what we were looking for, which we don't."

"So what can we do?" TJ asked.

Ethan turned to Scott. "I'm sorry, buddy, but I've got take you off this case. No choice. If we're going to get this guy, we can't afford even the slightest hint of impropriety. If we go to court, they'll try to use your relationship with Eric to shoe-horn their way into getting any evidence we might pick up from searches you do thrown out."

"Dammit, I came to you. I told you about Eric's lifestyle, his extra income. I deserve to be part of this."

"No question. But what you deserve isn't the issue." Christ, what to say to the man? If Ethan had a brother, he'd feel the same damned way. And what if Ethan alienated Scott too badly and he decided to spill the beans to Eric? After all, he clearly didn't believe his brother capable of any serious crim-inal offense.

"Scott," Lucy said quietly, drawing all eyes, "Eric's your brother. You've said you aren't close. But if you expect, or even hope, to come out of this with any kind of relation-ship, you have to back off now. He'll need you, and he won't trust you if you're part of the investigation."

Ethan's heart wrenched. How could she say she didn't deal well with emotions? She understood relationships better than anyone he'd ever met. He'd find a way to get her to accept him into her heart. He had to.

Scott shoved his chair back and began to pace the room. "Yeah. Okay. But what does that mean for me? I should go give speeding tickets until the rest of you close the case?"

"No," said Jake. "I'd like you to help me, if your boss can spare you."

"And what are you going to be doing?" Scott asked sullenly.

"Figuring out who killed Renee Josephs."

⌣

JAKE ALWAYS DID like to make a splash, Lucy thought. And he'd drawn everyone's attention, including her own, with his words.

"That is, of course, if y'all want my assistance."

"Hell, yes," said Ethan, and Lucy's already soft heart melted a bit more. She'd spent half her life among cops. Most of them had no use for outsiders, even well-trained ones. They hated to share, refused to give up a single iota of their authority.

"Do we need to make this official? Call in the feds and get you an assignment?"

"No. I'm sort of on a leave of absence." He waved away the vagueness of his situation. Really? Wasn't a leave like a light switch, either on or off? She saw the same curiosity reflected in Ethan's eyes. "My participation will be strictly off the record. But if you'll leave me Scott and Lucy, I believe we can make headway."

Under the table, Ethan tightened his fingers around her own. He hadn't let go of her hand, not from the second she'd touched him in reassurance. The feel of his rough skin had reminded her, in the first moment he'd grasped her fingers, of how those calluses had rasped against her body in bed. But then, when the flood of sexual sense-memory had dissipated, his hold had become something more. A promise. A warm, possessive security that simultaneously weakened and strengthened her.

"All right, then. TJ, you and I will head over to the station and leave these guys here to work with Jake's program." A grin flashed across his face. "You might want to change."

"Oh, damn." TJ blushed and hurried down the hall to don her uniform.

Lucy, watching Jake, saw how his eyes followed her. "Hey," she said, reaching across the table to punch him lightly in the shoulder. "Watch yourself."

"No problem." He winked. "Warning received."

"Okay, then."

Still, when TJ and Ethan left, Lucy noticed that Jake kept an eye on her until the door closed behind them.

At the station, Bob O'Reilly waited in Ethan's office.

"Marge said you'd be right back, or I'd have had her call you," he said. "I need to talk to you about your John Doe. Then I am going home and sleeping for a week, and you'd better not find another effing body, because I won't be available."

"I appreciate everything you've already done," Ethan said.

"Yeah, well, appreciate this: the full report's on your desk, but I'll give you the main point: your John Doe was dressed."

It took Ethan a moment to grasp his meaning. "Like a deer?"

"Yeah. Gutted, had everything inside him pulled out, then had his skin taken off. After that, someone cut him up with a hacksaw."

"Jesus."

"You said it."

"So our guy is a hunter."

"In my opinion, yeah. And an experienced one. It's harder to skin a human than a deer. Deer hide is thick and can be pulled. Humans have thinner skins; they'd have to be peeled. More like a vegetable."

The coffee Ethan had drunk at TJ's roiled in his stomach and backed up into his throat. He swallowed. "Well, that's a lovely image. I do appreciate the insight, though. I don't know what we'd do without you."

O'Reilly grunted, then heaved himself out of the chair. Before he could leave, however, Ethan stopped him.

"Bobby, what can you tell me about the woman found in the woods the same day they discovered Dobbs at the construction site?"

"That's the sheriff's case."

"Yeah, it is. But it might relate to the Renee Josephs murder. If you tell me the two have nothing in common, I'll let it go. I'm asking for your opinion: did the same person kill them?"

O'Reilly glanced at TJ. Ethan caught her eye and jerked

his head. Though she made no secret of her displeasure, she left the office.

"So?"

"Well, if the same guy did do Jane Doe and Renee, he's been busy. The woman died before Renee, but only by a day or two. He cut her throat with a big knife, quite possibly a hunting knife, but that's where the similarities end. In fact, she's got far more in common with your John Doe from last night. Brown hair, brown eyes, brown skin—my guess is Mexican. And beaten severely. As was your guy. Even before he was cut up, he had broken bones.

"But even then, your John Doe was delivered into your hands. This woman was buried. No one intended her to be discovered."

"How did it happen?"

"Sheriff's boys were doing a grid search. Ran across freshly packed earth 'bout a half mile into the woods by the construction site and figured they might find evidence, even a weapon. Found her instead."

"Damn."

"That about sums it up."

"Thanks for your help, Bobby. Now, go home and get some rest. And send TJ in, if you don't mind."

"Good luck, Donovan." The older man waved on his way out, and TJ slipped back into the office. Ethan settled into his chair and gestured for her to take one of the other seats.

"So we're looking for a hunter," he mused. "Eric Allenby hunts. Of course, so do three-quarters of the men in this town. But he was part of the scene at Lucy's house a month before her mother's murder."

"You didn't mention that earlier."

"Scott didn't need to hear it. I doubt Eric had anything to do with Cecile's murder, anyway. He'd still have been a kid. Everything in that case points to a single assailant, and I doubt he could have taken her down on his own."

"But Jed could have. And he and Eric are thick as thieves." TJ grimaced at the expression she'd used. "I think I told you when you first asked me about Eric that he and Jed double date on occasion. And then there's the way Jed treated Eulie. He and Eric also hunt together."

"Indeed. But we can't go after Jed directly. His business is in Palestine, for one thing. Outside our jurisdiction, so we can't put a cop outside the place to follow him when he leaves the way we could if he lived here. Plus, we don't have evidence tying him to anything. Gut feelings and hunches won't earn us a warrant."

"What next, then?"

"Let me make a call."

As he picked up the phone, Ethan mentally crossed his fingers that Toby Brown wouldn't blow off his request. He could. Hell, he probably should. Dobbs Hollow was far from Toby's jurisdiction. But with any luck, his devotion to the law and his love of a test would bring him anyway. If, of course, he and his partner, Beau, had time off.

"A feed factory? You want to check out a feed factory?" Toby's incredulous tone when Ethan explained his plan had his heart sinking. "You really do like a challenge, don't you?"

"You told me Beau could sniff out drugs no matter what surrounded them."

"I did. And he can. All right, you're on. I've got today and tomorrow off. How long's the drive?"

"'Bout three hours. The plant operates eight to eight, six days a week. The guy I'm interested in is night security. His shift starts at four. There's another I'd like to see us nosing around, too, a manager who'll get in at eight. So I figured if I could get you down here tonight, we'd go in at six in the morning. Let the security guard get comfortable before we invade his space, and be waiting for the manager when he shows up for work."

"You're sure you can get permission for us to come in?"

"Shouldn't be a problem. One thing I've learned living here, no one likes scandal. I'll threaten a court order and state involvement and the owner will fall all over himself to be sure word doesn't leak."

"Sounds like a plan. E-mail me your address. We'll be there in time for dinner."

"Thanks, Toby. I appreciate it. I'll buy you both steaks."

Toby laughed. "Sounds like a plan. Don't forget Beau likes his raw."

"A drug dog?" TJ asked when he hung up.

"The best we had in Houston. Now, we just need to convince Sam Farmer that allowing us to search Farmer's Feed without a warrant is in his best interest. Both Chuck Hemming and Eric Allenby work for Farmer's. Having us come through there with the dog should provoke a reaction, even if we don't find the drugs. But I'm betting we do. Scott searched his brother's place, and they wouldn't leave them in the woods, no matter how secure Eric feels there. He'd worry having them that far out of his sight. But the factory's a perfect spot."

"Is that legal?" TJ asked.

"We can search with the owner's permission. That's perfectly legal. Whether we could actually make a case against Eric with the evidence we gather—especially since the ties to him might be weak, depending on where the meth actually is—is another story. But we're not trying to build a drug case that will stand up at trial, we're trying to get leverage and make the guy nervous. If he's a killer, it may not work. If he just has information on the murders, it very well may."

TJ nodded slowly, digesting his words. She'd be a fine detective one of these days if she ever got out of this godforsaken town.

"Let me e-mail Toby, and then we'll head out to Farmer's house and explain the situation."

Once Ethan and TJ had gone, Jake asked Lucy to pull out her computer so they could see what, if anything, the program had come up with for a pattern. Scott's cell rang, and he stepped outside to take the call. The minute he did, Jake leaned across the table and put a hand on Lucy's, drawing her attention.

"Your friend Donovan seems like a nice guy," he said, his eyes scrutinizing her in a way that made her want to squirm.

"So I have your permission to date him, Dad?"

He refused to be teased. "I haven't had a chance to run him."

"Jake! He's a cop, for crying out loud."

"You and I both know that doesn't mean anything. But if you insist, I'll skip the background."

"I insist. He's a good man, Jake." She couldn't pinpoint the source of her certainty, but she accepted it nonetheless. Ethan Donovan was a good man and, at least for the moment, he was hers.

"He's a good cop, I'll grant you that. They're not always the same thing."

Lucy knew Jake's mind had returned to his sister's overdose, a death he felt he could have prevented by leaving his job. She covered his hand where it lay on hers, wishing she could offer any advice, any words of healing. But there was nothing.

Scott returned, breaking the moment.

"No news," he explained. "Ethan just wanted to ask me to do the notification. He thinks it will come better from a local, though I don't think there are any Macks left around here." He grimaced and returned his attention to Jake. "So, what do we do?"

"Take your mother out of the equation," Jake instructed Lucy. "Have I showed you how to do that, to eliminate one case in a series?"

"Yes. But why? How can you be certain her murder isn't connected?"

"I can't. It may turn out we have to add that information back into the matrix. But for a minute, I want to focus on Renee. Your mother's murder seems to me to have been intensely personal as well as very disorganized. Renee's is neither."

"Cecile's murder could have been his first." Jake was the expert, and she knew she shouldn't argue with him, but to put aside her mother's murder, even for a moment, grated on her.

"It could have. But if so, this guy killed for a long time without anyone noticing women disappearing. The statistical anomalies didn't begin until a few years ago. It's not enough to rule out a connection, but it's enough to make me wary of relying on one."

"Fair enough." Lucy clicked the appropriate keys on her computer while Jake explained the program's design to Scott.

"Computer-based profiling? Not afraid of putting yourself out of a job?"

"Nah," Jake said. "The program doesn't interpret, it just finds patterns. Like a super-advanced ViCAP. In this case, that's where you come in. If we develop any kind of profile out of the information the computer analyzes, you're the one most likely to recognize it."

"You really believe Renee Josephs's killer could be local?"

"I do. And even if you don't recognize the man from the profile, you'll probably recognize the type. You can give us direction. While the program works its magic, I'll give you my impressions from the data you uploaded: This guy is organized. In his regular life, he's controlling in the extreme, probably because he has something to prove. As a kid, he was second fiddle at home, never good enough, though others may not have realized it because outside the home he put up a front. As an adult, he's playing out a fantasy of overcoming that."

"You think he killed all those missing women?"

"Most of them. Certainly the ones who reported stalkings prior to disappearing."

"And the rapes with a partner?"

"If he did those, and it's possible he did, his partner is the subservient one. This guy cedes control to no one under any circumstances."

The computer beeped.

"Ah. The first true test. Let's see what the program has come up with."

"It agrees with you. No surprise there," Lucy teased. As she read, however, humor deserted her. "The computer notes similarities in victimology. Not in appearance, but in position in society. All middle class or better, no poor or homeless, no prostitutes. Women who'd be missed. As far as we can tell, none of these women were even having affairs, let alone taking money for sex. The rapist had no reason outside of his own mind to call them whores. The program has flagged that as an anomaly.

"Most of them were also last seen in very public spots. Malls, churches, schools. Jeez."

"How in hell could we not have known this was going on?" Scott muttered. "Eight years' worth of women."

"It's easy," Jake replied. "Predators like this guy count on it. They switch municipalities, switch counties, relying on a lack of communication to keep them safe from detection. And he muddied the waters by killing off a few so they wouldn't show up as his victims."

"But why allow us, even force us, to find Renee when he's hidden the rest of the dead women?"

Scott asked "You tell me."

"I told TJ he had used Renee as a billboard."

"I agree," said Jake. "He's tired of hiding out, not being recognized for what he considers his genius and importance. Something changed for him."

"You," Scott said. "You're the only thing that's changed in this town. And even though Renee wasn't from here, he left her here. So stands to reason she's meant for you."

"Again, I agree. He knows you, Luce. Either from your past, or from your books. Renee's murder may have been his idea of a challenge to you: Solve this if you can. You're his nemesis."

Lucy fingered her scar and thought about Billy Pike. But Pike hadn't killed Cecile, and TJ had checked his alibi for the rapes. Unless, of course, the man hadn't committed all the crimes, only some of them. And why would he have waited so long to begin his reign of terror? Billy hadn't left Dobbs Hollow for any appreciable length of time since high school.

Before she could ask Jake what might trigger the rapist's behavior, her phone rang. When she saw Artie's name on the readout, she slipped into the bedroom to answer it.

"Tim?"

"He's not with you?" Artie's gravelly, familiar voice held a hint of desperation, and Lucy's knees went to spaghetti. She sat down hard on the bed.

"He's supposed to be in Dallas!" Her shout brought both Jake and Scott to the door.

"I got home from work and found a note that he'd left to go home to you. Says he was worried. But I haven't been able to reach him on his cell."

"Oh God."

"Luce, I know Timmy's handwriting. He wrote this. Maybe his phone's off or has run out of juice and he doesn't realize it."

"No. He wouldn't do that to me. They have him."

"They? You know who's gaslighting you?"

"Maybe. Maybe not." She scrubbed her face with one hand, and consciously tried to loosen her grip on the phone. "Ethan and Jake both seem to think we're chasing more than one person. Possibly one who killed my mom and doesn't want me digging into the past, and a separate, serial offender who killed Renee Josephs and has been active in the area for a while and could also see the investigation as a threat."

"And you think one of them might have . . .what? Driven

up here and forced Tim to leave a note? Because I'd swear on my life, he wrote that note himself."

"I don't know!" Behind her, Lucy could hear Jake on the phone speaking in a low, urgent whisper. "What have I done, Artie? This wasn't supposed to affect anyone else!"

"I'll be there as soon as I can."

"No, really, you don't have to—"

"Of course I do."

Jake had apparently hung up his own phone, because he sat beside her on the bed and held out his hand. She passed him her cell, and he spoke to Artie. The two had met when Lucy was working on the Paxton book.

"You stick with your contacts up there. See what they can find out. We'll want the roads searched between there and here. If he did leave of his own accord, he'll be in his own car. Get an APB out on it. When did you last talk to him?"

Scott's phone rang and, although he stepped out into the hall to answer it, she missed some of what Jake and Artie were discussing. "Yes, we've got it from this end. Don't worry. We'll get him back safely."

He flipped the phone closed at precisely the same moment Scott came back into the room.

"I'm leaving," Scott said. "Chief changed my orders. I'm to drop by the station, pick up that list of chores that was found in the woods, and drive back out to Jed Martin's place. Make one of his employees go over the list with me, show me each and every item and where it would be done, what products would be used. And while I am there I'm to check and be certain Jed's on the property and hasn't taken off for Dallas for an afternoon."

He reached out hesitantly and touched Lucy's shoulder. "We'll find your brother. Ethan's on his way back here."

"Thanks." She tried to smile, but failed.

Scott took off, and Lucy began to pace.

"There has to be something I can do."

"You can," Jake assured her. "Let's sort out who's who in this screwed-up town."

"What do you mean?" Her mind was whirling, still too focused on Tim to understand what Jake was getting at.

"As you said to Artie, there's a lot going on and we don't know who's involved in what. So let's back out for a minute and get a broad view."

"Okay."

"We need a big piece of paper, since I am pretty sure your friend doesn't keep a whiteboard in her apartment."

They hunted around until they found a large pad, and Jake made several columns on it. The first he labeled Cecile, the second Renee, the third Drew, the fourth Rape Victims, the fifth Richie and Truck Guy, and the last Buried Victim.

"Hell of a lot of violent crime for one small town, even if the rape victims are from surrounding areas."

"I know." And when she saw them all laid out like that, it seemed crazy to believe they could be connected. She ran a finger down the page, allowing her brain to switch modes.

"But given the geography, at least some of them virtually have to be. The idea that you could have so many different killers running loose at the same time doesn't make any sense."

"So our first goal is to figure out which ones fit with which others?" "Or which doesn't. And the first one that stands out to me is Richie Mack and the mysterious body in the truck bed. Them and Drew Dobbs. The victimology is all wrong. Renee is almost certainly related to the rape victims. Right social class, right gender, victim of rape before her murder, and the writing on her body would be in line with what the victims reported being said during their attacks."

"And my mother?"

"I don't think so. Can't be sure, but a guy who kills a woman doesn't go into hiding for ten years, then become a rapist for several years before he kills again. No, I think she belongs to a different group, if she doesn't turn out to be a lone, aberrant victim of a personal vendetta."

"Well, Drew and Richie are opposite ends of the social spectrum, but they were buddies in high school."

"Drew's murder was extremely impersonal: rifle shot from a distance. Nothing like the kind of rage evident in the other killings. I wonder whether he just knew too much."

"He was always glad-handing people around town, like his father. I suppose he might have seen or heard about the crimes in his travels. But why wouldn't he have spoken up right away, and why would he have gone out to Belle Pointe in the middle of the night?"

"Generally, those two questions point in a single direction: blackmail." Jake scrawled *Blackmail?* in the column beneath Drew's name.

"Yeah. So Drew's in a catch-22: he knows about a killer, but that killer also has dirt on him. He goes to meet the guy — to make an exchange possibly? — and the guy kills him."

"Which implies that he knew the person well enough to trust him," Jake mused.

"That's a pretty large group, because he had an ego that wouldn't quit and probably thought no one would dare touch him."

"So, let's exclude him from everything for the moment." Jake chewed the back of the pen he was using for a few minutes, then spoke again.

"Socially speaking, your mother fits better with the buried woman and Richie and Truck Guy than she does with Renee or Drew. She lived on the edges, didn't have anyone to make a fuss over her murder. Low risk to the killer."

"She also fits the emotional tone better. At least, with Richie and Truck Guy. You don't skin a guy and cut him into pieces without being pretty damned pissed off. That was true in my mother's case, too." The clinical tone of her voice surprised even her, and she felt Jake's stare, but refused to acknowledge it. Her mother had been dead almost twenty years. Tim was still alive, and she was going to find him, no matter what it took.

"There's a certain degree of planning involved in those murders, but it's nothing like what the other three sets took. I'm inclined to divide these into two, possibly three offenders. One who is responsible for the rapes and disappearances, Renee's murder, and possibly Drew's as well. I'd put Richie and Truck Guy, along with the buried woman, at someone else's door. Your mother—she fits in with them or she's alone."

"Yeah," Lucy said slowly, "but the thing that bothers me is that, as alike as they are in victimology and emotional intensity, those three killings are completely different in terms of disposal. My mother he left in her home. Possibly she was his first kill, and he hadn't thought about it. Or he thought it wouldn't make any difference whether she was found or not. The buried woman he made at least a nominal effort to hide. She wasn't buried too deep, and within a few weeks the wildlife would have gotten at her and there wouldn't be much left to analyze. But Richie he used to make a statement. It's . . .inconsistent."

"Could be an arc," Jake offered. "Cecile's his first kill. It's exciting and he likes it. As you said, he didn't believe it mattered whether she was found or not. But as time went on, he realized that if he was going to indulge himself, he had to be more careful. In which case I would expect there would be more victims in the woods. Likely low-risk targets for him. Took them out there and killed them, buried them. Somewhere along the line he started selling drugs or partnered up with someone who did. This gave him access to a whole new set of victims. Life was good. And then you came along and started asking a lot of very inconvenient questions."

"Not to mention that suddenly someone else is in his territory killing people."

"Exactly. In fact, the idea that the two of these unknown

subjects—the rapist and the killer—may never have known about each other if not for you is one we should look at. They're probably both trying to figure out what the hell is happening.

"But back to our killer. He, or he and his drug-dealing partner, need to get you out of town. You're a high-risk target. They may wish they could kill you, but you're way out of their league and they still have enough self-preservation left not to want to take that risk."

The front door opened, and in one smooth move Jake pulled a gun Lucy hadn't even realized he was wearing from a holster in the small of his back. But it was Ethan.

A sudden rush of emotion paralyzed her for a moment. The fear for her brother's safety that she'd tucked away during her work with Jake came flooding back, followed immediately by relief. Tears filled her eyes.

Ethan suffered no such hesitation. In seconds, he'd tugged her out of her chair and into his arms. She found herself pressed against his broad chest and felt his hand stroking through her hair.

"They took Tim," she managed.

"I know, sweetheart. But we'll get him back. I've sent Scott—"

"He told us," said Jake.

"Good. Keith is on his way to Eric's. He'll keep an eye on him until Eric goes to work." As Ethan explained what he'd learned about Jed and Eric, and his plan to confront Eric at the feed factory, Lucy saw Jake nodding.

"When Jake called me about Tim, I asked TJ to take over the job of getting Farmer's permission to search—as a Dobbs, she has the best chance of getting him to agree—and I came back here."

"So they're being watched, then? Eric and Jed?"

"They are. We'll get them, Lucy."

"I hate to be the one to throw a wrench into things," Jake

said, "but from the little I've heard about these two, I sincerely doubt they're capable of organizing a kidnapping. They're much more likely to be our disorganized killers, the ones responsible for the body buried in the woods." He filled Ethan in on what they'd worked out before Artie's call.

"Then we have two serial offenders, or two sets, operating in close proximity to each other. Is that even possible?" Ethan voiced the same objection that haunted Lucy.

"Statistically? It's not probable." Jake shrugged. "But that's why you can't rely on probability alone, and why machines won't ever take the place of cops. Let's say our guy killed Lucy's mother in a rage, and felt no remorse. Given how careless he was about the scene, I'd peg it as his first. Afterward, he wanted to share his triumphs, and he found a friend. I doubt the friend ever would have come up with the idea on his own, but he didn't object, either. We want to lay those murders at Jed Martin and Eric Allenby's feet. That means there's someone else in this town as cruel and unfeeling as they are.

"That lack of empathy, the lack of objection, is probably the key to your second set of crimes. I'd lay odds your ViCAP guy comes from Dobbs Hollow as well, even though he's been operating over several counties. He's a product of the same culture of violence, for want of a better phrase, that spawned Jed and Eric." He flicked a troubled glance at Lucy.

"Small towns are like little petri dishes. Whatever's planted can flourish. And all you have to do is think about your own childhood to know what was cultivated in Dobbs Hollow: violence, prejudice, bigotry. That they're bearing fruit now isn't such a great surprise."

"They'll know each other," Lucy insisted. "Or if they're not sure, they'll have an idea. This is a small town! How could they not? I want to be there when you go after Eric."

"You can come down for the interrogation. Both of you.

In fact, I may need you to come in on it, to provoke him. But you can't be there when we go to the plant for Eric."

"If he's heard something—"

"If he's heard something, we'll get it out of him. I promise you, Lucy."

"But Tim's my brother. I need—"

"What you need is for the case to be workable against whoever killed your mother and kidnapped your brother. And that means I can't let you come to the plant."

Jake coughed. "I'm going to take a walk. Clear my head. I wrote my cell number on the pad we were using to sort things out if you need me before I get back." Lucy nodded, but she wasn't really paying attention as he slipped out the door. Rather, she focused on Ethan.

"I know gathering evidence the right way is important, and I trust you, I do—" To her surprise, Ethan stiffened and gently set her away from him. Lucy felt suddenly cold, and rubbed her arms.

"Ethan?"

"Maybe you shouldn't trust me," he said. He moved away and sat on the couch, refusing to look at her.

"What are you talking about?"

"Christ, Lucy, I'm so sorry." He massaged his knee and stared at the floor. "I tried to tell you earlier, but things kept getting in the way."

"Tell me what?" She dropped down on the sofa next to him and took his big hand in hers, rubbing his long fingers between her own. Still, he didn't raise his eyes.

"After my injury, I had surgeries. Several of them. My knee was a mess. I was on painkillers for months. It wasn't the first time. I'd gone through a similar round of pills and therapy for my shoulder a couple of years earlier. I was still taking the occasional pill when I hurt badly. Not often, maybe one every few weeks. I knew getting off the drugs would prove difficult the second time around; I just didn't realize how much I'd come to depend on them. When I couldn't get the doctors to write scrips for me anymore, I went to guys I knew from my time in Narcotics." He shook his head.

"Eventually, I had to stop. I asked my old lieutenant for help, and he got me into a rehab joint. But withdrawal's a bitch, no matter how nice the environment and how much support you have.

"I was an addict, Lucy. Like your mom. I had taken oxy the morning my partner got killed. If I hadn't, my reaction time might have been faster. I might have realized what was about to happen. My old lieutenant helped me straighten myself out, then told me he'd recommend me for any job where I wouldn't be around drugs or carry a gun, but he'd never give me a recommendation for a job on the force. When Dobbs's job offer came through, I jumped at it. I'm not good at anything but being a cop."

"I doubt that very much. But I've also known any number of cops who've been through AA and NA. What your lieutenant said wasn't fair."

"Yeah, it was. Because, even without the addiction, I couldn't pass the physical, not every day. My shoulder hurts, my knee buckles at random times."

"You forget how long I've spent around police. A whole lot of them can't pass the physical once they've been on the job for a few years."

"I wasn't one of them. If I can't do the job right, I don't want to do it. I came here because I figured the position wouldn't require as much physically or expose me to as much temptation. I was wrong. And now . . .I don't know how involved Dobbs or Billy Pike are in what's going on in this town, but they obviously don't care for you, and it's pretty clear Dobbs knew about my background before he hired me. He thinks he can use my past against me, force me to do what he wants."

Finally, Ethan met Lucy's gaze, and she barely recognized the man she knew in his bleak expression.

"He can't. Ethan, whatever Dobbs thinks, he won't be able to push you."

"Are you sure? Are you certain you can trust me?"

"Of course I am."

"God, Lucy, I'm so sorry for not telling you sooner. I was—" he shook his head, and Lucy felt the fist squeezing her heart ease a tiny bit. "I needed you to believe in me, and I wasn't sure I could even believe in myself."

She hadn't even realized she was holding her breath until she released it in a long, low whoosh. "It's all right. I wouldn't have understood then. Not with my mother's history."

"I swear to you. Whatever it takes to find Tim, we'll do it." His cell rang, and he snatched it from the holster on his belt.

"Donovan."

He didn't speak for several minutes, merely grunting occasionally. Lucy wanted to tear the phone from his hands and listen. Was it about Tim? About the raid they had planned? About Jed Martin or Eric Allenby? Ethan slid an arm around her shoulders and began to absently stroke her neck with his thumb. Her nerves jumped.

"Yeah," he said at last. "See you in a bit." He hung up and turned to Lucy. "That was TJ. She got Farmer's approval for tonight. She's going to go check on the mayor—she's worried about him, hasn't heard anything from him about Drew, and she's used to him haranguing everyone within shouting distance every five minutes—and then she'll be back. She's going to check in with both Scott and Keith, too."

"I'll call Jake, tell him to come back." She pulled out her phone, but Ethan took her hands before she could dial.

"Lucy, I—" Once again he shook his head rather than finishing. With a slight tug on her hands, he pulled her close, then wrapped his arms around her.

For the first time since Artie's phone call, Lucy's muscles unwound. Tim's fate still consumed her mind, but her body recognized the security Ethan offered and sank into it. His lips brushed the top of her head, and she turned her face up for his kiss. He hesitated a moment before loosening his hold and running a calloused finger over her mouth. His eyes were still filled with grief and shadows, and Lucy's heart wrenched. She slipped her arms around his neck and pulled herself up to press her lips to his.

With a groan, Ethan slid his hand into her hair and returned the kiss, his lips warm, at once both soft and hard. His tongue, hot and spicy, laved hers, sending a cascade of sparks through her system. Digging her fingers into the taut muscles of his back, she practically sobbed with the need to be even closer. He was dragging her up and into his lap when a strident beep interrupted them. Ethan closed his eyes for a moment, then set Lucy away while he pulled out his phone once again and glared at the screen.

"It's Keith," he said. "Eric's right where he should be. And he checked in with Scott. Jed's at the dealership, too. Keith will trail Eric until he goes to work, and Scott is going to be sure Jed gets home, at which point Cal will take over. If either of them has Tim, they won't have a chance to get to him without us knowing about it."

He was back in work mode, so Lucy picked up her own phone and called Jake to tell him to come back to the apartment. Now they could do nothing but wait until the time came for the raid and hope that nothing happened in the meantime.

# CHAPTER SIXTEEN

Blood cries out for blood, and I've always believed that
if I caught my mother's murderer I'd kill him on the
spot. For years, that ambition alone kept me in weapons and self-defense classes.


*FROM A BAD DAY TO DIE*

BY LUCY SADLER CALDWELL [DRAFT]

WHATEVER ELSE HE might have been, Eric Allenby was
a lousy security guard. At precisely six twenty-four in the
morning, Ethan punched in the gate code he'd gotten from
Jim Farmer. In the squad car, TJ and Keith followed him,
Toby, and Beau in his truck up the drive to the factory. No
one came out to meet them. Was Eric watching them on
security monitors? Flushing drugs? Sleeping on the job? No
way to tell.

At the front door, Ethan pulled out the key—another
present from Farmer—and let them into the building.
None of them attempted silence. The rubber soles of TJ's
sneakers and Toby's shoes squeaked, Ethan's boots thudded,
Keith's hard-soled shoes slapped, and Beau's nails clicked
on the marble floor of the entryway as they approached the
security desk, but still no sign of Eric. Ethan went around
the desk and looked at the bank of monitors. On the screen
showing some offices, he saw Eric rifling through a file cabinet. Perfect.

Ethan pulled his map of the plant's campus out of his evidence kit and spread it out on the security desk. They stood
in the atrium of the building that housed all the offices. The
factory itself was housed in a separate building connected by
two walkways. They'd be more apt to be successful searching the factory before the machines came to life at eight, but

"

nothing in his experience led Ethan to believe Eric would hide his drugs on the factory floor.

No, he was far more likely to hide them, for example, in a filing cabinet inside the plush inner office of the plant manager. Ethan signaled for the others to follow, and they made their way to the office. The door stood open, and Ethan stepped inside. The security guard sat behind the manager's desk, his feet up on the scarred oak, and Ethan was reminded of the day he'd found Billy Pike sitting in his own office.

"Eric."

"Chief Donovan." Eric dropped his feet, but didn't stand. "What brings you out this way?"

Ethan stepped aside so Toby and Beau could edge by him into the room. As soon as Eric laid eyes on the dog, his expression shifted from casually confident to alert and secretive.

"What the hell is going on? You can't have an animal in here!"

"That's where you're wrong. See, Jim Farmer is concerned that you might be up to no good here all alone in the wee hours of the morning." Ethan nodded to Toby, who slipped off Beau's lead and gave him the command to find.

The dog sniffed around a bit, then headed for Eric, who scrambled to his feet and backed away until he hit the wall.

"Get that creature away from me! I'll hurt him if he so much as touches me!" But Beau was pointing, his nose aimed at Eric's left pocket.

"Eric Allenby," Ethan said, feeling a tight, triumphant smile stretch across his face, "you are under arrest for the possession of methamphetamines." He grabbed Eric's shoulder and turned him to face the wall, then cuffed his hands behind his back before allowing him to face them again. "You have the right to remain silent. Anything you say can and will be used against you in a court of law. You have the right to speak to an attorney, and to have an attorney present during any questioning. If you cannot afford an attorney, one will be provided for you at government expense. Do you understand these rights?"

"Based on what? The word of a fucking dog?"

"Do you understand your rights, Eric?"

"Yes, I understand my fucking rights. My brother's a cop for Christ's sake."

"So's this dog," said Toby. "And in the four years we've been partners, he's never been wrong, not once, about a suspect."

Ethan held Eric still by means of a forearm braced against his chest, restraining him without actually hurting him, while he reached into the pocket at which Beau had pointed. He pulled out three glassine packets.

"Yessir, yessir, three bags full," he said with a grin, dropping the three packets into a brown paper evidence bag and handing it off to Keith. "Now, I wonder whether your customers come to you, or you go to them. I'll say you have a spot out in the woods where you meet. Or at least, you don't allow them near the plant. Maybe you meet them at Rosalita's. Or at Belle Pointe, where Drew was murdered."

"Fuck you. That's for personal use."

"Yeah? We'll see what Beau says. When we search the rest of this place, I'm betting we find more than enough to put you away for distribution."

"Yeah, especially after we go over your house with a fine-tooth comb."

Eric's face paled.

"Besides, Eric," Ethan leaned in, "you don't look like a tweaker to me. I'd lay odds you don't use at all. I'm also betting we find more than just drugs when we start tearing your life apart."

"You won't find a damned thing."

"No? Well, that's good. Because maybe if we can't find any evidence of your other activities, your partner won't feel the need to get rid of you. You wouldn't much enjoy being dressed the way poor Juan Ramirez was, would you?"

"I have no idea what you mean." But Eric wouldn't meet his eyes. He'd done it. Or at least he'd taken part.

"Of course you don't." Ethan turned to TJ. "You and Keith take Eric here down to the station and get him booked while Toby and I let Beau do his thing here. Make sure when you get him back to the

station you Mirandize him again. I don't want anyone letting him off because he's ignorant."

"Gotcha."

"And call the DA and let him know what's going on. Tell him we'll be amending the warrant soon enough. Distribution, possibly murder."

"Murder! Fuck that! You can't pin that spic's murder on me!"

"Who said I meant Juan Ramirez? We've had a lot of murders around here lately, Eric. Drew Dobbs, Renee Josephs, Richie Mack . . ."

"I didn't do it! I didn't do any of them!"

"We'll see." He stepped away and let TJ and Keith drag Eric, still screaming curses at him, from the room.

By seven fifteen, Beau had located Eric's stash behind the kick plate beneath the cabinets in the break room. Toby and Ethan collected and catalogued it, then settled in to wait for Chuck Hemming.

When Hemming arrived a few minutes later, Ethan recognized him. He'd seen the man around town, at Maxie's and Rosalita's. Pudgy and pasty-faced, he didn't present a threatening image, but Ethan wasn't letting him off the hook. Hemming hung around with Eric Allenby, and he was about to pay for his choice of pals.

"Sorry to bother you at work, Mr. Hemming," Ethan said,

gesturing to one of the chairs in the room, "but we need to have a little chat. See, this morning before you got here, we arrested your pal Eric Allenby for possession. By this afternoon, that charge will be updated, as we intend to include several other charges before he goes to trial."

"Eric?" Hemming stared at him, then sank into the chair. "You arrested Eric?"

"I have to tell you up front, everyone I've asked has mentioned how close the two of you are, so I'd have a hard time believing he kept you in the dark about all his activities."

"He did!" Hemming's fair skin flushed. "I don't know anything about his business. We're not close at all!"

"Really? Because Eric's name, along with yours and Jed Martin's, keeps popping up everywhere I turn."

"No! Those guys, they're good buddies. I hang out with them sometimes, sure, but it's a small town and we went to high school together. It's nothing more than that. Like the other night. Jed called me and said we should get together for drinks at Rosalita's. When I got there, Eric was already there. Jed must have called him first. Those two are tight as twins!"

"What night was that?"

"Friday. Night before last."

The night of the truck crash. Ethan's muscles tensed, but he locked the reaction inside, breathing slowly, refusing to give away his hand. "What time?"

"I don't know. Maybe nine? Ten?"

Ethan felt frustration eat at his stomach. If it were nine, no way could Jed and Eric have been responsible for the truck. They couldn't have gotten all the way to Rosalita's in time. Ten, though, was a different story.

"Which one. Nine or ten? Whichever you tell me, I'll check out with the bartender, so think hard about your answer."

"Closer to ten, I guess. I was . . .ummm . . .thinking about going to bed."

Oh, there was a lie. What had Hemming really been up to the night of the crash?

"So Jed called you at home?"

"Yeah."

"And your phone records will bear that out?"

"Well, he called my cell number, but I was at home. Everyone uses my cell. It's easier."

"I see." Ethan waited for three beats. "How much do you know about cell towers, Mr. Hemming?"

Not much, he hoped. Just as he hoped Hemming didn't realize he'd need a warrant, for which he had no probable cause, to examine his phone records.

The man squirmed in his chair. "I wasn't doing anything wrong!"

"No?"

"No. I had come into town, it's true. But I wasn't doing anything wrong."

"So you said. Mind telling me what you were up to?"

Hemming's eyes slid to the side. "There's this woman. I've been trying to work up the nerve to ask her out. I was in front of her apartment complex when Jed called."

An apartment complex? TJ's complex? Where Lucy had spent the night? But how could Hemming have found out so quickly? If the man didn't know, Ethan wasn't about to enlighten him.

"You do know stalking is illegal?"

"I'm not stalking anyone! Shit! Do you have any idea how embarrassing it is to have to admit I can't just walk up to a woman and ask her out?"

"Okay. So you're sitting in front of this woman's apartment and Jed calls and invites you for a drink. You get to Rosalita's and find him and Eric Allenby already there. What kind of mood were they in?"

"I don't know. Normal." Hemming was practically crying.

If Ethan hadn't been so pissed off and so damn worried, he might almost have felt sorry for the guy. Almost.

"Is it normal for them to invite you out at ten o'clock on a night you have to be at work the next morning?"

"Actually, no."

"Did they give you a clue as to why they should have done so this time?"

"No. And I didn't ask. If Jed's been dealing drugs with Eric, no one told me. And whatever else they did, I wasn't part of it."

"All right, then. You're free to go for the moment, Mr. Hemming. But please keep yourself available in case any further questions arise."

Hemming stared for a moment, then bolted like a rabbit.

"Hinky," Toby commented.

"Yeah, but I doubt he had anything to do with Juan Ramirez's murder. He's too skittish to manage that kind of brutality. He'd vomit all over the place and have an ulcer the size of Texas."

"True that. So what's next?"

Ethan grinned. "Next, I get to go after Jed Martin. I can't tell you how much I'm looking forward to it. You want to stick around?"

"I'd love to, but I have to get back to Houston. Can I ask you a question?"

"Shoot."

"You don't plan to stay here forever, really? Watching you today . . .you're wasted here."

"I'm not making friends here, so I doubt I'll be reappointed. But the HPD sent me off with disability, and I don't know how to do anything but police work." Ethan shrugged. "Whatcha gonna do?"

"Hell if I know. I'm coming up on my twenty-five in two years. My wife wants me to retire. What the hell would I do all day?"

Ethan laughed bitterly. "You figure it out, you let me know."

"Will do. Now, let's get the hell out of here. Poor Beau can't take the smell of dog food any longer and neither can I."

⌒

KEITH AND TJ met Ethan outside the interrogation room at the station.

"How's he doing?" Ethan asked.

"Sweating bullets and spitting mad," said Keith. "He asked for his lawyer, so we called the man. Thing is, he takes long weekends in the summer. It'll be another hour before he gets here from his lake house."

"Damn shame."

"Ain't it just? How do you want to tackle this? We have nothing on him for the murder."

"TJ, call your house and get Lucy and Jake over here. Tell Scott we've brought his brother in. Ask him to come in and talk to me. I'll explain everything to him face to face."

TJ headed for her desk, and Ethan turned to Keith. "Where's Sullivan?"

Brian Sullivan had been the Adams County DA for eleven years. Ethan had met him twice, but hadn't had to deal with him professionally since taking office, as most of the crimes committed in Dobbs Hollow were too minor to merit his direct oversight. Murder, on the other hand, required the man himself, not one of his underlings.

"He's over at Maxie's. He said to call him when we had a suspect for him."

"Get him over here. I don't want to wait when I get grounds for an arrest warrant for Jed Martin."

Keith made the call, then asked, "What do we do now?"

"How well do you know Jed Martin?"

"Hardly at all, though I bought my car from him."

"Anyone in the house close to him?"

"Not that I know of. Cal recommended his dealership. I think his sister might have dated Jed in high school."

"Okay. Then take Cal with you and drive out to the dealership and ask Jed to come in for a chat. Tell him we've picked up Eric Allenby on drug charges and Eric's pointing a finger at him, but that for the moment we just want to talk to him. When he gets here, we need to be sure he and Eric see each other."

"Gotcha."

Keith went to fetch Cal, and Ethan let himself into the observation room to keep any eye on Eric. Keith hadn't exaggerated about the man's nerves being shot. He checked his watch, got up and paced the room for a while, checked his watch again, and sat back down. He jiggled his knee, tapped his thumbs on the metal table, checked his watch again, and went back to pacing.

Scott arrived at the same time as Brian Sullivan and joined Ethan in the viewing room. He looked awful. This was killing him, but he was trying to hang on. Ethan laid a hand on his shoulder, and they stood together in silence for a long moment.

"He's waiting for his lawyer?" Scott asked at last.

"Yeah. I'm sorry it has to go this way, but we got him cold on this."

"Drugs."

"Definitely drugs. And from what Chuck Hemming said, chances are Eric was involved in Ramirez's murder, or at least the disposal of his body."

"No way."

"Then maybe his buddy Jed did it alone. But unless Eric gives us a wedge to use against Jed, we can't help him. You know it."

"You really believe he did it?"

"I'm sorry, Scott. I wish I could say different, but I can't. It's possible Eric found out about the murder after the fact, but right now everything points to him. He's the one whose business Ramirez was stealing, he's the one Richie Mack trusted and bought from."

"Hell. Can I talk to him?"

"Go right ahead. But remind him that everything he says will be recorded and that if he wants to wait to talk to you until after his lawyer gets here, he has that right. And no interrogation; he's asked for his lawyer. If we screw this up and it comes back to bite me on the ass in court, I won't be the only one."

"Yeah, okay."

Ethan turned up the sound as Scott greeted his brother. While Scott was explaining the fact that their conversation could be recorded, and that Eric didn't have to say anything, TJ slipped into the observation room.

"You think he'll talk to Scott?"

"Not to him, no. But at him. If I have their relationship pegged right, Scott will piss him off. I only hope he can provoke a response before the lawyer gets here."

"Do you think Eric has anything to do with my brother's murder? Or Renee's? Or Cecile's?"

Ethan rubbed a hand through his hair, trying to push away the headache plaguing him.

"Hell if I know. When this all started, you said the week Cecile was killed made Dobbs Hollow seem like Stepford }to you. Remember?" She nodded. "I'm beginning to understand what you meant. Every town has drug dealers. And where there are drugs there is violence. But this . . .I don't see how the hell it all ties together."

In the interview room, Scott had leaned over, pressing his palms into the table and staring at Eric. Through the loudspeaker, his voice crackled and hissed, but Ethan doubted it sounded so great in person, either.

"You need to tell the police whatever you can about Jed. I know you didn't kill Ramirez. You couldn't do that. But they'll pin it on you if they can't get Jed." Even with the crappy sound system, Ethan could hear the plea in Scott's voice, and it tore at him. He shouldn't have let Scott go in. It was too much to ask of anyone.

"I couldn't do what?"

"Kill a man! For God's sake, Eric, listen to me! They have you dead to rights on the drugs. You can't get out of that one no matter what kind of tricks your lawyer tries to pull. But you don't have to take the fall for Jed's actions."

"You don't think I could kill a man? Why not? Lack of balls? Lack of brains? Shit, killing is easy."

"Don't say that. Jesus, Eric."

Ethan's cell buzzed with a text message, but he ignored it.

"Why not? Destroys your precious image of your baby brother as an idiot? Well, too fucking bad. Yeah, Jed came up with the idea of hunting the Mexicans. But the truck—" before he could finish his thought, the door banged open and a heavyset, florid man in a suit shoved his way in.

"Shut your mouth, and shut it right now, Eric."

After a moment, Ethan recognized the stranger as Thom Henderson, a criminal attorney.

"You"—Henderson pointed at Scott—"out. Now. We'll have a chat later about the conflict of interest your presence here embodies."

Ethan turned off the sound so Eric could talk to his lawyer in private and looked at the text.

*Lawyer on the way in. Pissed.*

"Well, that was illuminating," he said to TJ.

"Hunting Mexicans? Please tell me that doesn't mean what I think it means."

"We'll find out when Jed gets here. Let me go talk to Scott. You see whether Lucy and Jake have made it over yet."

Ethan stepped out of the room and found Scott leaning against the wall, doubled over. He rested a hand on the man's back for a moment.

"Where did I go wrong?"

"Scott, you didn't create Eric. He's your brother. And we still don't know how deep his involvement runs. He said something about Jed hunting Mexicans, but he never admitted to being part of those hunts. It's possible he only found out about them recently, when Jed needed his help to deal with Ramirez."

"You think so?"

No, Ethan didn't think so. But Scott needed an assurance to grab hold of at the moment. "Right now, we have to work with what information we have, not with speculation."

Scott straightened. "Yeah. Yeah, okay."

"Keith and Cal have gone to pick up Jed. You know him better than any of us, so if you're up to it, I'd like you to watch the interrogation and give me your impressions."

"Okay."

"I don't have history with this guy, so fill me in. He was a big football star, right?"

"Yeah. Big star, big ego, which he's never lost." Scott's brow wrinkled, and Ethan saw him transform from worried brother to analytical cop. "He has a tendency to blame others for his problems. He got sacked on the field—normal accident in play—and it ruined his chances at pro ball, which he blamed on the school for not providing enough protection, stuff like that. He married his high school sweetheart, then divorced her because she supposedly wasn't supportive enough in his time of need. Load of crap. He wanted adoration, not marriage. When the dealership ran into financial trouble, he blamed his salespeople, fired a couple of them over it, even."

"He a bigot? From what Eric said, he chose Mexicans to kill." Suddenly several mismatched pieces of evidence fell together, and Ethan knew where his interrogation would begin.

"He could be. His dad definitely was. But Jed's also crafty.

He could have chosen illegals because no one would report them missing."

A knock on the door signaled the arrival of Jake and Lucy. Before Ethan could explain where they stood, the door opened again, and Sheriff Pike barged in. Lucy stepped backward, and without even thinking Ethan stepped between her and Pike.

"Can I help you, Sheriff?"

"What the hell? You make arrests in my county and you don't call me in? I have to hear about it from the DA?"

"We're not working your case, Sheriff. Nothing indicates that Eric Allenby had anything to do with Drew Dobbs' death."

"Sorry, Donovan, I have to overrule you there," Sullivan said. "If Eric was, indeed, killing Mexicans in the woods, chances are good he's responsible for the dead girl they found buried near Dobbs's murder site."

No arguing that logic, so Ethan shrugged and caught Pike, Jake, and Lucy up on where they stood. By the time he had arranged a code with Sullivan to buzz Ethan's cell when he'd heard enough for an arrest warrant, Keith and Cal had returned with Jed Martin. Since the station had only one interrogation room, Ethan shifted Eric and his lawyer to his own office to continue their private conversation, posting a guard outside the door to be sure Eric couldn't leave. Then he led Jed into the interrogation room.

"I've tried to be patient with you, Donovan," Martin blustered as soon as he entered the room. "But seriously, I have a business to run, and you're interfering with it. I came down here of my own accord today, but this is the last time."

"And we're very appreciative of that, Mr. Martin." Ethan had to work to keep his tone smooth and even. "Good cop" had always been his partner's role. But they had nothing concrete on Martin yet, and he needed to proceed carefully.

"You're a smart man, Mr. Martin. You know we have too

much on our plate right now to worry about minor code enforcement issues, little infractions people might feel the need to hide. Am I right?"

"I don't know what you're getting at."

"I got the sense when we came to see you that you might be hiding something from me."

Martin narrowed his eyes.

"I'm betting you were worried when you saw the list I brought you, the one with your company's name on it. Because you hire illegals to clean your shop, don't you? One of them dropped the list in the woods at some point, and we picked it up. If that's all you're hiding, you can go ahead and tell me. I swear to you, all you have to do is stop. I'm not going after you for it. It's not like I can even prove it without more than the list, anyway. I need to figure out whether that list has anything to do with Renee."

Martin thought for so long, Ethan almost lost faith, but at last he answered. "You're not going to string me up if I do?"

"Hell, no. They're illegals." Ethan managed a little laugh, though it turned his stomach. "Not good for many jobs other than cleaning toilets. You want me to get the DA in here to swear you're off the hook for hiring illegals, or can we talk about it?"

"Maybe it would be safer if we did that. You know, just in case."

"Sure. Let me go call him."

Ethan left Jed at the table and walked back into the viewing room. "Let him sit," he said to Sullivan, who was preparing to go reassure Martin. "I don't want him to know you've been here all this time."

He turned to Lucy. "If we need you, you'll be okay to come in and push his buttons?"

Pale but composed, she nodded. He wished he could wrap her in his arms and take her far from this windowless little room, far from this inhospitable town, somewhere she would be safe and happy. But he couldn't. He settled for laying a hand on her shoulder while they waited for Jed to become anxious enough. Just as he appeared to be considering walking out of the interview room, both Ethan and Brian Sullivan headed in to join him.

"Sorry that took so long," Ethan said. "I had a hard time locating the DA, but here he is. Do you two know each other?"

"I don't believe we've met," said Sullivan, holding out a hand.

"Yeah, well, not exactly the best circumstances," Martin said.

The two men shook hands, and Sullivan smiled. "Well, I hope I can ease your mind a little. Ethan tells me you've agreed to talk to him about your hiring practices under condition of immunity against prosecution for hiring illegal immigrants?"

"Yeah."

"That's not a problem. I just want you to be aware that this immunity only counts toward previous violations. If you're arrested at any point in the future for hiring undocumented workers, this immunity won't count toward offenses after today."

Sullivan was good at this. Ethan supposed most attorneys, most criminal attorneys at least, had to have some acting skills. They'd agreed Sullivan needed to be disapproving, but not overly harsh, and he was playing his role perfectly.

"Yeah, I get that."

"All right, then. We have a deal." He held out a hand again, and once again Jed took it. "That's it?" he asked suspiciously. "We don't need any forms?"

"Our conversation's all on tape," Sullivan assured him.

Martin nodded. "Okay."

Sullivan excused himself and left. Ethan smiled across the table at Jed. "So. We can talk now?"

"Yeah, we can talk."

"You hire illegal immigrants to work in your shop?"

"Yeah."

"And the list I showed you, the list that was found in the woods near Renee Josephs's body, that was an assignment list you would have given to one of those men or women?"

"Yeah. If you don't lay things out very specifically, they don't get done."

"Of course. You're running a business. You have to be clear about what you want."

"Exactly."

"But you never hired Renee Josephs?" Feel safe, feel as if you have nothing to hide.

"My God, no."

"Where do you find the people you hire? A service?"

Martin's eyes shifted away. Guilty as hell.

"No, no. It's not that structured. They're just from the day-labor stations."

"Could you find one of the ones who's worked for you in the past? I'm just trying to cross my t's, you understand. To be sure the list is what it appears to be and no more, and that it's not related to Renee Josephs in any way."

"I could probably find one. But, you know, they move around all the time. They might not be at the same place I picked them up before."

"Okay. Do you have any of their names?"

"Names?"

"Yeah. See, I am trying to trace one guy in particular, see what kind of jobs he worked, and I thought you might know him since you occasionally delve into that community."

Jed's eye twitched. "I don't usually ask their names, and I pay them cash, so I don't have to write their names on checks or anything. And they're mostly women. Women clean better than men."

"Huh." Ethan leaned back in his chair and steepled his fingers under his chin. "That's confusing to me, I have to admit.

Because Eric Allenby says you knew Juan Ramirez. In fact, he says you killed him."

"What the fuck are you talking about?"

"I'm talking about murder, Jed. And you have no immunity for that." He read Jed his rights and Jed reacted precisely the way he'd expected.

"I don't need a lawyer," he spat. "I don't even know any Juan Ramirez."

"That's quite possible. See, your buddy Eric told us all about your little hunting game. I haven't had a chance to ask him yet whether you asked your victims' names. But one of them screwed you, Jed. What did you do, wait around after work and ask her if she needed a ride home?"

Ethan stood and leaned over the table, getting into Jed's face. He needed this to work. Even if it did, there was a good chance they wouldn't get Jed on the murders without finding evidence on the bodies they now knew were out there. But at this point, Ethan had moved on, though Martin didn't need to know that.

"You set her loose in the woods to have your fun, but she had that chore list in her pocket and she dropped it. I'm betting once you're behind bars, we find someone in the Mexican community willing to stand up and say she worked at your shop. Or maybe I'll just go down the hall and ask Eric."

"I have no idea—"

"Yeah, yeah. No idea what I'm talking about. I've heard it all before. But, see, at the moment Eric's primary concern is saving his own ass. He claims all he's ever done is help you dispose of Ramirez's body once you were through torturing and murdering him. And, to be frank, he doesn't seem like a killer. A drug dealer, sure. But not a killer. So I'm inclined to believe him. Plus, there's the fact that his brother is a good cop. That carries a lot of weight."

Ethan let that sink in for a few seconds, then pulled a

swab out of his pocket. "Want to volunteer your DNA, or shall I get a court order?"

"No judge in this county will give you a warrant to invade my privacy like that!"

Ethan shrugged. "You're probably right. After all, I'm still an outsider. Which is why I won't be the one requesting the warrant; Tara Jean will. She may not have turned out the way folks here expected, she may have disappointed her daddy, but she's still a Dobbs of Dobbs Hollow. She'll have that warrant minutes after she asks for it.

"Of course, if you've done nothing wrong, you shouldn't worry about us checking your DNA."

"Shit. Go ahead and swab me. You won't find anything."

Ethan took the swab, then handed it Keith. "Take this in to Jake and see if he can get the FBI to run it for us. They'll be faster than the state labs."

"The FBI! Why the hell are you bothering the FBI with one dead Mexican? Or even two?" Jed swallowed. "If there are two, I mean. I wouldn't know. As that DNA will show you, I haven't ever touched any damned Mexicans."

"Did I say the immigrant murders were the only ones we were investigating? I don't recall saying that."

"What, you think I killed Drew? Everyone knows your girlfriend shot him. And it's Billy Pike's case, anyway."

Ethan remained silent.

"The Josephs girl? Shit, the night she was killed, I was playing poker. You know that! You've got nothing on me. Nothing."

"I'm actually concerned with DNA from an older case, Jed. See, twenty years ago, criminals didn't know about DNA. Hell, most cops didn't know about it, and those that did didn't have access to labs for testing. If a woman pulled out your hair while you were stabbing her, the most the cops could do was a microscopic comparison of the found hairs to yours. If the ME found skin and blood under her nails, the best they could hope for was a type match, which still left a lot of room for doubt. Even fingerprints only worried guys who were already apt to be suspects, because a lot of small departments were still doing manual fingerprint checks and IAFIS didn't exist until 1999."

Jed shifted in his chair, and Ethan smiled. "You sure you don't want a lawyer, Jed? Not that you have a hope in hell of getting out of this, with or without one. Not when Cecile Sadler died with a fist full of your hair and your DNA under her nails. But you should have a sporting chance. Maybe he can get you life in prison rather than the death penalty." Before the man could speak, Ethan rushed on. He needed his offer of legal representation on the record, but he didn't want Jed to seriously consider it.

"Or maybe what you'd really like, given that you're about to spend the rest of whatever life you have behind bars, is to tell Lucy why you killed her mother. Would you get a charge out of that?"

He knocked on the mirror behind him and a couple of seconds later Lucy entered the room. He'd never seen her face so expressionless. Even her eyes, usually filled with life, betrayed nothing. Was this too much to ask of her? But they had no real evidence, despite his threats. Only a few hairs had been preserved, and they'd never been tested to see whether they carried follicular tags. The tips of Cecile's fingernails had been kept, along with the skin she'd scraped from her attacker, but Ethan had no idea what time might have done to that evidence. He desperately needed a confession, and Lucy presented their best hope of prying one loose.

"Hello, Jed," she said.

"Well, if it isn't little Lucy Sadler. Still playing the prude, or have you let the chief here into your pants? Probably not. Is that why he's so anxious to solve your momma's murder? Did you promise him a little sugar if he did what no other man has been able to do?"

Ethan wanted to vault across the table and strangle the man, but Lucy just stared calmly at him as if he were a strange species of insect she couldn't decide whether she needed to crush or not.

"Poor little Jed," she said at last. "Not even good enough for the town whore. I watched from my window night she told you to get lost."

"You bitch!" Jed lunged for Lucy, but she skipped back out of the way and Ethan slapped his hands on Jed's shoulders and pressed him back down into his chair. His hands, so close to Jed's neck, itched to close around the man's throat. Jed would be dead long before anyone could pull him off.

Lucy seemed to sense his rage. Her eyes met his, and now, far from empty, they were filled with determination. She gave her head an almost imperceptible shake.

"Face facts, Jed," she taunted. "You're a poor substitute for a man."

"You think you're so superior?" Beneath Ethan's hands, Jed struggled to rise.

"You're going to make it worse on yourself if you get out of that seat, little man," Ethan taunted. "You know even if I let you get to her, she'd take you apart in thirty seconds flat."

"I'm not like those poor Hispanic women you chased through the woods," Lucy said, leaning over. "I fight back. I'm stronger than you are. Better than you in every way."

"Yeah? Your mother thought she was better, too." Beneath Ethan's hands, fury vibrated through Jed's body. "But I showed her. She begged at the end. Begged for her life. Didn't do her any good, though. I slaughtered her. I should have done the same to you, the minute I heard you were back."

The phone in Ethan's back pocket vibrated. The DA had heard enough. Ethan could read Martin his rights, but he had more questions of his own first. Lucy had done her part; now it was up to him. He eased his hands off Jed's shoulders and leaned down on the table next to him, drawing his attention away from Lucy.

"And Tim? Where's he?"

"Tim? You mean her brother?" Jed's face went blank with confusion as he glanced from Ethan to Lucy and back. "What the fuck does he have to do with anything?"

"Make this easier on yourself, Jed. You know we have you cold on any number of counts. Anything you do to help us can only help you."

"I dunno what you want." A crafty look entered Jed's eye. "Did something happen to your brother, little Lucy? Did you misplace him? I could help you find him. I know everyone in this town. They respect me. They talk to me. I can find him for you."

Ethan avoided the plea he was sure he'd see in Lucy's eyes, focusing on Jed instead. The man knew nothing. No point in prolonging the interrogation.

"Don't even think about it, Martin. You can't con your way back onto the streets. Jedediah Martin, you are under arrest for the murder of Cecile Sadler. . . ." Even as Ethan recited the familiar words by rote, his attention shifted to Lucy. Her composure never faltered, but he could almost feel her nerves humming.

Seeming dazed, Jed stood, and Ethan cuffed his hands behind his back. He pushed Jed out the door, leaving Lucy standing alone, and passed him off to Cal to take down the hall to the holding cells, where he would wait to be taken over to the county courthouse for arraignment. After that, presuming he was denied bail, which the DA had promised would be the case, he and Eric would both await trial in the county courthouse.

He hurried back into the interrogation room, where he found Lucy sitting on the floor with TJ next to her.

"He killed her because she wouldn't sleep with him." Impending hysteria added a sharp edge to Lucy's voice. "Of all the men she could have turned down and didn't, she had to pick the psychotic killer to get some standards with."

Ethan jerked his head at TJ, who rose and left. He took her spot, putting his arm around Lucy and pulling her into him.

"She always had standards, sugar. She'd never have slept with anyone in your school, and she never brought men into the house. You stressed that yourself. He broke her rules, rules she set to protect you and Tim, so she sent him and his pals on their way. You've lived in Dallas. I'm sure you saw women there who truly lived without standards, whose lives had beaten any fight out of them. You can't say that about your mother."

"No."

"I'm sorry I didn't push harder about Tim, Lucy. But Jed—"

"Didn't know anything," Lucy finished for him. "I could tell. I just don't know what I'm supposed to do now."

"We'll figure it out. C'mon." He stood and held out a hand to help her up. She took it, then leaned into him and wrapped her arms around his waist. His throat clogged with an emotion he didn't dare put a name to, and he stroked her soft hair, soothing them both.

He pressed a kiss to the top of her head. "Let's get out of here." With an arm over her shoulders, reluctant to let her go, he led her out into the hallway. "I have to talk to Sullivan for a minute to be sure everything goes smoothly, and then I'll take you back to TJ's. Okay?" He tilted her face up. The loss and fear in her eyes hit him like a bullet to his heart.

"We'll find him, sweetheart. I swear it."

Lucy nodded. He gripped her hand, refusing to be separated from her, and slipped back into the observation room where DA Sullivan was chatting with Keith and making notes on a small pad. TJ stood off to one side, but Billy Pike had left, for which Ethan could only be thankful.

"What did Jake say about the swab?" Ethan asked Keith.

"He'll do it. He's not happy about it. Says he's supposed to be on leave of absence from the Bureau, but they'll work it up for him anyway. I explained the issue keeping the evidence at the county lab."

"He wouldn't explain it to me, however," said Sullivan.

"Pike left right after Jed confessed to killing Cecile," Keith explained. "I guess he couldn't take hearing the murderer his dad never found had been under his nose the whole time."

Sullivan made a rolling motion with his hands. "What does that have to do with anything?"

"I don't trust Billy Pike," Ethan stated. Better to get the truth out there, bald as it might be.

"Why the hell not? His father held your very position until he keeled over from heart failure on the job eight years back. Billy started going on rounds with him when he was still just a kid. Hell, Al Pike took Billy to Cecile Sadler's murder scene. He's been working as a cop since eighteen. No one has a better background for the job, and he's proven himself a great sheriff."

"But his father didn't solve this crime. And that presents a conflict of interest." Ethan hoped that would be enough, but still Sullivan protested.

"It presents a motivation."

Ethan pulled out his last card. "You heard Eric and Jed. They were hunting Mexicans in our woods. If this turns into an international incident, do you really want it on your plate? Hell, no. We dump the evidence of our serial killer on the FBI and let them cope with the fallout."

"Serial killer?"

"Sir, with all due respect, you didn't see Juan Ramirez's remains. He'd been carved up like a deer, and it sure didn't look as if any first-timer had done it. I can't hide that fact. Everyone in town already knows. And then there are the remains the sheriff's men found in the woods. Also probably Mexican, also with her throat cut by a hunting knife.

It's only a matter of time before the news spreads across the border. If we don't appear to be taking this seriously enough, we're in for a world of hurt."

Sullivan nodded slowly. "Good thinking."

THE COMMANDER PUSHED the chair into its place and grinned at the man sitting in it, bug-eyed with hate and anger. Today was going to go down in history as one of the greatest days in his life. It would only be better if he could take the credit for what was about to happen himself. But the plans had fallen into place too well. He'd always planned on blaming Drew for the rapes if anyone found out about them—which that fucking bitch Lucy and her weakling, drug addict boyfriend Donovan had—but that had been pure necessity.

This was art. In one swoop, he was going to take down everyone who'd ever sneered, ever looked down on him. And he was going to have Lucy Sadler at his mercy. His cock twitched just thinking about what he could do to her. With a helpless audience watching, no less.

He snapped a few pictures while the man in the chair struggled against his bonds and screamed behind his gag. In the corner, another body lay trussed like a Christmas goose. That one was out cold, but he didn't matter, anyway. Not yet. He'd have his turn in the spotlight soon enough. Still, getting a shot in now would complete his pictorial journal of the day.

He always kept photos. The invention of the digital camera was the best thing ever. No developing, no evidence anyone could find. He'd printed out a couple of the pictures from the games he and Drew had played with of the ones who had lived, and he'd hidden them in Drew's room. Eventually, the cops would get around to searching there. For the moment, Drew was a victim, and the Dobbs home sacrosanct. But not for long.

He put the camera down and took out a bottle of chloroform, a rag, and a hypo filled with oxycodone. Always better to knock a victim out with chloroform first, then inject. He'd learned that early on, when a needle broke off in the vein of a struggling girl.

"Time for you to go to sleep," he said. "When you wake up, your darling Lucy will be here to join you."

LUCY WANTED TO scream as the DA went over a seemingly endless list of questions with Ethan. But at last Sullivan had everything he needed, and he went to get the ball rolling on the arrests, leaving TJ, Lucy, and Ethan alone. The minute he did, Ethan let go of Lucy's hand and pulled her into his arms again.

"We found your mother's killer, sugar. If we can solve a murder nearly two decades cold, you know we can find Tim." She could feel the promise, like a blood-sworn oath, sinking into her.

TJ blew out a long breath. "I think my father may have him," she said. "He wasn't home yesterday when I tried to see him, and I went to his usual haunts and couldn't find him. The thing is, I don't know how he would have done it. How could he know Tim was coming back to town? How could he get him alone?"

"And why?" Lucy asked.

"If he believes you killed Drew, he may try to use Tim to get back at you." Ethan's grip tightened. "We can ask him when we find him."

Lucy's phone rang. When she pulled it from her pocket, the display read "Tim," and her stomach clenched as she held it to her ear.

"Don't say a word," a low, electronically disguised rumble warned, "or I put a bullet in your darling brother's brain. And wouldn't that be a damned shame."

Lucy began to shake. She heard Ethan say her name, but his voice came from miles away.

"I'm going to let him say a few words so you'll know he's still alive."

Tim's voice trembled when he spoke to her. "Don't come, Lucy! Don't—"

But then the strange, electronic voice returned. "Here's how it's going to go down. You will make whatever excuse you need to get away from your friends. You will drive to your house. We'll be watching, so we'll know if you're not alone. Don't piss us off. More instructions when you get there."

The phone went dead, but Lucy continued to hold it to her ear, unable to let go for a long moment.

"Lucy!" Ethan shook her slightly. "Talk to me, sweetheart."

"They have him. Dobbs, whoever. He has Tim. He's going to kill him."

"No, he's not. Tell me what he said."

Lucy shook her head, trying to pull free of Ethan's grasp, but he only held her tighter. "Talk to me, Luce. You know you can't do this alone."

"They said I had to." She repeated the instructions she'd been given. "They said . . .I know them, Ethan. They'll torture him. I can't let that happen."

"And if you do as you're told, you think they'll miraculously let him go? It's not happening. And you're not leaving here without me."

"I can't let anything happen to Tim on my account. I can't."

"I'm not asking you to. All I am saying is that if you're going, I'm going."

"No, you're not. Whoever this is, I don't want to set them off if they really are watching."

"I can't let you do this by yourself. Lucy, please. Whatever else you want. Anything. Just don't ask me for that."

"There's no choice. You'll have to tie me up to stop me, and if anything happens to Tim I'll never forgive either of us."

Ethan ran a hand through his hair and her heart ached. Had their roles been reversed, she wasn't sure she could manage what she was asking of him.

But he was stronger than she was. "Give me a minute. Do not move." He glanced at TJ, who nodded—apparently, they were ganging up on her. Ethan disappeared for a moment and returned with a small device. "Give me a minute to program in my cell." He punched a bunch of buttons on the palm-sized yellow-and-black gadget, then handed it to her. "It's not much, because they'll find it if they look, but it's the best I have right now."

"What is it?"

"Personal GPS tracker. A bunch of companies make them. Works on satellite rather than cell towers or anything, so it usually doesn't fail. Just press this button"—he pointed to a rubber button with a little globe on it—"and it will send your location to my cell. Press the one that says SOS on it, and it will inform emergency services.

"At least this will allow me to keep track of you for a while, because for damn sure the house isn't the last spot they'll have you go. It's a crime scene, after all. Unless they're planning to shoot you on the spot when you arrive—"

"Which they aren't. Anyone who wanted me dead that badly and that quickly could have done the job easily by now. There's more to this."

"Lucy." She saw his Adam's apple shift as he swallowed. "I can't find you tomorrow laid out like Renee Josephs."

She stepped into his arms for a quick, fierce hug, a comfort to both of them. "You won't. I'll send you a GPS link as soon as I get to the house, and then after I move."

"I'll call the others, update them. We'll all be waiting for your signal. And we'll be as close behind you as we can."

Suddenly near tears, Lucy nodded. She leaned up and pressed her lips to Ethan's, then ran for the door.

ON THE DRIVE to her old home, she checked her mirrors compulsively, but could see no one following her. Still, she didn't dare call Ethan, though hearing his voice would have been wonderful.

Crime-scene tape blocked access to the house itself, but a red SUV sat at the curb. No sooner had she pulled up than her cell rang.

"What took you so long?" asked the voice. "Get out of your car, and get in the Jeep. The doors are unlocked and the keys are on the passenger side seat. There's also a prepaid cell there. Hang up this phone, then drop it on the driveway. I will call you back on that one."

Lucy did as instructed. While adjusting the driver's seat in the Jeep, she reached behind her to the small of her back and pushed the GPS tracking button on the device Ethan had given her.

"Leave this line open," the voice ordered as soon as she answered the second cell. "Follow my directions, and I don't want to hear you talking to anyone else or repeating my instructions."

"I'm not wearing a wire. You have my brother."

"Better safe than sorry. If you need me to repeat a command, just say so. Don't ask if you have it right."

"That's fine, but I want to talk to Tim again before I go anywhere."

"You don't get to set conditions."

"Then I'm staying right here." Was he watching? Lucy

opened the door of the Jeep. "Stop that! You don't leave the vehicle, or I'll hurt him. Tell her I mean it, boy."

Tim came on the line. "Luce, don't be stupid. He won't let either of us go."

"Just hang on, Timmy. I'm coming."

"You spoke to him. Now close the door and head down the Post Road to where it turns onto the Lake Trail."

"I don't know where that is."

"Don't worry, I'll tell you when you get close."

Turn by turn, that creepy, digitally altered voice guided her deeper into the woods around the lake as if he were a personal GPS. He'd meant it when he said he was watching. He might just have a tracker on the Jeep, but he might also have video inside. With every turn, she found a way—by stretching, adjusting her seat belt, pretending to scratch—to surreptitiously press the button that would send Ethan her location.

"Now, you walk," the voice said when she reached the end of any drivable road and the trees became too dense for the Jeep to negotiate. She put her hands on her back and stretched her spine, triggering the tracking device once again, then set out as directed.

⌒

"Where the hell is she going?" Ethan and TJ sat in his truck a block from Lucy's old house. Without any idea what kind of surveillance might have been set up, they couldn't get closer. At least the tracker was working, though Ethan's map of the county showed precisely nothing in the area where she was.

"Can I see that for a minute?" TJ traced the spot on the map where Lucy's last signal had originated. "We're well out of the city limits now. Technically, we should be calling in the sheriff."

"Not a chance."

"Yeah. Okay." She examined the map again. "Shit. If you go another mile or so through the woods, you'll find a hunting cabin. No car can get through there, though. It's pretty rough hiking. Al Pike and the mayor used to go there. They took Drew and Billy, and a couple times I went, too, though I wasn't invited."

"That's where they'll be. Let's go." He gunned the engine on the truck, and they took off at full speed.

⌒

Lucy stood in the shade of the trees, sweat trickling down her temples, searching for any clue as to the whereabouts of the man watching her. He might have had GPS on the Jeep, but now that she was on foot, he'd have to have her in sight.

"Take off your shirt," said the voice on the phone.

"No." The hell was she doing a striptease for this guy.

"No? Your sister says she won't help you out." An explosion, then a shriek of pain. "Shut up, boy, you don't need that hand. Or do you? I forgot to ask whether you were left-handed or not. Oh, well."

"Stop it! Just stop!" Lucy pulled off her shirt. "See? No recording! I told you I wasn't wearing a wire!" Even as she struggled out of the top, she pushed the SOS button on the GPS tracker hard. She'd heard both the shot and the scream live as well as over the phone. They'd come from over to her left, so she turned in that direction and began walking.

"Stop." Said the voice. "Leave the pants and boots, along with whatever weapons may be in them."

She wanted to tell him to go to hell, but the sound of Tim's shriek still echoed in her ears and she shivered despite the humid heat collecting on her skin. She sat on the damp earth and pulled off her boots and socks. As her enemy had surmised, she'd tucked her Glock into one of her boots. Nothing for it now but to leave it behind. As she shimmied the jeans down her legs, she let the GPS device slip down inside one leg, pressing the SOS button one last time. With luck, the man wouldn't check the clothes.

In only her bra and panties, she felt extremely vulnerable. Probably his intention. How the hell was she supposed to rescue Tim? Please, God, let Ethan be close.

"Move forward until I tell you to stop."

Lucy took small, careful steps, watching where she put her feet. The earth seemed to seethe with insects, and shudders ran up and down her spine with each touch of her toes to the dirt. The ground here, beneath the canopy of the old oaks, lay in constant shadow and decay. The rain had brought all the grubs to the surface, and God alone knew what else lived beneath.

Moving slowly also gave Ethan more time to find her. Now, in so far over her head, she wondered why it had been so hard to admit she needed his help, so hard to trust him. She should have gone to him straightaway—should, at least, have told him before she left that she trusted him.

"Turn left," the voice ordered. Lucy did, and saw the outline of a structure through the trees. "Head for the hunting shack and let yourself inside."

Slowing her steps even further, Lucy made her way through the trees to the shack. The door was closed and swollen, so she had to yank it hard to get it open. The sudden release almost sent her sprawling backward. She clung to the splintery wood, however, and remained upright.

Until her legs almost failed her at the sight of what lay inside the cabin.

The mayor had been tied to a chair, a piece of duct tape strapped across his mouth. On the floor next to him, Tim cradled one bloody hand, bandaged with what looked like a kitchen towel. His feet were bound with rope, but he was not gagged. The entire place reeked of gasoline, and two gallon-sized cans stood next to the chair.

Across the room, Billy Pike held a pistol pointed directly at Tim's head. At her entrance, he tossed away the cell phone he'd been holding in his other hand. His eyes swept derisively over her body.

"Good to see you know how to follow directions. But then, you always were easy to lead into a trap. Pathetic, really. Get over there with the rest of your family."

She stared at him.

"I said get! Or didn't you know that the esteemed mayor was also your dear daddy? Your momma let it slip one night and my father passed it on to me. So, what we're going to have here is a tragic family accident. Murder-suicide."

Lucy didn't move. She shoved his allegations about her own parentage to the back of her mind and focused on the one wedge she might be able to use

"Tim's not Mayor Dobbs's son, Billy. DNA will prove it when they run the tests to ID the bodies. It's not my family or the Dobbs family that will come under scrutiny, it's yours. Tim's your brother."

Fury flared in his cold eyes. "Shut up, bitch. Your lies won't help you now."

"No lie. You had other siblings, but they didn't live. They died because they had a genetic abnormality called spinal muscular atrophy, though at the time their deaths were probably put down to crib death or the like. Tim has it, too, though his is very mild." She hoped she was doing the right thing. Having to face his genetic heritage this way would devastate Tim, but she couldn't see anything else that might force Billy to stop.

"Bullshit," said Billy. "You'd say anything to save your precious brother. Just like he'd do anything to save you. It's so sweet. That's how I knew he'd be coming back to town sooner or later. That's why I had my good buddy Drew drive up to Dallas and take his picture for me to use, and put a tracker on his car so we'd know when he was coming home. Of course, poor old Drew didn't live to put that information to good use. But since you'd never told Tiny Tim about the fun times we shared in high school, he was only too happy to pull over for an officer of the law."

*Shit. Oh, shit.* She'd been so busy protecting herself from the shame of her experiences, she'd never given a thought to the fact that she could be putting Tim in danger. Begging forgiveness, she glanced at him and found no condemnation in his eyes, only support.

"You'll be found out. There's no reason for Mayor Dobbs to hurt Tim. And once the DNA comes back—"

"There won't be DNA. This is my county, my jurisdiction. I'll close the case personally. Even if they do find out Tim's not a Dobbs, Pike DNA isn't on file anywhere. They can't trace it to me. Case closed."

"That won't satisfy Jake. Or did you forget the FBI is involved?"

"As I said, this is my jurisdiction. In order for them to get involved, I have to invite them. I haven't. And your drug addict boyfriend won't be able to help, either. There's a county-wide spot check for drugs set for tomorrow. He's going to fail. It will be my sad duty to take his badge and report him to the state police."

*Oh, Ethan.* "Ethan's never missed a call. Never shown up under the influence. People in town will know he's no user."

"Knowing and proving are totally different things. Or hasn't your illustrious career in true crime taught you that? Right now, what matters are the numerous times the mayor here mentioned wishing you were dead. The members of this town won't find it hard to believe his grief over Drew's murder pushed him over the edge."

Dobbs shouted behind his gag, and Billy sauntered up

to him, keeping the gun leveled on Lucy, and pulled the tape from his mouth.

"Something to say, old man?"

"I never said I wanted her dead. I wanted her gone. Out of town so she wouldn't ruin my reputation or Drew's chances at a senate seat. You fucking idiot, you're just like your father, taking everything one step too far." The mayor started to laugh, choking on his words. "She's my damn daughter. Once the will is read, people will know I didn't kill her."

The statement shocked Lucy possibly more than the original sight of Billy Pike with his gun. She'd suspected Billy right from the beginning, had recognized the evil that lived within him. That Andrew Dobbs should provide for her in his will, on the other hand, was beyond the scope of even her imagination.

Billy seemed as shocked as she was. He stood for a moment, his attention fixed on Mayor Dobbs, and the gun wavered. Only slightly, but Tim took the opportunity to push off the floor and tackle him.

Lucy leaped to join him, and for a moment the tide seemed to be turning in their direction, but then Tim let out a howl and fell away as Pike ground his boot heel into the bloody pulp of his wounded hand.

Lucy tried to hang on, but despite her martial arts training Pike escaped her grip and backhanded her across the face. She fell away, then pushed herself back to her feet, determined to get to him while he remained off-balance from the fight.

But Pike was too fast. Before she could reach him again, he had the pistol up against Tim's head.

"That's enough of that." Pike's eyes swept over Lucy, focusing on the scar above her breast. "You know, you and I have unfinished business. Seems a shame to waste such a perfect opportunity. And I so rarely get an audience for my work. At least, while I'm creating."

Lucy took a step backward. "You're not going to touch me, Billy."

He smiled then, and she felt her stomach heave. "Oh, yes. I am. You were my first. No matter how many times I've tried, none of the others have even come close. I never could figure out why. I got to watch them for a lot longer than I watched you afterward. Of course, maybe it was that they didn't know, when they ran into me in the street or came into my office to see how their cases were progressing, that I was the one who'd forced them to submit."

"Raped them, you mean."

He inclined his head. "It was better when Drew helped. More fun. More like it had been with you."

"You didn't rape me."

"No. Not then." That smile again. And his eyes were completely dead. At some point, Billy Pike had slipped over the edge into complete insanity. "But we were so young, weren't we? We only wanted to mark you for what you were. Or at least, I did. Drew just wanted to do anything I asked of him."

"Drew?" Dobbs sputtered. "My son was in on this with you? He helped you?"

"Hell, yes. He loved me. Got down on his knees and sucked me off whenever I told him to. Raped women. Killed them. Whatever I wanted.

"But, damn, he was a fucking pain in my ass. Always whining, requiring me to discipline him over and over. Guess you didn't do a good job with that, Mayor. And he was too unreliable, too weak. That's why I had to kill him. He completely panicked over Lucy's reappearance, saw it as a threat, not an opportunity to finish what we started.

"In a couple of weeks, after the furor over your murder-suicide dies down, I'll solve his murder. It will turn out that Lucy here killed him. Everyone knows she hated him. You found out, killed her and her brother, then yourself."

"Why are you doing this?" Lucy asked, still trying to

reason with him, despite the fact that he'd obviously moved out of the realm of logic. "You were at the station. You know Ethan caught Jed Martin. Why not let that investigation run its course? Your secrets could remain hidden."

"Not likely. No, this is your fault. You brought in the FBI. Sooner or later, one of your boyfriends would look more closely into the murders and rapes in the area. Drew was in on enough of them to provide a perfect fall guy. I'll connect him conclusively to three or four, and everyone will buy that he committed the others, too. He has alibis for a couple I did on my own, but not enough to convince people to look further."

"No one will believe you. Think this through. Ethan and Jake and TJ—they all know I didn't kill Drew."

"Ah, but you told me yourself you were alone that night. None of your friends can alibi you. They might not believe you killed Drew, but they won't be able to prove it. Now"—he traced the gun barrel over her scar—"if you're finished being nosy and wasting my time, we can get down to business."

On the final word, Lucy lunged forward, pressing her shoulder into the gun. If he shot her, so be it—with luck, the bullet wouldn't damage anything important—but she couldn't sit still and let him kill them all.

The blast shook the small cabin, and the smell of gunpowder and burned flesh filled the air. She thought she'd prepared for the pain. She hadn't. She staggered backward, her shoulder burning. But over the pain, she remembered one of her self-defense instructor's admonishments: When you're fighting for your life, you have two choices: ignore the pain and keep fighting, or give in to it and start dying. She plowed headfirst into Pike's stomach, knocking him off balance. The gun went flying, and she heard Tim scrabbling across the floor in search of it.

"Bitch!" Pike grabbed her by her shoulders and smashed her into the wall three times. Her head slammed back each time although she tried to tuck it toward her chest. Dizziness and nausea assaulted her, but she aimed a knee at Pike's groin nonetheless. He stepped back, then grabbed her arm and swung her around so she landed on top of Tim, who was still searching the floor for the gun.

At first, Lucy was too relieved that Pike had stopped beating her to realize his intention. When she looked up, he stood near the door, fiddling with something in his pocket He pulled out an emergency flare and a lighter. She tried to hit him again, but she couldn't move fast enough. He lit the flare and opened the cabin door.

"You should have let me shoot you. It would have been a less painful way to go." Pike tossed the flare into the corner, and the walls went up with a whoosh as he stepped outside, pulling the door shut behind him. Lucy raced for the door, but he'd either locked it or wedged something against it outside, because it wouldn't open. The metal knob burned her hand, but the pain was only a dim addition to the fear for her own life and her brother's.

⸺

RED FLICKERING LIGHT burst through the shadowy darkness of the woods, and Ethan's heart clutched. He'd been running, following TJ's directions to the hunting shack, but with the fire in sight, he didn't need assistance, and he left her behind as he sped up beyond what even he would have believed possible.

The entire cabin was in flames. Ripping off his T-shirt, Ethan wrapped it around one hand and grabbed the door handle. It wouldn't budge. From the side of the structure, he heard glass breaking, and he followed the sound. In the uncertain light, he could make out Lucy standing by the window, trying to help Tim climb out. But the window was too small and too high off the ground—no way would they make it. And the fire was rising.

Ethan ran back around the front and began kicking the door. The first time, he felt almost no give, and a shock ran all the way up his leg, through his bad knee and into his back. Damn. Who the hell built a shack with a door like that? He went after it again, with much the same result. On the third try, both the door and his knee began to fail. Then TJ was next to him, and on the fourth try, with both of them slamming the wood at the same time, the door gave way.

Where were Lucy and Tim? Was he too late? Surely they'd heard him and TJ. The smoke and fire were blinding, and the smell of gasoline overpowering. He pressed the T-shirt to his nose and mouth and waded into the cabin.

Whoever had set the place on fire had evidently doused all the walls, but left the center part clean. Lucy and Tim huddled there, alone with a bulky figure Ethan could almost swear was the mayor, if he hadn't been certain Dobbs was behind the whole thing.

"Dirt!" Ethan hollered out to TJ. "Pack it in the doorway, keep the floor clear of fire!" She nodded to show she'd heard him and began grabbing armloads of the thick, clay soil still heavy with water from the storm and tossing it on the flames in the doorway and on the floor nearby.

Both Ethan's knee and his shoulder throbbed. He staggered forward and bent to help Lucy up, which was when he realized that the odd coloring of her skin he'd noticed when he'd seen her through the window wasn't due to the flames. She was covered in blood, as was Tim. And neither appeared fully conscious.

"Lucy!" He shook her slightly. Light as she was, he'd never be able to carry both her and her brother in his condition. "Come on, woman, get up!" She stirred slightly. "Lucy! Tim needs you! Tim's going to die!" She roused at that, as he'd known she would. Her dazed blue eyes met his, and her focus sharpened.

"Ethan—"

"C'mon, sugar. You have to help me here." Despite TJ's efforts, the fire was creeping inward toward them, closing their escape route. "We need to go. Now." Lucy shook her brother. Tim responded only sluggishly. His face was chalk white, and Ethan wondered whether he'd survive the smoke inhalation and loss of blood.

"Can you manage on your own?" he asked Lucy. She nodded and began crawling toward the door. Ethan watched until he could be sure she'd make it out, then put his hands beneath Tim's armpits and began dragging him in the same direction. Outside, TJ had Lucy seated against a tree and was applying pressure to her shoulder.

"The mayor," Lucy gasped as Ethan set Tim next to her. "We have to help him. Billy tied him to a chair. He can't get out on his own."

Billy? Sheriff Pike had been behind this?

The man couldn't be conscious, or he'd have made a fuss over Lucy and Tim being evacuated before him. The damned cabin was an inferno. Still, Ethan made his way back, intending to attempt to haul the man out. But Dobbs surprised him. Two steps inside, Ethan found him. He'd turned the chair on its side and was squirming his way forward. With TJ's help, Ethan managed to get him out, chair and all. They stripped the rope off, and Dobbs staggered to his feet.

"We'll never get an ambulance out here," Ethan said. "We need to get back to the car." He and TJ had pulled up behind the Jeep he assumed Lucy had driven.

"I'll take the boy," said Dobbs, shocking Ethan speechless. "You don't look as if you can handle much more than your own weight, and TJ will have her hands full with Lucy." He coughed, spat, and leaned over and hauled Tim up into a fireman's carry. "Let's go."

They'd almost reached the truck when the first shot rang out. Dobbs's head exploded in a spray of red and gray, and

Lucy shrieked. Ethan grabbed her and rolled to cover near a fallen tree. Damn, damn, damn. Where the hell was Pike? Lucy squirmed beneath him, but Ethan wasn't about to let her up until he knew where the danger lay.

"Ethan."

"Give me a minute." He poked his head up and saw TJ crouching behind a nearby tree.

"You see anything?"

"No. Where the hell is he?"

Lucy ignored them both. "Pike!" she shouted, struggling against Ethan. "You fucking coward. Give it up! You can't explain your way out of this one!"

A shadow shifted in the woods off to their right, and both Ethan and TJ fired.

"Get moving," Ethan ordered. "TJ, take Lucy. I'll bring Tim along in a minute." He had no idea how. Tim's breathing was fast and shallow, and he'd be dead weight, but Lucy needed to be protected, so Ethan would do whatever it took. "Radio for help. They ought to be on their way already, but be sure to get the EMTs. And for God's sake, tell them the sheriff's on the wrong side of this one before they get here."

As TJ and Lucy ran through the woods, Ethan fired another volley off into the woods along their route. Pike returned the fire, and Ethan wedged himself behind a bulky oak for protection. He waited until TJ and Lucy were leaning up against the truck, out of range of Pike's gun, and called out again to draw fire so TJ could get Lucy inside.

"Come out, Pike! Don't make this any worse!" Bullets buried themselves in the tree he hid behind, sending slivers flying everywhere. The truck door slammed, and he let out a quick breath of relief. Lucy was inside, out of harm's way as long as she and TJ stayed down.

In the distance, he heard sirens.

"Hear that, Sheriff? That's the bell tolling for you! It's over!"

"Fuck you, Donovan! These are my woods, this is my county.

You can't win. You'll never find me. I'll haunt you, and I'll haunt your girlfriend. And one night, when you're relaxing after a couple pills and a glass of whiskey, I'll come knocking on your door." Another round of bullets, then silence.

Emergency vehicles pulled up behind Ethan's truck, and two EMT's headed in his direction. Ethan covered them as they lifted Tim and trotted back toward their ambulance. Johnny Wilson climbed from a county cruiser.

"What the hell is going on out here?" he shouted before he'd even reached Ethan.

"Keep your voice down, you damned fool. He's still out there." Ethan grabbed him by the shoulders and pulled him down into a crouch, eyes scanning the tree line the whole time. The hell if anyone else was dying on his watch.

"Tara Jean said the sheriff was trying to kill y'all?"

"It's true." Ethan took his eyes off the surrounding trees for a minute to emphasize the point. Wilson met his gaze with skepticism.

"I've known that man my entire life, Donovan."

Christ, he was tired of these townies treating him like an outsider instead of a cop. "No longer than you've known TJ."

Wilson conceded the truth of the statement with a nod, and Ethan relaxed a fraction.

"Look, I understand it goes against the grain." He tried to sound encouraging, but damn, he was too pissed. "You don't have to go gunning for him. Just bring him in. And do it carefully."

A fire engine arrived, and heavily outfitted men began jogging through the woods toward the blazing cabin, talking into their radios about the logistics of containment. Surely that would be enough to send Pike on his way?

TJ leaned on the horn. "Hey," she shouted out the window of Ethan's truck. "The ambulance is taking Tim, but we need to take Lucy ourselves! Get over here!"

"Gotta go," Ethan said to Johnny. "This is your jurisdiction, anyway, so I guess you're in command. Just be careful. There's an armed man out there, and whether or not you've always considered him your friend, he's insane."

Without waiting for an answer, Ethan dashed for the truck. TJ sat in the driver's seat, and she ordered him to get in the back with Lucy. He didn't argue. He needed to touch her, to check her over and be sure she was still alive. Apparently, she felt the same because, even before he closed the door, she slid across the seat and wrapped her good arm around him. He pulled her closer until she sat across his lap, her head tucked between his neck and shoulder.

Under the front seat, he found a blanket they kept on hand to warm shock victims, and he wrapped it around her, being careful not to jostle her shoulder wound. Why had Pike made her undress? Fury slid through him again, and he had to reassure himself that Pike's intentions remained unfulfilled. Lucy was safe, and he would keep her that way.

He didn't know what to say to her. Everything had changed, but nothing had changed. He could no longer imagine his life without her, but he still had nothing to offer her. So he sat quietly, stroking her hair as TJ wove through the emergency vehicles and out toward the road.

LUCY CLUNG TO Ethan, relishing the feel of his body against hers. They had made it. He was here, with her. But how much damage had he done to his bad knee, his shoulder? She buried her face in the crook of his neck and tried not to weep. His life was in shambles. Between the truth of his past and his ruined knee, he would never be able to go back to police work.

"I'm so sorry," she choked out.

"Don't even think it. None of this was your fault."

"If I hadn't come back here, you wouldn't be hurt. Tim wouldn't be——"

"If you hadn't come back here, Billy Pike would still be raping and murdering women. Jed Martin and Eric Allenby would still be hunting down illegal immigrants like animals in the woods."

The truck thumped over a rock and off the dirt road out of the woods onto the road near Lucy's house, and TJ turned toward the highway to take them to the hospital. A sheriff's department car passed, headed into the woods. A minute later, a Hummer came up the road from the same direction.

"It's Pike!" TJ's shouted warning came the very moment she twisted the wheel to avoid hitting the Hummer head-on. Their right wheels left the road, but Pike had prepared for the action, and the Hummer hit them with a screech of metal, locking driver's side to driver's side. Both vehicles shuddered to a halt with the Hummer's front fender hung up beneath the rear wheel well of Ethan's truck.

"Down!" Ethan shouted, forcing Lucy to the floor.

TJ, too, slid down in her seat, just in time to avoid the two shots that came through her window, shattering the glass. Lucy felt Ethan shift to reach between the seats.

"I'm out of ammo. He's going to come around the other side the minute he can get free of his airbag, and we'll be sitting ducks. Pass me your weapon." TJ did, and Ethan popped open the passenger door and fired off a couple of blind rounds. When he pushed the door fully open and slid one leg out, Lucy had to force herself not to clutch at him, to drag him back inside where they had at least the illusion of safety.

MORE SIRENS WERE approaching, but Ethan couldn't afford to wait for them. Pike had evidently given up his plan to trap them in the truck and kill them. He was loping off toward the deepest part of the woods. His khaki shirt was covered with blood and he wasn't moving well.

"I'll be right back," Ethan promised.

"No! Let him go. Let someone else get him. Please, Ethan." Tears were pouring down Lucy's face, more devastating than bullets. "Do you remember what you said about not being able to find me like Renee? I can't let him take anything else from me. I can't. I can't lose you."

Ethan wanted to shout, to roar in a primal combination of pain and joy. Instead, he cupped her face in his hands and kissed her. "You won't lose me, sugar. I swear it. But I can't let him go. Don't ask me to."

Silently, she nodded.

"Radio the EMTs. Make them take you to the hospital," he told TJ. "I'll meet you there." He couldn't wait for an answer. Even bleeding and on the run, Pike had too great an advantage for Ethan to give him much of a head start. He set off after the sheriff as swiftly as his aching and swollen knee allowed.

The woods closed in quickly, overwhelming him. The scents, the sounds remained foreign even after nine months on the job. As TJ had reminded him more than once, he was an urban cop through and through. But he'd spent enough time in back alleys and slums, tracking down suspects. He couldn't let this be any different or he might lose the most important prey he'd ever hunted.

Ethan's skin crawled from the unfamiliar surroundings, and his body burned from unaccustomed abuse. He forced the sensations away. Gradually, his senses sharpened and his focus narrowed. Pike was out there, and Ethan had no intention of letting the man get away.

A spot of blood caught his eye, glistening in the last rays of summer sunlight sifting through the trees. Ethan held his breath and listened. From off to his left, a quiet rustle of leaves and branches alerted him to his quarry's direction. Pike's injury was causing him to drag through the groundfall, and Ethan followed the trail, moving tree to tree, protecting himself as best he could while keeping up a decent speed.

The shot came from his right and took him off guard, scoring a screaming hot path through the skin where his neck and shoulder met. Two inches left, and it would have gone straight through his jugular. He hit the dirt and rolled to the side. Dammit, Pike had suckered him with the trail.

But he had to be close. From his vantage point behind a large rock, Ethan searched the area. Movement in the brush gave him a target, and he squeezed off two shots. He heard Pike's cry and his fall.

All too aware that this could be another trap, Ethan approached the spot slowly. From behind him, he heard voices. Reinforcements. He kept moving, however, in case Pike had merely pretended injury to get away.

And, indeed, when Ethan stepped through the brush, no body lay there. The unmistakable click of an empty weapon being fired came from his right, and he turned just as Pike came barreling toward him.

Pike's body hit with brutal force, sending both men to the ground. Though he was several inches shorter than Ethan and injured more severely, his anger lent him strength.

"Why won't you die?" Pike lifted his fist, and Ethan blocked the blow with the side of his forearm and tried to wrestle the smaller man off him. Pike raised his knee and slammed it into Ethan's injured one, sending a spear of paralyzing pain through his body.

Instinctively, Ethan grabbed for Pike's neck with both hands. Pike tried to fight back, but Ethan's longer reach gave him leverage, and he forced the other man back, off, and over until their positions were reversed. But Ethan didn't let go. Pike's face reddened and he choked, his fingers scrabbling for purchase and pushing against Ethan's chest.

The voices Ethan had heard before came closer, Lucy's among them.

"Ethan! Let him up!"

He felt their hands on him, but all he could see was Pike's mottling face.

"Ethan, please." Lucy, still clad only in her underwear and blanket, knelt beside him, dragging his attention away from the man beneath him. "Please. I need you to let him live. Let Keith deal with him. He's not going anywhere."

Gradually, Ethan forced his muscles to unclench, forced himself to let go and roll away from the other man. Keith Arlen and two deputies grabbed Pike—still gasping for air—and dragged him away. Ethan tried to stand, but his knee gave way. TJ hauled him to his feet, shoving one shoulder beneath his.

"I thought I told you to take Lucy to the hospital."

"Yeah, well, I don't know which of you is more stubborn. I almost had her in Keith's car when we heard the shots. Then she had to follow you."

He looked over at Lucy, stumbling along beside them, her beautiful face far too pale. How much blood had she lost from that shoulder wound? And the smoke inhalation. She should have been in the hospital, but she'd come for him instead. He longed to reach for her, but the geography of it defeated him: with his left arm looped over TJ's shoulders to keep him on his feet, he could only take Lucy's left hand, which would surely hurt her wounded shoulder.

At last they reached the road, where an ambulance waited. The paramedics loaded Lucy inside. Ethan crawled into the passenger seat of Keith's cruiser while TJ slid behind the wheel, and both vehicles took off.

# CHAPTER SEVENTEEN

I thought I left my mother behind when I left Dobbs Hollow. Now I find that, all these years, she's lived in me. I hope I can preserve some sense of her for my brother, for all of you.

FROM *A BAD DAY TO DIE*

BY LUCY SADLER CALDWELL [DRAFT]

LUCY FELT AS if she were at the same time floating and impossibly heavy. She could hear people moving around, but couldn't be bothered to open her eyes. Even thinking was an effort, but eventually she sorted out what had happened. She forced her lids up and encountered the brilliant white of a hospital room.

Ethan slouched in a chair, one leg encased in an immobilizer and propped on the edge of her bed. A bandage covered a wound at the base of his neck an inch above his shoulder, and blue shadows lay beneath his eyes. He looked like hell, but he was alive and that was all that mattered. He must have heard her sigh of relief, because he opened his eyes and gave her a lopsided smile.

"Hey, sleeping beauty."

"Hey. How's Tim?"

"He came through his surgery like a champ. The docs say he probably won't regain full fine motor control in his hand, but that's relatively minor compared to what might have happened."

As if her brother didn't have enough to deal with already. "It's my fault. I started this whole mess by coming down here."

"It's not. Lucy, for God's sake, you have to cut yourself some slack here. Tim doesn't care. He's worried about you. They put him in a room two doors down, and he keeps saying he's fine and he wants to get up and come see you. I told him as soon as you woke up I'd let him know."

Tears rose in the back of Lucy's throat, clogged her nose, and leaked out the corners of her eyes.

"Hey, hey, stop that." Ethan rose from his chair and pivoted carefully so he could sit on the bed. He grabbed a tissue from the nightstand and wiped away the water dripping down her temples. "You already look like hell, sugar; we can't have tears, too. You've got a room full of friends out there waiting to be allowed in."

"Not unless this hospital has the world's smallest waiting room," Lucy joked with a watery grin.

"Nope. Jake and TJ are here, Josh and Megan, Maxie and Buddy. Even Eulie is showing her support, probably because she feels guilty. She treated you badly, and then it turns out that her ex killed your mother. And a bunch of other people, too. Jed's activities are competing with Billy Pike's for the number-one slot on the gossip charts."

"How does everyone know? How long have I been here?" Instinctively, she looked toward the windows, but they were draped in heavy, light-blocking shades.

"It's seven in the morning."

"How are Maxie and Buddy here, then? Who's running the diner?"

"They left the B team in charge. It's just breakfast, and most of the people congregating are enjoying the rumors, not the food.

"On the other hand, there are a few less-than-friendly faces, too. A couple detectives from the sheriff's department. I'm afraid they get first crack at you. They'd have liked to kick me out, but they couldn't quite manage it. I even managed to squeeze in while they interviewed Tim."

"Thanks. I guess."

"You guess?"

"I guess I have to admit he's grown up now."

"Is that so hard?"

Suddenly, with Ethan by her side, it wasn't. Tim would always be her little brother, but he'd shown himself more than capable of holding his own under the worst possible circumstances. And she'd found someone else she trusted. Now, to find a way to tell him so.

"While we were in the cabin, I wanted to tell him not to worry, that you were coming, but I couldn't let Pike realize we had a plan. He—Tim—he did great, even without the reassurance."

"Of course he did. You raised him." Ethan winked at her. "A kick-ass sister like you wouldn't put up with anything less. He did great on his interview, too. Stayed really cool. Of course, that could have been the morphine. Now, let me go get TJ and Jake, along with the detectives, and we'll get yours over with."

Lucy thought about objecting, about telling him she could handle herself without the backup, but she wasn't at all sure it would be true. Her emotions careened from one point to another, and she didn't know how she'd deal with an interrogation.

"I'll just pop out and tell them they can come in, okay? Better to get this done and behind you."

"Yeah. Sure."

Ethan grabbed a pair of crutches and swung himself out of the room. He returned a few minutes later with TJ, Jake, a dark-haired stranger, and a man who introduced himself as Johnny Wilson, acting sheriff.

"Lucy," Johnny nodded at her. "We have Sheriff Pike in custody, and we have your brother's statement about what happened inside the cabin. But I'd like to get the details from you."

"Sure."

She relayed the story, starting with the phone call she'd received while at the police station. For the most part, Johnny let her talk, interrupting only occasionally for clarification.

She left out Pike's references to his actions in high school. Tim wouldn't have understood what Pike was talking about, so he probably would have skipped that part of his account as well. Besides, her high school experiences had no bearing on either her mother's murder or Pike's killing spree.

"So you never suspected it was Sheriff Pike on the phone?" Johnny asked.

"No. I had no reason to." She looked directly at Johnny, avoiding TJ and Ethan, who knew about her history with Pike.

Johnny and his sidekick left, and an awkward silence filled the room. Ethan broke it.

"Why did you tell him you had no reason to suspect Pike? After what he did to you in high school—"

"TJ and I had talked about him. She looked at his alibis."

"No." A frown creased TJ's forehead. "We talked about Drew. Not Billy. I saw Drew stuff that note into your locker back then. Saw him downstairs waiting for you. I didn't even know Billy was involved. I should have, seeing how insepara-ble they were, but it never occurred to me."

Jake glared at TJ and swore. "All this could have been avoided! All of it! You call yourself a detective? Hell, you call yourself a friend?"

"Jake! Lay off!" But Lucy's warning came too late. TJ was gone.

"What's the matter with you?" For all his faults, Lucy had never seen Jake go off half-cocked.

"You could have been killed, Luce, and all because she let you believe she'd checked into Pike's alibi when she hadn't."

"It was a misunderstanding." Lucy fought to remember TJ's exact words. "She said she'd looked into 'him.' I thought she meant Pike, but she was talking about her brother. She was a little kid the first time she came to my rescue. If you blame her, you have to blame me, too. I should have found out exactly what she remembered, but that part of my past is embarrassing, and I don't like talking about it."

"Fine. You both acted like idiots."

"Maybe so. But it's over. And you don't get to criticize, anyway." She fixed Jake with the sternest expression she could manage from her prone position. "Now, go find TJ and apologize."

"You're a hard woman, Lucy Caldwell."

"Just get." With a nod at her and Ethan, Jake got.

Ethan stroked her hair back from her face. "How you holding up? It can't have been easy telling strangers about the mayor being your father."

Lucy shook her head. "He wasn't my father. He contributed half my genes, and he gave my mother money, maybe even bought her that house, but none of that makes him a father. Imagine leaving me money in his will, as if that would make up for the treatment he allowed my mother and us to face all those years. What she said to Megan's brother about following her heart . . . I guess she loved him. It's probably why she stayed here, even though he would never acknowledge her. Us."

"Love is complicated."

Lucy waited for Ethan to elaborate, but he didn't. "I hated this town, you know. Hated everyone in it. And yet, I believed what they said, too. I studied her death, and how her life might have caused it, but I never gave a single thought to how she got so lost. Not until I came back."

"It doesn't sound as if she had a great childhood. And then she fell for the wrong man. But nothing you've ever said has led me to believe she was a bad person."

"She wasn't. And somewhere along the line, I forgot that." The tears were dripping down her face again, and Lucy swiped at them.

"I'm a wreck."

"Nah. Just a fender bender. You ready to see the rest of your fans?"

"Not yet." She patted the edge of her bed, and he maneuvered himself so he could sit, his bad leg propped on the chair. "We've talked about me, about Tim, about Billy Pike, but what about you?"

"As you can see, I'm fine."

"What about your job? How long's your knee going to have to be stabilized? Will you need more surgery?"

"I haven't really talked to anyone about the job. I assume I get to keep it for three months, until my term's up. They'll have a damned hard time justifying getting rid of me before that, what with Eric, Jed, and Billy all going down on my watch. After that, the deputy mayor will appoint some-one new."

"You don't think he'll ask you to stay on?"

"Whether he asks or not, I won't."

"Really?"

"No." He met her eyes, and she felt the weight of his words. "I've had time to think. You were right about what my old lieu-tenant said being wrong. I would never take another job as a narcotics cop, or even one where I was exposed to that kind of temptation regularly, but I can handle myself on a day-to-day basis. I can carry a gun. I can do what needs doing.

"In three months' time, when my contract with the town of Dobbs Hollow is up, I'm going to see about getting a PI license. I can't go back to the Houston PD, but investigation is what I do. It's who I am."

He took a deep breath. "Thing is, my contacts for that stuff are all in Houston. I could move, but I'd have to start over. I'd do it, though, if—"

"If?" She could hardly breathe.

"Lucy, you said I'd leave you one day because I didn't need you. You were wrong. I do. I need you because you believed in me even when I didn't, and because you make me stronger. You make me better. But you need me, too. Not just to feed you and make sure you come up for air when you're working too hard, but because I love you."

"You do?" The words came out on a strangled, choking

breath. She sucked in another to finally, finally tell him she loved him, too, but he was still talking.

"Yeah, I do. And I'm not sure anyone else ever has, not properly, not without you feeling like you had to take care of them, or that you owed them. So, here's the thing: it will be harder for me to get started in my PI business if I don't go back to Houston, but I'll move to Dallas instead, if you ask me to. And not because you feel like you should. Just because you want me to."

The tears started again, and she started to wipe them away, only to realize that at some point he'd taken her good hand.

"I won't ask you to do that." His grip and his expression tightened. He'd misunderstood her words. "Ethan, I can work anywhere. Tim's in college. He's also old enough to decide for himself where he lives." She gulped in a huge breath. "I love you. When I was in the cabin, I wished I had told you. I can move to Houston a lot more easily than you can to Dallas. If you really want me to."

"Oh, yeah," he said, swinging his leg around so he could lie next to her on the bed and pulling her close with great care. "I really want."

She closed her eyes and snuggled into the heat of his body. Everyone else would have to wait. For once, she was going to take what she wanted. She felt the vibration of Ethan's chest beneath her ear and realized he was humming. She fell asleep, teary-eyed, to the tune of "If Ever I Would Leave You" from Camelot.

# ACKNOWLEDGMENTS

What you hold in your hands is not my own work, or at least not mine alone. Because it was first acquired and published by Penguin, it has been through the hands of extra editors, extra copy editors, extra proofreaders.

First, I have to thank my agent Jessica Faust, who took me on when I was writing cozy mysteries and stuck with me despite the rocky road to publication. My first editor, Theresa Stevens, helped shape everything you see in this book. Leis Pederson, my editor at Penguin, continued the refinements. My copy editor there, Andy Ball, caught any mistakes that might have slipped through the cracks. And finally, when the Leis left Penguin and the book came back to me, Lynda Ryba proofed it for me again, Keith Snyder made it look beautiful, and Carrie Devine gave it a fabulous cover.

My companions at the Women of Mystery blog, my Sisters in Crime chapter-mates, and the many good women of RWA who read and commented and helped me with research deserve more kudos than I could possibly give them. Writing organizations can help keep you sane when the publishing world is making you crazy.

Clare Toohey, my commuting partner, helped hash out plot points time after time, and my writing sprints pal K.M. Jackson kept pushing me onward. I owe them both my gratitude for keeping me on target.

And last, but definitely not least, I must thank my husband, who takes care of everything when I am under deadline…and sometimes even when I am not. My own, private hero.

I am sure I have left people out, and I apologize profoundly for doing so. If I included everyone who deserves to be thanked, the acknowledgements would be longer than the book.

# ABOUT THE AUTHOR

Laura K. Curtis gave up a life writing dry academic papers for writing decidedly less dry short crime stories and novel-length romantic suspense and contemporary romance. A member of RWA, MWA, ITW, and Sisters in Crime, she has trouble settling into one genre. She has published four romantic suspense novels (*Twisted*, 2013; *Lost*, 2014; *Echoes*, 2015; and *Mind Games*, 2015), two contemporary romance novels (*Toying With His Affections*, 2014; *Gaming the System*, 2015), and a host of short stories, many with a supernatural bent.